STORM
AND THE
WALL

MARK BACHAND · EMILY BACHAND · MEGAN BACHAND

STORM
AND THE
WALL

CONTENTS

Acknowledgements

The girls and I would like to thank all of our friends and family that had to put up with us talking about this crazy story that the three of us have made up over the past two years.

A special thanks to the weird voices we all have in our heads that provide us with an endless source of material to write about.

If you are interested in following our stories, please sign up for our mailing list at www.bachandbooks.com. Signing up will also get you a *free copy* of our new novella ***Bendati the Sorcerer***.

CHAPTER 1

Wrong Place, Wrong Time

i

Please don't let him die! Please don't let him die! This was the frantic thought replaying on an endless loop in Tom's head as he watched the paramedics lift the stretcher to standing height and begin the trip to the hospital two miles away.

Just a few short minutes ago, he had been heading down the back stairs of his high school. The tight spiral staircase that was recessed into the wall was a well-used shortcut from the gym and locker room area above, to the band and art classrooms below. School had been released about 45 minutes ago, but it was getting close to the end of the school year, and Tom had needed to stay late to work on a history project. With that behind him, his walking speed to collect his things in his locker was right at that uncomfortable speed - the one that hovered between a walk and a run. It would have been easier to break into a run, but Tom was already two warnings into getting his next detention, so he flew down the back hall with burning calf muscles and took the stairs three at a time. Lost in his thoughts of what he was going to do when he got home, he didn't really pay attention to what the voices in the hall were saying until he pushed the door at the bottom of the stairwell open and stepped through. It was just as his hand left contact with the door that he started to register the intense scene in front of him.

Pale with anger, Tony DeMarcus towered over the much smaller Rick Beauregard as he pinned the smaller boy against the lockers, less than twenty feet away. "I didn't ask you. I am telling you. You will be selling my merchandise here on campus until you have paid me back what you owe me! Did you think the weed was free?"

Tom froze and held his breath. He knew immediately that getting caught overhearing this would mean whatever happened to Rick would happen to him. And in that instant, Tom prayed that Rick had all the street smarts of a trained hostage negotiator.

"B-b-but Tony! You never said I would have to pay it back!" Rick stammered.

Aww crap! thought Tom.

Tony still had Rick pinned with one hand, while the other hand moved like lightning from being poised to hit Rick to snatching a gun that was tucked into his pants behind his back.

"We ain't dating. Why would I be giving you gifts like that, Rick?" Tony leveled the gun at his face. "I gave you the weed so that you would owe me, and now, you are going to start selling to your friends and if..."

However, Tony never got to finish the sentence because it was at that point that the heavy door at the bottom of the stairs finally closed with a boom that echoed down the hall.

What happened next was surreal. His brain seemed to slow the scene down. Upon hearing the door close, Tony spun to see what the noise was behind him. Tom sucked in a huge breath as the gun, still going in slow motion, swung toward him. At that moment, Rick realized he had a chance to escape and bolted like a startled jackrabbit. The sudden movement caused Tony's attention to snap back to focus on Rick, bringing the gun barrel up to point directly at Ricks exposed back. "Stop!" yelled Tony. Far too terrified to obey that command, Rick continued at top speed down the hall just as Tony closed one eye and started to pull the trigger.

Tom was never sure afterward if Tony was really going to fire the gun or not, but it was at that point that something snapped in him. His hands came up and as he yelled "No!" he felt a surge of power leave his body. The result was amazing. It was as if a small bomb had gone off with Tom at the epicenter. Tony was hurled forward like he had been launched from a catapult, hitting the lockers with enough force to cave in the door and bend the frame. Rick, who had been several feet further down the hall, was much luckier and was only shoved off his feet to slide down the hall on his stomach. As both boys came to a rest, they were covered with parts of the drop ceiling that was blown free by the blast.

ii

"Had to be some sort of explosive." Tom snapped back to the present as the fireman next to him was explaining to one of the police officers while he critically examined the cracks in the cement wall and shattered floor tiles where Tom had been standing during the altercation. "No natural gas pipes in this area…" More was said by the firemen and police milling about, but Tom was already lost in thought trying to wrap his head around how he had done it. There was no mistaking it. He knew he had caused the blast. He had felt it, and while Tom redoubled his introspective efforts on trying to make sense of it, the firemen and police continued to try to do the same.

Most of what had happened since the blast was a blur. Everyone in the school had felt it. The police and fireman had been called, and a couple of the teachers had come down the hall to see if any of the students were hurt. By then Rick had gotten back on his feet, found the first teacher that he looked like he had a set of functioning ears and launched into telling them how Tony was trying to force him into selling drugs for him "or else."

iii

Being a small town, Tom already knew some parts of Tony's story, but over the following days the newspapers would fill in the rest. As it turns out, Tony had been born and raised in New York City, and when his parents had seen that he was getting involved with gangs and drugs, they had shipped him off to live with his uncle in northern Vermont. They thought that the "clean living" and being hundreds of miles from his gang friends would prevent their son from continuing on his journey to becoming a criminal. What they hadn't known is that Tony had already fully committed to the gangster lifestyle, and when he arrived in Vermont, he didn't see farms and close-knit communities. All he saw was potential customers for the drugs that he was going to get shipped to him. He was determined to start his own branch of the gang, but to do that, he needed members, willing or unwilling, to distribute for him.

"So, did you see him drop it?" It was the police officer speaking.

"Drop what?" Tom asked coming out of his fog.

"Drop the explosive!" At that, Tom's mind seemed to jump back on track. No one would believe what really happened. Heck, Tom wasn't even sure if he believed it! Then the firemen and the police had postulated the next most possible explanation: It had to be some sort of explosive. After all, they had found Tony's pistol. It made sense.

"It all happened so fast. I'm not sure." Not quite a lie, but not what the policeman wanted for an answer either.

"Think, Tom," He pressed "did you see anything or hear any sounds before it went off?"

Thankfully, before he could answer, his mom was there. "Okay, Denis. That's enough grilling my boy. You know as well as I do the effect this kind of trauma has on a child." Tom's mom was an ER nurse at the local hospital and must have heard about the incident from one of the EMTs; although he flinched being referred to as a "child," he was glad his mother was there to prevent further grilling.

They walked outside of the building, and his mom paused and gave him a hug. "I am so glad that wasn't you that got brought in earlier." She pulled him away and looked him up and down as if inspecting him for damages. "That boy was in really rough shape, but he will make it." She shook her head. "He looked like he had been hit by a car." She hugged him one more time before catching and holding his gaze. "You didn't have anything to do with the explosives that boy was playing with, did you? I mean, this is the second explosion for you in three months…"

Leave it to mom to be direct. "No mom," he said looking straight into her eyes.

"Good. I have to go back to finish out the shift now that I know you are okay. Would you like a ride home before I go?"

Tom declined, and they parted company. He started his walk home, glad to be out in the fresh air of a late spring afternoon so he could think.

υ

As Tom started the walk to his house on the far side of the town, he slowly turned the problem over in his mind. How had this happened? What was that energy he had given off? Will Tony live? Could he have killed someone?

Tom shuddered at the idea of what could have happened. He never wanted to hurt anyone. He had been born and raised in this same small town. His dad had passed away in a car accident when Tom and his brother, Levi, were still quite young, leaving his mom to raise him as best she could on her limited means. In typical New Englander fashion, he was raised conservatively, and his moral compass was influenced by a decade or so of Christian upbringing. Intellectually, he was smart and a bit of an idealist, but not a genius. He would listen in his Current Events class to how messed up the economy is, how corrupt the government officials are and how bad the environment is getting and just pray that somehow the "good guys" would win. At 17, he was still young enough to see most of those topics in black and white. There was a right side and a wrong side.

Socially, Tom was challenged. He had a tough time making friends. He was too smart to fit in with most of the jocks, too sober to want to be around the stoners and not shallow enough to fit in with the social elite. It was entirely possible that if it weren't for his brother Oliver, or "Levi" as he was called; there would have been days that no one would have talked to Tom at all. Even his mom would tell him "when you are older people will realize how amazing you are, and you will have more friends than you will know what to do with." This announcement would always be met with an eye roll from Tom. *Yeah. Just what every teen wants to do; sit and watch people to see if they miraculously got nicer as they age.*

Levi, though, was great, and the bond they had from having to rely on one another was a strong one. With their mom frequently working two jobs to provide for them, they had to learn responsibility a little earlier in life than some of the other kids. What really drew them together was "Levi's little problem." He had a fairly severe form of epilepsy. Under normal circumstances that would have been a frightening thing for a young boy to have to deal with, but in this case, they also had to deal with the fact that there were frequently no adults in the house when the seizures happened. Because of this, it would fall to Tom to make sure that Levi didn't hurt himself and that the seizure didn't last too long. So far, in his 16 years, Levi had been hospitalized three times. Two of those times, the seizures had been broken in the ER, and he was just admitted for observation and to readjust his seizure medications. The other time had been truly scary. Levi's seizures hadn't broken in the ER, and he had spent three days in a drug-induced coma in the pediatric ICU. After that, there were another three days of observation. It had been a scary time for both boys, and Tom had stayed with Levi for as much of it as he was allowed. It was with that admission that Levi found that his biggest trigger to having a seizure was stress. The more upset he was, the more intense the seizure. So before he was discharged, the doctors focused on teaching him ways to remain calm, everything from breathing exercises to meditation, and pills of course. There were always more pills prescribed. Levi left with two new prescriptions in addition to the two he was already taking.

To make things worse, when the hospitalization was finally over, the return to school had been pretty rough. Levi's big seizure had started in school where he was surrounded by other kids; by the time he came back to school, some of the older kids had already started referring to him as "twitchy" and mimicking seizures when he would walk into the room. Knowing that stress could cause another seizure and seeing Levi getting upset by the three older boys picking on him, Tom didn't even try to talk them out of it. He just walked up and punched the biggest guy in the mouth. He dropped like a brick, holding his lower lip, but the other two immediately jumped in and started punching Tom. The teachers were on it in seconds and fortunately, all Tom got out of it was a bloody nose.

While he sat on the floor pinching his nose, one of the girls in his class showed up. She had long black hair that fell in loose curls and bright green eyes. "Hi. I saw what happened and ummm… they totally deserved it. If it had been my brother, I would have clocked the guy too." She started digging through her purse and pulled out a small Ziploc with a few items in it. "Although I may have started with the leader of the group and not just hit the biggest one." She paused as if thinking. "If you take out the leader then the other two might have run. Bullies are a-holes, but in groups, they tend to be more like dogs with only one alpha." Satisfied that she had the right bag she dropped it in Tom's hand. "Here. I used to get nose bleeds a lot. It's a bunch of gauze and a chemical cooling pack to stop the bleeding." She smiled, "Just crack the solid doo-hickey inside the pouch, and it will get cold as ice."

"Thanks. Uh…?"

"Reagan. Reagan Hill."

Tom gave a start. Reagan Hill had been in his class since the fourth grade, and she had always been sick. Tom had heard a bunch of other kids talking about how they thought she had some really slow form of cancer. This couldn't be the same girl. She was vibrant, beautiful, and nothing about her seemed ill or withdrawn like the girl he had known.

She immediately picked up the shock on his face. "I know; I changed a lot." She stood up and patted him on the shoulder. "Yoga and smoothies" and giggled as she walked away.

As it turned out, Tom got suspended for that one for two days. On the upside, the older kids stopped picking on Levi.

vi

Tom smiled as he passed the old Catholic church that marked the halfway point to his house. After the suspension was over, he had run into Reagan in the hall between classes. She was still hanging out with the same kids he had seen her hanging out with before her "transformation." The only difference was now there was a group of boys that were trying to get her attention a few feet away. It didn't take Tom long to figure out from her body language that she was not interested in them. She did, however, notice Tom right away. "Hey, tough guy!" she hollered waving. "How's the nose?" He inwardly groaned. It had only been three days since the fight, and he knew that his nose was still several shades of black and blue.

"Back to normal," he quipped with a huge grin. "Can't ya tell?" She giggled, and her face lit up. She stepped out of her ring of friends as he walked past and fell in step with him on the way to his next class.

"Don't worry. Bruises from defending another are badges of honor."

Tom chuckled. "Thanks again for the cold compress. It was entirely possible I would have bled to death in the hall without you." he exaggerated.

"You did seem well on your way…" she agreed.

Tom chuckled. "Maybe."

"Well, I thought it was as good a time as any to pay you back for when you helped me."

Tom looked confused.

"Oh my God! You don't even remember!" she exclaimed reading his confusion. "Seventh grade. I was puking in a garbage can outside of math class and some of the boys in my grade were making snarky comments about me being pregnant. You came up to them and said we were dating and that you knew I wasn't pregnant." Her smile left Tom speechless. He had totally forgotten the incident. "Then they started picking on you for not knowing how to get a girl pregnant, and they left me alone."

"Oooh yeah!" Tom remembered. "Ben and Danny. Those guys were always horrible to someone."

"Well, no one ever defended me before that. And certainly, no one ever claimed to be dating me, even if it was just to get two jerks off my back." Reagan commended.

"Uh. Yeah. No problem." Tom stammered out.

Tom was having a hard time thinking of what else to say. These few sentences had been the most he had ever spoken to a girl like Reagan. And what was she wearing for perfume? It smelled like vanilla mixed with cotton candy. It was distracting.

Before he could pull his thoughts together, they had reached his physics class, and he stopped at the door. He turned and looked at her. She still had a half smile on her lips, and her eyes sparkled bright green.

He wanted to say something funny. Something that would get her to want to hang out with him outside of school, but what came out was "Umm… I guess this my class." Brilliant.

"Yeah." She sighed. "Well, I'm glad my patient is doing okay. I guess I'll catch ya later." Then, on impulse, she reached up, pressed her index finger to the tip of his nose, said "boop!" and hurried off toward her class.

He stood there as if paralyzed for a second before stepping into the class with tears in his eyes from the pain in his nose and smile on his face.

vii

Tom rounded the corner onto the street his house was on, and his thoughts flipped back to the events of the day. Man! He wished he knew how Tony was doing! He had never hurt anyone like this before. Sure, there had been times that he had rough-housed with his brother and accidentally hurt him, but that was nothing like this. DeMarcus had been knocked out at the school and hadn't woken up when the EMTs had picked him up and brought him to the hospital. How had he done it? And what was it that caused things to move? Was it magnetic? Radioactive? Electric?

He knew that when Tony had leveled the gun against Rick, he had wanted to push Tony and the gun so that he wouldn't hit Rick. At more than twenty feet away, Tom had raised his hands and yelled. Then whatever-it-was had been released, and everything went flying. Tom stopped his walk and looked around. There was no one around to see him, so he picked a target - a little kid's tricycle was sitting in a driveway he was passing. After one more quick glance around, Tom raised his hands and pointed at the trike. He took a deep breath and forcefully said "No!"

Nothing happened.

He tried it one more time. "No!"

"Hey kid!" hollered a lady from the upstairs window of the house. "Don't lose your mind. I'll get Cameron to move his trike in a minute."

Tom was mortified and hurried on past the house with his face burning red.

viii

As Tom passed the last couple of houses before arriving home, he wondered if it was just a fluke and wouldn't happen again. No, that didn't feel right. He could feel the energy in him. He may not be able to trigger it right now, but he could tell it was there. Waiting. Thinking that he wouldn't use it was like thinking he could tell himself never to use his right hand again just because it had fallen asleep. He could try, but the odds were it would happen again sometime when he was not paying attention.

ix

As Tom took all three steps in one bound onto the back porch and started fishing out his keys, all he could think was how thankful he was to be home. He felt like it had been ten years since he had left for school that morning. Grabbing a large glass of water, he turned on the TV and sank into the recliner in the living room. He had just settled in and had let the opening notes of his favorite sci-fi series start to lull him to sleep when someone right next to him said, "You're home late."

To say that Tom was jumpy after today would be an understatement. At the same time that he was jumping out of the chair and yelling "Faaaaghh!!" his hand came forward, and that same energy shot forward, blowing a baseball sized hole in the window.

12

Levi paused soaking in the fact that he had just scared his brother half out of his mind and that the window shattered with no one near it. "Damn dude! How did you do that?" Not waiting for an answer, he turned toward the shattered window, "Mom's gonna be pissed!"

CHAPTER **2**

The Experiment

i

Tom never got the chance to answer Levi's question, for it was at that moment that they heard their mom holler "Boys? Guess who was let out early to be with you?" as she entered the house. Tom was instantly in panic mode as he realized that he would not have an excuse for the small circular hole in the window in the living room. Levi saw his brother's eyes grow wide with concern and instantly knew what his brother was thinking. Without a word, he quickly crossed the room over to where the floor lamp was standing next to the recliner, looked at Tom and winked, and then reached out and pushed it over into the already broken window. The rest of the window blew outwards in a hail of glass and lampshade pieces with a loud crash.

Their mom was in the room in seconds. "What happened?!" She demanded as she took in the two boys standing next to the broken window.

Before Tom could open his mouth, "Sorry, mom! We were fooling around and accidentally knocked the lamp into the window." Levi covered smoothly. Then, before she could say anything, "We are really sorry. I'll go get a broom and stuff to clean it up." Then to Tom, "Can you go get some plastic and duct tape and cover the hole?"

Tom didn't even answer. He left the room in search of something to patch the hole while Levi was off to get the cleaning supplies, leaving their mom standing in the living room shaking her head.

ii

Dinner that night was tense. Tom's mother had whipped up one of her regular meals, and as they all sat down to supper, the questions began. 'Do either of you boys know this DeMarcus boy? Did you know he had a gun in school? Tom, did you see the explosive that he used?'

Tom answered "no" to all of these and offered little else for information which seemed to just irritate his mom to no end. It wasn't intentional; he just didn't know what else to say.

Then Levi, who had been practically squirming in his seat the entire time, saw his opening. "So, Tony had an explosive that just knocked everybody over, but didn't set anything on fire? That's weird."

"Yup. Very." Tom answered and shot Levi a "shut up" look when their mom wasn't looking. "So, how was your day mom?" It wasn't a subtle change of subject, but it worked. The topic changed, and the stress of questions died away.

iii

Somehow, they managed to get through the rest of the evening, even watching a couple of TV shows and unwinding before heading off to bed. However, Tom hadn't even been in bed for 20 minutes, when there was a light rap, and Levi's face peered in around the door.

Tom groaned.

"Come on, dude!" Levi begged, "You can't just leave me in the dark like this." He slipped into Tom's room and closed the door before taking two steps and jumping onto the foot of Tom's bed. "What the hell is going on? And don't feed me that crap you told mom. I saw what you did in the living room! I know there is more to the story."

Tom sighed. He knew that he was going to tell Levi everything eventually. He just hadn't planned on it being before he even had a chance to process it himself. "Honestly, I don't know man. You're right. It didn't go down like I told Mom at the dinner table. I did that thing that I did in the living room to Tony at school, except a lot bigger. It was terrifying. I could have killed him. I don't know what it is yet - all I know is that I can't control it and that it's dangerous."

"Sweet!" Levi clasped his hands together and smiled excitedly. "How long have you been able to do this? Do you know how you're able to do it? How is it dangerous?"

Tom started to laugh. "Calm down, you spaz! You don't want to trigger another seizure."

"Whatever." Levi blew off the advice "I'm not going to seize. Now out with it!"

"Okay but it's kind of a long story..."

iv

Three months ago, Tom had received a text from his mom to grab her salad out of the fridge and bring it to her at the hospital after he got out of school. As soon as the final bell rang, Tom jumped on his bike and swung by the house to grab the salad before heading up to the hospital three miles away.

Once at the hospital, he had texted her that he was there. She met him in the breakroom and fished around in the fridge for a second before pulling out a brown bag with her name on it. "You have my salad?" She asked holding out her hand.

"Yeah. Here you go." Tom handed her the Tupperware container with her salad in it. "You have to be the only person I know that can bring a salad for lunch and forget the salad;" he jibed, "so what's in the bag?"

"Dressing, fork and an apple." She replied without taking her eyes off the salad.

She had already worked eight straight hours without food, and she was famished.

Tom had a pretty good idea why she had forgotten the meal. This was her second double shift in a row, and she was exhausted. As usual, she had focused that morning on getting the lunches for her sons put together and had ultimately forgotten to pack her own. It wasn't the first time that this had happened.

As she ate, they chatted about Tom's day at school while he looked around the room. It was mid-sized with a large conference table and several chairs as well as a refrigerator and table sporting a microwave that was so dirty you couldn't see inside it. On the far side of the room were the employee mailboxes and a large bulletin board that dominated most of the rear wall.

Tom loved the bulletin board. Frequently, it would have jokes or things for sale - like snowmobiles or jet skis. As he got closer to the board, one of the ads caught his eye. It was a full-sized ad with little tear-away contact numbers that read:

> **Research Topic:** Testing the cure for epilepsy.
>
> **Attending Physician:** Dr. Edward Mobien
>
> **Needed:** 50 Men and 50 Women. Age must be over 18. Non-smokers. Chemical free.
>
> **Conditions:** Free lab work and physical during the term of the research. Upon successful completion of the study, each candidate will receive $500.
>
> Please call Terry at 802-555-1256 for further details.

Tom froze. "Mom! There's a cure for epilepsy!?" He snatched one of the contact tags and held it up.

"Woah. Slow down champ." She said looking up from her meal. "That is just another research study from another doctor thinking that they have the cure to something big." She stood up and walked over to the board. "Yeah. I've heard of this guy. He is good, but from what I hear, his study involves giving people drugs that permanently alter a person's brain chemistry." She shook her head. "Talk about high risk. Jesus!"

The idealist in Tom was already kicking into overdrive. "But mom! If there is even a chance that this medication could fix Levi, shouldn't we do everything we can to help?"

"Tom. That is not how this sort of thing works." She explained "These studies never fix something completely on the first go. From what I heard, the Review Board is even making him add steps to his study because it is such a high-risk thing he is doing."

"But mom!" He objected.

"No Tom!" She countered firmly. Then, she turned back to the ad on the wall, tore it down and threw it in the trash. "I won't hear any more of this. You are too young to be in the study, and I am not interested in you being a guinea pig. If Dr. Mobien comes up with a proven cure that has been thoroughly tested, then we can talk to Levi about this. Otherwise, this discussion ends here."

"Fine," Tom said through clenched teeth. "I think I have some homework to do."

"Maybe you should go start that now?" His mom agreed, grateful to have an end to the tense topic.

"Okay." Tom agreed as he slipped the contact tag he had in his hand into his pocket and turned to leave the room. "See ya in the morning."

υ

The very next day Tom called the number and spoke to the nurse, Terry, at Dr. Mobien's office. She asked him a few questions, and he answered all of them as best he could. The only one he exaggerated on was his age. He was only seventeen years old but rounded up to eighteen so that he would qualify.

His logic was simple. This study had the potential to save his brother from a life of seizures, and even if it didn't completely cure him, what if it helped him a lot? What if this study contributed to another study that actually did cure epilepsy? It was certainly worth it to Tom to do everything he could to help his brother… and of course, getting $500 at the end wouldn't hurt either.

By the end of the call, Tom had an appointment on a Saturday that his mother worked to meet with Dr. Mobien to do the physical and lab work. He showed up at 8 am sharp and by 10 was in a conference room with 10 other test subjects. There they were shown a 30-minute video. It started out by giving the background on Dr. Mobien. It talked about how he had two graduate degrees - one in biomolecular science and one in biology from Stanford as well as a medical degree with a specialty in neurology from Yale Medical School.

Then, the video went on to explain all the research that was involved in discovering this medication. It seems there are a handful of tribes in the Amazon rainforest area that have no reported cases of epilepsy at all. More importantly, these tribes were not genetically isolated. In other words, it had to be something that they were doing that fixed the problem. After years of searching, Mobien had narrowed it to a handful of compounds that were present in certain foods they ate. For almost two years, these compounds couldn't be replicated in a lab, but Mobien wouldn't give up. He refused to believe that the cure was something that could only be cooked up in Mother Nature's kitchen. Finally, after another year, he was able to produce a working compound. He then collected a group of two dozen dogs that were going to be put down for having severe epilepsy. After getting permission to run the test, Mobien administered the compound in IV form to all the dogs. He administered between one and twelve times the recommended dose of the medication. Twenty-three of the 24 dogs were cured entirely with no adverse effects - even at the higher doses. The one dog that was not cured died from an unrelated heart defect.

The evidence seemed to overwhelmingly support Dr. Mobien's compound. However, when he applied to the review board to have it tested on humans, several of the doctors on the board were reluctant to approve it. They wanted more testing to show that it wouldn't harm someone with a non-epileptic brain. As a result, Dr. Mobien agreed to take 100 healthy test subjects and administer one to five times the usual dose of the compound while monitoring them closely. Since his compound only normalizes the excitability of the brain cells, there should be no effect on anyone that already has normal brain cells.

Once that part of the study was done, he could move on to seeing if the compound would cure humans with epilepsy in the second phase of the study. If all went well, the cure could be on the market in as little as three years.

Tom could not have been more excited to participate in the study. Before he left that morning, he signed up to have the compound administered two Saturdays from then when his mother was again at work.

vi

On the day of the test, Terry met him at the door of the small suite of research offices in the oldest part of the hospital. "Again, sorry about the accommodations. Neurology isn't a big money maker for the hospital, so we tend to be located in whatever space is left over."

"No problem," Tom replied.

"If you will have a seat, I will go let Dr. Mobien know that you are here." She flashed a smile and didn't wait for the answer.

Tom looked around the waiting room and found it to be a narrow room with cement walls that had been painted over so many times that the lines between the cinder blocks were all but indistinguishable. The lights were the standard institutional fluorescents that cast a slightly yellow glow on the few pieces of furniture and occasional magazine that made up the room.

It wasn't long before Dr. Mobien stepped into the waiting room. He was a tall man with dark-rimmed glasses, dark hair and a goatee. "Tom! Good to see you. Please come on back with me, and we can get started." He shook Tom's hand and ushered him back toward the study area with his lab coat trailing out behind him.

Tom had already decided that he liked the good doctor based on his previous interactions with him. There was just something about him that exuded confidence without stepping over that line into the world of cockiness and condescension that afflicted a lot of physicians he had met. He followed him down a hallway and through a massive set of double doors. After Tom stepped in, Terry placed a sign on the outside of the door stating, "TEST IN PROGRESS – NO ADMITTANCE" and pulled them both closed tight explaining "We need to keep out any extra sound and light distractions."

vii

Tom nodded and continued on behind the doctor past a small room that was filled with all sorts of electrical equipment and into the following chamber that had an overstuffed recliner facing a large flat screen TV. As he got closer to the recliner, he could also see a couple of video cameras pointing at the recliner and a table with a small box and many wires coming out of it. Finally, just behind the recliner at head level was a standard hospital monitor, complete with all the usual attachments to monitor heart rate, breathing, blood pressure and how much oxygen is in the blood.

"Well, this is it. Have a seat, Tom."

He did and got a little better look at the room. He was still in the old part of the hospital judging by the aging stone architecture and oak trimmed doors. To the left of the TV, was a massive support beam for the hospital. To his right, he caught a glimpse of his reflection and realized that they must have installed a two-way mirror so that they could watch their subjects from the small equipment room next door without being watched back. As Terry and Dr. Mobien placed countless leads on his head and even a few on his chest, Dr. Mobien explained to Tom what he could expect during the compound administration part.

"So, once we are done attaching the leads, Terry will place an IV in your right arm. This study has a control arm and a variable arm. That means that some people will get an IV of fluid, while other people will get the compound. You are not allowed to know which one you get. In either case, when we start, we will be playing a nice soothing soundtrack, and a peaceful movie of the ocean will be on the TV. We will get a reading of what your baseline EEG, or brain waves, looks like. Then we hit a button that will trigger the IV pump to start giving you whatever is in the IV bag. The IV will infuse over 20 minutes, and then we will monitor you for 30 more minutes. That's it." He concluded just as he finished attaching the last of the head leads. "Any questions?"

"Nope. Fire away." Tom said, and with that Dr. Mobien smiled and left the room, pulling the door closed behind him. The room was as silent as the grave. The thick cement walls and plush carpet deep in the basement absorbed all sound and left him acutely aware of how loud his breathing was. After a few more seconds, Dr. Mobien's voice came over a speaker so loudly that Tom couldn't suppress an involuntary jump even though he knew it was coming.

"Can you hear me?" Mobien asked.

"Yes," replied Tom.

"Good. There will be a 10-second pause, then the music and video will turn on, and the study will begin. Okay?"

"Sure."

Not even a full minute had passed when the red recording lights on the cameras blinked into life along with the TV and stereo. On the screen was a beautiful beach with crystal blue ocean water just a few paces away. The music that played along with the sound of the waves was soft and rose and fell like waves. It was apparently chosen to be as soothing as the video. The camera then went down to the water and seemed to float along, riding the waves.

viii

In the observation room, Dr. Mobien and Nurse Terry Krenshaw were hard at work. Both of them had a "pre-study checklist" to go through to ensure none of the things they were supposed to be checking on got missed. Mobien had to check the video and EEG leads, and Terry was responsible for vital signs and keeping everything on time.

Typically, it took several minutes to set everything up and get a decent recording of the subject's baseline readings. He had just finished fine tuning the video feed when he looked down at the EEG tracing for the first time. "Whoa!"

Terry looked up from what she was doing "Everything okay over there?"

"I don't know." Came his tentative reply.

"What do you mean?"

"This guy has some weird brainwave readings. He has theta waves while he is awake. That all by itself isn't all that abnormal. It happens when people daydream sometimes, but he also has these crazy slow, HUGE delta waves!" Mobien explained as he watched in open wonder as one of the most abnormal readings he had ever seen ran across the monitor.

"Okay… So, what does that mean?"

"I have no idea," Mobien muttered. "Normally, delta waves while the person is awake only happen in developing brains of infants and small children. This guy is way too old for this." He squinted up at the monitor and then hit the "continuous print" button. "I mean - we know that delta waves are helpful in releasing hormones to aid the body's healing process and that they play some role in learning and committing things to long-term memory, but as for what they are doing at this frequency…" He shrugged. "Maybe we should stop the infusion. I can't say this isn't a reaction to the medication."

"That would be hard to do." Terry frowned.

"Why is that?"

"Because I haven't started it yet." She replied looking back at the screen.

Mobien looked up at her, surprised. She shrugged back.

"Oh wow… So, this is all him. This is his resting brainwave pattern." Amazed, Mobien looked back at the monitor.

"Dr. Mobien," Terry said, getting his attention. "We are approaching the five-minute marker where we either give the IV infusion, or we abort. What is your call?"

"Crap. Right." Mobien quickly went through his list of things that would cause him to abort. Tom had stable vital signs and was in a peaceful state. It really didn't matter that his baseline brainwave reading was abnormal as long as it didn't change when he gave the compound. "Go ahead."

Terry paused a second with her finger on the button that would start the infusion. *I hope he knows what he is doing* was all she could think as she pressed the button.

Tom had been watching the video for almost a half an hour now. It had started out with waves crashing. Then, it went on to things that floated along on the water. First, it was a beach ball that was bounced around in the surf. Next, it showed deeper waters and an empty rowboat floating on the waves. Once it got close enough, you could make out a fishing pole and a couple of bags of rice in the bottom of the boat. It wasn't an exciting film, but it was mildly interesting enough to keep you from falling asleep.

As it turns out, Tom was so completely engaged in the film that he didn't even notice the dimming of the lights or the abrupt pause in the images and music as the main power was shut down. However, a split second later, the energy from the backup generator flooded the circuit to the EEG machine attached to Tom's head. The resulting blast of electricity screamed through the leads and into Tom's head with enough force to vaporize the conductors that Dr. Mobien had so diligently attached moments earlier.

The next few minutes were a blur. Tom screamed, and the room he was in seemed to simply explode in a burst of blue light. The blast blew apart the two-way mirror that separated the two rooms, flattened everything in the observation room and knocked the door off from one hinge. The explosion could be felt as far away as the emergency room across the road.

Dr. Mobien was the first one to rise as the dust began to settle in the small observation room. He slowly pushed broken pieces of equipment off from himself until he was able to stand. As he started to register what had happened, he spotted Terry half-buried a little further toward the door. Mobien realized that he had been standing between her and the blast and so had taken the brunt of the flying debris. Catching his eye, she smiled weakly at his bloodied face as she pushed away from the smashed equipment. "I'm okay Ed." She said, momentarily forgetting her decorum. "Tom…?"

Mobien was already moving toward the door. Hooking a sharp right toward the testing room, he was not quite prepared for what he saw. The heavy oak door to the room had been blown completely off from its hinges and had slammed into the far wall with enough force to embed it about four inches deep into the cement. Even more impressive yet was the room itself. With all the lights in the room smashed, it was difficult to make it all out at first until his eyes adjusted to the light filtering in from the small antechamber outside the door. Fine dust from the explosion still drifted lightly in the air. The TV that dangled loosely off from one fastener was one of the few pieces of equipment that had not ended up in a pile in one of the corners of the room. The two video cameras were crushed into several small pieces on the floor of the room just below two large depressions, one in the wall and one in the large support column at the front of the room.

It was then that Mobien saw him. Still in semi-sitting position in what was left of the recliner, was Tom. His clothes seemed to have steam rising up from them and what was left of the EEG was smoldering on the floor. Mobien ran to him and grabbed his wrist and placed a hand on his chest. The pulse was strong, and his chest rose and fell with a steady rhythm. Thank God. "Tom, are you okay?" he asked gently shaking him…

x

He had been okay, in spite of having been at ground zero in what the fire department swore classified as an "atypical minor natural gas explosion." The full report spoke about a pipe that must have leaked a small pocket of gas into the room that was ignited by the electrical arc from the power surge. The fire department's report sounded almost like a fantasy novel. It just didn't seem like it could possibly be true. The leak was never found, but the matter was eventually laid to rest.

Of course, Dr. Mobien had immediately called for an ambulance to take Tom to the ER, and thankfully, he had still been unconscious when he arrived. He missed the "talk" that his mom had with Dr. Mobien. A talk that ranged from accusing him of gross malpractice for admitting an underage subject into his study to demanding to know the exact chemical compound that Mobien had used on her son to inform him of what would happen to him if there were any lasting bad side effects from this "incident."

To his credit, Dr. Mobien listened to the entire tirade with a solemn face and repeatedly apologized for any part he played in Tom ending up in the ER. It would be several days before Ms. Woods would get the official letter from the fire department explaining it was not Dr. Mobien's fault at all.

It was around Mobien's fifth apology that Tom woke up. Aside from an intense headache from a mild concussion, he had handled it reasonably well. No, the real impact of the incident didn't start to show up until about a week later when the nightmares began...

xi

"Dude!" Levi had been spellbound listening to the story. "That's crazy... AND awesome!"

Tom looked at him like he had three heads. "What's awesome about it?"

"First, that was super-cool of you to volunteer for a study that could help with curing epilepsy! Extra bonus bro-points." He held up a hand for a high five and waited. Tom groaned and gave him a "high one" by just using his index finger to return the high five. "Whatever." Levi shrugged. "Next, awesome that you didn't die after getting blown up like twice in three months!"

"Okay, I'm with you on that one." Tom agreed.

"So, short version: you may have some sort of weird thing you can do after being drugged and electrocuted. Did I miss anything?"

"Just the dreams and sleepwalking."

"Woah. You sleepwalk now too?" Levi was impossible. He found just about everything exciting.

"I think so" Tom conceded. "I go to sleep and have these crazy nightmares about the ocean. I dream that I am getting pulled into the water. When my toe touches the water, it's like I am getting electrocuted or catching fire or something. My whole body is one big nerve ending, and then when I wake up, a lot of the stuff on my desk and the dresser is on the floor or scattered all over the room."

"Well, that sucks." Levi agreed. "I have a hard-enough time keeping my room clean without my electrified-sleep-zombie-self messing it all up."

"Seriously." Tom agreed.

"What's the plan?"

"I have no idea. I guess I have to just wait and see if these dreams go away…"

CHAPTER 3

A Visit with the Good Doctor

i

Tom's dreams had been getting stronger each night, and were now in the process of becoming full-blown nightmares. The water had taken on a more powerful quality with each repetition of the dream, and the irrational terror it evoked had become equally more intense as had the furniture rearrangements in his room. He was now even waking up to find things as large as his bed had been moved.

ii

It was these dreams that finally made Tom seek out Dr. Mobien again. Tom had wanted some explanation of why he was feeling this way and what the ocean images meant. Mobien was the only doctor he knew that might have some insight into something this weird. All the same, Tom was surprised when Mobien called him back and offered to meet with him the following afternoon.

He is probably worried that my mom is going to try to sue him, thought Tom on the way to the restaurant. Mobien had wanted to meet but had explained that since the "incident," the clinic had been closed. It seems that the support post that had been in the room was one of the central support posts for the entire building and it had suffered some minor structural damage. More to the point, there were two fair sized cracks in the post which required the eye of a trained engineer to see if they warranted cause for alarm.

"Thanks for meeting me here, Tom." Mobien began as they both sat down at Rutnies, a local restaurant. "I was hoping that you would want to talk again."

"Really? Why is that?" asked Tom, genuinely surprised.

"Well, before the incident, your EEG was very interesting." Mobien began "Your delta waves were the largest and slowest I have ever seen. I would love just to monitor you some time and ask you some questions."

"That's great doc, but at the moment, I am all studied out." Tom interrupted. "I don't think my heart could take another one of your studies right now."

"I don't mean *right now*" interjected Mobien quickly. "I only want you to keep an open mind for the future. I would love to get some more readings from you once they have the repairs completed and a lot more safety features installed. *And* this would not involve any drugs." He finished trying to sell his request.

"Okay. Maybe someday… I will have to let you know if and when I feel up to it," Tom countered. "I do have a question though."

"Let's hear it."

"I would like to know why I keep having nightmares about the ocean," Tom asked.

"I don't know." Mobien mulled over the thought as he rubbed his chin and sipped on the coffee he had ordered. "I suppose it is possible that you are having some sort of post-traumatic stress response from the incident. The image I used for the study was a scene of the ocean. Maybe your subconscious borrowed the image since it relates to the incident."

Tom frowned. There was more to it. He was sure of that. "I don't know…"

"I understand that you may be a bit skeptical. You should give it some time and see if they go away."

"I guess so…" Tom was still dubious.

"It should be about two more weeks before all the engineers will let me back in there. If you are still having this issue then, we can try something else and see if that helps. I have had some luck with hypnosis for this sort of thing."

"Really?" Tom felt hopeful this might help. "You'd do that for me?"

"Of course. We just need to get the engineers to sign off that it's okay for us to go back to the clinic."

Tom did not have high hopes that the dreams would go away over time. If anything, they seemed to be intensifying, but he was willing to be patient and wait.

iii

John Cummings had lived on Temer Avenue for almost 42 years, and at the age of 85, it made him the oldest resident on that little stretch of pavement. John found it odd that with old age had come the inability to sleep on a regular schedule. "Part of the circle of life" an older friend of his had joked several years back "You come into this world on your own sleep schedule and if you live long enough that is just how you leave it." He hadn't understood then, but he sure did now. He would sleep for two to four hours and then be up for six to eight hours, around the clock. Never mind that this meant that he was usually awake at nearly three in the morning each day – for all rights and purposes the deadest hour of the clock.

All the same, it was a beautiful night, and John decided it was time to go for his usual summer moonlit stroll down the road. It was when he was a few houses down from 115 Temer Avenue that John saw the lights. They were bright blue flashes like bursts from a camera flash. "What the hell…?" John wondered looking up. The more he looked, the less it seemed like camera flashes. No, John decided, one of the Woods boys must be welding something up there. There is a steady blue light with bright flashes on top of it. Suddenly there was a flash brighter than the rest that lit up the street like it was daytime, then a loud thump and the room went dark. "Huh. He must have dropped his torch." John mused. "Serves the fool right for trying to weld like that in the dead of night," he muttered continuing down the road.

iv

Tom landed on the floor with a loud thud that jolted him into being fully awake. "What the h…!"

"Tom! You okay?" Levi asked bursting through his door in his pajama bottoms and t-shirt.

"Yeah. Just fell out of bed after another crappy dream." He replied rubbing his bruised bum. "I am so sick of this! I was waiting to see if the dreams would go away, but after what happened at the school, they are getting even worse!"

"Well, from what you said Mobien told you, they should be back in their offices. It's been way over two weeks." Levi suggested. "Let's go see he can fix this."

v

And so, promptly at 8 am, Tom called Dr. Mobien's office and told the secretary that he needed to talk to the doctor today. "It is an emergency. Please tell Dr. Mobien that my issue is escalating."

"Just a moment please." There was a long pause. Tom could imagine her finding Dr. Mobien and repeating his request. "Dr. Mobien happens to have an opening this afternoon at one. Would you be able to make that?"

Tom smiled with relief. "Sure. I'll be there."

vi

Tom and Levi arrived at Mobien's offices at five minutes to one. Tom had told Levi he didn't have to come with him, but after all the strange events surrounding the experiment, there was no way that Levi was going to miss this.

In truth, Tom didn't mind having him there. He and Levi may fight like cats and dogs at times, but they always had each other's backs, and if he did get hypnotized, he wanted someone there that was fully awake to remember everything that happened.

It wasn't long after they had checked in that the secretary opened the door into the offices and ushered the boys down the hall. They both followed her down a small corridor lined with hardwood doors and ducked into the fourth one on the right labeled "conference chamber: room 314."

"Here you boys go," she said indicating to the chairs around the conference table. "Have a seat, and the doctor will be right here in a bit." With that, she disappeared back through the door.

Not even five minutes later, Dr. Mobien appeared in the doorway. "And who do we have here?" He asked in his most ingratiating voice as he held his hand out for Levi to shake it.

"This is Levi, my brother," Tom answered as the two shook hands.

"Ahh. This is the young man you told me about with epilepsy that inspired you to become involved with the study." His smile deepened in genuine appreciation.

"Uh. Yeah." Tom muttered, a little embarrassed that Mobien had voiced his motives in front of his brother.

As they all took their seats, Dr. Mobien led the conversation "so the secretary said you are still having nightmares and that they are getting worse. Why don't we start there?"

So, Tom told him everything – the dreams about the electrocutions when he touches the ocean, the sleepwalking, a detailed account of the incident at the school and finally the window at his house. He didn't hold anything back. After Tom was done speaking, Mobien sat in stunned silence with his fingers interlocked on the conference table for a time.

Finally, when he did speak, Tom could tell he was carefully weighing his words. "I think that you have been through a lot lately Tom. You had a frightening experience with the test, and then not even two months later your life is threatened at school. It is enough to unsettle anyone. I do have a friend though that could help you…"

"Hold on now; I am not crazy!" Tom interrupted, now that he could see where Mobien was going. "These things have to be related to the experiment. How else would you explain what's happening?"

"I don't know. I wasn't there, but I certainly wouldn't opt for the supernatural explanation for my first choice." Mobien shot back. Frustrated, he reached into his lab coat pocket and pulled out a bottle of pills and slammed it down on the table. "Look at this." He indicated the pills on the table. "This is my life's work. It's the final pill form of the IV medication you received during the study. It's a medication that I have spent years researching that will permanently cure people like Levi here from having any seizures. One dose, no ongoing prescriptions. Bam! Done." Levi's eyes locked onto the bottle with undisguised longing. "The theory behind it is sound and *real.*" He stressed the last word.

"Now, I am not sure what you are trying to get me to believe here, but if you are asking me to believe that my medication - which is just a combination of rainforest fruit extracts - gave you superpowers… Well, you might want to think that one through again. It's. Just. Not. Possible." He emphasized each word. "Besides, if I even entertained the possibility that it might be true, I might as well kiss my ability to practice medicine goodbye. No one would believe it, and then this medication would never be approved for use."

Then, he quickly regained his composure. "Look, maybe your mind is playing tricks on you." He saw Tom roll his eyes and Levi shake his head. "That is much more likely to be the case, and if you really want to know for sure, maybe we should try the hypnosis. I have been known to have some success with regressing people to the time of a traumatic event through hypnosis to help them understand what actually happened. Or at the very least, it may be able to help you with the nightmares."

"And if I am hypnotized, and tell you the exact same thing I just told you…?"

"I will be stunned." Mobien began reluctantly.

"Would you agree to help me figure out how to fix it?" Tom asked earnestly.

"No matter what we find, I will tell you everything that I know about the medication I gave you and about the monitoring - maybe that will help you get past the stress you have felt since the explosion at the lab." Mobien affirmed "However, I am not going to waste my time with parapsychological research. I don't believe in it, and I have spent too much of my life building a solid reputation as a person of medical science to have it all illegitimized by talk of me being into anything occult."

"Fair enough" Tom conceded. "You have my word and Levi's that we will never tell anyone you were involved, but we want the same promise from you. From this point on, I was only a person in your study. I never came to you with questions and no mentioning hypnosis to anyone. I want this to fall under that 'doctor-patient rewards thingy.' Is that a deal?"

"It's 'doctor-patient privilege,' and yes, it's a deal," Mobien confirmed with a half grin. Then he paused for thought. "Okay, let's get this started. Why don't you boys move the table out of the way and get our chairs facing each other? I need to go dig up a candle." He said rising and heading for the door. "I'll be right back."

vii

In two minutes, Mobien was back in the room with a medium sized dinner candle. He and Tom sat facing each other in their overstuffed conference chairs as Levi looked on from a chair set off to the side. After advising both boys to be quiet and Tom to relax, he explained that he was going to use a rapid hypnosis technique that many carnival workers use to achieve a level of deep relaxation in their subjects quickly. He then lit the candle and began talking in a soft voice. In short order, he had

Tom in a deep state of hypnosis and began to regress him to the time of the incident in the hallway at school. "Okay Tom, we are going to walk through this memory slowly, so that you can tell me what is happening before it happens. We are going to start on the day you found the two boys arguing in the hallway at school." Mobien began "Now you just came down the stairs, and you see Tony and Rick arguing."

Dr. Mobien watched as Tom's hands clenched into fists at his side. His eyes were closed, but his brow was furrowed as he remembered the tension of the situation. Quickly checking the notes he had made about their encounter, Mobien lead him further into the memory "Tony has just threatened Rick. Now he hears the door close and turns toward you."

"He doesn't get turned that far around. He hears Rick start to run" Tom answers.

"And how does that make you feel?" Dr. Mobien presses.

"I get a sinking feeling in my stomach. Tony is spinning back around toward Rick." Tom's voice is tense and anxious. "He is raising the gun!" Tom starts to squirm in his seat.

"Now we will advance slowly," Mobien said as he started to move Tom toward the crisis at the root of which he knew must be a delusional state while Levi looked on with interest. "We now are at the point where Tony is pointing the gun at Rick. What happens next?"

"DeMarcus yelled 'STOP!'" Tom almost shouts, now highly agitated. "I can't seem to move. I can see his finger starting to squeeze the trigger!" Tom stiffens as he relives the moment.

Dr. Mobien is just about to interject and calm Tom down when he notices a complete shift in Tom's demeanor. Tom stops fidgeting and sits up straight. His body language completely changes from anger and anxiety to one filled with purpose, but nothing could have prepared

Mobien for what happened next. Tom's eyes seem to start to glow, and an intense wind picks up with Tom at its center. In a flash, the candle is blown out, and the notebook Dr. Mobien was using is blown off his lap. A second later the wind is strong enough to push Mobien and Levi out of their chairs and up against the wall. As Mobien squints his eyes against the light and the wind, he cannot look away from Tom who seems to be rising up out of the chair. As he floats six inches above the floor in the gathering gale, his hands start to glow with the same energy as is emanating from his eyes. Slowly, his arms begin to rise up in front of his face as waves of energy rippled down toward his hands.

Mobien realized in that instant that everything Tom had told him had happened just as he had described. In a near panic, Mobien's mind jumped ahead in the story, and he knew with certainty that Tom was about to unleash enough energy that he may utterly destroy the office… and anyone in it. In fact, the only thing that had stopped that from happening already was the fact that Mobien had told Tom to tell him about events before they occurred…

"Tom!" Mobien shouted as he was pinned against the wall by the rising wind "on the count of three you will be awake!" He quickly shouted as the wind continued to intensify. "One! Two! THREE!"

Instantly Tom came wide-awake. For a split second, he hovered in the air above the chair, his eyes wide as he took in what was happening. Then, he was crashing into his seat, and the wind and glow were gone.

Dr. Mobien staggered as the wind suddenly died out, his eyes wide. "Holy crap!"

"Oh my GOD!! THAT WAS AWESOME!!" Levi crowed between deep breaths.

Tom was shaking visibly but still picked up on Levi using his breathing techniques so that he wouldn't stress out and cause a seizure. "Careful, Levi."

"Don't sweat me, man!" Followed by more breaths and a huge smile "Let's see if we can get you to float home!"

Tom groaned.

"Dude! We can tie a string on your leg, and you can do all the 'glowy-balloon-thing' you want!"

Tom gave his brother a withering look while at the same time started to relax knowing his brother wouldn't have a seizure.

"So, you remember everything?" Mobien interrupted the boys.

Tom nodded.

Mobien grabbed his tipped over chair and gracelessly sat down at the table. Nothing that he had learned could have prepared him for what he had just seen. It just should not be possible! How could a person just radiate such power and not even know how they were doing it themselves?

"Are you okay?" Levi asked, not liking the look on Dr. Mobien's face. "You don't look so hot."

"Yeah, I just have to collect my thoughts. Give me a second."

His mind was already spinning forward. How could the experiment have led to this? Was it because of the test compound or was it because Tom already had something odd with his brain and this just let it out? Could the medication have a different effect when exposed to electricity?

Tom couldn't help it anymore "So… What do you think? You believe me now, right?"

Mobien looked up and started to chuckle nervously. "Yeah, Tom, I think you make an excellent case."

Tom and Levi started to laugh a little too. "Good."

Dr. Mobien sobered a little. "To be honest with you, this is waaay out of my league. I have never even heard of this happening to anyone." He replied honestly. "I can tell you that your brain wave tracing before the incident in my office was really… unique, and that after the incident in the lab, I did look up your IV and it was the one with medication in it. It wasn't just fluid. What I don't know, is what the effect of having electricity added to the medication would have had on you. A combination of these things could have caused it. Without further testing and research, I have no way of knowing."

Even this relieved Tom to a degree. "That is fine with me. I didn't even have a working theory at this point. I will take whatever I can get."

Mobien sat for a minute as his thoughts raced through possibilities. "It is fascinating to me that none of the other subjects had *any reactions* at all," he mused. "From the brainwave readings we got on you before the testing started, I would have to say that you must have had some genetic anomalies before chemicals and electricity. If that is true, that would mean that others in your family could suffer from the same condition, and they may have a similar response if exposed to the medication. Further research would be required to know for sure." Tom immediately raised an eyebrow. "Oh, don't worry, Tom. The medical review board shut me down because of the explosion. I need to get cleared by the fire marshal before we can start up again, so there won't be any further testing for quite some time." Tom seemed to visibly relax as Mobien continued. You know, the genetic anomaly may even have something to do with Levi's severe form of epilepsy."

"Great!!" Levi cut him off in midsentence. "I get to take handfuls of medications to keep from twitching like a frog on a hot plate, and he gets to throw stuff with his brain! So not fair!"

Mobien sighed and continued. "As far as *what exactly* this ability is… I guess if you believe the stories about old yogis meditating and bending spoons, it would be theoretically possible that with Tom's weird Delta and Theta waves, the right chemicals and some electricity, that he could also be able to move things with his mind…" He wondered out loud. "It seems that it has given you some form of telekinesis. I have to say, though, that I have no idea what the glowing or wind that seemed to kick up is about or how it all works."

"Telekinesis…?" Tom asked with skepticism.

"That *is* pretty sweet." Levi conceded.

"Yes," Mobien answered Tom and ignored Levi. "It would explain throwing DeMarcus without leaving a burn on him, the window at your home and even what happened here in this room." Mobien collected his thoughts for a moment. "This is a bit of speculation on my part, but I wonder if your flashes of the ocean are directly linked to the electrical shock and the initial triggering of this ability. It could be your brain made a connection between that experience and the video of the ocean. If that is the case, then focusing on the image of the ocean may bring your new 'talent' out."

"Bring it out?" Tom asked reluctantly.

"Yes. A lot of trauma victims are able to remember an image from just before their accidents. Frequently, focusing on these images helps them to remember more of the accident so that they can work through the emotional trauma of the event." Mobien explained. "I wonder if focusing on the ocean image will allow you to manifest your new ability consciously. If you are doing it on purpose and not reacting to danger, it is very likely that you will have a lot more control and focus. It is like learning anything. The more you practice, the easier it should become to do it. My guess is that you will need to make a choice. Do you want to have control over it when this happens again, or do you want to suppress it and hope that it doesn't happen at all?"

"Oh. I don't know, but I do know that it is nothing that I am in the mood to experiment with right now." Tom shuddered as he considered the damage that he might accidentally do in such a confined space.

"Aww… Come on, Tom" Levi chimed in with a grin. "This little room could use a few more windows, don't ya think?"

Dr. Mobien suddenly looked a bit uncomfortable. "No boys. I didn't mean now, but if you want my advice - I think you should consider learning to control this ability. It has already popped up three times because you can't control it. One of those times you punched a fist-sized hole through a window. Have you ever wondered what would have happened if a person had been standing in between you and the window?" Tom started to look sick to his stomach. "Yeah. I didn't think you had."

Dr. Mobien rose from his chair and slowly started walking around the room while looking at the floor and occasionally under the chairs as he continued talking. "I think you should find someplace where no one is going to see you and start trying to figure out what triggers it. I would be glad to help in any way I can, so please don't hesitate to call me."

"Yeah. Maybe that might not be a bad idea." Tom agreed. "I guess I have a lot of thinking to do."

Tom and Levi rose to leave. "I appreciate the help" Tom told Mobien and shook his hand.

"Anytime," Mobien replied, half distracted, as he continued looking around the room for the missing bottle of pills. "Anytime…"

CHAPTER 4

Basic Training

i

"I have a plan to help with your sleepwalking." Levi offered as he burst into Tom's room.

"Levi! How many times do I have to tell you? Knock first!!" Tom snapped as he pulled up his pajama bottoms.

"Yeah. Yeah. I know. Privacy. Whatever." He mocked and flopped on the foot of Tom's bed. "Here's the thing – I want to watch you do your 'Woods Brothers Midnight Movers' routine!"

"What?"

"I want to watch you sleepwalk – duh!" Levi explained "No. Seriously. Check it out." He pressed forward noting Tom's frown. "Not in a creepy way. I want to see if I can make out why you are trashing your room and moving your furniture." He offered.

Tom considered it and then shook his head, "I would never be able to sleep knowing that you are here watching me."

"Then we can try something else. I can set up a camera to record you. Could you sleep like that?"

Tom broke into a grin. "Okay, but I get to look at it first – just in case I do anything embarrassing."

"Deal!" Levi agreed. He immediately ran back into his room and grabbed his hunting camera. "So, let's do this."

"Tonight?" Tom asked eyeing the motion-activated video camera that the boys used to see what kinds of animals were around during hunting season.

"Of course, tonight!" Levi replied over his shoulder as he set the camera up on the desk in the corner of the bedroom. "This is a safe spot, right?"

"I have no idea," Tom replied and crawled into bed just as Levi finished fidgeting with the camera. "Alright, let's do this."

"Okay. This is going to be awesome." Levi smiled and flipped off the light switch as he slipped out of the room.

ii

Tom woke with a start at the sound of a loud thud, followed by a groan.

"Jesus! Tom!" Levi complained. "I think your dresser is up against the door again!"

Tom smiled to himself. He had clearly done some redecorating in his room again last night. *At least my nocturnal activities have one good side effect.* He thought as he got up and pushed his dresser away from the door. *I get my privacy.*

As soon as it was clear, the door flew open, and Levi burst into the room, fully dressed for the day.

"Dude! I almost couldn't sleep last night! Have you already looked at the footage?" He walked straight back to where the desk was supposed to be. "Crap! Where is it?"

Tom looked around. The desk that had occupied the far corner of the room was now on its side in the opposite corner.

"Never mind!" Levi called. "Got it!" he announced triumphantly holding up the camera.

Two minutes later the boys had the camera plugged into Tom's laptop, and the video footage queued up.

"Hold on." Tom stopped Levi before he pushed play. "I get to preview it first, right?"

Levi seemed to almost physically deflate as he moved around to the stand on the opposite side of the laptop so that he couldn't see the screen. "Yeah… If you have to…"

"Cool," Tom said relieved and pressed play.

From the far side of the computer, Levi watched Tom's face as he watched the video at "4x" speed. After a couple of minutes, Tom's eyes grew large, and he clicked a button to make the video play at regular speed. A minute later and he was pale and shaking when he clicked the "stop" button.

"Dude. You okay?" Levi asked, concerned.

Tom just nodded and motioned for Levi to come around and look. He spun back the video a few minutes and hit play as Levi sat next to him and started to watch. At first, it was just Tom lying in bed. Then, the covers seemed to begin to ripple like waves on a lake. After a few seconds of that, they flew off, and Tom started to glow. A wind picked up blowing papers and small objects all around the room. Tom, glowing and hovering above the bed, held his hands out and the dresser and desk started floating in a circle around the room. At that point in the film, the video camera must have flown off into a corner because the footage became unrecognizable just before going dark.

Both boys were spellbound as they watched the impossible evidence of what had actually been happening every night in Tom's room.

Still shaking, Levi looked over at Tom as he let out a low whistle. "I suspected, but dang!" He breathed, then immediately broke into a grin. "So… how about we figure out how this thing works so that you can stop going all Jedi every night?"

iii

"Dude! Who the hell is 'Uncle Lester?'" Levi asked as soon as they were done talking with their mom.

"Really Levi?" Tom asked disbelieving that he didn't know. "He is dad's brother. You know - remember the farm we use to go to once in a while when we were little? The place with 'Kevy Bacon?' That baby pig you used to talk about?"

"Jesus, Tom! I was four!" Levi shot back with an annoyed look and then smiled. "And that pig was the only cool thing about that place!" He laughed. "It almost made up for that weird friggin farmhand they had with the huge hillbilly beard that chewed tobacco all the time. Dang, he smelled bad!"

"You really don't remember much." Tom laughed. "That 'farm hand' was Uncle Lester!"

"Oh my God… This just keeps getting better." Levi started laughing too now. "Did he really just ask us to work on his farm today?"

Tom scoffed. "Nope. According to our cousins, he found some woman online that says she wants to marry him, so he left to go to Florida to meet her. That was six months ago."

Levi whistled. "Damn. I hope he isn't in a ditch somewhere."

"Me too" Tom agreed "But he sent an email to Grams two months ago saying he would be back in the fall, so who knows." Tom reached his desk and looked at the word processing program he had used to write a fake email he had shown his mom before hitting "delete."

"All I know for sure is that he isn't going to be around for months. The email I made up asks us to take care of his farm for the summer, so it should give us a ton of free time far away from anyone – that way I can get some control over my abilities."

"Brilliant idea. Except for one thing - We aren't farmers!!" Levi pointed out.

"Well, neither was he, really." Tom countered "He has a vineyard. Not a bunch of cows and chickens and crap like that." He explained. "I think all we need to do is make sure they don't get over or under watered and we are good to go."

"But won't mom check with Uncle Lester? And what happens when he comes home?" Levi asked.

"That's the best part. Mom hates him. I'm not sure why, but she won't talk to him unless she absolutely has no other choice."

"And that is why you run this merry little band." Levi laughed. "When do we begin our farming careers?"

"The last day of school is this Friday. So… Monday?" Tom offered. "Mom works a double that day anyhow."

"Sweet." Levi grinned.

Tom and Levi lived on the outer edge of town, but Uncle Lester's farm in the next town over was another 4-mile bike ride from their house. Their uncle had purchased a farm that was set back about a half of a mile from the road, and the long curving dirt driveway was starting to show signs of not being used. The two boys noticed sumac bushes had begun to encroach on the sides of the path as they turned off the main road.

"How did Uncle Lester think he was going to keep the farm going if he wasn't around?" Levi asked between breaths as he stood on the peddles to maintain his speed up a short hill.

"I don't know. Maybe he was just going to let it go for one year and not grow anything." Tom suggested as he worked his way up the hill behind Levi. He, again, found himself regretting the fact that the only car the family owned was the one his mom took to work every day.

They had just crested the short hill when Levi let out a "Wooohoooo!" and started down the steep descent on the other side at top speed. He was barely out of sight around the corner at the bottom when Tom heard Levi yell "CRAP!" followed by the sound of tires locking up on gravel and a crash.

Tom was already on his way down the hill and slowed his bike as he came around the corner. What he saw immediately made him start laughing. Laying across the road was a huge, old sugar maple. On the ground, right before the tree trunk, was Levi's bike, and about fifteen feet past that, on the other side of the tree trunk, was Levi - already brushing off his clothes and sporting a new rip in the knees of his jeans.

"Are you okay, man?" Tom asked getting off his bike and looking over the massive trunk.

"Yeah," Levi replied trying to get away from the cloud of dust in the air that he had made when he brushed off his clothes. Then, as if noticing the tree trunk for the first time "Hey! It looks like you have your first test of your telekinny-thingy."

Tom followed Levi's eyes to the tree as it dawned on him what Levi was suggesting. "What?! Use telekinesis? Are you kidding me? On this thing?" Tom asked incredulously. "Just the section covering the road has got to be close to a thousand pounds! There is *no way* I can move something that big!"

Levi laughed at his brother's reaction. "Come on man! What is the worst thing that could happen? You could pull a muscle in your brain and think with a limp for a week?"

"Mocking me is not going to make the tree any lighter."

Levi shifted gears and started being serious "Look, we need to move the tree because we don't want to have to stop at the end of this hill and carry our bikes over this thing every day this summer. And more importantly, we don't have any idea if weight even comes into play with your ability. I say you just give it a shot and see what happens."

"I guess I can try…" Tom, conceded reluctantly.

"Do or do not. There is no try." Encouraged Levi in his best Yoda impersonation.

Tom paced a little. He had not been expecting to try this so soon and hadn't really had time to consider how he was actually going to trigger his powers intentionally. He had no idea what would set them off or what the outcome would be. He just knew that he could feel… something buzzing inside his body. It was like the feeling you have after you let go of an electric fence – just an intense tingling.

He started thinking it through. The tree trunk was about four feet in diameter, and over eight feet of it needed to be cleared from the road. Would he just strike it in the middle? Would it snap there and move off the road? He had no idea. "Okay." He said, getting Levi's attention. "Stand behind me in the trees so I don't accidentally hurt you."

"Oh. Good point." Levi walked a dozen or so paces behind Tom and grabbed onto a young maple. "Ready."

Tom looked resolved as he turned to face his target. Then he raised his hand with the palm facing out and his fingers extended, pointed it at the tree and willed the tree to slide back out of the way.

Nothing happened.

Maybe I am going about this wrong. Dr. Mobien said that the trigger might be thinking of the ocean. Extending his hand once more, Tom called to mind the image of the sea that he had seen during the test and focused on it. His mind calmed, and he could feel… something. Minutes dragged by as Tom tried and tried again to refocus on the image – make it clearer, but still, nothing happened.

It was infuriating. It was like feeling the edge of a feather with your fingertips. He just couldn't grasp it. As the shadows started to fall directly beneath the trees, Tom knew that it must be closing in on lunchtime. He was pacing again. *This is stupid!! Why is this so **hard?** I did it by acci-dent twice now!*

That is when it hit him. It wasn't hard, and when he had done it, he hadn't thought about it. He had simply reached out with his mind and done it as if moving things with his mind was the same as using his hand.

Tom stopped pacing, faced the tree and reached out with his mind as if to feel it. There was that odd sensation again - the tingling - and then… a new sensation. He wasn't touching the tree with his hand, but in his mind, he knew he was sensing the energy that made up the tree. The tingling grew stronger as he realized what he was doing. As he continued to explore the sensation, it became clear that it wasn't like the physical feeling of touching a tree. He was feeling the energy in the molecules that made up the tree. In his mind, he could even sense the bonds that held the tree together. It was fantastic, and the power that was contained - even in the weaker bonds - was powerful to the point of being scary.

Tom was lost in a world of new sensations, so it was Levi screaming over the wind that had spontaneously sprung up on the narrow dirt driveway that finally brought Tom back to the present. "Tom, I think it's working!! Why don't you try moving it?" He yelled.

Yikes! How long have I been standing here? He wondered to himself. Not taking his eyes or his concentration off the tree, Tom gave Levi a "thumbs up" and got back to the task.

The first thing he could think to do to tackle this problem was crack the trunk about the middle of the road and then push the pieces off on either side. With that in mind, he brought his attention to the center of the trunk. He focused and tried to shove the tree with his mind. It wiggled slightly, but it didn't move. Not satisfied, he decided to imagine a crack forming down the middle when an odd thing happened. It was as if the bonds in that area came into sharper focus and he could almost see them breaking. Yes! Tom thought and poured more of his energy into that thought.

With a loud crack, the middle of the tree shuddered and split partway down through. Tom staggered backward a couple of steps. Levi was immediately trying to run through the gale wind to get to Tom. "Dude! Are you okay?" He asked clearly concerned for his brother.

Tom turned and assured him. "Yeah! Once I figured out how to do it, it was a lot easier than I thought it was going to be." He smiled. "It was like expecting to swing an ax into a solid stump but only hitting cotton candy!" His smile widened. "Oh man! I know I can move this thing out of the way now. Watch this!"

He had felt the difference the last time. This wasn't all about thinking, or physical energy. This was all about will. He needed to reach out with his mind, feel the energy of the tree and will it to do something. Tom turned back to the tree with the ragged cut down the middle and refocused his mind. He felt the energy of the tree. He expanded that sense until he had included all of the section of the tree trunk that sat in the road. Once he had a firm understanding of that energy, he imagined it moving. However, Tom was still really new to using this ability, and when he pictured it moving in his mind, he simply imagined it moving up and out of the way. This time, though, he put all of the will he could muster behind it.

The result was immediate and terrifying. The wind coming from Tom blasted outward in all directions, knocking Levi flat on his back and blowing leaves and loose debris in all directions. With bright flashes of light and a noise like thunder erupting from the edges of the tree, the section that crossed the driveway separated from the rest of the collapsed tree. A split second later, that entire section shot straight into the air as if it had been launched in a rocket.

Startled by the sudden movement, Tom flew backward to land a handful of feet from where Levi had fallen. Both boys watched as the tree shot straight into the air and quickly became a small dot in the sky. They then looked at each other as it dawned on them both that the flying chunk was bound to reverse directions soon enough. Eyes wide, they scrambled from the middle of the driveway and bolted toward the cover of the woods.

They quickly found a spot that was between a large rock and an even more massive tree. Figuring that even if the one ton of sugar maple did decide to come down right there, they would be safe due to the tree and rock, the boys sat, looked up and waited.

υ

As the seconds ticked by and the suspense mounted, Tom chanced a glance at Levi and saw him slowing his breathing in an effort to keep calm. Briefly, Tom marveled at his brother. He could not imagine a life where he had to maintain such rigid control of his emotions. Another glance and he could tell Levi was losing his fight against having a seizure. Grimly, Tom watched his brother as he chose a spot on the ground, laid down and waited for it to start.

Thankfully, the seizure was a short one. Levi briefly got a distant look that was accompanied by rapid twitching around the eyes. After a handful of minutes, it was over, and Levi sat up. "So, I take it we weren't crushed by the tree trunk while I was out?"

"Not even close," Tom confirmed.

"How far did you throw that thing anyway?" Levi asked as he started to get up.

"How should I know?" Tom replied squinting up at the cloud-smattered sky. "I've never thrown anything like that before."

Levi started to giggle. "Well… I guess we will hear about it in the news." Then, imitating a news announcer: "one-thousand-pound sugar maple trunk lands on farmer's tractor. Farmer says this confirms his suspicions about aliens stealing his cows. News at eleven."

Tom leaned back against the rock and started laughing. Levi was back to normal. Both boys relaxed as the laughter ran its course. Eventually, they got up and walked over to the new opening in the driveway. Tom walked up to the tree on one side, and Levi took the other.

Levi let out a low whistle as he inspected where the section of the tree had broken free. "Holy crap! Is your side like this too?" He asked as he ran his hand over the severed stump.

It was amazing. Tom had cut many trees down for firewood, but he had never seen a tree cut like this. It was as if someone had ripped away just the section of tree that was lying in the driveway. More interesting still, the edges of the cuts were perfectly smooth. There were no slivers or stray fragments anywhere to note an imperfection in the cut. It was as if the wood in the tree had simply stopped being connected in a perfectly flat plain.

"Yeah." Tom agreed. "It's like it was cut with a laser or something." They both pondered it in silence for a few more minutes. Then, Levi walked back to his bike.

"Okay. We should probably keep going now." He said as he glanced up at the sky again before throwing a leg over his bike. "We can talk about what just happened after we get some distance from here."

"Probably not a bad idea." Tom agreed, and with one last look around, he picked up his bike and started peddling the rest of the way up the driveway. "I would pay good money to know where that section of tree ended up…"

vi

Tom and Levi breathed a sigh of relief as they came around the last bend in the driveway and were greeted with the sight of the old rambling farmhouse and barn that marked the start of the land that Uncle Lester used for the vineyards. Off to either side of the barn, one could see the fields of grape vines and blueberry bushes that combine to form his signature blueberry wine.

It wasn't the vineyards though that made Tom smile. No, it was the winding road that skirted the edge of the fields. Like seaweed along the contour of a lakeshore, the path followed the side of the fields back past the grapes and blueberries, past the small pond that their uncle used to irrigate the fields during the hottest months of summer, and back until it disappeared around the corner of the hill in the distance.

He knew that if they followed that path all the way to the end, they would eventually reach a horseshoe-shaped set of hills where generations of previous owners would throw their garbage. Not the little stuff, like household goods, but big things like old cars, metal milk jugs, and tractor accessories. It was a place their uncle used to call "the farm equipment graveyard," and they knew it would be the perfect place to practice where no one would be able to see or hear them.

The boys stopped in the house using a key they recovered from a nail above the fourth stall from the door in the barn. Once inside the house, they snatched up their uncle's water canteens that he brought with him when he was planning a day of work in the fields and quickly filled them with water. Then they were back out the door on their bikes heading toward the equipment graveyard.

As soon as they arrived, Levi was off his bike and into everything at once. "This place is awesome!! Look at all this old stuff." He crowed holding up a rust-eaten pitchfork in one hand and pointing at an old haying trailer with the other. "What do you think, Stormy?"

"Stormy?"

"Yeah." Levi grinned. "If you are going to have superpowers, you need to work on your superhero name."

"Oh man…" Tom groaned. "I am no superhero."

"Sure, you are!" Levi insisted. "You have powers, and you even protected an innocent - Rick Beauregard."

"Rick is dumb. Not innocent. There's a difference."

"Rick may have been stupid for smoking that crap, but he didn't deserve to be shot in the back, and from what you told me, you protected him." He smirked. "Super. Hero. Bam!"

Tom couldn't help himself and chuckled a bit. Levi's excitement was as infectious as his laugh. "Whatever. It can't be silly like 'Stormy' though."

"Okay. What about 'Death Blow?'"

"No! I want to be a good person. Not a villain. That's a villain's name." Tom explained.

"Oh. Well, that rules out some other names then too." Levi crossed some others off his mental list. "You really didn't like Stormy?"

"'Storm' would have been better." Then, changing the subject, he continued. "Anyways - ever since we decided to work on learning to control my abilities, you have been making non-stop suggestions. So how about it? What should we do now? Other than coming up with a name."

Levi beamed. "Well, we need to do a few things. First, I need to know what you figured out with that tree in the driveway."

"It's kind of hard to explain, but I'll give it a shot." Tom sat on the carcass of the old hay trailer. "First, I learned that I could feel the energy of stuff with my mind. It's like having another set of hands that can feel the energy in the molecules."

"Do different things feel different?"

"I don't know. I haven't tried to feel anything except the tree." Tom answered as he contemplated it. "I'll have to experiment and see if I can figure things out. Anyway, I also figured out that if I focus my will on moving that energy, it actually works."

"Isn't that the same as saying you can move stuff? Why all the focus on the energy?" Levi asked, trying to wrap his head around what Tom was telling him.

"No. It's different. When I don't focus on the energy, I can't move anything at all."

"But you didn't focus on energy when you blew Tony half way through his wall locker."

Tom groaned at the memory. "True. I think that when I am super emotional, I can use my powers without focusing on them, but that's when it's most dangerous. I can't control what happens when I do it that way."

"Good to know." Levi agreed. "Let's not do that. I could teach you some of the meditation and calming techniques that they showed me at the neurology clinic. You know – the one that I use so I don't get worked up and 'do the synaptic shuffle?'"

Tom chuckled at Levi's nickname for seizures. It was just like him to make light of something scary. "That would be very appreciated."

"Cool. We can work on that tonight, but let's not waste this chance to use your powers in privacy. We need to get that wind that kicks up when you use your power under control."

"Wind? That's what you want to focus on?" Tom was surprised. He had thrown a thousand pounds of sugar maple tree into the air, and Levi wanted to focus on the wind that it generated?

"Ummm. Dude? I don't know if you were paying attention or not, but you were glowing and generating winds that blew over trees and threw me backward. It would suck if you used your talent to rescue a cat stuck in a tree just to impale the kid waiting for the cat with flying debris." Levi pointed out.

Tom was stunned. He had known that he generated a wind but must have been so focused on the task at hand that he didn't notice how powerful the wind was. "Okay. Good point. What do we try first?"

CHAPTER 5

The Wall

i

As the three black vans pulled up outside the building, James Neuwin breathed a sigh of relief. It had been a solid four hours since they had pulled out of the parking lot of their headquarters in Boston, and he was more than ready to get started setting up their temporary field office. The company he worked for bought it several years back along with similar buildings around the country with a substantial grant from the Department of Homeland Security.

It had all started when the first people that would later become known in classified circles as the "Changed" had shown up. They seemed to be people that were born ordinary but had developed some sort of unique ability. On one fateful day, a low-ranking member of the FBI stumbled onto a young man that could shoot energy bolts out of his fingertips and had immediately panicked. He reported the finding to the director of the FBI, Dean Emerson, and in typical government fashion, the discovery was made a top-secret matter.

It did not take much research to confirm that the man with the energy bolts was not the only person that was starting to change. Over a dozen had already been identified. Most of the reports were from tabloids, but a legitimate news source had previously reported one young lady that could set fires with her mind as being able to "unconventionally start fires." To Emerson's way of thinking, the FBI needed more information on these people. In fact, his head swam with questions. What was the extent of the powers? Were they working together for any nefarious purposes? What caused the change? Would it eventually happen to everyone? How long had this sort of thing been going on? If it got out that the government knew nothing about these people and had no way to control their abilities, it might lead to a national panic. He decided to hire an outside group to investigate the matter further.

The group the FBI hired to investigate, Great Wall Incorporated, was what some like to call "aggressively patriotic." It was comprised mostly of scientists and ex-military personnel that were willing to do whatever was needed to protect America. Of course, in the past, "protecting America" had been a very lucrative business for GWI. They had definitely profited from the fact they were not an official government agency. Feeling free of accountability, they had felt at liberty to take on projects that would even make the CIA wince. They had used outlawed chemical and biological weapons, killed civilians, displaced entire towns and assassinated high ranking foreign officials. They had toppled regimes and built arsenals. They had then sold the weapons to opposing foreign terrorist cells and then provided intelligence to both sides, so they would fight one another instead of threatening the US. To their way of thinking, they were making money supplying information and weapons, and the terrorists were too occupied with killing each other to ever focus on harming US interests. It was definitely a win-win situation for them.

Now, GWI was to use its considerable scientific resources to find and study the Changed. To their way of thinking, if there were individuals with abilities like the ones the FBI was saying might exist, then these things could not be human and had the potential to be a threat to the security of the country. Equally important in their line of reasoning, GWI saw the potential of getting these "assets" under their control. If they could force the Changed to work for them, they could charge their clients for the services of these new "weapons." Between charging the government for the research and charging their customers for this new service, they would make millions; it was this combined mission that they approached with something close to a religious fervor.

Within a couple of months, they managed to discover, capture and study about twenty of the Changed. The tests were thorough, to say the least, and when they were over, none of their test subjects were left alive to complain to anyone about how they had been treated. However, in spite of the wealth of information that GWI had managed to accumulate regarding the extent and variety of the Changed's powers, they never were able to pinpoint a reason for the change taking place. Finding out that bit of information would have been the crowning achievement in their research; it would have given them a way to trigger the change in otherwise ordinary people and create an army of Changed that already worked for them. Equally confounding, they found that the change itself was not new. The Changed lived among the general population. Hiding in plain sight worked for many of them. Unfortunately, the ones that couldn't pass for human were usually driven into hiding.

In the end, when GWI reported back to Emerson what they had discovered, and how, he was shocked. Using torture and murder on foreigners was one thing, but GWI had done this to American citizens, and that was several steps too far. Slightly unnerved by the genie he had let out of the bottle and the possible repercussions if it was traced back to him, he released the group from any further contracts with the FBI. GWI, however, could not get over what they had learned about the Changed. It was potentially the most significant development in the history of warfare since the atomic bomb, and the FBI just wanted them to walk away? These were individuals that could cause serious security issues for the U.S. if they were left with no government oversight. How could the FBI expect them to pretend that they didn't know about this?

It didn't take long for the CEO of GWI, Greg Buckner, to decide to continue without government approval – figuring that the government would eventually change their tune and seek him out. The first thing he did was divest GWI of its public business presence and went underground. Then, he doubled his efforts to start military coups in developing countries so that he could sell them arms and information in order to finance what he considered his new primary business venture. He was going to be the sole provider of specialty mercenaries that had abilities. Using the information his team had gathered, he coerced several newly identified members of the Changed into joining The Wall – as it had become known. Not many of them wanted to join, but all of them did. It was amazing how compliant people became when you threatened them and their families.

Once the Changed were brought back to the newly established training site, he brainwashed them and developed ways to get them to become proficient in how to use their abilities in tactical situations.

In the final step of his plan, he leaked information about the existence of the Changed and The Wall to several government organizations with which he had previous business dealings, telling them "if you ever have problems with one of these types of issues, just let me know. We have dealt with them before."

Now ten years later, James had risen to the level of lead field agent for The Wall and was intimate with the business model on which Greg Buckner had settled. It was fairly simple. First, you look for individuals that may have special abilities. Frequently, in the early days, one of his government contacts would feed him intelligence on where to look for them. Later, The Wall developed software to help make the process more efficient. Then, you observe the subject from a distance and try to confirm that they have an ability. If they do have an ability, he would determine the nature and extent of that ability. Once he had an idea of what they are capable of, he offered them a high paying job using their ability to defend the country by working at The Wall. If they refused, he threatened them with anything he had to in order to get them to change their mind. He would tell them he would wipe out all their bank accounts, kill their family or shoot their puppy. It didn't matter – as long as they joined The Wall.

Now, if they still refused, he had standing orders to kill them. After all, in this business, you do not want to have super-powered people with a grudge roaming the countryside. Of course, if they did join, there were instantly spirited off to the indoctrination and training camp where loyalty and ruthlessness were drilled into them. It was the ultimate "carrot and stick" approach: try to entice them with a carrot and if that didn't work, whack them with the stick.

As brutal as his job was, James loved it. He was granted responsibilities that few people ever experienced. When he would go out on what people at The Wall had come to call a "Simple Shakedown" of a potential Changed person, he was the first and only authority that would decide their fate. He was in total control of each operation that he ran. It was mainly a matter of necessity while he was on the job since no electronic communication was permitted with headquarters. With other government organizations performing randomized phone traffic taps, scanning e-mails and monitoring internet traffic to catch terrorists, there was simply no mode of communication that was secure enough to warrant the risk. All reports were digitally encrypted with the most robust encryption available. They were then hand carried to the Wall's technical staff where they were loaded into the headquarters servers. These servers were on a separate system from the one that connected to the internet. With that being the case, no one could hack into their network. No paper reports were allowed outside any of the facilities as they may fall into the wrong hands; anything printed inside a facility was burned by the end of the day.

The other critical aspect of James' job was to collect all supporting data and to destroy any public evidence that the person had an ability – even if that evidence was an eyewitness. After all, it is pretty difficult to train someone to be a top-secret assassin after they have made international headlines that they are the world's first super-powered person.

Currently, he was on the trail of a new "candidate" in Vermont. Hours ago, the supercomputer, referred to as "KIA," at their headquarters in Boston had posted an alert. KIA, short for "Know It All," was the comically named brainchild of a group of super-nerds that worked at The Wall. They had taken the simple program that The Wall had initially developed to find the Changed and fed it into a multimillion-dollar quantum computer. The result was an artificial intelligence driven computer that could perform risk assessments based on known and implied threats. It did this by scanning through massive volumes of social media, emails, texts and phone calls every day looking for anything that might point to an enhanced person. When it finds one, it correlates all the information and calculates a Probability of Talent score. The higher the score, the more likely the person is Changed, and today's top hit looked promising.

SUSPICIOUS PERSON ALERT!!

Newspaper Article #1

Date: June 2, 2017

Title: Boy Survives Research Lab Explosion

Person of interest: Thomas Woods, survivor

Newspaper Article #2

Date: August 7, 2017

Title: Gang Violence in Local High School

Person of interest: Thomas Woods, witness

Police Report for Northeastern VT on August 7, 2017

Report Keywords: Gang Violence, Explosion

Eye Witness: Thomas Woods

NASA event report

Status: Classified

Date: August 19, 2017, EST

Overview: "The North American Telcom Satellite (NATS) unexpectedly went offline in the afternoon of August 9th. A sister satellite showed a streak of light that originated from somewhere in New England that hit the satellite just before it lost service. A crew was dispatched to collect the debris. Intermingled with the wreckage were the remains of what seems to be a large amount of sugar maple tree…"

Candidate Name: Thomas Woods

Location: Northern Vermont

Probability of Talent: 83.7%

Strength Level: 7.1

Talent: Unknown

James smiled. He smelled blood in the water on this one. Anything more than a 75% Probability of Talent score usually ended up being correct, and in this case, either someone had figured out how to make a rail-gun out of a tree trunk, or there was a super-freak out there somewhere – possibly working for someone with a beef against America's telecommunications industry. Up until now, none of the Changed that James found had ever been working for anyone, or at least none of the ones he had suspected had ever admitted to it before they died.

But why would you take out a satellite if you didn't have a really good reason? It's not like things get launched into space by accident!

James paused. KIA also scored potential contacts on a scale of one to ten for how powerful they are. The Strength Level score was logarithmic and so was more like the Richter Scale than a timeline, with each number being close to a 30-fold increase over the previous number. Most people scored between one and three. Only a couple of dozen in the last decade had scored above a 5, and none of them were on record as being a 10. However, if someone had the kind of power needed to put something in space, then they could possibly be the most powerful Changed they had found in months.

He picked up his pace unloading things from the trucks and began setting up the satellite office.

ii

By the following morning, the temporary field office had been set up. Each of the field offices had been chosen for two main reasons. First, they each were close to the largest metropolitan areas in each state while still maintaining some degree of privacy, and second, and more importantly, they had basements that extended at least fifty feet underground. With technology improving exponentially and an ever-evolving system of spy satellites, The Wall was taking no chances that anyone would discover their work.

James yawned as he climbed out of the van. He had worked well into the night setting up the self-contained network of computers that the team would be using to formulate their report as well as the chamber that Thomas Woods would eventually occupy.

Dr. Mobien's office was just opening when Lead Agent Neuwin pushed open the door and walked in. He briefly surveyed the office and made his way straight to the receptionist's desk. "Could I speak to Dr.

Edward Mobien, please? My name is Agent James Neuwin of the FBI."
He casually lied to the secretary as he flashed a fake badge that he had
picked up at a carnival outside of Salt Lake City eight years ago.

"Yes, of course. May I ask what this is regarding?" She asked rising
from her chair.

"You could, but I wouldn't be able to tell you." He said cutting off
further questions. "Sorry Miss."

She frowned slightly and then disappeared down the hall toward
Mobien's office. Less than five minutes later, Dr. Mobien was meeting
with James in the same conference room where he had met with Tom
just a few weeks prior.

"Sorry to disrupt your morning Dr. Mobien. I will try to keep this
as brief as humanly possible." James said without preamble. "I am here
from the FBI checking on the mishap in your research lab in June."

"The FBI is investigating botched lab experiments now?" Mobien
was incredulous.

"No... not all botched lab experiments. We only investigate the ones
that look like they may have had some form of explosive used." James
countered, expecting that response.

"And you are just getting around to investigating this now?" Mobien
asked, still not trusting Neuwin's motives.

"Unfortunately, the government is just as short staffed as the medical
field." Replied James shaking his head. "We knew about it but couldn't
get anyone out here sooner."

"Fine" Mobien relented "so what can I do for you guys?"

James smiled. "I only need two things. First, I understand that
the local authorities returned all the equipment and reports that they

collected from your lab that day. We will need the reports and such. Second, I would like to conduct a brief interview with you.”

Mobien rose and gestured for James to remain seated. In less than two minutes he was back in the room with a modestly sized cardboard box. “In here is the debris from the explosion. There is what remains of the EEG electrodes, a couple of smashed digital video recorders and several other pieces that we can’t identify. We were going to toss them out, so please feel free to do so after you are done with them. They are completely worthless now.” With that, he unceremoniously dropped the box on the table. “As for an interview, I will tell you what I told the fire marshal and the police: The room blew up. I wasn’t doing anything illegal. I was conducting the study I had outlined in my Application for Human Trials paperwork that is filed with the University. That is all that I know.” Mobien shook his head. “There was no reason for that explosion even with the power surge that we got from the load test. We weren’t running any flammable gasses or liquids.”

“I see.” James was staring hard at Mobien’s eyes, watching his expression and body language. “So, this is everything that was used in the experiment?”

“Except for the medication that we were testing, yes.”

“What about after the experiment?” James asked browsing through the box.

“Excuse me?”

“What about your write up on the case? What about the printout of the live time data? Didn’t you get an EEG and EKG? Where is your report on the case?” James pressed. “I don’t see it in here.”

“These devices record to a simple hard drive where they can be printed out later. As you can well imagine, we never got around to printing anything out. As for the reports, I never wrote one because the experiment was halted immediately and there was no point in writing it." Mobien explained.

James, however, was not buying that. Mobien was holding something back. He was sure of it. "So, there is no case summary of any sort? Not even with the Department of Health and Human Services or the FDA?"

Dr. Mobien raised an eyebrow, and red flags went up in his head. If Agent Neuwin really was from the FBI, he should already have access to those reports. "As I am sure you know Agent Neuwin, I cited finances as the reason for scrapping the study. There simply was not enough money in the grant I received to replace an EEG, EKG, oxygen saturation monitor, two digital cameras, a recliner and remodel the rooms that were affected by the blast. There is no point in trying to salvage data from a handful of destroyed hardware so that I could sort through volumes of data in order to write a report that would be little more than conjecture due to the limited number of subjects that participated prior to the explosion. It would have been a waste of my time."

"I see…" James mused. He quickly decided to switch tactics with Mobien who was obviously starting to get suspicious. The last thing that James needed was Mobien calling the real FBI to confirm his credentials. He needed to calm this guy down a little. "I would like to thank you for your assistance with this case Dr. Mobien. I see no real need to drag this investigation out any longer than it needs to be. We will assess the materials here, and we will be back in touch to let you know the outcome of the investigation." He smiled disarmingly. "I am sure you will be as interested to know the reason behind the explosion as we will."

"Absolutely. I know I would certainly feel better about working in this office again if I had a real reason for the explosion – unfortunately, that sort of work is better left to the fire department and you guys. Now, is there anything else you need here, or can I get back to seeing patients?" Mobien asked trying not to sound like he wanted Neuwin gone as badly as he did. Something about the man just gave him the creeps, and he wanted to wrap up the interview as fast as he could.

James smiled. "No. All set here. I can show myself out."

It was not until Dr. Mobien sat down to eat his lunch that he had time to think about the interview and realized that Agent Neuwin never asked him a single question about possible reasons for the explosion. How odd. That was why he said he was investigating the incident to begin with…

iii

The following morning found James at his desk in the field offices subbasement replaying the slow-motion footage that his men had recovered from Dr. Mobien's cameras late the night before. James was pleased. The case against Thomas Woods was building quickly.

He dragged the progress indicator back to the beginning and watched the digital recording of Thomas during the drug administration as it played out on his laptop screen. Fortunately for James, the room where the experiment took place was old, and there were a limited number of outlets for all the equipment. This meant that the cameras had to rely on batteries and so were not affected by the power surge. All the same, most of the footage was of Tom quietly watching the video which contained about the same entertainment value as watching paint peel. That all changed however when the power surge hit. Tom arched his back as the electricity arced around the lead wires and into his head. Then, there was a bright flash of light followed by a black screen as the footage ended. James backed it up and reduced the footage speed of the last second of the recording to its slowest setting. The first camera was looking from Tom's right straight at his face. The power surge was hitting him, and he had his eyes screwed shut in pain. Then, just before the screen flashed, his eyes flew open for a split second. They looked as if there was lightening trapped within them and glowed with a life of their own. James froze the screen and looked down at the printout of the driver's license he held in his hands.

> **Name:** Thomas Woods
>
> **Hair:** Brown
>
> **Eyes:** Brown

Gotcha! That can't be a reflection of light in the room, and there is no way a person can change the color of their eyes like that. There has to be something going on here. He called for Trevor Merrola, his second in command. "We need to call in a couple of favors with the folks in the FBI. We need to scan for unexplained light flashes from any satellites that cover the New England area then subtract out any that are just due to lightning or any other known phenomenon. Do whatever you have to in order to get it done, and don't let anyone trace this request to our current physical location. Understood?"

Trevor nodded and turned to walk back to his desk. He knew that the best way to not come up missing on one of these shakedowns was to give James Neuwin wide birth. Do whatever he asks immediately and get rewarded. Questioning his methods or actions had been known to end with your loved one receiving your company sponsored death benefit.

Okay, thought Neuwin, *this guy's powers cause a flash, so I may be able to find him if he is using his powers outside at night. But what I don't know is what his powers are.* James thought about it further and considered what he knew. According to Thomas Woods' statement to the cops, he had been standing about twenty feet away from where the would-be gang member dropped some sort of explosive device. The device detonated almost precisely where Woods said he had been standing before the blast threw him backward. The explosive had no shrapnel and caused no fire marks. It just knocked everything away from where it detonated. In short, it was not like any explosive Neuwin had ever heard of. It was no small wonder the local authorities had decided to investigate the matter.

What bothered him even more was that if there was such an explosive, how had Woods been the closest one to it and not been the most injured? The DeMarcus boy had fractured ribs, a broken arm, a concussion, and a dislocated shoulder. James had run DeMarcus' injuries through the computer model, and the report he got was that the injuries were consistent with what one should have expected if a medium duty truck had hit DeMarcus going approximately 40 miles an hour. No, this was not how explosions worked. It was purely a mechanical trauma. Something had hit DeMarcus – hard. After doing dozens of shakedowns, Neuwin knew that one of the worst mistakes to make was attempting to make contact without at least knowing the nature of the talent in question.

Every time The Wall had attempted to make contact without a firm understanding of a subject's abilities, they had been burned. One of those occasions had been by a person that could sense other people with abilities. James had been on that mission, and his former lead field agent had brought some Changed people to make first contact. The subject saw them coming from a great distance and shot four people, including the lead agent before he could be subdued. James had beaten the man mercilessly during his reconditioning as an agent of The Wall. When he had finally got through his anger, he had petitioned the next lead agent to make first contact with regular agents and leave the enhanced ones in reserve.

James looked down at his watch. Not long now and visiting hours would begin at the hospital. Today was lining up to be a great day. According to the agent that James had stationed at the hospital to watch the DeMarcus boy's recovery, he was starting to wake up after a month-long coma. That was great news. James had a few questions for him, and he had yet to meet a person that he could not persuade to answer his questions.

CHAPTER 6

Tony Meets James

i

Jacob "Pops" Merrill had acquired his nickname in Tony DeMarcus' gang simply because he was the oldest person Tony had recruited. At the ripe old age of twenty-two, Pops had decided to join the gang to make extra money. Tony had deliberately targeted and recruited someone that would be able to drive the carloads of drugs from New York City to northern Vermont, and since Pops used to work as a Pepsi distributor, he knew the route well. The lure of more money, no taxes and a little sample product on the side were just enough to make it worth the effort of working for someone like DeMarcus.

Pops had seen kids like Tony before when he lived in St. Louis, young and hungry. They could risk more since they were minors and if they didn't do anything stupid and get busted by the cops and tried as an adult, a guy could get rich working for them. The trick was always knowing how close to work with one of these new gang branch leaders. Too close and you go down with them if they do something dumb; too far away and they start to question your loyalty, which is more life-threatening than jail time by far!

Pops continued walking quickly down the hallways that lead to the ICU. He hated this place with its sterile smells and its fluorescent lights. It all brought back bad memories. He had an uncle that had died in a similar hospital when he was younger, and he remembered going with his parents to visit as his uncle slowly deteriorated. *Intensive Care Unit my white ass!!* thought Pops. *It's more like what my old man used to call it… "God's waiting room."*

Pops let out a bitter chuckle as he rounded the last corner leading to the ICU. It had been a little over two hours since DeMarcus had called him and asked for him to come to the hospital, and Pops was pretty sure that his boss's temper would be wearing a little thin by now. Pops took a deep breath, and he braced himself as he stepped into DeMarcus' room.

"It's about time you got here, Pops." DeMarcus griped as soon as Merrill entered his room. "I was starting to think you weren't going to show."

Pops winced at DeMarcus' tone. "Easy man, I had to pick up a shipment. It slowed me down a little."

DeMarcus visibly relaxed. "So, business is doing well then?"

"It's almost as good as when you are running it, Chief." Pops offered, knowing what a careful line he was walking. If he said things were too good, the young and self-conscious DeMarcus would be nervous that Pops would try to replace him, but if he did not do well enough, then DeMarcus would be upset that he was losing money and that could get ugly as well. When his response didn't get any reaction, he pressed on.

"We were hoping that you would wake up and tell us how this happened. The other guys and I have been talking, and we want some payback."

DeMarcus' grin was predatory. "Good. I am still a little fuzzy on the exact details, but I know who did it. The kid that walked up behind me – Tom Woods."

Pops jaw dropped. "One guy did this? What did he do – beat you with a pipe?"

With his good arm, DeMarcus rubbed his bandaged head trying to remember. "That is the part I am a little fuzzy on. The stuff that I remember couldn't have happened the way I remember them." He paused and thought. "I heard some of the nurses talking, and they say that little bastard used some sort of home-made bomb. It must have messed with my head, 'cause I can't remember how it really happened. One thing I do know though… I want him to feel all my pain and more before he dies."

He had been thinking they were going to beat up some high school kid but murder? "Uh. Okay…"

DeMarcus' dark eyes burned as he glared at Pops – almost daring him to question the order. "Well? Are you going to wait for him to find you somehow? Go get some of the guys and get it done."

Pops jumped, not realizing that he had already been dismissed. "Right. Of course, boss. We're on our way now." He said making his way to the door. "Get better soon man."

DeMarcus just grunted.

ii

James Neuwin passed Pops in the hallway as he headed toward DeMarcus' room. It had taken him hours longer than he thought to get out of the makeshift field office. The satellite scan had required some serious negotiating to secure. It had finally taken James getting on an encrypted cell line with Greg Buckner, himself to seal the deal. Greg had been reluctant at first, but after he realized that James was in pursuit of the person or persons responsible for the satellite mishap, he finally relented. "That sort of person – at the very least – needs to be under our control." Greg had said. And as far as James was concerned, being dead would make Woods very under control.

Now, it was shortly after 2:00 pm and James was anxious to have this critical interview over and done with before the nursing staff started their shift change at 3:00 pm. The hospital volunteer that had escorted him throughout the hospital finally came to a stop in front of one of the rooms in the ICU. "Here you go, sir." She said indicating one of the doors.

"Thank you, dear," Neuwin said dismissing her with a smile and a wave as he slid past her into the room.

DeMarcus took one look at Neuwin's dark grey suit and rolled his eyes. "Great! More cops – just what I needed. I am not talking to any of you without my lawyer, so you might as well leave."

James smiled viciously as he looked around the room to make sure they were alone. "Well, I am not going to do that… and you won't be needing your lawyer."

"How do you figure that?" DeMarcus froze as he watched Neuwin prop a chair against the door handle so that no one would be able to get in. "Oh shit!"

James was on him in a second, ripping the nursing call bell out of his hand and pinning him to the bed by his throat. "Before you choke to death, you should nod your head telling me that you will not scream.

If you scream, I can promise you I will kill you long before anyone gets through that door."

DeMarcus nodded.

Just then the doorknob started to jiggle. "Hey, what is going on in there?" came the nurse's voice from the other side.

"The door closed and got stuck" shouted James "can you call someone to get us out of here?"

"I will call now. Please stay calm, and we will get you out. It should only be a couple of minutes." And with that, she was gone.

"Okay." Neuwin turned back to DeMarcus and lowered his voice. "You are going to tell me everything I need to know about your encounter in the high school hallway. You have less than two minutes, or when they open that door, it will be to take you to the morgue. Got it?"

DeMarcus nodded again as his mind raced. He was not sure who the man in the grey suit was, but he was sure his initial impression of him being a cop was dead wrong.

"Speak fast, dirt-bag or I may change my mind and kill you when I leave here out of spite." Neuwin threatened. DeMarcus started telling his tale immediately. He told James about his gang roots in New York City, how he had been sent to Vermont by his parents, how he had decided to sell drugs in the school and how he had been pressuring underclassmen to distribute for him. When he got to the point where he was threatening Rick with a gun, he paused for a second.

James put his thumb on one of the pins that were protruding from DeMarcus' broken arm and pushed. DeMarcus sucked in a breath as pain ripped through his shattered arm. "Then what?" Neuwin demanded.

"That freak started to float, and then everything flew away from him like he had exploded or something. Then I hit the lockers, and I don't remember anything else." DeMarcus finished in a rush as he turned pale from the pain.

There it was – proof that Thomas Woods was one of the Changed! And as an added bonus, James had a feeling that Woods' talent was some form of telekinesis. "That's it?" Neuwin asked.

"I don't remember anything else after that. He just raised his hand and sorta pointed at me then I woke up here." DeMarcus was sweating profusely, and half expected Neuwin to kill him now that he had what he wanted. He was amazed when James jumped off the bed.

"Okay. Here is what happens next. I am going to open the door, and you are going to say that I am your attorney's assistant and that we had a great visit in spite of the door getting jammed." He quickly walked over to the door. "And if I hear you so much as think very hard about me, I will track you down, and you will die a very slow death, and that little pea-shooter you threatened Beauregard with would not be able to stop my team and I. Understand?"

DeMarcus nodded his head, and James whipped the chair away from the door, grabbed the doorknob and yanked with everything he had. The nurses and maintenance team that was outside the door looked on in open amazement as the door flew open and James theatrically went sprawling onto the floor. "Whoa!"

"Are you okay?"

"Yes, fine. It looks like we got the door to open." James said getting to his feet. "Well, I am late for an appointment. I will see you later Mr. DeMarkus. Best of luck on a speedy recovery!" James quickly walked out of the hospital room and down the hall toward the elevator. A man in hospital scrubs stepped into the elevator with him just as the door was sliding shut.

Alone in the elevator, they stared at each other for a second. "Did you get everything you needed Sir?" asked the man.

"Yes, Agent Robins," James responded coldly. "We no longer have a need for Mr. DeMarcus. Kill him tonight. Make it look like a drug error."

iii

James arrived back at the field office that evening around 5:00 pm. It had taken him longer than expected to find the Woods boy. Getting the mother's address had been easy, but the kid was almost never there. It seemed that on days that the mother worked, the subject and his sibling would leave on their bikes and not come back until just before the mother came home. That would not do. He needed to be able to observe the subject and witness his abilities. That meant he would need to locate where they went every day and set up an observation point. James smiled to himself. No one could avoid him for long.

CHAPTER 7

Training Continues

i

It had been two weeks since the boys had started their daily training and they had discovered a lot about the way that Tom's talent worked. He had attained a degree of mastery over moving objects. The only significant casualty of his education was a basketball shaped hole in the wall of his uncle's kitchen. It had been a minor control problem that had occurred when trying to grab a cup from the shelf; however, it had reaffirmed his need for further training in the equipment graveyard or the "Yard" as it had come to be known. In spite of this minor setback, he continued to improve and eventually no longer needed to concentrate when calling up his power. It flowed from him without effort allowing him to move everything from massive boulders to the air itself.

The side effects of hurricane force winds and emanating a glow had also been significantly improved upon. Now, if he concentrated, the wind was barely perceivable, and the glow could be eliminated entirely.

Tom had hoped that his insomnia would improve with training, but the best he could achieve is 6 hours on days that he really used his talent a lot.

All-in-all, it was a very productive two weeks, and both boys were in a great mood as they finished packing their lunch and jumped on their bikes for the 4-mile trip to their uncle's farm. With the wind at their backs, they were making great time when Levi noticed it.

The same brown car with Massachusetts plates passed them a second time. With one glance at the driver, Levi's intuition kicked into high gear. After some consideration, about two minutes later, he called over to Tom who was in the lead, "Water break!" Tom nodded and pulled over.

"Dude. What's the issue? We haven't even gone three miles." Tom asked, knowing that his brother had never needed a water break on the four-mile ride before.

"It's that flatlander in the tan Camry. He has passed us twice." Levi explained in a soft voice.

"Well… That explains everything then. Maybe we should take breaks when the dump truck passes us too."

Levi punched him in the arm. "Hey! I'm serious. It wasn't the fact that the car passed us a couple of times. It was how it slowed slightly when it passed, and the driver was wearing a suit and sunglasses and seemed more focused on us than he did on checking out mailboxes to see if he was getting closer to wherever he was going."

"Really?" Tom asked.

"No. I'm making it up because I like to invent drama." Levi's reply dripped with sarcasm.

Tom squinted as he looked up and down the road again. "Okay. Here's the deal then. If we see the creeper in the Camry again, we will cut through the trail in the woods past Greenia's Pond and take the spur trail that comes out behind Uncle Lester's farm. There is no way in hell some old businessman is going to be able to catch the two of us on our bikes as we off-road it on that trail, and even if he knows that trail, he'll have no way of knowing which spur trail we took to get off of the main trail. And it's 'bye-bye Creepster.'"

Levi considered it and then nodded once. He knew Tom wasn't taking this entirely seriously, but it was a sound plan in the event the car went for a third pass.

In silent mutual consent, both boys stowed their water bottles and started off for the farm again. It hadn't been five minutes when Tom noticed the Camry was coming up behind them again. This time he did see the middle-aged man in a suit and sunglasses looking at them. Neither boy needed to say anything. They both sped up on their bikes. The trail to Greenia's Pond was only 300 yards down the road. The man in the Camry noticed the change in the boys' speed and seemed to slow down a little.

Interesting move. Thought Tom. *I would have expected him to accelerate if he was going to try to pull something.* Counting their blessings, Tom and Levi barreled down the road at top speed, and after a quick glance to make sure they wouldn't get hit, made a sharp left turn across the road and disappeared into the tree line.

After passing about 50 feet into the woods, Levi chanced a glance back over his shoulder and saw that the Camry had come to a stop at the trailhead with the man in the shades glaring down the path after them. Levi's middle finger shot up as he half-turned on his seat and blew the man a kiss. The last thing that the driver of the Camry heard was Levi's voice shouting "Creeper!" as he continued down the trail at full speed, laughing as he went.

ii

Once the ride was finally over, and both boys were laying breathless in the tall grass with their bikes on the ground next to them, they finally had time to look back on what had just happened.

"Who do you think he was?" Levi asked.

"An off-duty cop that had heard two boys were hanging out on the farm while the owner was away?" Tom suggested.

"In an out of state car?" Levi countered.

"Good point. Probably not."

They were both silent a moment as they considered what to do about the man in the Camry.

Levi was the first to voice what they were both considering. "So… If push had come to shove, you could have…" and he left the thought hanging in the air between them.

Tom winced. "Geez. I don't know if that is a great idea. I mean, I am pretty good when I am here with you with no pressure, but I don't know how I would do if someone was freaking me out by following us home, or even worse, shooting at us!"

"Then that is what we need to train for!" declared Levi. "Let's level up our training. You seem to have the basics. Now let's make things difficult."

Tom groaned. "I thought lifting one-hundred-pound rocks and throwing things accurately without touching them *was* difficult!"

Levi was on his feet. "No. I mean really difficult. We can start with this: I will charge you, and you stop me from touching you."

"I've never moved a person or animal before."

"Sure, you did! You threw Tony-the-dork halfway through his locker!"

"I don't know…" Tom hesitated, but Levi had already backed up about thirty feet to get a good running start for the tackle.

"Ready or not, here I come!"

The distance wasn't all that big, so Tom didn't have time to really think about it. He simply reached out with his mind and tried to stop Levi in mid-stride, yet when his mind came in contact with the energy that made up Levi, it was as if he was covered in grease. Tom couldn't focus on Levi enough to control him, and a split second later, all the air was knocked out of Tom as Levi's shoulder nailed him in the midsection and both boys landed in a tangle of arms and legs on the ground.

"What the hell, Tom?" Levi exclaimed as they both rolled onto their backs. "You were supposed to stop me."

"You think I didn't understand that part?!?" Tom snapped back. "It was weird. I couldn't get hold of you. The energy that makes up your body seems like it is moving and changing all the time. It's like trying to grab a handful of tadpoles. They just slip right through your fingers when you try to close your hand."

"I'm a tadpole?" Levi already had a smile on his face.

"You're a dork." Tom laughed.

"Well, this dork has a theory," Levi said, getting back on his feet. "I bet you can't move live stuff."

"You just said I could because of DeMarcus." Tom corrected him.

"That was before I used you as a tackling dummy. Now, I think I was wrong. I bet you threw something into Tony and that's how he moved. Maybe it was his clothes that you moved or even the air around him. It doesn't matter. What matters is – we need to test this crap." And he was back on his feet looking up at the treetops closest to him. "There." He pointed. "Bring that crow off the tree limb and down here."

Tom got up as well and walked a little closer to the tree. He reached out his hand and willed the bird to move toward it. As he reached out with his mind, he felt the same moving energy. He took a deep breath and tried to slow the energy so that he could move it. The response was immediate. Tom felt as if someone had turned the feedback on a speaker up to its highest setting in his head. He let go with his mind as bright colors flashed behind his closed eyes. Grabbing his head his knees buckled and he fell to the ground.

Minutes later, when he was able to register something other than pain, he heard Levi asking "Jesus! Tom! Are you okay?"

"Yes. Wow!" Tom shook his head to clear it. "I'm not doing that again."

"What did you do?"

"I tried to slow down the moving energy, so I could move the bird," Tom explained.

"Huh. Well, I think the bird felt a little something because it shivered and flew off."

"Did I hurt it?"

"I don't think so. He didn't squawk or anything to indicate pain." Levi offered.

"That's good," Tom said in a relieved voice. "I think we just found out something important. I think that there is a force around living creatures that protect them from this sort of energy manipulation."

"How so?"

"I don't know. That movement of energy almost seemed to have a life of its own. Maybe it was the animal's soul. Maybe it was something else. I don't know." Tom trailed off.

"I guess so" Levi agreed. "Okay, so what if you don't stop them? What if you just use your power to move a shield in between you and them? I don't know where you'd keep it, but…"

Tom's face lit up. "That's genius! And I know exactly what I can use for the shield!" Tom jumped to his feet. "Okay. Let's do it again. Try to tackle me!"

Levi looked a little dubious, but he backed up thirty feet or so and set his feet like he was a track star waiting for the starting whistle.

"Go!" Tom yelled, and Levi took off at a sprint. Tom squinted, and the air around Levi seemed to shimmer like the air directly above a fire. Levi was running full-tilt at Tom when he stopped like he had hit a brick wall.

"Ooof!" He grunted on impact with the invisible wall. "Hey! What gives? What did I hit?"

Tom started laughing. "Dude! This is awesome! I have control of the air molecules around you!"

"No way!" Levi breathed the words in amazement. Then he tried to move his fingers and found he couldn't. "I can't move anything."

"Nope," Tom confirmed. "I could even push you back if I wanted to." Tom made a pushing gesture with his hand and Levi's entire body, still frozen in the same position, moved back a few feet.

"Sweet," Levi said impressed. "Can you let me go now?"

"Oh. Right." Tom had been so impressed with his new-found ability, that he hadn't thought to release it. He made a shooing gesture with his hand, and Levi dropped to the ground as the frozen molecules released.

"How did you know to do that?" Levi asked moving his fingers and arms to make sure everything still worked.

"I guess I knew that I could control the air molecules because I could feel their energy when I would go to pick up the wood and rocks that we have been practicing on," Tom explained. "Air feels different. The energy seems more dispersed, but it is still there."

"So, instead of stopping all the molecules around someone, can you also stop all the air in the shape of a wall?" Levi asked. "What I mean is, can you block something without capturing the person?"

"I don't see why not. Why don't you throw a rock at me and I'll try to block it?"

"Okay." Levi agreed. He backed up to a distance of about twenty feet and picked up a small rock.

Tom raised his hand, and the air in between them seemed to shimmer. "Ready."

Levi threw the rock at Tom, and it bounced off the wall of air as if it had hit something solid. "OH MY GOD! THIS IS AWESOME!" Levi yelled in excitement, and immediately picked up two more rocks and pecked them as hard as he could at Tom. Both harmlessly bounced off the wall. "Dude! We should see if this would work with bullets."

Tom dropped his hand, and the shimmering stopped. "Bullets?"

"Yes!" Levi was practically dancing in place as his mind raced ahead. "You are going to be a superhero, right?" Not waiting for an answer, "If you are going to be a superhero, you need to be able to protect yourself against people trying to shoot you with bullets." He paused thoughtfully for a second "and it would be super cool if you could fly."

"Fly?" Tom started to laugh but immediately stopped. "Holy crap! I could! Well – sort of."

He instantly had Levi's attention. "Look." He squinted in concentration, and the air in front of him started to shimmer. Then, as Levi watched, Tom stepped up onto the shimmering air as if he were mounting the first step of a staircase.

There he stood, hovering in the air in front of Levi.

"No shi…" Levi began to say but immediately had to stop, turn his back to Tom, close his eyes and started breathing with long, slow respirations.

Tom knew that this meant that Levi was battling not to have another seizure and again questioned his decision to bring Levi in on what was happening with his powers. As soon as his attention wavered from the step made of air, it dissolved, and Tom dropped to the ground and landed hard on his butt.

Levi turned around and saw what had happened and immediately started laughing.

At the sound of Levi's laughter, Tom started to chuckle in spite of himself.

"Do you know what this means?" Levi asked, excited.

"What?"

"You can fly." The statement hung like a bubble ready to pop in the air.

"Yeah…"

iii

In less than four days, Tom had mastered some of the basics of holding himself aloft using the air around him. It all seemed to be going so well that he decided it was time to give it a try.

The morning of the test run Tom was in good spirits, and as he slowly rose up above the Yard – twenty, thirty, and then forty feet in the air - he felt his spirits soar to equal heights. It was then that his mind started to get the better of him. *This is so cool, but how reliable is this power? What if it falters? I could…* No sooner had he thought it than his concentration slipped, and he started falling. Fast! He had made it up to sixty feet in the air by now and was directly over a large birch tree. As he picked up speed, he looked down and saw the topmost branches rushing up to meet him. Instinctively, Tom thrust his hands out in front of himself. A bright burst of light erupted from his hands and formed a protective wall of glowing air between him and the fast-approaching trees. The branches of the tree hit the wall and shattered, barely slowing him. The ground, however, was a different story. The impact of the makeshift shield into the ground was, to say the least, impressive. It sounded like a cannon blast as rocks and wood flew in all directions. Tom hit next with a loud thud in the center of a small crater that had been formed at the base of the tree.

It was several minutes before Tom could catch his breath again and was able to try to move from under the pile of branches and debris that had landed on top of him. *Okay… mental note: Do not get distracted again.*

iv

Most of the summer had passed before Tom was willing to try it again. He knew that his free time to experiment would be more limited with his senior year of high school starting in three days, so with a healthy amount of caution on his side, he slowly lifted himself gently off the ground and up to just above treetop level.

"Wooohooo! You got this man!" Levi yelled to him. Tom smiled and waved back down at his brother. He had been practicing for days now and was finally willing to try a more advanced test run again. As he turned North, he sailed higher and higher into the air causing Greenia's Pond to take on the look of an evaporating puddle beneath him. He was several hundred feet up when he hazarded a glance back and saw the smoke columns from the campgrounds to the north and east of his uncle's land.

Riding a cushion of air was still a very new sensation for Tom. With the wind in his face, he concentrated as he continued to manipulate the surrounding air molecules, to propel himself forward. He then spent a few minutes getting a feel for how to turn, speed up and slow down. The power flowed out of him, shooting him over trees and roads. However, keeping the pocket of air firmly locked in his mind was proving to be a mentally taxing experience. Tom quickly realized that flying in this manner was not going to be something that could be done over long periods of time and decided that he would need to start looking for a place to land.

Getting his bearings, he followed the main road to where his Uncle's small private road split off at a sharp 90-degree angle. He had just located it when he saw something move out of the corner of his eye. It was small and white, and when he slowed down so that the sound of the air rushing by him softened to a dull roar, he heard it - the soft hum of a drone. Whoever was flying it, was taking care to keep the drone located behind and above him. It was the one spot that even if he suddenly turned around it wouldn't be in his direct line of sight. It was as close as one could get to a blind spot when flying out in the open.

Crap! Someone's watching! More than that, someone might be recording him. He tried to reach out with his mind to crush the drone, but it was too far away, and it kept moving around making it hard to grab. Unfortunately, as soon as his attention was divided, he lost his focus on staying aloft and instantly started to fall. *Damn,* he thought. *I have to get control again, but I can't let that drone get away!* He looked back up at the drone which had accelerated and dove to get in close to see what was going on with Tom. It was a fatal mistake on the drone pilot's part. Tom knew he might not be accurate enough to grab the drone, so as they both fell, Tom created a solid wall of air directly in front of the drone. At its maximum speed, the large, professional-grade drone was doing close to 50 mph, and when it struck the invisible barrier, it shattered like it had been blown up with explosives. Tom was relieved for an instant before his attention returned to his own rapid descent. He had picked up a lot of speed since he started to fall and with the ground zooming toward him, he found that concentrating was quickly becoming a complicated thing to do. The air molecules were passing him too fast to grab them and use them to slow his descent.

The last time he had been in this position, he had only been about 60 feet up, and his reaction of bracing for impact rather than flying had ended in an earth-shaking crash that had leveled several trees and left a four-foot-deep hole in the ground. Unfortunately for Tom, he was quickly approaching panic mode as the details of the ground below him grew into hyper focus as he failed time after time to slow the air around him as he fell. At 200 feet up, rational thought left him, and he gave up his final attempt to slow himself and again shoved a barrier of energy out in front of him. Tom was aware of his mistake but couldn't help himself any more than someone can stop themselves from wincing when they place their hand on a hot stove. A lifetime of natural reactions took over, and the burst of adrenaline hit his power like jet fuel on an open flame. Bright energy burst out of him in all directions, and a hurricane-force wind erupted as his fall started to look more like a comet entering the atmosphere than a man falling.

υ

James looked up from his position near Greenia's Pond. He had been using a clearing right next to the pond as a launch site for the drone for several days now as he continued his reconnaissance on the subject. He smirked to himself. He had been right to think that Woods would be playing with his new abilities. All the subjects seemed to love to test them out when they first discovered them, and Tom had been no different.

James was proud of his decision to send his second-in-command, Trevor Merrola, to follow the boys. Even though Trevor had spooked the boys near the trailhead to the pond a few days ago and ultimately lost them in the woods, it had given James the idea to use drones to continue his pursuit without being seen.

It hadn't taken him too many flights to establish where the boys were going every day and so it was that James had set up his launch site at Greenia's pond. It was near enough to the hills the boys were using to let the drones get within video range, but far enough away that he wasn't worried that the boys would stumble upon his location. There he had his entire crew set up with telephoto lenses and video cameras so that he could catch it all on tape.

Today, though, had been a defining moment. He had been caught by the subject. The subject had stopped trying to fly and had focused on bringing down the drone - or at least that what James thought had happened. The last clear image he had was the subject spinning in the air to face the drone and then the drone lost contact. Most impressive though was when James ripped off the VR goggles and looked up to spot the falling youth. What he saw was like a sign from God – a massive ball of flaming energy that was shooting toward Earth like a scene straight out of the apocalypse. He knew immediately what it was. "Woods" he muttered under his breath. "Wrap it up, boys! If he survives that, we'll need to pick him up before he gets even stronger."

It was a simple fact of the hunt. If you make first contact with one of the Changed too late, they tend not to want to join the Wall. They start to feel like they can do things on their own and become loose cannons, a liability that must be eliminated.

vi

From Levi's position at the top of one of the rises in the Yard, he could just make out Tom starting to fall with his uncle's binoculars. He had seen Tom spin in midair and begin to fall, then a small puff of smoke as something near to Tom burst apart. The last thing he saw was the tell-tale glow which told Levi that Tom was in an uncontrolled fall again!

"NO! TOM!!" Levi screamed. *This can't happen! Not from that height! He can't survive that!* He felt himself getting worked up as he started a frantic run for his bike at the bottom of the hill. *I'll never get there in time!* he thought as he willed his legs to move faster toward the bike. He could feel a seizure coming on, and it was going to be a big one. It was this crossroads that finally made Levi grab the bottle of pills from his pocket that he had "borrowed" from Dr. Mobien's office. The pills that promised to cure his epilepsy… *Tom needs me! I can't be out of it seizing in the Yard when Tom might be dying in the woods somewhere! Maybe this will at least lessen the seizure — if not cure me altogether.* It was the last argument his mind made before doing what he had been debating about doing for weeks. He grabbed four of the large blue pills, put them in his mouth and washed them down with a long pull from his water bottle. Then, he continued his charge down the hill toward his bike.

As soon as he reached it, he snatched it up and threw his leg over - his foot finding the peddle without looking. It was then that he felt it hit him and knew that he was never going to be able to check on Tom. "Aww cra…" was all he got out before his eyes rolled back in his head and he fell to the ground in a twitching tangle of arms, legs and bike parts.

CHAPTER 8

Tom Meets James

i

Holy crap! It's going to take years to fill in that crater was about all Tom could process in his condition as he limped his way through the woods toward the road leading to his Uncle's farm. He had been walking for about twenty minutes now and still was in a daze. How could he have survived that!?

To put it mildly, the landing had been rough. He had been able to slow down a little, but something had happened just before he had hit the ground. He had been falling at what should have been a terminal velocity. He had seen the trees shatter on his glowing shield and knew that he was about to die. The next thing he knew, he was waking up in a smoldering crater roughly 400 feet in diameter and about 40 feet deep with nothing but a fading image of the ocean in his head to explain what had happened. He felt foreign. His body tingled, and his senses struggled to take in what he was seeing. It was like he was waking up on the surface of the moon. Not a tree stood in the newly established depression. *I should be dead… nothing should have survived that.*

Confused, Tom now sported a bruised right hip and leg which was making his progress through the woods slower than usual, so it was with a huge sigh of relief that he finally broke through the underbrush and popped out onto the main road about a mile from his Uncle's driveway. *Thank God!* he thought. *I have to hurry. If Levi saw me fall, he may have had a seizure!*

It was as if the universe had heard his need to hurry. A white van pulled up beside Tom, and the driver rolled down his window. "Damn, son! I'm not sure what you've been up to, but you look like you've had a hell of a day so far. Do you need a ride?"

Normally Tom would have politely declined and kept walking, but the thought of his brother seizing at the top of the knoll in the Yard made him willing to risk it. "Sure. If you could drop me at the end of my Uncle's driveway, that would be super helpful. It's only about a mile from here."

"Yeah. No problem. Hop up in the back." The driver called through the window.

Tom pulled the sliding door open, and one of the men slipped from the second row of seats to the third to make room. Tom hopped up onto the second-row bench seat and pulled the door closed behind him. As the van picked up speed, Tom used his feet to move the expensive camera cases so that he didn't step on any of them. "So, what are you guys doing up this way?" Tom asked.

"What do you mean?" The driver replied.

"Well, you guys are all wearing clothes from LL Bean, and you have all this camera stuff… Nobody takes a lot of pictures of their own back yard that I know of." Tom began "Do you work for one of the nature conservation groups?"

The smile the driver had sported when he got in the van seemed to slide off his face.

"Hey! Stop here. That's my uncle's driveway." Tom instructed barely noticing the drivers change in demeanor.

"Damn." The driver said under his breath. "Good catch kid, but we aren't stopping here."

Fear gripped Tom's stomach as he realized something was very wrong with the group in the van. "I said STOP!" Tom yelled, and the metal walls of the van started to ripple as Tom's power flared back to life.

It was then that Tom felt the sharp pinch in his neck. "Woooaaah! There kiddo. We can't have you doing any of that now."

Tom's hands flew up, and he felt the needle protruding from his neck. *That bastard drugged me!* was the last thing that went through Tom's mind before he lost consciousness.

ii

As the agents arrived at the field office carrying Tom Woods in on a collapsible field stretcher, James started barking orders to the group of men that had assembled.

"I want Sanchez to go collect the subject's younger brother. We know that siblings have a higher chance of having abilities so take at least a dozen men with you." James instructed. "Merrola, I want the subject to have an IV with a continuous drip of sedation going, and I want *him tied the hell down!!*" He emphasized. "I will not have another Los Angeles happen under my watch."

At the mention of Los Angeles, the men carrying Tom eyed him wearily, sped up and headed straight for the room that had been set up to contain a person with abilities. The room had been made fireproof and had reinforced metal walls and a camera that was embedded behind bulletproof, heat resistant glass. The only furniture in the room was a chair made out of carbon fiber that was welded to the floor. The men quickly set Tom up in the chair with the IV and then shackled him to it by his wrists and legs using handcuff-style restraints, and by the waist with a special heat resistant spun fiber that was capable of handling hundreds of pounds of pressure without snapping. It was excessive, but The Wall had come to realize through painful experience that the power some of their "guests" possessed could be fatal - especially if the person in question didn't even know how to control it.

"What are you ladies waiting for!?" Neuwin bellowed. "Sanchez – why hasn't your team left yet? All you had to do is grab twelve other men to go with you!" He scoffed. "And remember –stay on your toes with the sibling. We may need leverage to make his brother work for us, and that won't happen if we don't get him here in one piece. Now get moving!"

iii

Levi woke with a start. *Something is wrong. Where am I?* were the first two thoughts to fly through Levi's head. *I didn't have a seizure!* Which was immediately followed by *it's not morning anymore!*

He was right on all counts. Somehow, he had the sensation that something was very wrong. He had always had a strong intuitive sense, but what he was feeling now was much stronger. He had a sense that danger was coming for him. There was no questioning it. He knew it as surely as he knew that he was standing next to his bike in the Yard.

What he didn't know is what had happened to his brother. The last thing he had seen was a glowing streak headed toward the ground out past Greenia's Pond. In spite of the danger vibe, Levi got on his bike and started peddling for all he was worth to the trailhead by the farm that would lead him in the direction of where he last had seen Tom. Figuring out how he had avoided a seizure and what this meant would have to wait.

As he rounded the corner by the barn, Levi caught sight of the three black SUVs pulling up into his uncle's door yard. He knew without a doubt that they were the source of the danger vibe. It was a thousand times stronger now.

There is no way I am going to make it across the open field next to the house to the trailhead without them seeing me. Levi knew that with 12 of them between him and the safety of the trees, there was no way he would make it. *Wait a sec – how did I know there are 12 of them?* The knowledge had just popped into his head as the first man out of the lead SUV had started getting closer to the house. *Who cares? I gotta get something to protect myself!* He quickly ditched his bike and slipped through the sliding glass door in the back of the house that lead to the dining room. *If I can get Uncle Lester's 12 gauge before they get in here, I can at least stand a chance of getting through this!*

It was then that he heard the first agent enter the front door and knew his chance of getting to his uncle's room, grabbing the shotgun behind the door and loading it was almost impossible. The gun may as well be on the far side of the moon. Levi knew that ten of the twelve men were approaching the house. Two had stayed behind with the vehicles. Four of the ten men would take up positions on the four corners of the house, preventing any chance of sneaking out without being seen. The remaining six men would now enter the house and go room to room "clearing the house." *How do I know that is what Special Forces calls it when they check each room in a building?* It was a brief but frightening thought. Levi stayed frozen in the kitchen, which was the last room in the far-right corner of the house. There he remained completely motionless and silent as he weighed his options. Surely if he did nothing, he was going to be caught or killed. He knew that to survive, he needed to think his way out of this and to do that he needed to remain calm.

By now the calming exercises that he had learned to control his seizures came like second nature to him, yet this time, as he closed his eyes and slowed his breathing, he suddenly noticed that he was still able to see flashes of images of the house! He wasn't sure what was happening, so he focused on one of the flashes, and it solidified into an image.

What he was seeing was the back of the agent that seemed to be standing in front of him. In the vision, the person glanced around, and Levi was able to put it together that he was seeing through the eyes of one of the other agents, and that soldier was on the other side of the wall on which that Levi was leaning… *Holy crap! How is this possible?* Dozens of questions popped into his mind, but he immediately suppressed them. *There will be time for answers later. Right now, he needed to survive this.*

Levi focused again on the soldier on the opposite side of the wall and found himself picking up stray thoughts. The voice over the communications device in his ear had told him that they had found Levi's bike out back and knew he was in the house. He looked down at the weapon in the soldier's hand. Just looking at it, he knew that it was a tranquilizer gun that was designed to subdue but not kill whatever it hit with the wicked looking darts that filled the clip. He also knew that there was a 45-caliber handgun loaded with hollow point bullets in the holster that was on the man's hip in case the dart gun didn't pan out. Unbidden, the knowledge that this man had used both weapons with the cool detachment of a professional mercenary came in cold wave to Levi.

These men would not stop. There was no doubt of that. Levi quickly looked around his immediate area of the kitchen and found a long-bladed carving knife with a wooden handle. He snatched it up knowing that he needed to slow these men down. If he wounded one of them, maybe the others would rush to help him, and, in the confusion, Levi could make it out the front door. He didn't take the time to think through what he would do about the men outside, but he knew he only had seconds before the two-person team in the next room rounded the corner and he would be caught.

Without any further hesitation, Levi concentrated on the man on the other side of the wall and got his position. He then immediately plunged the knife at thigh level through the wall. The blade ran true into the man's upper right leg, but what Levi hadn't planned on was the electrical wire that ran down the inside of the wall at that particular spot.

With the wooden handle insulating Levi from injury, the full force of the current ran into the agent on the other side of the wall causing his muscles to contract and his finger to squeeze the trigger of the tranquilizer gun. The first two darts hit his teammate – once in the bulletproof vest and once higher in the back of the neck. As his teammate pitched forward, the next several darts headed straight down the hall and into the foremost agent coming from the bedrooms area of the house.

Levi felt the changes. He knew that three of the six in the house were now down and the other three had dropped for cover when they heard the scream and the weapon firing. He knew he wouldn't get an opportunity like this again. He bolted around the corner in the chaos and ran for the front door.

The second man in the hall saw Levi run and had a faster reaction time than Levi had expected. He knew the man was raising his weapon and felt the man's emotion as he squeezed the trigger. Levi froze for a split second knowing that the man had aimed slightly ahead of him to account for the fact he was running. The dart sailed less than two inches in front of Levi and embedded itself into the far wall of the living room.

Not missing a beat, Levi was already moving forward again and was out the front door just as the second agent in the hall squeezed off three more rapid-fire shots.

As Levi burst through the front door, he jumped over the three steps that lead up to the old farmhouse and landed with both feet. He instantly knew that the men stationed at the two front points of the house been anticipating this and had their guns raised to fire. He froze standing directly between the two men. The man at the right front corner was faster on the draw and fired his dart gun straight at Levi. As he squeezed the trigger, Levi was off again. The dart, having missed hitting him in the chest, flew past him and hit the agent on the left corner of the house in the thigh.

The agent at the right corner shook his head in disbelief and unleashed a barrage of darts. Levi zig-zagged as he ran in a pattern that would have been considered "inspired" except for the fact that he was actually seeing where the agent was aiming and course-adjusting as he ran. He was halfway to the woodline as the two agents that had been at the rear of the house joined in with their own volleys of darts.

At 50 meters to the trees, Levi lurched forward and hit the ground. He hadn't been hit, but he knew that the men firing at him would only stop when they saw him hit the ground. He waited as if unconscious until he sensed them starting to get up from their firing position to walk over to him. Then, he was on his feet and at a dead run again.

At 25 meters, a dart brushed by his cheek but didn't puncture his skin as his feet flew over the remaining ground. *Oh my God! I am totally going to make it!* He couldn't believe his luck as he flew past the first couple of trees.

However, his excitement came to an abrupt end as another agent in tactical gear stepped out from behind a tree and clotheslined him with his tranquilizer gun. Levi's feet flew out from under him, and he came down hard on the ground as the air rushed from his chest.

Looking up at the man in disbelief as he struggled to catch his breath. He heard someone from the house yell "Did you get him, Sanchez?"

The man named Sanchez casually looked down as he flipped his dart gun around and pointed it directly at Levi. "Yeah, I got him." He replied touching what must have been a communication device at his neck and speaking in a quiet tone of voice. "Bet you didn't see that one coming." He chuckled and pointed the dart gun directly at Levi's chest.

"Hold on now guys. That stuff that happened in the house was just an accident! I didn't mean to stab that guy. Can't we all just calm down and talk this all out?" Levi pleaded.

As the sensation of falling replaced the sharp pinch of the dart, the last thought that went through Levi's mind was *Man! I couldn't read that guy at all. I couldn't even sense his presence. It was like he wasn't... even... there.*

CHAPTER 9

The Job Offer

i

"Mr. Woods." A tinny voice started to penetrate the fog in Tom's head. "Mr. Woods…? Tom?" came the voice again.

Tom slowly started to become aware as the sedation was lowered again by the agent behind the camera.

"Tom? This is Agent Garra. Can you hear me?"

When Tom didn't respond, a sharp click could be heard over the intercom as Garra shut off communications between the interrogation room and the control chamber in the adjoining room.

ii

"I don't know, Mr. Neuwin…" Garra began. "The initial dose that was given in the field should be wearing off, and I have already turned the drip rate down enough that he should be waking up now."

"So, what are you saying, Agent Garra?" James sneered. "That a 17-year-old boy is savvy enough in the ways of enhanced interrogations to be faking unconsciousness so that he can take out 20 armed men in an underground bunker while chained to a chair?"

"No… what I am saying is that he should be awake by now. His heart rate and blood pressure say that he probably is awake." Garra countered.

"Jesus man! Even I know you can't tell if someone is awake by their heart rate." James snapped. "According to our records, the only other time this kid has had drugs is when he had his wisdom teeth out! Isn't it more likely that he is just a lightweight?" then, not waiting for the answer "lower the drip rate one more time and if he doesn't wake up, we can… stimulate him."

Garra sighed and decreased the drip rate again from the control panel in front of the monitor screen.

iii

By now, Tom was feeling less like his head was full of sand and more like he was just very, very calm. He remembered getting in the van, driving past his uncle's driveway and the sharp pinch of the sedative just before he lost consciousness.

Now, as he was able to start processing what was happening to him and he realized just how much trouble he was in, he began to think through what his next steps should be. First, he knew that he was alone in a room and tied to a chair. He also managed to get a peek at the video camera embedded in the wall in front of him. Slowly he put tension against the cuffs holding his wrists to the chair behind his back. They were secure and held fast. Of even more interest to Tom, when he contracted his muscles in his hands to test the restraint, he had felt a sharp stinging feeling on top of his right elbow. He had given blood enough times at school to recognize the feeling of an IV. *Interesting. I wonder what that is about.*

He then tried to use his powers on the cuffs to unlock them, but when he tried to focus to use his power, he realized he couldn't. *Ahhh… There is the reason for the IV. If I am drugged, I can't use my gift. But who are these guys? How do they know how to suppress it?* Tom's still fuzzy mind couldn't think through any answers, but he immediately realized one thing – if he was going to get out of here, he was going to need his powers, and if he was going to use them, he would need to get the drug stopped.

Further musings were interrupted by a sharp click of the intercom switching on again. "Tom? We know you can hear us! Look up at the camera, Tom."

It had to be that Agent Garra again from earlier.

Tom's fuzzy thoughts ran ahead of him. *I can't pretend to be sedated forever. Eventually, they are going to catch on. More importantly, I need answers. Who are these guys? What do they want? What do they know about me? Where am I?* The questions, once started, continued to bubble from his head like springtime brook in the mountains.

"Okay, Tom… Don't say I didn't ask you nicely first." Garra's tinny voice belied the seriousness of his treat.

An instant later, Tom's entire body jumped as a mild electric charge coursed through the chair.

"Okay! Okay! Okay!" Tom quickly yelled at the camera. "I am up. Stop!"

Silence.

Then "Good to see you are awake, Tom" came Agent Garra's reply. Tom could practically hear the amusement on his lips. "I trust you are awake enough to answer some questions for us now… Or should we help you wake up some more?" Garra's greasy voice was almost dripping with eagerness. In that instant, Tom understood Garra. This was a man that enjoyed questioning people. He loved to pry their secrets from them. He liked seeing how much pain someone was able to take before they cracked, and he took pride in the fact that he could always break them. This was a man to be feared.

"No. No, that won't be necessary." Tom quickly offered. "What do you want?"

"Not much. I just want to know you a little better." Garra offered, but even drugged Tom knew that wasn't all of the truth.

"Oh, that's good." Tom sighed as he made an effort to act as if that relaxed him. "I would like to get to know you better too." The words were out of his mouth before he could think through how Garra would take them.

An instant later, he had his answer as the electricity from the chair wracked his body in pain. "Not quite so much cheek please, Mr. Woods" came Garra's reprimand over the speaker.

As the pain stopped, Tom briefly had a moment of clear thought. *I need to be more careful. This guy loves that button and needs to be in charge.* "Okay." Tom croaked "Sorry… Sir."

"Much better" Garra gloated. "Now, the first question we have for you is: how long have you been aware you have powers?"

Tom saw no value in lying to him. "Only since the end of the school year. Maybe three months?"

"Good. Nice that you have decided to cooperate." In the background, Tom heard another man's voice. So, Garra wasn't the one calling the shots in this. "What are your powers, as you see them?"

Ouch! I don't want them knowing exactly what I can do. He thought through the returning haze of the medication. "I can move stuff with my mind." He offered, knowing that it was safe to say since they probably already knew that.

The jolt was almost immediate and stronger than the last one, ripping away the effects of the sedation. "We already know that Mr. Woods!" Garra snapped. "We want to know what *else* you can do. What are the limits of your power? How did you get them? How does it work?"

Tom took a deep breath as the pain left him and clarity from the meds lingered. "I am not 100% sure how it all works." Tom conceded. "I was taking part in a study, and the place blew up. Next thing I know – I can move things without touching them. If you can connect the dots and tell me how this happened, I would love it. I want my normal life back."

Another pause. Then "Why is that Mr. Woods?" came the voice over the speaker. "You are a young man that can fly. Why would you want to give that up?"

"Why?" Tom couldn't keep the contempt out of his voice. "Oh, I don't know…" his voice dripped sarcasm as he looked down at his arms and made a show of trying to get out of his restraints. "Maybe because this just isn't working out so well for me?!?"

The shock was the strongest yet and was immediate. "Temper, temper, Mr. Woods" chided Garra over the intercom.

That was it! Tom had had enough. "I am not answering anything else until you answer something for me!" he growled through the pain.

There was a pause then "Really?" It was a different voice. "What would that be?"

"Who the hell are you people and what do you want?" Tom fired back.

Click. The intercom went off again. Tom waited, suspecting that the next thing he would feel is the electricity again. To his surprise, the door to the cell opened and in walked a man of about 35 years in a dark blue business suit. When Tom got a look at his face, he realized with a start that this man was the one that had been driving the van earlier that day. "Good afternoon, Subject Woods." He began perfunctorily. "My name is Special Agent James Neuwin. I work for a company called Great Wall Incorporated – or 'The Wall' as we call it. We are the first, last and only line of defense against things deemed 'special threats' by the US government." James told him, skipping the fact that they did not currently have any government contracts.

Tom paused in complete shock. *What the hell did this guy just say? Did he say that he is electrocuting me for the government?* He couldn't even formulate a question as his mouth hung open.

James chuckled. "I know. You are thinking: how could you work for the government when you have me tied up and have used electricity on me?" It was like he was reading Tom's mind. "At your age, I would have been confused too. I would not have known how serious a threat the Changed – that's how people with abilities like yours are known – could be. But I know now Mr. Woods." James had been pacing as he talked but now stopped directly in front of Tom. "I have seen with my own eyes how destructive these powers can be in the hands of those that aren't on our side. I have seen my men – good agents – killed by these monsters, and because of that, we have had to draw a serious line in the sand." He went back to pacing. "When we discover the newly Changed, we make contact and ask them: Will you come work for us?"

Tom almost choked on his own tongue "You mean this is a *job offer?*" He was floored.

James smiled like a man that just bit into something sour. "Sort of… If you come to work for us, you have to give up your life here in Vermont. You will do *whatever* we instruct you to do. Your family will never see you again. The reason for this is simple. We don't let people stay at home with tanks or nuclear weapons, so why would we allow one of the Changed to walk around with that kind of unchecked power? No. They need to be constantly accounted for."

"You want me to use my powers against people? And do what? Hurt them? And you want me to leave my life here behind? You're asking me to give up *everything!*" Tom shuddered thinking of what James and this agency were asking of him.

James immediately cut him off "Not everything." Then much more quietly "You get to live…"

Tom's heartbeat pounded in his ears. *Did this guy just say he was going to kill me if I refuse?* Then, after pausing a second to collect his wits. "Does that mean if I say no…?"

"You never leave this room alive." James finished.

"Are you *kidding me?!*" Tom yelled. "This is Northern Vermont if you haven't noticed. The government doesn't just kidnap and kill people!"

"Really?" James quipped making a show of looking around the room in which Tom was located. "And why is that again?"

"People would notice! You would be discovered. It would be all over the news!" Tom was angry and starting to lose his patience with his captor's line of reasoning.

"Shhhhh." James had heard enough. "I have been more than patient with you Mr. Woods, and normally this is the point that I would simply have Agent Garra give you a lethal dose of something if you refused me. Unfortunately, I suspect you may have powers that are strong enough that it would be worth my while to see if I can get you to come over to our way of thinking. Sadly, that can get a little messy as I am forced to look for your weaknesses." He turned his back to Tom. "First, I will use pain…" and with a gesture, all Tom could feel was pain as the electricity poured through him at a near lethal level.

When it finally stopped Tom slumped forward breathing raggedly and barely conscious. "Or through using the lives of those you love the most as leverage…" James finished.

As James motioned for the door to be opened, the final words sunk into Tom's pain-soaked mind. "What do you mean? 'Using the lives of those I love?'"

The door swung open, and James glanced back. "I mean – I sent a team of men to collect your brother from your uncle's farm. If he survived, he should be here soon, and then we will see how compliant you are when it is *your brother's* screams you are hearing…" was the last Tom heard as the door clicked shut.

"NOOOOO!!! NEUWIN! YOU BASTARD!! DON'T YOU TOUCH LEVI OR I'LL…" But Tom couldn't finish his threat because Garra had turned the electricity back on.

iv

Garra had heard enough of the subject's threats and hit the button to shock him again. This time, though, the adrenaline and electricity both combine to overcome the effects of the sedation, and Tom could feel it the instant it happened. The first thing he did was use his ability to rip the electrical wires that were attached to his chair out of the ground and shove them into the two sets of fluorescent lights in the ceiling causing them to blow out and throw his cell into darkness.

The silence was palpable for several seconds in the control booth as everyone stared in stunned disbelief at the screen. Did the camera break or did the lights go out? How had it happened? No one had ever been able to focus enough to use their power with that much medication in them before. It should not be possible. It had to be an electrical glitch.

No one was quite sure what they had just seen. "Come on Carl, get that thing back on." James snapped at Garra.

Garra quickly regained his composure and started flipping switches to see where the malfunction had occurred. Nothing seemed to work. Then, one of the guards in the room seemed to go pale. "L-l-l-look!" he stammered, pointing at the screen.

The camera, they all discovered at once, was working just fine, as a dim battery powered backup light flared into life from inside the room revealing Tom sitting there with the disconnected wires on the floor in front of him. Garra threw on the switch to the intercom "What do you think you are doing? Do you think that electrocuting you is all we can do?" he demanded.

"No," Tom answered. "But that was one of the top two things bugging me."

"What was the other one?"

"The IV, but that's not a problem now either," and in the dim glow of the backup light, Garra could make out the IV that was now laying on the floor with the electrical wires in front of Tom.

Garra and James exchanged a nervous glance. "Not possible" James mouthed to Garra.

"We have plenty of other ways to get what we need from you Mr. Woods. I suggest you stop fighting the inevitable." Garra said into the intercom mic at the desk.

Tom looked up directly into the camera. "It's not inevitable if I can get out of here." and as he said the words the cuffs that could have held a man with ten times Tom's strength, snapped off his wrists like they were made of cheap plastic. He stood up, snapping the restraint belt.

Garra visibly flinched and took a step back from the screen.

Tom stepped forward, and the leg restraints made popping sounds as his ankles broke free of the metal shackles. "I would never work for a group like this!" Tom yelled at the camera. "Now, I am leaving to go get my brother!"

As the men in the observation room watched, Tom reached out and made a slow gesture with his hand like he was crumpling a ball of paper, and to their amazement, the camera behind the protective glass also crumpled, leaving the men in the observation room staring at a blank screen.

James spun to look at Garra, his face a mask of anger. "This has gone far enough." He said through clenched teeth. "Hit the gas and put this kid down!"

Garra didn't need to be told twice. All interrogation rooms run by The Wall had a built-in failsafe device. Poison gas could flood the room at the touch of a button, and Garra's hand slammed down on that button now.

υ

From inside the room, Tom heard the metal grates open behind him and the hiss of the gas being released. Being raised on spy films and political thrillers, it didn't take Tom two seconds to realize what was happening.

He needed to hurry. He needed to survive this, and he needed to get to his brother. As he spun to face the rear wall, the thought that he might not live to save his brother flooded him with anger and determination. Reaching forward with his arms, Tom grabbed the vent covers with his mind and slammed them shut, fusing them in place.

Then, he turned to face the only door in the room. Behind that door were freedom and his brother. Without any further thought, Tom took a deep breath and went to work on the door.

vi

From outside the interrogation chamber, Agent Gilman was standing guard and beginning to think there may be a problem. He had heard several small detonations emanate from the cell. He had seen a lot of weird stuff during his two years as part of The Wall, but something was making him think that this latest kid may be more trouble than they had originally thought he would be. As his father used to tell him "Having a tiger by the tail ain't too bad, son – until you let go of the tail." The thought of losing control of one of the subjects they interrogated was unnerving and had him playing with the holster safety on his sidearm.

Gilman knew the phase of the process they were in now very well. He knew the time for dart guns had passed, and if the subject broke free, they would have to put him down with lethal force.

Then, it started. It was an incredibly loud, high-pitched whistling sound. Next – impossibly – the reinforced, vault style door, began to shake on its hinges. Agent Gilman quickly started to back away down the hall – his eyes wide and his firearm now in hand. *How can this even be happening? We've set off explosions in these rooms, and the door didn't even wiggle!* But here it was in front of him – a 200-pound door shaking like an aluminum tea kettle lid as it came to a hard boil.

Gilman felt a hand on his shoulder and turned to all the other agents pouring down the hall with weapons drawn. No alarm had sounded yet, but everyone could feel what was coming. He extended his arm out to keep the other agents from moving past him, closer to the door.

In the next instant, all was chaos. The door finally blew outward into the hall embedding parts of the wall and door frame into the cement wall opposite the interrogation room. The blast of wind that followed the door blew all the agents back down the hall like leaves before in an autumn storm.

Agent Gilman looked up from the floor in time to see Tom emerging from the room. He immediately opened fire, but the bullets just ricocheted away several feet in front of Tom.

vii

Tom looked down the hall and saw the exit sign past all the agents pointing left down an adjacent hall and immediately started walking toward the men. Several of them dove into rooms off the hallway, knowing that they would not be able to stop Tom with conventional firearms. Some agents continued to fire. Tom held up one hand, palm outward and a shimmering shield of air surrounded him, protecting him from the storm of bullets that flew his way.

Tom rounded the corner, and the elevator was only twenty feet away.

Just then, red lights and alarms sounded throughout the facility. Someone must have finally hit the lockdown alarm. The elevator would surely not work now.

Tom spun around as he heard the pop, pop, pop of gunfire from behind him. Some of the agents that had ducked into the rooms had regained their composure and were trying to mount a defense. Tom didn't have time for this. Levi needed him. He quickly reached up into the roof of the tunnel above the hallway and pulled it down. The hall filled with dust and debris as large rocks began to rain down sealing the tunnel between Tom and the agents.

Finally clear of interfering agents, he turned and ripped the elevator apart leaving a clear path up the elevator shaft. Stepping onto a cloud of air molecules, Tom rose up the shaft with increasing speed, and in minutes, he had sailed out into the evening sky.

CHAPTER 10

Standoff at the Farm

i

Sanchez had restraints on the younger brother and an IV providing continuous sedation was in place and running. He wasn't sure if the kid had a power or if he was just the luckiest little brat he had ever met, but there is no way he was going to give this kid another shot at escape. Neuwin would be furious if he lost him, so Sanchez was taking every possible precaution. Levi had been blindfolded and his restraints secured to an 80-pound cement weight. This kid wasn't going anywhere.

Content with these measures, Sanchez turned his attention back to the scene at the farm. He would have liked to return to the field office sooner, but he had been forced to clean the extraction site first.

The agents that were hit with the tranquilizer darts were all dragged to the SUVs where they could sleep off the effects. Then, everything from the hole in the kitchen wall to the footprints outside were either documented for the repair team that would be coming later tonight or were swept clean so that there would be no evidence that anything had happened at the house. It was one thing that The Wall were firm believers in: never let there be proof of anything that would scare the neighbors.

Now that all the tedious parts were done, Sanchez was anxious to get moving, knowing that Neuwin would be getting irritated at the delay. He was just about to radio for the remaining men to come back to the SUVs when the first one hit.

A fifty-foot maple landed in front of the lead SUV. The second, mature maple was seconds behind the first, landing with an explosion of dirt and leaves behind the rearmost SUV in the convoy.

Sanchez had been in war zones for most of his adult life, and he immediately knew he and his team were in trouble. "All agents – on me! Now! We have contact." With the speed of a well-trained military squad, the remaining agents all dropped their tranquilizer guns and locked and loaded their weapons as they found cover behind the trees and the vehicles.

It was only seconds later that Tom landed a short distance from the convoy. "Where is my BROTHER!?!" he demanded.

"Oh, crap," Sanchez muttered under his breath. He knew that he had just seen this kid drugged and strapped to a chair from which no normal human could have escaped. If the kid just flew here, that meant he had somehow escaped an underground bunker and over twenty armed men while drugged and shackled. Then, touching the transmit button on the device at his throat, he issued orders in a low voice to his men: "Someone get in the middle vehicle and put a gun to the brother's head. The rest of you need to form a semicircle around the threat. Be prepared to fire only if I give the signal, and if I do - shoot to kill."

Sanchez released his mic and stood up from his crouching position and faced Tom. "We have him, and he is okay." He announced in a loud voice.

Tom turned to face Sanchez and noticed the other agents attempting to circle him. "Where?"

"Somewhere safe." Sanchez countered knowing that one of the only pieces of leverage he had was Levi.

"I want him handed over to me now," Tom demanded.

"That's just not going to happen young man…" Sanchez replied. "There are a dozen men here with guns. I would hate to see you or your brother get hurt because you made a rash decision."

Tom smiled, and Sanchez knew he had pushed too far. He also knew without a doubt that this subject was not afraid of being fired upon. In his experience, only two things will cause a person not to care if someone threatens to shoot at them. One was if the person didn't care if he lived or died, but Sanchez knew that was not the case with Tom. The other reason was if the person knew he wouldn't get hurt if they did open fire. In Sanchez's mind, that was far more likely, and if that was the case, his only chance of ending this quickly was to take Tom by surprise.

Without another thought, he raised his gun and yelled "NOW!" and in an instant, the air in the small clearing was filled with smoke from eight separate automatic weapons. It was only when all the clips were empty that the shooting stopped, and the group of agents that surrounded Tom waited for the breeze to blow away the smoke that obscured their target.

As the smoke cleared, the agents slowly started backing up and reaching for additional clips. In the middle of the clearing, surrounded by a shimmering wall of air stood Tom Woods – without a scratch on him.

"I gave you a chance" was all that Tom said. Then he made a grabbing gesture with his hand, and all of the agent's guns flew from their hands to land at his feet. Several of them turned and ran. Tom started walking straight toward Sanchez, and when Sanchez looked like he was about to bolt, he held up the same hand and made a grabbing motion.

The air around Sanchez suddenly seemed to come alive and wrap tightly around him, blocking his escape. "I asked you a question," Tom said quietly. "Where is my brother?" The invisible hand wrapped around Sanchez squeezed harder and lifted him from the ground.

One agent ran up behind Tom, with a long wicked looking hunting knife. Tom heard him, glanced back and made a flicking motion with one hand. The agent flew back like a horse had kicked him.

"Last chance," Tom advised.

"Middle car." Sanchez rasped out.

"Good." Tom turned his attention from Sanchez to the cars in the driveway. With a wave of his hand, Sanchez flew back several feet and landed in a pile in the grass.

Tom placed both his hands together, palms in and then opened them like a book. The middle car shuddered, and then the roof split down the middle. The agent that had been assigned to hold a gun to Levi's head stood up and pulled Levi up with him. "Stop, or I shoot!" He warned.

Tom froze, and the car stopped moving. "Easy, mister." Tom urged, holding both hands up palm out. "Don't hurt my brother."

"That's all up to you, Woods." The agent warned. "We just need you to come with us back to the office and have a talk."

"I've seen your office and how you ask questions," Tom answered. "My brother and I are not going anywhere near that place ever again."

"I guess that depends on whether you would rather have a bullet in your brother's head than make the tri…" the agent trailed off as one of the SUVs floated up into the air to rest above the agent and Levi.

"You do realize that the only reason you are alive is you have my brother with you, right?" Tom asked in a deadly serious voice as he walked closer to the car. "Are you really willing to shoot him? Because if you do, I can promise you, I will drop this car."

Tom didn't wait for an answer. All of the agent's attention was focused on the car floating over his head. Tom took two more big steps toward the agent and was finally close enough to extend his shield around Levi.

The agent realized what was happening a split second too late, panicked and pulled the trigger. The bullet bounced off the wall of air and buried itself in the agent's thigh. Howling in pain, he tumbled from the wrecked SUV as Tom dropped the floating SUV into the yard and rushed to Levi's side.

Levi had fallen back to the seat when the agent had let go of him. Now Tom reached out with his ability and picked him up in a cloud of air molecules. The IV, blindfold, and shackles all fell away like a spider's web under Tom's direction as both boys coasted up into the evening air and headed home.

ii

It had taken hours to get all the personnel and equipment up the twenty flights of stairs to the relative safety of the ground floors of the field office. James was furious. This subject had the potential to be one of the most powerful Changed that The Wall had converted in quite some time, but it had all gone south somehow. The lower sections of the field office were unstable and no longer usable, and Agent Sanchez had just radioed in and told him that they had lost their leverage as well as the subject himself. Woods was so angry now that James knew the odds of turning Woods to their side were virtually zero.

There was no other choice. James needed to go back to the main office in Boston and get a cleaning crew. From what Sanchez had told him, Woods had not seriously hurt any of his men during the encounter at the farm. Nor had he hurt anyone at the field office. He chuckled. Well… The crew James was about to bring, had no such reservations at all. Tom Woods would be eliminated, and by this time next week, there wasn't going to be any evidence that Tom Woods had ever existed.

CHAPTER **11**

The Aftermath

i

It was the first day of school, and the pressure of waiting was almost unbearable. Tom and Levi had agreed to meet in the library during the fifth period. Tom had an open study period, and Levi had lunch. They both grabbed a random book off the shelf and sat in the back with their heads close together so that they could talk without being overheard.

"Man!" Tom began "I…"

"Yeah. I know." Levi interrupted. "I can't believe it either."

Tom made a face. "Dude. You do that all the time now. Cut it out!"

"Do what?" Levi asked with a blank look on his face.

"Finish my sentences. It's getting weird."

"Okay. Sorry." Then quickly changing the topic "So, what's the plan?"

"What plan?"

"It's been three days since they came for us." Levi began. "That day, when the fighting finally stopped, we circled back to that weird warehouse they were in, and we found out that their leader had gone somewhere for reinforcements." He shifted in his seat and readjusted his book to better cover his face. "From what you told me, that guy isn't someone who is just going to let bygones be bygones – especially after the spanking you gave him. So, again: what is the plan for when they come back?"

Tom sighed. "I wish I had never gone back there, but I had to make sure that those guys weren't trapped in the lower rooms."

"Don't worry bro. Your halo is still just as shiny as it used to be." Levi joked. "I just don't want him showing up without us being ready. It almost didn't turn out so well the last time."

Tom looked hard at his brother again. "I have to say; I was really amazed that you almost escaped with that many agents after you."

"I wouldn't call being drugged, bound and gagged when you got to me, *amazing* per se..." Levi made a face.

"Yeah, but from what I saw of the condition of the agents there, you gave them a run." Tom's eyes continued to bore into Levi.

"Well, that's what they get for hiring people from Bad-Guys-R-Us." Levi scoffed, and a smile flitted across his face before his frown came back. Tom had noticed the frown was there more often than the smile over the past few days. "Tom. We need a plan. Now."

"Right. Right. Right." Tom put his head down lower behind his book. "The way I see it, we have several disadvantages. First, we don't know much about these guys at all. How long have they been doing this? Who do they have working for them? Do they have any of the Changed on their side and if so, what can they do?" Tom started writing it all down in his notebook. "Once we know what they are capable of, we can move on to step two: how do we develop a defense?"

"Now that's what I'm talking about!" Levi agreed. "That is the beginning of something solid. I have a couple of friends in the computer science club. I will hit them up to do some dark web research. I'll give them a fake story about wanting it for an extra credit assignment…"

"Way to dodge doing any of the work yourself." Tom grinned at his brother's laziness.

"It's a gift," Levi replied beaming from ear to ear.

Just then, the bell sounded indicating the end of the period, and both boys sighed and headed off to their next class.

ii

It was eighth period, and Tom was in his least favorite class – gym. He had hated it so much that he had put off taking the remaining one-credit class that he needed to complete his college prep curriculum until his senior year. Now he no longer had a choice.

In typical fashion of the gym teacher, she had all but skipped reviewing the syllabus and just jumped right into a sport. She was four years out from retirement and didn't want to focus on the teaching aspect as much as she wanted to focus on the having fun part.

"Alright, class! Our first stop on this trip to getting you to enjoy being healthy and active will be soccer! So, let's see who is up for this. Let's do five laps around the field to warm up. When you are done, meet back here for stretches." And with that announcement, there was a collective moan from the class as they started their first lap around the field.

Tom wasn't done his first lap when another runner bumped into him. It was Reagan. "Howdy stranger!" She said between breaths.

"Hi." Tom tried to smile back, but it looked more like a grimace.

"You're running a lot faster than you were your freshman year."

"Yeah." He huffed. "I have been feeling the need to get into better shape lately."

Reagan smiled back at him. "Me too. What do you say we make this into a game?" She quipped and playfully punched him in the arm. "Tag! You're it." Then she took off ahead of him with a burst of speed.

Tom's jaw almost hit the floor. Again, he was struck by how different Reagan was from the chronically ill girl he had known growing up. She was smart, witty and in excellent shape!

"Keep moving Mr. Woods!" Came the gym teacher's voice over the loudspeaker on the field.

"Crap!" he muttered under his breath as he picked up his speed to a jog. "I'd take Agent Neuwin's electric chair over that lady any day..."

iii

"That's total bullcrap!!" Levi snapped as he and Tom walked toward the door leading out of the principal's office.

"Watch your tone young man." The assistant principal warned.

"Yes, ma'am." He said over his shoulder as he hurried out the door and into the hall.

"Really?" Tom asked shaking his head. "So, you didn't cheat on a pre-test in biology, and you somehow managed to get a perfect score without studying in the first week of school?"

"Would you believe me if I said yes?'" Levi asked.

"Not a chance. You suck at sciences. You're just lucky that they called mom and arranged to have me pick you up after school instead of making her leave work to do it herself." Tom was not impressed.

"I didn't cheat." Levi reasserted.

"Right. You're just suddenly..." Tom started.

"…a Nobel scholar in biology." Levi finished. "Har har. Very funny."

Tom stopped dead in his tracks his eyes huge. "What the?!?" He began. "How did you know I was going to say that?"

Levi looked at the ground. "Crap." He exhaled and looked hard at Tom. "You are waaay past me talking my way out of this."

Tom stayed frozen and stared at him. Waiting.

"So, you remember when we went to talk with Dr. Mobien, and he had the epilepsy cure in pill form?" He began.

"Yeah…"

Levi pulled the bottle from his pants pocket and shook it, so it rattled in front of Tom.

"Levi! My God! Tell me you didn't…"

"…take them?" Levi rolled his eyes. "Of course, I did. How do you think I am able to read your thoughts?"

"Read my…" Tom was in shock.

"Yup. Back when I saw you start to fall out of the sky it triggered a seizure, so I took one of the pills hoping that it would cure my epilepsy, but instead, I got the ability to read people's minds." Levi confessed.

"What about your epilepsy though?" Tom asked, fearing the answer.

"Nope. Still alive and well. I didn't take my meds for a day and a half after you sent the agents packing, and I ended up having a small seizure last night." He stated with a dark face.

"Sorry man. I know you were hoping that Mobien had the cure. We both were."

Levi didn't comment.

"So why don't you tell me about what you can do with your ability – other than cheat on tests." Tom tried changing the subject.

"For real Tom, I didn't try to cheat. That teacher's thoughts were just so loud!" Levi impishly defended himself. "It's cool. Thoughts are in the air and normally are like the buzz from a beehive. However, sometimes someone will think something really loud, and it will stand out, or I will concentrate on what one person is thinking, and I can make it out. It helps to be closer physically to them to do that though."

"Is it just listening that you can do? Can you talk to someone? I've read books about people that can."

"Naw." Levi cut him off. "I tried telling mom to pass me the potatoes last night, and she didn't seem to hear anything. I think my talent is kind of passive."

"Maybe." Tom pondered. "Or it may be like mine, and it will take a while to figure it out."

"Maybe," Levi agreed. "The cool thing about mine is that it's not as flashy as yours and I can use it without people knowing." They passed the Catholic church which marked the halfway point on the trip home. "So, what are we going to do when they come back?" Levi asked, changing the subject. "I know that we need more information on them and such, but I was in their heads, and they seemed to be really determined. And you said that guy, James, told you that if you didn't join, they were going to kill you. What if he comes back and just keeps trying to kill you?"

Tom scowled. He had been wondering the same thing for the past three days too. "I don't know. If he really is a part of the government like he said, he will have the police on his side." Tom kicked a rock and sent it skittering down the street.

"Yup, so we can't get him locked up, and all he needs is one clean shot," Levi added, worried.

"I know. I can't keep a protective shield up all the time." Tom agreed.

"But where does that leave us? Kill or be killed? Because if James gets some of the Changed on his side and they are trained to be as bad as those agents were, they will try to kill us!"

Tom was about to pass the rock again, but this time when he kicked it, he pushed with his ability at the same time that he kicked, and the rock shot out from his foot like it was fired from a cannon, sailing past trees and down toward the lake miles away.

"Subtle." Levi scoffed and kept walking.

"Sorry." Tom conceded. "I don't know where that leaves us, but I am not willing to kill someone. There *has* to be another way."

iv

It was two days later, after school, that Tom walked into Rutnies to find Levi already sitting in a booth in the back as far from the other guests as possible.

"Hey. I got your text to meet you here. What's up?" Tom casually asked as he slid into the booth on the same side as Levi so that their backs would block people from seeing what was on the table.

"Bad things. Terrible things. I talked to my friends in the computer science club, and I have the results of that dark web search I asked them to help me with." Now that Tom was closer, he could see Levi was pale and looked nervous.

"Calm down, bro," Tom said picking up the soda that Levi had already ordered for him and taking a sip. "What are we looking at?"

"This group, the one that tried to grab us, they are the real deal. The info my fellow nerds collected was some real Grimm Brothers fairy tale kinda crap!" He pulled a folder out of his backpack, opened it and spread the contents on the table.

"Look at this," Levi said shoving one of the reports toward Tom. "I had them start with what Agent James told you. He said he worked for a company called Great Wall Incorporated. That company used to exist up until about eight years ago. They were a group that various government agencies use to contract to do stuff that they didn't want to get caught doing themselves. They sold guns, performed assassinations, and blackmailed some pretty dangerous people. Then eight years ago, poof! Gone." He pulled out another article that read. *Eccentric CEO, Greg Buckner, of successful security professionals' company, GWI, closes doors after 15 years.*

"That's the last legit newspaper article on The Wall. Now, the rest of these are tabloids and blog posts. This one says that The Wall grabbed his kid brother. The weird part is he was out of the country when it happened. He got this text message from his brother saying 'Agents from The Wall are after me. Help!' Then, when he got home, his parents didn't remember that they had a second child. None of his brother's things were in the house. Even crazier than that, the younger brother had been removed from all the family pictures and his birth certificate and driver's license no longer existed."

Tom got chills.

"Dude! They friggin *erased* him!" Levi hissed the word through clenched teeth.

"That's not even possible." Tom began. "This would have to be a conspiracy of epic proportions for someone to do that."

"I thought that too, but what if they have one of the Changed that can erase you?"

"Oh man... Is that even possible?" Tom questioned.

"It's a lot more possible than having every branch of government and hundreds of civilians be in on a conspiracy to snatch people with abilities." Levi reasoned.

"And Tom, there are dozens of stories like this one, but they are hard to find. The techy guys said they were amazed at how deep they had to dig to find this stuff. They even had to shut off their computers a few times because software viruses were targeting them while they were doing the searches."

"Okay." Tom could see where Levi was going with this. "I take it you told the guys to stop looking? We don't want anyone to trace those searches back to the computer club."

"Way ahead of you." He confirmed. "I had them stop as soon as they told me about it."

"Is there anything else significant in there?" Tom asked gesturing at the pile of printouts.

"Yes and no. A lot of the other information is from tabloids, but each one describes what might be one of the Changed. I just can't tell which ones are real and which are complete baloney." He shook his head. "Take this one: maybe there is a bigfoot in Northern California, or maybe it's one of the Changed." He shuffled some more papers. "Here is a guy in Massachusetts that can talk to plants." He tossed the pile back on the table. "There's just no way to know for sure."

"Know for sure about what?" Came a female voice from the booth behind theirs.

Both Tom and Levi jumped and spun around to see who it was, and there with her hoodie pulled up was Reagan. "Hey boys." She said smiling and waving as they both tried to regain their composure.

"Dang Reagan!" Levi snapped, scowling. "You almost gave me a heart attack."

"What are you doing here?" Tom asked as Levi smoothly slid all the papers back into the folder and then returned that to his backpack.

"Umm... let me see..." She tapped her cheek. "What could I possibly be doing in a restaurant?" Then, snapping her fingers like she had just remembered something important, "Eating."

Tom went crimson. "Uh yeah. We were just about to order too."

But it was too late. She had already turned back around in her booth to face the guy that had brought her.

Levi chuckled. "Damn, man. You really do suck with girls. You know that, right?"

Tom went another shade of red and made furious hand gestures to keep quiet.

"Don't worry," Levi said tapping his head. "Now that I know she is there, I can tell she isn't paying attention to what we are doing anymore."

Tom's eyes grew round. "You are listening to her thoughts?"

"Yep." Levi laughed. "And I bet you would pay me every allowance you will ever get to know what she was thinking when she was talking to us..."

"No way!" Tom objected. "That's an invasion of her privacy!"

"So, you don't want to know what she thought when she looked at you?" He pressed.

"No. I can't do that to her." Tom was obviously struggling. "I just figure she thought I asked her a dumb question and then she went back to her... date."

Levi rolled his eyes. "Man, I didn't realize you had it this bad." He paused for a second. "Okay, I won't tell you what she was thinking, but

I will tell you one thing that I didn't need to read her mind to know: ask her out. You will be glad you did."

Tom held up his hand. "No more Levi. Just let me worry about it, okay?"

Levi stood up and shook his head. "You got it, bro. Let's head home."

υ

The trip home was mostly in silence. Each of them had a lot on his mind that he needed to sort through. Twice on the trip, Levi had to pause to get his breathing under control as he replayed what he had read about The Wall in his mind.

When they got home, he went to his room and brought some of the medicine to relax him into the kitchen. Tom was sitting at the table doing his homework.

"This is freaking me out," Levi announced as he grabbed a glass from the shelf. "You want some lemonade?"

"Sure," Tom replied not looking up.

Levi handed him the glass. "After reading what they are capable of, I just don't think we stand a chance if they come after us."

Tom put down his homework and took a drink. "I know. I feel the same way."

"We need to up our game." Levi downed his pill and most of his drink in one gulp. "If we could just amp up the abilities we have, we might stand a chance. Especially if they have a lot more people on their side."

Tom dropped his pencil. "I got it! I know how to get them off our case!"

"How?"

"They only get away with this crap because most people don't believe in people with abilities. We need to tell people about us and make them believe. Then, when the spotlight is on us, they won't be able to do all this sneaky cloak and dagger crap! It's hard to make someone disappear when they are nationally known. It would just be too big to erase."

Levi, who had been looking hopeful, was suddenly crestfallen again. "Dude, that will never work!"

"Why not?"

"Because we will never make it that far. If we schedule an interview, they will be waiting to make us disappear before we ever walk through the door." Levi countered. "Read the articles. It has been attempted before."

"Then we don't make an appointment. We do it spontaneously. If they don't know who we are going to tell, they can't stop us." Tom offered.

"And if they somehow find us before we can get our story out?" Levi asked. "What then?"

"I don't know."

"Well, I do. We need to take what is left of Dr. Mobien's formula." Levi said quietly.

Tom was instantly on his feet. "No way! We lucked out last time, Levi. We have no idea what a second dose would do to us!"

"We are going to find out…" Levi said even more quietly looking at the glasses of lemonade.

Tom followed his gaze and then looked at the shelf and saw the empty pill bottle when the realization struck him. "My God… Tell me you didn't…"

"Sorry, Tom. I knew you would never do it, and you weren't in those guys heads! You don't appreciate what they are capable of. I felt them pull the trigger on me. They did it like they were putting in a load of laundry!" Levi pleaded for him to understand.

Tom was on his feet and headed to the sink. All he could think of to do was stick his finger down his throat and make himself puke it back up, but as soon as he was on his feet, he knew it was already too late. The room began to spin, and his knees buckled.

vi

Wake up… Was the first thing that Tom could hear, but he wasn't hearing it. It was like someone was saying it in his head.

Sweet! It looks like he is waking up!

"Yes. I am awake. Now please be quiet!" Tom snapped, grabbing his pillow and cramming it over his ears.

"Wow! You could hear that?" It was Levi's voice.

"It was kinda hard not to!" Tom complained. Then, his memories kicked in, and he was instantly furious. He sat up and tossed the pillow. "You put drugs in my lemonade?!?!" A brisk breeze seemed to spring out of nowhere in Tom's bedroom.

"Nothing you haven't taken before!" Levi cringed.

"You had NO right!" Tom yelled.

"I know, but like I said last night, you weren't in those agents' heads," Levi said as his ability allowed him to see the anger come off his brother in waves. "I was trying to protect you!"

"You have a funny way of showing it!" Then, looking around his room "How did I even get in here anyway?"

"Oh. The first pill I took was the medication so that I wouldn't have a seizure. I gave you half of Mobien's pills in your lemonade at the same time. When you passed out, I moved you to your room, and then

I went to my room and took the other half of the pills. They knocked me out too, and I woke up this morning, and you were still out cold." Levi finished.

Tom heard Levi's voice in his head. *I was really starting to get nervous.* He looked at Levi as his anger slowly subsided. "Yeah. I can imagine you wouldn't have wanted to have to explain a comatose brother to mom."

Levi realized that Tom could hear his thoughts and blushed. "Uh. No."

"So, does this mean that I can hear other people's thoughts, or does it mean that you can make me hear your thoughts?" Tom asked.

"Geez. That's a good question. We'll have to test it." Levi was already grabbing a notepad.

"That will have to wait. What time is it?"

"Half past eight," Levi answered after a glance at his watch.

"Then we have already missed the beginning of the school day." Tom surmised getting to his feet. "I say we blow off school today, go to the radio station here in town and tell them all about the Changed and The Wall. We can see if and how our powers were affected later. This is too important to put off."

Levi nodded in agreement while staring at Tom but didn't move.

"Well? Aren't you going to go get ready?" Tom asked.

"Yeah. I was just noticing something new."

"What's that?" Tom stopped and looked at his brother.

"You are kind of glowing."

"Glowing?" Tom quickly looked in the mirror in his room. "I don't look like I'm glowing to me."

"No, you are definitely glowing to me," Levi said walking around Tom and staring at him.

Tom grabbed Levi by the shoulders. "Levi. Focus. We need to get the word out, or we won't be safe." He spun Levi around and pointed him at his room and gently shoved him. "Now go get that folder of info on The Wall and change your clothes. You smell like you slept in those."

"I did!" Levi called over his shoulder as he entered his own bedroom.

"Ten minutes Levi, and we are heading out" Tom called and quickly started changing his clothes as he went over how he was going to tell someone about the crazy experiences that he and his brother had been having over the past several months.

CHAPTER 12

The Plan Goes Awry

i

Trevor Merrola paced in the moderately sized auditorium while agents quickly filed in and took their seats. Trevor had received a text moments ago from James instructing him that his caravan of reinforcements were twenty minutes out and to assemble all agents in the briefing room.

After working with James Neuwin for almost five years, Trevor knew he would be furious when he got back to the Vermont field office. He had received reports of how James' trip back to the main office had gone. James had arrived there in the early hours of the morning the day after the attack. By 8 am, he had already been reprimanded for allowing the field office to be partially destroyed, failing to recruit one of the Changed with powerful abilities, failing to provide any useful intelligence on the subject's younger brother and priming the stage for information about The Wall to be leaked to the general public.

Rumor even had it that the CEO, Greg Buckner, had threatened to throw him in the Lower Reaches of the training center. However, that was probably just a rumor. The Lower Reaches were said to be where The Wall put subjects that were too powerful to control. There they would run experiments on them that grew more and more horrific with every telling of the story. Trevor scoffed as he caught himself considering it.

No, the stories of that place couldn't be real, but if they were, James would probably give them a run for their money. He was one of the toughest men Trevor knew. In addition to being a world class tactician, he also was an expert in hand to hand and small arms combat. Now combine that with the emotional capabilities of your average serial killer and the blind patriotism that borders on an extremist religion and Trevor couldn't think of a place that Neuwin couldn't handle.

But instead of being lunch for the Lower Reaches, Greg had sent James on a mission out to the Midwest. The trip took him a couple of days, but when he returned, Greg approved the additional resources, and James was on his way back the very next morning.

Just then, the double doors to the auditorium were thrown open, and James Neuwin came marching in with an almost palpable wrath emanating from him. Trevor didn't bother trying to call attention to the assembled group. You could already hear a pin drop in the room.

When James got to the podium, he switched on the mic and started his briefing without preamble. "As you all are painfully aware, we were not prepared for Subject Woods. He was far more powerful than we expected. Let this be another reminder, never to skim on reconnaissance before picking up a subject!

"On top of failing to retrieve him, he now has information on us, including our location and what our general mission is. We have word that he has already started spreading that information to his classmates, some of which have been searching the web for additional information on us.

"So here is what is going to happen next: First, Sanchez and his team are going to go sanitize the farmhouse. I want all the evidence that we were ever there to be gone. Fix the yard, and anything else didn't get done when you were there last time. I don't want a shred of evidence to back up their story if we can't get ahead of this leak. They might be able to prove they have abilities, but they won't be able to prove The Wall was ever there.

"When everything else is done, that team will be staying behind for three months to surveil the younger brother. That seems appropriate considering the fact you had such difficulty apprehending a 15-year-old boy! If he, like his brother, is Changed, we will make a trip back to collect him. If not, Team Sanchez will close up this office and return home.

"The second thing that will happen is that Agent Merrola will take three other agents and round up the two hackers that were researching the Wall. They used two computers in the computer lab at the local high school. You will pose as telecom professionals and swap out the hard drives on those computers for ones that are clones of a clean computer in the lab. Then, you will find the little bastards and make it look like they drown while swimming.

"Third, Agent Blake will take a group to the Woods home. Remove every trace that the Subject ever existed. Have the IT team hack into Amazon or wherever mom shops. Figure out her favorite hobby and convert the subject's room into something centered around that hobby." He found Agent Blake in the crowd and got eye contact. "And this time, don't forget to remove him from ALL family pictures, Blake."

"Finally, I have brought a group of Resource Agents to capture and clean the subject." James continued as thirteen people in street clothes filed into the auditorium and came down to stand behind Neuwin.

Trevor was stunned. He had never seen so many of the Resource Agents used to put down a single subject. Each of the Resources was one of the Changed themselves that had been recruited and indoctrinated. Usually, the cleaning crew consisted of one or two people to alter memories, one person to remove the subject's online presence and two people to dispose of the subject. The more dangerous subjects might get three Resources assigned to him but ten? It was overkill.

"We will place a call to the school telling him to meet his mother outside for an appointment she forgot. When he comes out, we grab him. Make no mistake people; this is a scorched-earth mission. Anyone that would raise questions about this subject is to be fed a story that they won't pursue, fed new memories that they won't question or fed a bullet."

Trevor swallowed hard. Yup. His boss was pissed. He looked at the lineup of Resources. Some of them he recognized well enough to know the codenames The Wall had given them. There was Streak with the ability to turn himself into electricity and move up to 50 feet in the blink of an eye. If he remembered correctly, Streak also could shoot lightning at people although Trevor had never seen it himself. Next, there was Slash who could enhance any sharp object to be able to cut through almost anything. Then, Stonehenge who could move rocks at will. The only other person in the lineup that Trevor knew was Maul – James' personal favorite resource. Maul was insanely strong, invulnerable and did not need to eat, sleep or breathe. He was unstoppable by physical means. If he could catch up to a subject, the fight was over, and of course, there were the twins. They had been born joined at the head but were separated during their second year of life. Both of them had a moderate ability to control and manipulate memories, but together, they could virtually rewrite your entire life and get you to believe it. The twins were the Walls' go-to resource when a serious leak had occurred. Together they didn't even have to be in a person's presence to alter their memories.

It was at that moment that one of the agents that had been assigned to monitor the local media sources came flying into the room. All eyes turned to him. "Sir! We have a problem. I just intercepted a call to the local radio station asking them if they had a reporter that would be around this morning for a big story. KIA's voice recognition program gives it a 96% match to the younger brother, Levi!"

James' face went pale with anger. "Okay people! That's the starting gun." He turned to face the Resource Agents. "Small change in plans. We aren't going to the school. Let's get set up outside that radio station and wait for them to come to us!" Everyone was still standing stock still listening to orders. "Now people! Now!" James barked, and the room erupted in activity as agents quickly prepared to leave for their missions.

ii

Tom and Levi passed several people going about their morning routine on the street as they walked toward the radio station. Levi was abnormally quiet as they passed people. Then, breaking the silence "Tom, you wouldn't believe how easy it is to hear what people are thinking now."

"Shh!" Tom hissed as they walked past a woman pushing a baby carriage that shot Levi a strange look. After she had passed them, he whispered sharply to Levi "You need to be quiet about this stuff!"

Is this any better? Levi's voice sounded like thunder in Tom's mind.

"Jesus!" Tom jumped. "Does that thing come with volume control?"

Sorry. Levi smiled impishly. *Is this better?* He asked at a quarter of the volume.

"Much." Tom agreed as he relaxed into his normal stride. "So, have you noticed any other changes in your abilities?"

Maybe. People seem to have a cloud around them. He paused in his description. *The word "cloud" isn't right, but it's close. You have a bright blue cloud, and it is super well defined. Almost everyone else though has a much dimmer cloud and harder to see. I don't know if I have a cloud. They don't seem to show up in mirrors. I suspect that it may have to do with you having an ability. Maybe since I can hear thoughts, it is related to thought-energy? I don't know. It's a guess. How about you? Have you noticed any changes to your abilities?*

"No, but I haven't tried to use them either," Tom admitted. "We'll have to look into it this weekend at Uncle Lester's place."

They rounded the corner onto Main Street, just three blocks from the radio station when Levi grabbed Tom's hand and yanked him through the closest door.

"What the hell, Levi?" Tom exclaimed as he realized that Levi had brought him into a pharmacy. "This is a bad time to suddenly get the urge to pick up deodorant."

Levi gave him a sharp look. "That is not why I dragged you in here!" Then, noticing people were looking at them, he snatched a comic book off the newsstand and thrust it into Tom's hands. "Here. Check out this issue of Superman! It's awesome!" At the same time, Levi's voice was in Tom's head again. *Dude! There are three people out there with clouds just like yours!*

Tom sucked in a breath at what Levi was suggesting. "Are you saying that three villains attack Superman in this episode?"

Tom could hear Levi's laughter in his mind. *Hey. 007 – all you have to do is think your question, and I'll hear it. You don't need to say it in code, ya dork!*

Fine. Tom shot back, embarrassed. *It's not my ability. I am still getting used to you being able to do it.*

No worries. Levi replied. *Now about those super-agents…*

Okay. We need info. Can you read any of them from here? Tom asked.

Only that they are thinking of your face as they scan the crowd… Anything more detailed, and I would have to be closer.

Close enough. I take that to mean that they aren't after you. Tom concluded.

So what? Levi countered. *That doesn't help you at all.*

Actually, it does. Tom explained. *We now have an advantage that they don't know about – you.*

Levi smiled.

Now, tell me which people out there do you think have abilities. Tom instructed.

No problem. See the guy by the bookstore that looks like he has been living in a gym and popping steroids like they are breath mints? Him. Levi watched Tom's eyes until they focused on the mountain of a man. *Yup. Then, there is the couple having coffee outside of Karen's Café. Both the greasy looking guy and the hot blonde next to him.*

Tom picked out the other two and got a good look at them. *Got 'em.* Then, turning back to Levi *We have one other thing to worry about. They must have someone that can see the future or read minds from a distance. How else could they have known we were coming here this morning? If that is the case, we will need to play things by ear so that even we don't know what we are going to do next…*

Levi frowned and then looked guilty. *Umm. I don't think they have anyone like that.*

I'm listening. Tom had a sinking feeling.

I might have called the radio station before we left to make sure we weren't going there just to find out that there are no reporters there to interview us. He admitted. *I never gave them either of our names though! I thought it was safe…* He looked miserable.

Tom brightened a bit. *That's actually good news. That means that they probably just had the phones monitored and they don't have anyone that can see the future or read minds or any other crazy stuff.*

Levi relaxed seeing that Tom wasn't going to get angry. *Sorry.*

Nothing we can do about it now, but I am not willing to put this off either. I doubt that they are eager to use their abilities in the middle of a busy street, so here is what I am going to do. I want you to stay here and pick up any info you can. Use your ability to tell me if I am about to get ambushed or text me or whatever works. I am going to walk right up to the front door and do the interview.

Levi's face reflected his disbelief. *That's a horrible plan!*

Think about it, Levi. If they got a handful together to pick me up on short notice, how many can they get together the next time we try. Of course, that's if they let us try again. I am betting that if there is a next time they would be showing up at our house or school to try to pick me up. Imagine if mom was home!

At the mention of his mother being in danger, Levi winced. *I wish I had uncle Lester's 12 gauge.*

Maybe I should call the cops…

No way! What if these guys are with the FBI? If the police show up and talk to them, they will be after us too. Tom shook his head. *I need to get in there and get our side of the story out.*

Your call. I will do what I can, but being able to read minds doesn't really help crack heads…

"Are you boys going to buy that comic or are you just going to stand there and read the same page over and over all morning?" came the cashier's voice.

"Sorry Mrs. Mahoney!" Levi called back to her.

That's our queue. Tom thought to Levi and put down the comic.

Hold on a sec. In a moment of foresight, Levi grabbed a pair of reflective sunglasses and ran to the register.

When he got back to Tom, he slipped the glasses on his brother. *Now we are ready. This way you can look at whoever you want, and they won't know you are doing it.*

Taking a deep breath, they stepped out the door and onto the sidewalk.

Levi walked directly behind Tom, past two more stores before ducking into a toy store and immediately turned to watch through the window.

It's all you now. I don't sense that anyone saw me.

Good. Tom acknowledged and kept walking toward the radio station. The couple at the coffee shop was the closest. He watched them intently from behind the reflective glasses as he approached. They seemed relaxed but paused their conversation as he walked by.

They are getting up to follow you! Levi advised. *Can you hear me?*

Yes, please stop shouting!

Okay. Sorry. I don't know what the range is on this thing!

It was then that the large man spotted Tom and slowly moved over to stand in front of the door to the radio station.

Oh crap! Levi moaned. *That's pretty definitive body language bro! They aim to stop you from getting inside.*

Yup. I got that too. Tom agreed. *Tell me if the couple tries to jump me from behind.*

Levi continued to watch as Tom closed the distance to the radio station.

CHAPTER **13**

Things Heat Up

i

"Well, what do we have here?" The huge man said in a rumbling baritone as Tom approached him. "Looks like someone is cuttin school."

"No. I have an interview with one of the radio personalities for class." Tom countered smoothly.

"I really don't care who your interview is with 'lil fella. You are coming with me." The mountain of a man informed Tom and reached toward him, while at the same time the two behind Tom raised their hands pointing them at Tom's exposed back.

BEHIND YOU!! Came Levi's voice in Tom's head like a starters gun firing.

In that instant, Tom's mind played out each of the different ways he could handle this. He knew that the agents were all there to essentially keep the existence of the Changed a secret. He also knew that if he allowed the agents to take him anywhere less public, the odds that they would succeed in covering it up got higher, and his odds of surviving got lower. What he needed to do is attract more people to watch – not less.

He bent forward, ducking under the big man's grasp and pushed backward with his ability. The force of the blow knocked the two approaching from behind off their feet and threw them back into the tables. Then Tom stood up and slammed his ability into the man in front of him… and nothing happened.

"Heh. Heh. Heh." The huge man chuckled. "You thought you was gonna knock me over?" He shook his head and reached for Tom a second time.

Knowing that he couldn't knock the big man down, he quickly grabbed the air around himself and flew up in the air about 20 feet.

People started to notice, but not enough.

By now the couple were back on their feet. "Now that wasn't very nice." The lady said through clenched teeth. Then, she leaned back as balls of fire burst into life around her hands, and with a shoving motion, a geyser of flame shot into the air at Tom. He tried to dodge to one side, but she just followed him with the blast.

Tom spread his arms wide and then brought his hands together at the same time as he flooded the movement with his ability. The clap was like a bomb detonating as it shattered windows for several blocks in every direction and set off car alarms. The explosive blast of air dispersed the fire from the lady agent and sent her flying a second time. The greasy man that had been standing next to her was nowhere to be seen.

An instant later he reappeared. "I may have been caught off guard once, but you are going to have to try a lot harder if you are going to get me again." A split second later he was almost under where Tom was floating. He reached up with both hands and lightning flew from his fingertips.

Tom barely had time to get a shield up, but it wasn't enough. The lightning smashed into his hastily erected barrier, shattered it and hit him a glancing blow in the shoulder. Even diminished, the blast knocked him from the air and sent him sprawling at the feet of the large man.

Tom scrambled to get to his feet with his entire body tingling from the blast of energy, but he wasn't quick enough.

Look out!! He heard Levi scream in his head just before the man's enormous hands grabbed his shoulders. The pain from the grip brought Tom's attention into focus as he screamed.

The big man shifted his hands to get a better grip. "What was that?" He smiled as he mocked Tom and started to squeeze his shoulders again.

Tom reached down and into his adrenaline infused body and brought his will into razor focus. "I said. LET GO!!" as he poured all the energy he could into his right hand and then brought that fist up into Maul's stomach. The power behind the blow would have gone straight through an ordinary man, but the big man just bent forward, loosening his grip and took a couple of steps backward. Tom instantly was free of his grasp and running back up the street.

Looking down the street, Tom could see people coming out to see what was happening. Some had their phones out, recording the brawl. Others were on their phones telling friends what was happening. It didn't matter to Tom. It actually accomplished his goal of getting the word out. He just wished it could have been presented in some way other than violence.

Pulling his attention back to the situation at hand, he knew he just needed to get away from the big one, yet in his haste, he forgot about the couple until another blast of heat hit him from his right.

Tom would have liked to have been able to say that it was his fantastic reaction time that saved him, but the truth was, he was still reeling from the pain in his shoulder, and he had tripped. The flames brushed him causing his clothes to smolder, but most of the blast hit the street sign right where his head had been an instant before.

The greasy man that had thrown lightening was also there and had just raised his arms to fire at Tom a second time as he lay scrambling to get back on his feet when the skinny man suddenly collapsed to the ground.

Tom looked up to see Levi standing over the man with a baseball bat from the toy store. The brothers exchanged a brief smile before Levi's eyes went wide and he pointed to the door of the radio station where four more people came running out into the street.

Holy crap, Tom! They ALL have abilities! came Levi's voice in his mind. Tom knew there was no way they could win this.

Take cover! Tom yelled back at Levi who immediately ran for the store.

Tom spun to face the new threats and was thrown backward onto the ground as the earth under him heaved like a wave. Tom rolled to one side as three knives buried themselves to the hilt where he had just been laying.

Then, he was back on his feet. He bowed his head and grasped his hands together in front of himself. The air shimmered in a bubble around him. Gunshots rang out, and the bullets flew off the shimmering wall. Huge chunks of rock and concrete flew at the barrier making cracking noises as they slammed into the invisible shield.

"Stonehenge, step back and let Maul deal with this child." A woman in a black dress yelled instructions to the group.

"That won't hold me back, lil man." Maul bellowed. "Not now that you've pissed me off!" And with that, he slammed into the barrier with all his weight. Tom tried holding the air molecules in place, but it was like the man's hands were inside his mind ripping it apart.

It was too much. Tom dropped the barrier and the six agents advanced. They had almost made it to Tom when the one with the knives flew backward like he had been tackled. Then Maul staggered back as small bursts of light hit him all over.

Tom looked back over his shoulder and there, coming down the street were three people in ski masks. The one in the lead had drawn a skull on her mask, was firing the light blasts from her hands and was running at full speed into the fray. The second one wore mostly white and had a sword in each hand. The last one was dressed all in grey and simply ran straight at the agents with a complete lack of regard for his own well-being.

It only took the agents a moment to readjust to the new threats. Bullets flew from one of the agents as he fired weapons from both hands with uncanny accuracy only to have them bounce off the guy that was unarmed. He never paused or slowed down. He just ran straight into the gunslinger knocking him to the ground unconscious.

"Billy!!" The woman in the dark dress screamed as the agent hit the ground.

"Nice job, Rhino!" The woman in the ski mask called out.

"Get him Ink!" Maul yelled. She was immediately after the man, enveloping him in a darkness that seemed to flow out of her.

"Hey! I can't see!" Tom heard Rhino yell as the woman called Ink disappeared into the dark cloud with him. He tried to think of what he could do without hurting his would-be rescuer.

The second man had gone after Stonehenge his blades rang like bells as they made contact with the Agent's thickened skin but did little by way of damage. Stonehenge threw several large rocks at the swordsman, but the man parried them away or dodged them with an agility that was undoubtedly superhuman.

Tom threw up a barrier as another blast of fire flew toward him. Then, seeing an opening, he grabbed a car from the side of the road and slammed it down on top of Stonehenge.

Freed up from his struggle with the rock throwing superhuman, the swordsman turned to face another agent that had glowing hunting knives in each hand. The swordsman swung his blade expecting it to connect with the hunting knives, but when he felt no resistance, he almost fell over from the force of his swing. He quickly got his balance back and stood to face his enemy only to realize that the short hunting knives had neatly sliced through his sword and was now sticking out of his stomach.

Without a word, the swordsman quietly sank to the ground.

"Blades!" The woman in the ski mask cried out as her friend fell to the ground.

Tom had no time to mourn the fallen as the fire-spewing woman continued to hammer him with blast after blast.

"Stop playing with him, Inferno!" The man with the hunting knives called out.

"I will do as I please, Slash." She chided him. "Now go play with your knives before I get upset with you."

Tom had been waiting for a just such a distraction and immediately flew up into the air again.

"Not this time, little bird," Inferno called after him, and he looked down in time to see fire surround her as she floated up into the air, smiling. "You didn't think we would let you fly away, did you?" She laughed. "Why don't you just give up, boy? I was worshiped as a god not too long ago, and I when I get angry, I only grow more powerful! You don't stand a chance!"

The bolt of fire she shot was massive. Tom threw up a shield and was pushed like snow before a plow through the sky above the town. Focusing more on the shield than the flight he allowed himself to drop suddenly and slipped under the blast.

Looking down, he saw the woman with the white energy bolts running from Ink, Maul, and Stonehenge. Neither Maul nor Stonehenge was fast enough to get her on their own, but with Ink blocking her escape, it was just a matter of time before they closed in and caught her.

Tom knew that this was a losing fight. Two of his would-be rescuers had already fallen. One was most likely dead, and the other just seemed to be unconscious. The girl fought with inspiration and Tom decided right then that if he were going to lose, he would rather his final stand was with her.

With that decision made, he sent a pickup truck from the street straight at Inferno and while she was busy ducking that, he dropped to street-level next to his last rescuer.

"Hey, need a hand?" He asked.

"I was about to ask you the same thing," the woman quipped from behind the ski mask.

"I was thinking it's about time for a hasty retreat?" He offered.

"Now you're talking." She spun quickly and faced Ink as she unloaded a barrage of white bolts into the darkness that oozed from the woman. With each impact, the dark shuttered and Ink stopped her advance. "I told ya, lady – you don't want to try touching me!"

Ink just smiled as she stepped backward and out of the dark cloud around her came Maul at a run. Ink's advance had been a ruse to hide Maul. "She wasn't gonna, lil girl. But I will!" Maul bellowed and reached for her. The girl didn't have time to sidestep him.

The second Maul's hand made contact with her; white electricity flew in all directions. Maul screamed in pain as his knees buckled and his momentum drove him face first into the ground.

The girl righted herself and brushed off her shoulder where his hand had been. "And that is why I am called Ghost Touch!" She snapped.

Tom took it all in while throwing anything he could get his hands on at Inferno, but when Maul hit the ground, he saw his opening. "Run!" He yelled and pointed at the opening in the circle of agents. The girl was through and firing bolts to keep the hole open as Tom started to make his run for safety.

"NO!" Screamed Inferno upon seeing her prey get away. She immediately launched herself into the air and sent a blast of flames down to close off Tom's only escape route. "That's enough! Now you die!!"

Tom knew it was coming a second before it hit him – a massive blast of fire slammed into his shield. She continued to push herself harder and harder as Tom dug in deep for every last ounce of strength, he could find to keep his shield in place. Seconds ticked by as the cement outside of his shield bubbled and turned to liquid. Trees in the park behind Tom burst into flames, and electrical lines overhead melted and fell to the ground. All the other agents ran for cover from the heat as the two faced off. Inferno continued to burn brighter and hotter as the air around her seemed to blaze like the sun.

Down on street level, Tom held his hand above his head, keeping his shield in place. Anger and desperation threatened to overwhelm him. *Tom! Focus!* His brother's voice was clear in his head. *You aren't going to win this if you panic! Watch your breathing!* Tom remembered the meditative techniques that Levi had shown him. With his shield in place, Tom imagined the imagery of the ocean that had haunted his dreams all summer. The feeling of power hitting his feet as his toes touched the water and he finally knew what to do. He gave in to the power and allowed himself to submerge in the ocean. He took it all into himself.

As Inferno got angrier and her blast intensified, she became determined to reign fire down on him until there was nothing left to burn. Even now, his shield was quivering – starting to crack. Soon, it would give way, and she would watch as his body turned to ash!

Finally, the shield flickered and went out… and the incinerating ray from Inferno slammed into Tom, obscuring him from sight beneath the onslaught. The force of the blast plowed a trail of destruction through the park as it pushed him back toward the gas station on the far side. In her anger, she continued to hammer Tom with the blistering beam, until he finally came to a stop amid the gas pumps. There, she paused her destructive assault to assess the damage.

As she floated above the gas station, she finally got a clear view and instantly saw the change in him. No longer was he a high school student fumbling as he tried to manipulate the energy in the things around him. Now he stood amid the flames from the pumps like a figure made of burning blue plasma. The charged particles that made up his body spun like a glowing fog stirred by a fierce wind. He no longer was manipulating the energy around him. Now, that energy was a part of him.

A chill ran through Inferno. Something big had changed in this subject. She knew that she had to get back to the other Agents and warn them, but it was at that moment that the pumps blew up, obliterating the gas station. Debris flew in all directions, and Inferno was hurtled across the park only come to a stop when a pipe from a severed street light protruded from her chest.

ii

Ghost Touch had known this would not end well as soon as she saw the beam of fire heading toward the pumps. She was nearly two blocks away when the blast threw her to the ground. Knowing the explosion was her only chance to get away before her adversaries had an opportunity to regroup; she took off her ski mask and her hoodie and quietly blended into the crowd that was ducking for cover on the street.

iii

Levi had been standing in the toy store ever since Tom told him to find cover. At first, he hefted the bat in his hand and waited for an opportunity to sneak up behind someone else that wasn't paying attention.

Then, he felt it. Like a tickling at the back of his mind. Someone with mental powers was looking for him. He knew it instinctively. It was like they were calling his name. Levi wasn't sure what the nature of the new threat was, but he was sure that he needed to find out.

He immediately sat down on the floor and focused on the voice. No. He caught himself. Voices. There were two people calling to him, but their minds were so similar that it almost felt like just one.

Levi stayed quiet allowing the two to push against his mind. By not responding to the two, Levi left them nothing to attack, yet the closeness went both ways, and as he sat there, he had a sense that these two were the ones that erased the memories he had read about in the dark web report. In fact, the longer they searched, the more details he was able to see. They had done this to dozens of other people. Entire families would never know that a son or daughter had been abducted or killed. They were made just to forget…

That was the final straw. These two had come here steal his memories of his brother! Levi pounced on the two. His rage was making up for his inexperience. The battle shifted back and forth across the landscape of three minds. After a couple of minutes of this, he knew that these two would never stop coming after him, and while Levi was a good young man, he did not share his brother's desire to turn the other cheek. No, if you hit Levi, he hit you back.

He knew what he had to do. He grabbed one of the twins and pushed deep into the boy's mind. He knew where he was going. After all, he went there every time he had a seizure. It was the dark, unmapped place in the most primitive part of the brain, and it was there that Levi shoved the first twin watching him begin a fall that would never end. The second twin witnessed what had happened, and he tried to run from Levi only to find that he had run back to the same place in his own mind. With grim determination, Levi repeated the procedure. He had no doubt that wherever these two were right now, someone was trying to shove wallets in their mouths.

The entire battle hadn't taken more than five minutes, but when he looked out the window again, so much had changed.

Levi watched as his brother was pinned under Inferno's heat blast. He reached out to Tom and could feel the panic slipping in. He knew his brother was starting to crack under the constant attack. *Tom! Focus!* He sent his voice out to his brother. *You aren't going to win this if you panic! Watch your breathing!*

He felt Tom starting to get control again. *Okay, now you need to know that I just found out: these guys are going to keep coming at us as long as we are alive. If we are going to survive, we need to make them think you are dead or we need to kill them.*

There was silence for a second, then *Understood. I think I know a way. I will find you later if I can* and then… nothing. It was like someone had flipped a switch on a radio and it just couldn't transmit anymore. A heartbeat later, Tom's shield failed utterly, and he was blown through the park and into the gas pumps. There was a brief pause as Inferno finally seemed to come to her senses, and he watched in horror as the gas station exploded. The windows to the toy store were blown inwards throwing Levi and the cashier backward over the display.

Holy crap!! I hope that was the plan you mentioned! Was all Levi could think as he quickly started using his breathing techniques to remain calm.

CHAPTER 14

Leaving Home

i

Tom sat, dazed, watching the water flow through Stevens Brook while the blare of sirens sounded from half a mile away. He was sitting under a small bridge off one of the side streets near his house. This was his quiet place. Hidden from sight from all but the occasional train, this is where Tom had gone all throughout high school when he needed to clear his mind. He knew they were still looking for him and probably not only with their eyes. They would most likely have telepaths or others with similar abilities. Because of that, he could think of no better place to go to achieve the emotionally and mentally quiet he needed to remain hidden from them.

Unbidden, the events of the day played out again in his mind. So much had happened. The people he had fought today had wanted to kill him - not beat him up or make him feel bad. They had been there specifically to end his life. Tom had only been in a handful of scraps in his life, and most of those fights had been broken up by either adults or friends. This fight had been very different. There had been no "go to your corner" from an intervening authority. He had seen the looks on the faces of the adults that came out of their stores to see what was happening and they had been terrified – and not just of the bad guys. The people in town didn't know what to make of Tom's abilities, yet their fear wasn't even the worst part. Tom had lost. He had tried his hardest and had failed.

He had been forced to dig deep inside himself and let the ability consume him. At first, he couldn't tell if the pain was Inferno burning him or if it was his own power tearing him apart as he tried to use it. He just knew it was too much and he couldn't focus enough to keep his shield in place. It fell, and the fire blast hit him in the chest, pushing him clean through the park and into the gas pumps. When the change was complete, the force of Inferno's blast was like trying to stand in a stiff wind. There as pressure, but the fire could no longer burn him.

It was then that Inferno paused to survey her damage. The brief respite gave Tom a chance to glance around as well, and that was when Tom saw the pumps on fire. He knew what was coming next. His mind, which had been running through escape scenarios ever since Levi had told him that they would never stop until he was dead, knew that the explosion would be his only chance. He braced for it, and in the instant that the pumps blew up, he poured all his ability into flying as fast as he could as close to the ground as possible.

The resultant burst of speed was beyond anything Tom had experienced so far. He shot like a streak past the gas station and the row of churches and historical buildings next to them. In the time it takes for a dropped glass to hit the floor, Tom had shot out past the city limits, still flying only a couple of feet off the ground to avoid being seen.

Once outside the city, Tom pulled up to treetop level and circled the city. He hadn't expected this. Using his power now was easy and flying felt natural. Effortless. He wasn't focusing on holding himself aloft by moving the air molecules around him. He simply willed himself to move, and his energy-infused body obeyed. He knew that he needed to land and hide. Flying around while looking like a burning blue road flare was definitely going to attract attention if he wasn't careful. He needed not to be seen. That was when he decided to land under the bridge. Once there, he focused and tried to push the power back down inside himself. The blue plasma flames flickered and faded leaving him standing there in smoldering clothes. He breathed a sigh of relief. At least he wasn't going to have to live the rest of his life looking like a life-sized sparkler.

He paced a few steps in the small space beneath the bridge trying to make sense of this new aspect of his abilities. He had suppressed the outward evidence of his power, but he could still feel it inside him. It felt like he had dammed up a river. It was still there – waiting to get out.

ii

It had been almost two hours since the gas station explosion. Levi knew that he would need to act like he had just seen his brother get blown up in case any of the agents were watching him. Initially, he had run out of the toy store and straight to the gas station screaming his brother's name. The gas station was in complete ruins. The original building had either collapsed or was in flames. Even worse, the initial explosion had blown out the support beams for the canopy, which had collapsed onto the pumps where Tom had been standing.

Privately, Levi prayed his brother had made it out of there before the explosion, but he had some serious doubts if that was possible.

Using a branch that had blown free from one of the trees in the park as leverage, Levi tied to pry open a corner of the canopy to look beneath it for his brother. Unfortunately, as soon as the corner lifted off the ground, a fresh blast of flame and smoke shot out ending any hopes Levi had that his brother could be hiding in that section of the debris. Refusing to give up he moved on to the next part that was not engulfed in flames and looked like it might have a space big enough to hide his brother, Levi dragged his branch over and repeated the process.

He was just about to move to the next section when a crowd of people pushed toward him. At first, he didn't recognize anyone, but then he heard a voice over the crowd "Levi!!" and a hand bounced up over the mass of faces.

"Reagan?" Levi asked, confused. "What are you doing here?"

"Are you kidding?" She quipped. "That big bang triggered the school evacuation protocol. They didn't know what was happening, so it was safer to send everyone home." She shrugged. "I used my phone to look through the cameras on Main Street and saw Tom getting attacked – and FLYING!!"

Levi glanced around and saw the traffic camera attached to the stop-lights. He had heard that some of the kids in school had figured out how to access those. Then, to Reagan "Yeah. I guess the cat is out of the bag now. My brother has powers – or had..." He trailed off as his eyes filled with tears.

Sympathy filled her face. "Let's not give up yet. Where was he standing when the pumps blew up?"

Levi swallowed. "He was holding onto the pumps to help him stand up after that bitch, Inferno, drove him across the park."

Reagan's eyes softened, and he heard her thoughts as if she was saying them aloud. *Oh my God! There is no way he survived that. No one is that fast.*

He looked away to hide his fears from showing in his face. Looking back at the burning building, it all became apparent. If Tom had been caught in the blast, he would be dead now, but if he had made it out, Levi wasn't going to find him here under the debris. Following that line of reasoning, if Levi continued to search, it would be the same as saying "I think Tom died, and I'm looking for his body," and he refused to do that. Satisfied with his conclusion, Levi tossed his branch into the flames and turned to face the crowd.

Then "Levi! Honey, where are you?" It was his mother's voice. Pushing her way past the other people searching for survivors, she made her way toward where Levi stood.

"Here I am, mom." He called waving her over.

She wrapped her arms around him and hugged him furiously. "Oh! I thought I had lost you. The other nurses in the ER told me that my kid was fighting on TV and then one of them said you died…"

Levi looked at her with tears streaming down his cheeks. This was not going to be easy. "Mom… That was Tom."

Her expression turned blank. "Who?" She asked.

"Tom – your oldest son?" He clarified.

Ms. Woods made a concerned face "Levi… Did you hit your head? You know you are an only child."

Levi sucked in a breath as what she said rocked him to his core. It seems that Levi had not been the first stop on the twins' memory erasing tour.

"Oh sorry." He covered quickly, not wanting to upset her. Without warning, he hugged her.

"That's okay honey. People do weird things when they are stressed. Some people crack jokes." She said patting his back.

The hug though had been to cover him as he reached out with his mind and searched her thoughts. Family vacations, birthday parties, grade school graduation – they had all been erased or expertly altered to remove Tom from his mother's mind. As far as she knew now, she only had one son.

Levi let out a small shudder as he cried. It was inhuman what the twins had done. They had stolen Tom's entire existence from the woman that had given birth to him. He had been wrestling with a moral dilemma of whether or not he should release the twins from the prisons of their minds. Now he wanted to go pull them out of there so he could put their worst fear in front of them before stuffing them right back in again. This time, permanently.

His anger could barely be contained. "Listen, mom, this was all really freaky, so I am going to bail and go home. Okay?"

"Sure thing hon. We can talk later when you aren't so upset. I am just glad you are okay. Do you want a ride?" She asked trying to be supportive.

"No. The walk will do me good." He replied as he turned to start his walk home.

"Okay. I have to get back to work." She hollered over the noise of the sirens. "See ya tonight."

Levi was just out of visual distance when he altered his path. *Screw this. Let me find one of those guys now!* He fumed. *I am going to do things to them that will terrify children around campfires for generations!*

Looking around he immediately noticed that there was no trace of the agents anywhere. Even Inferno was missing, as was the street light pole from which she had been hanging. *They took the whole street light? I hate them, but man, they are thorough.*

It was abundantly clear that The Wall had decided to take their agents and go home. Even in his anger, Levi knew that he would not survive if he went nose to nose with all of them – especially on their turf back at the bunker.

He kicked the ground in impotent fury. *God help them if Tom didn't survive this!*

Then, realizing how foolish he must look, he changed direction again and started walking back toward the house. *If Tom did survive, where would he go? Home? No. That would be the first place The Wall would look.*

iii

It was another half an hour before Levi jumped over the bridge railing, hugged the bridge support and then lowered himself from the support beams to the space under the bridge where Tom stood.

"Yes!" Levi crowed as he ran to hug his older brother.

"Hey Bro." Tom greeted him. "I figured you would look here eventually."

"Yeah, well, next time we fake your death, we need to have a prearranged place to meet and maybe a secret way that I can know that you are still alive." Levi shook his head. "How did you do that anyway? It really looked like you blew up at the gas station."

"Like this," Tom answered and released the restrictions he had on his ability. This time the change was not painful, and it was much faster. One moment, Levi was talking to his brother, and the next Tom just seemed to burst into blue light as a vast breeze blew outward from Tom in all directions.

"Holy crap!" Levi jumped back.

"Sorry. It was easier just to show you." Tom apologized. "This is what my ability looks like now, and it's about a thousand times stronger than it was."

"Holy crap!" Levi repeated as he continued to marvel at his brother's appearance.

"You already said that," Tom commented dryly.

"Yeah, but when your brother turns into a human butane lighter, I think you're okay to say it twice!" Levi quipped. "Can I touch you?" He asked putting his hand close to Tom to see if he was hot to the touch.

"I think it's plasma, not fire, you dork." Tom snapped.

"Plasma? Like the TVs? Do you get HBO?"

"Levi…" Tom growled.

"Okay, seriously, what is plasma?"

"Jesus, Levi. How did you graduate your Freshman year?"

"Sorry. Not all of us can be a well-educated night-light like you." He teased.

Tom immediately reigned it in, and the light flickered and died out, leaving him standing next to Levi in his street clothes. "Plasma is one of the four main states of matter. It is basically ionized particles."

"So, why do you light up now?"

"I think the way my power works is that I can manipulate the energy of non-living things." Tom started to explain as his blue flames winked back out.

"We already knew that." Levi interrupted.

"Yes, but what we didn't know is that if I call up enough of that power, it can ionize the molecules of my body turning them into plasma."

"Oh. Well, that's cool I guess." He approved. "Hey – look at it this way – you are supposed to be dead. When you go all propane on people, no one can make out your face. It's like a built-in super suit." He smiled. "You are going to save a fortune on masks."

Tom groaned. Then turning back to look at Levi "We didn't get to talk about it much, but you were able to pick out if someone has an ability just by seeing them?"

"Oh yeah." Levi agreed. "They glow. And, I can even make out how strong a talent they have by how bright they glow. I am pretty sure it must have to do with the amount of mind power it takes to use abilities. Well… I'm pretty sure that's it."

Tom chuckled. "Not exactly a firmest answer ever…"

"Whatever. You know what I mean." Levi continued. "And I might also be able to make people do stuff if I want them to, although that is not a well-tested thing and I think I have to be really close to them…"

"Make people do stuff?" Tom asked.

"Well, I can't permanently erase memories or any of that stuff, but I can do stuff like I did to The Wall agent that was following me here and make him think that he suddenly went blind…"

"What?!?" Tom choked. "Is he really blind?"

"Relax. God no." Levi told him in a soothing voice. "I just made him think he is blind for the next hour or maybe only a few minutes. I'm not really sure how long the compulsion will work."

Tom made a sour face.

"Come on Tom!" He said exasperatedly "He was a *bad guy.*'"

"It's still a horrible thing to do to someone, Levi." Tom chided. "You could have just told him to stand still and not follow you. Remember mom's rule about fighting 'do the least amount of harm to accomplish your goal,' and your goal was only not to be followed."

Levi winced. "Um. That's another thing we should talk about."

"What's that?" Tom asked.

"There's no polite way to tell you this," Levi took a deep breath and then blurted, "Mom thinks you're dead. Well, actually, she thinks you were never born. Meaning that she doesn't even know that there was a you, not to ever be born."

Tom stood there with his mouth open, stunned.

"Dude. Say something."

Tom sat down on a rock. "They erased me from Mom's memory?"

"I know this *looks* bad, but… um, yeah. It's bad." Levi slumped down beside Tom. "I want to say we can fix this, but I don't think we can. I looked into her mind, and those memories are gone – not blocked."

Tom straightened slightly like he had just made a decision. "Good."

Levi looked at him like he had lost his mind. "Huh?"

"If she doesn't know me anymore, then The Wall is no longer worried that she will be a problem for them, so she is safe." Tom stood and started pacing again. "And, they think I'm dead, so they won't try to use her to manipulate me." He started getting excited. "And, they won't recognize me, since the only one of them that has ever seen me with my new powers is dead and no one can make out my face when I use my abilities!"

"But your life here…" Levi began. "Tom, I stopped at the house before I came here. The Wall had already been there. Your room is a crocheting room for mom, and you aren't in a single picture anywhere. Now, I haven't checked, but if they did that, you could bet your last Pop-Tart that they have deleted all your online files too. No more birth records or driver's license, man. You've been erased."

Tom looked down at the floor as Levi continued. "Look, I don't know what you are going to do, but I know you can't come home. I am certain it is under surveillance from The Wall and on top of that mom would start to wonder who the hell the extra kid was after a while." He reached into his pocket and pulled out a wad of cash. "This is everything I could get for cash. I cleaned out my bank account and emptied every stash of spare change we have. I don't even know what to tell you to do next. I just know that there are still a few people that recognize you in this town because the memory wipers didn't get to them before I stopped them. If one of those people reports having seen you, we are back on The Wall's radar. You have to leave the area, man. Run and don't look back."

Tom stared at the money for a few seconds and then reached out and took it. "You're right." He agreed. "It's almost autumn, and it's going to start getting colder. With no identification or social security number, I won't be able to get a legitimate job. It's likely I will end up homeless for a while. I'd rather do that somewhere that has a larger homeless pop-ulation where I can blend in unnoticed. I'll head south." Tom dug his cell phone out of his pocket, smashed it on the rock he had been sitting on and tossed it in the brook. "Don't try to reach me, Levi. Watch the classified ads on Craig's List in the vacation rentals section. I will try to pass you info that way."

Both boys were in tears as Levi hugged his brother.

"At least mom won't have to go through the pain of thinking one of her sons died." Tom reflected as he called forth his power and burst into bright blue light. "Today Tom Woods may have died, but Storm was born. And this Storm is going to rain hell down on The Wall until that organization no longer exists." With that vow, he nodded to Levi, rose into the air, paused one last time to look around the town where he had grown up, and then in a flash, he was gone.

CHAPTER 15

Tom's New Life

i

Three months had passed since the showdown in Vermont had made international news, but for Tom, it felt like a lifetime. On his flight south, he had come to realize that if he went too far away from Vermont, it would make seeing Levi more difficult than it already would be, so he stopped at the next large city he saw – Boston. Unfortunately, in addition to losing his friends and family, his money had given out after only days of being in the big city, and he had been forced to live in a homeless shelter in the South End of Boston.

Each day all he could think of was how much The Wall had cost him. His future was ruined. He couldn't finish high school or even think about going to college without a past. He couldn't even drive a car without a driver's license. However, the blade that hurt the most and never healed was how they had taken his mother's memories of him. Knowing she would never look at him like she used to again almost broke him, and knowing that The Wall was still out there, possibly doing that to other families right now, made him nauseated with an anger that had no outlet.

It was fortunate that during those first dark days Tom never saw any activity from The Wall. Dark thoughts could have easily turned into dark actions. However, most days he faced challenges of an entirely different nature. Those challenges would frequently center around food or money. His prediction about the difficulties of not having any history were all coming true. Each day, he would find a discarded newspaper at one of the many coffee shops in the city and go through the *help wanted* sections. He would then walk down to the address listed and apply in person. It wouldn't take long. He had no work history, no home address, no social security number and no one to use as a personal reference. The only job offers he received were paid under the table to do one awful day of hard labor at a time – normally for less than minimum wage. Those jobs he did gladly and without complaint, but as the weeks passed, he knew that there had to be a better way.

It was on one of these jobs that he found a way to support himself. He had responded to an advertisement from a little retired lady that lived just west of Columbia Avenue. Her husband had passed away a few years prior, and her old Victorian house still burned coal during the winter months. As a result, once a year, she would put in an ad for a laborer to help her by getting a load of coal from a local coal company by the river and refilling the bins in the cellar. It was hot, dirty work, but she paid in cash at the end of the day.

It was during his brief lunch break that Tom made the discovery. He was sitting in the basement eating his sandwich when got the idea. He reached down and picked up a fist-sized chunk of coal and looked it over. It was hard to believe that diamonds came from this dull rock that people could afford to have delivered to their house by the truckload. All that was needed to make the change was pressure and heat.

Tom smiled. He had to try it. He set down his sandwich and closed the door of the cellar so that he wouldn't get caught. Bright blue light flooded the dark space as Tom allowed his power to run unchecked through him again. Turning the rock over in the glowing palm of his hand, he closed his other hand over the top of it and started to squeeze. He could feel the energy that made up the coal began to change. Harder and harder he squeezed, applying more force and pouring his ability into the rock. He could sense the heat emanating from the condensing substance and knew that if it weren't for his ability protecting him, the heat from the rock would have burned through his hands.

After what seemed like forever, Tom finally sensed that the rock was as compressed as it could get and quickly dropped it on the cement floor to allow it to cool. It was now a fraction of its original size and glowed red. Tom quickly made the change back to looking like a young laborer and went about filling the coal bins again.

At the end of the day, he went back to check on the lump he had compressed and found it to be what he thought looked like a decent sized diamond which he quickly scooped into his pocket.

When he got it appraised, he was shocked to find that the man at the pawn shop said it was a 1.5 carat diamond worth just under two thousand dollars. The following day, Tom took a portion of that money and purchased a duffel bag at a local department store. Then, he went back to the coal company and bought a duffel bag full of coal, and just like that, Tom was no longer poor.

He stayed two more days in the shelter figuring out his next steps, but things were definitely about to improve for him. The first thing he did was find the best forger in the city and created a new identity. He was now Thomas Ripley, a twenty-two-year-old sales representative from a little-known South African diamond mining company, and he was back in the U.S. to sell their diamonds. Then, he went out and bought a new wardrobe that consisted mostly of expensive business suits and bought a condo down by the water.

It took him about another month of selling diamonds to various upscale retail outlets and consulting with financial advisors before Tom was ready to hang up his hat as a diamond salesman. He knew that if he continued to pour fresh, unmarked diamonds into the area for very long, eventually someone would start to ask questions. However, a man that had almost two million invested and was living a modest lifestyle off the dividends really wouldn't raise too many eyebrows. He even had enough to begin giving regular donations to the homeless shelter that had taken him in when he first arrived. Things were starting to turn around for him.

ii

After taking care of his basic needs, Tom went back to work on preparing himself for tracking down and removing the threat that The Wall posed. First, he began a strict schedule of working out for two hours a day, six days a week with a personal trainer. The workouts were brutal as he pushed himself harder than he ever had in the past. He was sore constantly. However, he had only been doing that for two weeks when he added a two-hour training session with a self-defense company to his routine. His first trainer from the company was a former special forces hand-to-hand instructor that was making a living teaching mixed martial arts at a local gym. Tom paid him extra to teach MMA and to provide all the training he would give a special forces trainee.

To round out his day, he contacted the cyber defense department of the local police department. He told them he was doing a report for college about hackers and asked for the names or "handles" of the best hackers alive. The police proudly produced a "most wanted" list and shared it with Tom who promptly took the list home and tried to contact every one of them.

It took a couple of weeks of posting requests for contact on the web before a letter arrived via regular mail. At first, Tom just stared at the letter. He held the paper up and could see the impression marks on the paper from where the old-fashioned typewriter had impressed the letters on the paper. The message was a set of instructions on how to configure a computer to be secure and untraceable to the authorities. It also held the name of an anonymous chat account. Tom no sooner had the configuration completed, and the chat window pulled up than a message popped up on his screen.

> ► Hello Tom.

Tom jumped and open-mouthed, stared at the screen. He had not expected the hacker to be ready when he logged on.

> ► Tom. Close your mouth. You look foolish. Now, why are you searching for hackers?

Tom immediately started looking around the room for the camera.

- ► If you are looking for the camera, there is one in the computer and one in your phone. I have access to both. Please don't tell me that you didn't know that they can be on without your permission and without turning on the little red light...
- ► **Sigh**
- ► Oh well... Again, why are you searching for hackers?

Tom finally recovered his composure enough to answer.

- ◊ I am looking to hire someone to train me. I need to be able to search for someone that doesn't want to be found on the web.
- ► You have my interest. Why are you searching for them?
- ◊ That is my business.
- ► Not if you want my help, it isn't.
- ◊ I don't even know who you are. I put requests for help out to ten different hackers.
- ► Yes. I saw. That was cute. I noticed you used the police's most wanted list for hackers... They don't know it, but some of those names they listed are aliases for the same person.
- ◊ So, which one of them is you? What can I call you?
- ► I am not on the list. None of the best hackers are, but for the sake of giving me a name, just call me Iyr.

Tom did a quick web search for the word "Iyr," and all he got was that it was Aramaic for "Watcher" or "Angel." No articles had been written about hackers of that name.

◊   Okay. Will you help me?

►   Again, I will not help you if you don't tell me why you are searching for the unsearchable.

◊   Fine. Evil people are working for a company called The Wall. They erased my life and tried to kill me. I want to find them and make sure they don't do that to anyone else.

►   I have heard of them. They are fairly good. Hard to track on the dark web. How do you plan on making sure they don't harm others anymore? Kill them?

◊   I want them in jail, not dead.

►   Damn, you are naive. A jail cell won't stop them.

◊   I won't kill unless it is in self-defense and I have no other options.

►   I admire your idealism, but I sense you will have your resolve tested if you go down this path. I know of The Wall. They are the type of group where any indecision on your part could prove fatal.

◊   That will have to be my issue.

►   True... So, you are a person with abilities with a desire for justice to be served to a group that is out of control?

◊   How do you know I have abilities?

►   You know I have a camera on you. I ran your face through facial recognition software, and you came up as the same person that had a super-powered dispute in Vermont a few weeks ago.

◊   Oh.... Um. Yeah.

►   Well, then Tom Woods – now called Thomas Ripley – I will train you. Attached to this chat box is a document that will tell you how to make it so that you are relatively safe from being hacked and how to stay undetected while you are surfing the dark web. Download it. Disconnect from the internet and read the READ_ME document. It will instruct you on how to install a secure operating system called *Tails* on a USB drive. You will be able to pop this

USB drive into any computer and be safe on the internet.

◊   Thank you.

►   Don't thank me yet. You will also find my fee in that document. If you don't have any bitcoins, you will need to purchase some because that is the only form of currency I take.

◊   I will make that happen.

►   One final thing: In addition to the payments, you will owe me a favor.

◊   Hold on there.

►   This is not negotiable, but don't worry. If my favor conflicts with your moral code, I will allow you to veto it. Is that acceptable?

Tom thought it over for a couple of minutes.

◊   Yes. I agree to these terms.

►   Excellent. Then, download your files and let the learning begin.

With the addition of adding "hacking class" to his already busy physical training schedule and occasionally sneaking out of the city to practice using his new powers, Tom had the equivalent of a full-time job. He would come and go at roughly the same hours as his neighbors with regular jobs furthering their belief that he was just another hard-working local.

Days of intense study turned into weeks and weeks turned into months. After four months, Tom could tell that he was making some significant improvements in all areas. His body was becoming hard and lean, and his mind was becoming quick and agile. He was determined that the next time he fought The Wall, the outcome would be very different.

In his spare time, he had also been carefully observing how the general public was taking the knowledge of people with enhanced abilities. The discussion over what should be done dominated the media. People wanted to know everything, all at once. How many changed people were there? What can they do? How did they get changed? Why haven't we heard of this before? If one of these people could kill you with a thought, should that person need to be registered like a gun? The depth and breadth of the discussion was staggering, and people had very strong opinions on both sides.

Of course, the fact that no one in a position of authority in the government was stepping up and talking rationally to everyone was also a source of stress. It was exactly the kind of opportunity for which Greg Buckner had been waiting. It took him all of three days to secretly buy out an established personal protection agency that had specialized in providing high priced former special forces soldiers as personal bodyguards. He then came out on national television as the owner of *Max Protection* and announced to the world that he knew all about the Changed.

Tom was at home preparing his dinner with the news playing on the TV when Buckner's face caught his attention. He was certain the man getting interviewed was the same man, the CEO of Great Wall Incorporated, that Levi had shown him months ago at the table in Rutnies. Tom turned up the volume.

"What I am saying is that my company *Max Protection* works with the ones that can be trained to help contain those that can't be trained. We are the only security group that has this advantage, and I know what you are going to ask: Why is it necessary? Are they dangerous? And my answer is: absolutely!" Greg confirmed. "Their abilities drive them mad over time, but with the right training, supervision and sometimes medication, they can frequently be useful to society."

The news reporter leaned in "How do you mean?"

"I mean they can be useful. Like guard dogs, if trained properly. If not, well… You saw the Vermont footage of what happens when they go feral."

"But Mr. Buckner! These are *people* you are talking about." She countered.

"No, ma'am." He objected. "They stopped being 'people' when they became able to do things that normal, God-fearing, mortals can't do."

"So, what do we do with them?" She pressed.

"We train the ones that are willing to be trained and keep them under tight supervision. The other ones we will have to put in specially made detention centers." He explained.

"You mean jail?"

"I mean detention centers. We can't have them hurting people, but I don't believe in harming them." He clarified with his best, saintly smile, and just as the camera panned to Buckner's right, Tom saw him. The greasy man Tom knew as Streak was standing protectively at Buckner's side.

Tom felt sick to his stomach. If he had any lingering doubts, seeing Streak at Buckner's side had erased them. Greg Buckner was the man he needed to take down. He was the one that had sanctioned the wiping of his mother's memories. He was the one that allowed that animal James Neuwin off his leash with permission to hunt him down and try to kill him, and those were only the things that affected Tom personally. He knew that his same story had been played out, again and again, numerous times as James had worked to recruit his army of people that had Changed.

"And you have been working with these creatures for some time now? Why haven't you gone to the media with the knowledge that they exist?" The reporter's voice brought him back to the present.

"Let me ask you this, Nancy – would you have believed me a year ago if I told you I knew a 17-year-old boy that could fly and throw cars with his mind?"

The interview continued, but Tom was no longer listening. In a moment of insight, he could see Buckner's game. First, he had specifically *not* mentioned that he was a part of the government. If he were, now would be the time to claim that so that people would not be nervous that their leaders were unprepared for this sort of threat.

If that were true, why had James said that they were "the government's last line of defense…" That made no sense unless that had been part of the lies that his men tell new recruits to get them to join – just to make them think they are joining the right side. Maybe GWI was a contracted group like they had been before they went underground. In Current Events class in school, Tom had heard about the government employing such companies during the Gulf War and about how those companies had a tendency not to stick to the rules. Yes. That definitely sounded much more like Buckner and his group.

As for what Buckner was doing now with this interview, that also was obvious to Tom. He was making himself an authority on the Changed. Now people would start going to him as a resource. On top of that, by opening a second business, Buckner was separating his dirty work of using The Wall to kidnap and brainwash people from his public image of a guy that is trying to protect people from a potential threat. Truly, Buckner was playing both sides of the fence in this game.

Tom was about to shut off the TV, so he could calm down when the next announcement made him pause. "In later news, a group of people with special abilities have applied for and received a permit to have a rally in the Boston Common on Friday afternoon. Their message? Come and meet us. We are not your enemy."

The young, idealistic part of Tom loved the idea. They were trying to control the narrative by telling their side of the story in an effort to undermine the crap that Buckner was putting out there. This was a rally that he would have to attend.

CHAPTER 16

The Battleground Expands

"I am called Leaf, and I would like to welcome you to our little social gathering," greeted a large man over a microphone.

Tom had been to lots of pep rallies growing up and even one or two rallies for social causes in Burlington, but he had never seen anything like this. Boston Commons, which generally had well-tended trees, a manicured lawn, and a couple of flower beds, looked like it had been the recipient of an extreme makeover. Surrounding the area of the rally were beds of flowers that were utterly stunning. Bright shades of every color bloomed beside each other giving off their sweet fragrance.

Tom was no flower expert, but he knew he had never seen half the varieties that were on display. Behind the flowers were food-bearing plants and trees that he knew hadn't been there when he made his last visit to the Commons a month ago.

Then, there were the people… The Changed had made a point to have tables spread out in the space they had been allotted. Each table had free t-shirts, fliers and some fresh foods on them. Stationed at each table was a person wearing a shirt that said, "We are the same because we share differences." Most of the people wearing the shirts had nothing obvious about them that screamed *I am Changed*, but a handful of them did. Tom was able to see one that looked like she was made out of metal and another that had what looked like a small set of wings.

Journalists also dotted the scene interviewing everyone from the Changed at the booths to the people that came to see what the rally was about.

"I know there has been a lot of information coming at you about people with 'abilities' lately," boomed the big man over the amplifiers. "But we are not all that different from you. Most of us were born into families just like you were. We grew up and then something happened that made us different." He paused for effect. "Don't you have something about you that makes you different from a peer group? Maybe you can play the piano and your friends can't. Maybe you are excellent at sports, and your friends aren't. It doesn't matter. What matters is that if people look deeply, they will see we all have similarities and differences, but that should not stop us from treating each other with respect."

He smiled and looked around. "With a lot of help from mother nature and our volunteer members, we have set up some booths through-out this area of the Commons. Please check out the fliers. Each table has a different flier with the story of a different person that has an ability. These stories are to help you see that we share similar hopes and dreams. If you have questions, each person staffing a booth will be available to help answer them. If you feel the same, please grab one of our free t-shirts and show your support, and, of course, help yourself to the food."

Tom stood in the middle of the field as people walked all around him smiling as they enjoyed the food and conversations. This was precisely what was needed. This is why he had gone public and fought The Wall. Maybe now people with abilities could start to step out of the shadows and not be scared. It was an amazing feeling.

It was then that four black vans and a large cargo truck pulled up next to the Commons and stopped. Tom's stomach lurched as agents in their black tactical gear started pouring out of the back of cargo truck. Easily over fifty agents lined up with riot shields and tranquilizer guns at the ready.

The crowd of people that had been peacefully talking with the rally organizers all started to walk quickly out of the square, but true to their peaceful nature the Changed at the booths all held their ground.

Leaf's voice boomed over the speakers. "I don't know what you men are doing here, but we have legal permission to be holding this rally. We have broken no laws."

The agents never bothered to answer. They simply walked up to the first booth, grabbed the young lady working there, handcuffed her and started dragging her to the cargo truck. Leaf stormed over to the Agents. "Who are you people?" He demanded in a voice loud enough to be heard without the speakers. "I demand to see your badge and proof that you are with law enforcement."

Tom knew what was coming next and quickly walked back to a spot where the bushes and trees grew thick.

He was still watching when it happened. The first agent went to restrain Leaf. He grabbed his arm and tried to pull it behind Leaf's back so that he could apply the cuffs when Leaf lifted his arm and pulled the 230-pound man clean off his feet to dangle in the air in front of him. "You have no right to touch me." The other agents immediately converged on Leaf's position. One shot a dart that hit him in the chest but didn't penetrate his bark-like skin.

One of the rally members in a white, skin-tight suit with a red sash and white mask with a grinning skull on it ran to Leaf's side. With bolts of white energy shooting from her palms, she dropped several of the closest agents only to have twice that number continue to run toward the rally leader's position. "Leave him alone!" she screamed.

Tom couldn't believe it. He was almost too stunned to move. The woman's powers were the same as the woman that came to help him fight the agents back in his home town. His head spun as he paused for a second and watched her and the agents exchanging fire. *Is that you, Ghost Touch?*

A heartbeat later, he snapped out of his brief stupor and realized that he needed to act. Not only were these the same agents that had stolen his life, but they now were going after someone that had risked her life to save his. Without further hesitation, he dove into the bushes and released the restraints he used to keep his powers in check. In a blast of blue light and wind, Tom's form changed as the very molecules that made up his body became so charged with energy that they took on the form of a shifting blue plasma. Floating up into the air above the Commons, he was able to get an overview of the fight below.

Dozens more men were headed toward Leaf and Ghost Touch, but before they could close the distance, Leaf extended his arm, palm up, toward them and made a lifting gesture. Immediately grass and shrubs burst from the ground to grow to over ten feet in height between him and the agents. Tom was stunned. Leaf had created a living wall between himself and the agents. It was thick enough that the tranquilizer darts weren't getting through it.

Other agents were still trying to abduct more rally members, and small skirmishes had broken out in a half dozen places throughout the green. Seven more of the Changed were already down with darts in their now sedated bodies, while others rushed in to help drag their fallen friends away from the advancing agents. Two of the rally members could already be seen getting loaded into the truck by the agents.

Fire and lightning flashed sporadically against the almost constant *thump, thump, thump* of the darts being fired. The rally members were woefully outnumbered and outgunned by the agents. Tom created a shield for one group of rally members and blew back a group of agents with a blast of energy from his hand. As more firepower was concentrated on Tom, some of the rally members with no defensive powers started to flee through the woods at the far side of the field.

As the advance of the agents slowed, one of the SUV doors opened, and Stonehenge got out. Tom recognized him immediately and knew the rally members position had just become far more dire. The giant man took several steps closer to the battle, stopped, took a big breath and raised his arms. At first, nothing happened, but after a few seconds, the ground began to rumble. A heartbeat later a wall of stone burst out of the ground completely encircling the rally members in the Commons. The stone wall rose slowly. It was two feet thick and must have weighted tons as it grew from four feet to six feet and finally to ten feet tall as it effectively cut off any means of escape.

That was all Tom needed to see. He raised his hand and grabbed a fistful of air molecules. With his new powers infusing them, it quickly became a ball of flaming plasma which he then hurled at Stonehenge. The huge man took the blast square in the chest and was thrown backward into the SUV which crumpled like paper from the impact.

All eyes turned to Tom as the fighting stopped. "This fight is *over!*" Tom yelled to those below. He looked around and found a large group of people from the rally gathered in the southeast corner of the field several feet from the stone wall. Tom turned and focused on the wall. At two solid feet of rock, the wall could have withstood a tank slamming into it. He knew that he would not just be able to smash it down. He could try, and it might work, but the blast would likely hurt of the rally members. Instead, he reached out and separated the solid mass of rock into pebbles in the shape of a seven-foot door. Pushing all the pebbles out of the way to form an opening was much easier. In less than a minute, the rally goers were pouring through the opening.

A cheer went up as Tom floated back up into the air and threw a handful of flaming plasma at the ground in front of the advancing agents. "I don't recommend following us!" He warned them.

Tom quickly flew back to the opening in the wall. "Hurry everyone." He encouraged those fleeing. "It won't take long for them to regroup and head around to the back of this thing." Most of the Changed were running for the opening in the wall while a small group that had a means of defending themselves continued to provide cover fire. Tom looked back and saw the woman in white laughing as she advanced on a group of agents that were hiding behind an overturned table. "What are you doing?" He yelled at her.

"Cleaning up the park!" She yelled back with a huge grin. "Boston is dirty enough without us leaving these pieces of trash all over the park!" With that, she leveled another volley of her white energy bolts.

He could see she wasn't going to leave or back down from the battle. It was obvious she was enjoying this. He needed another strategy. "We need help carrying out the wounded!"

She stopped and frowned. "Ugh! Fine! Spoil-sport!"

Once she and Tom got back to the hole in the wall, he lifted his hand and the remaining unconscious rally members floated into the air and followed them through. "Hey! You said you needed help with that." The woman accused.

"I do need help. Where are we going to put them?"

"Follow me." She said and ran down a side street.

To his amazement, most of the group had piled into a large, beat-up looking bus that was parked on the far side of the Commons. "This is it." She said as she jumped on the bus. "Load them in the back."

Tom floated the sedated members into the bus. He had no sooner settled the last one into a seat when Leaf stood up. "We have to move now people. Those that are awake, please care for the unconscious." Then turning to face Tom. "You are welcome to come with us. You've earned it. If you decide to leave, do so now. We don't want the agents to catch up."

Tom was intrigued. He looked around and found a seat for himself not far from Ghost Touch. Then, they pulled out and started the drive.

CHAPTER 17

New Friends

The bus had been on the road for an hour when it pulled off the main road and started down a smaller road for several miles. It continued taking smaller and more remote paths until it finally came to a shuddering stop in what amounted to a clearing in the middle of nowhere. The driver turned off the engine which sputtered and wheezed like an asthmatic in pollen season before giving one final cough and shutting down. Leaf looked at the bus like a doctor that knew his patient only had a few days left before rising and motioning for people to follow him off the bus.

Tom got out and followed the small group as they quietly walked over to the far corner of the clearing. After everyone was off the bus, Leaf stood beside them and raised his arms. In no time at all, the clearing was full of thick, lush vegetation that completely obscured the bus. Tree limbs covered it from above, and dense shrubbery and undergrowth filled in so thickly that someone could be standing within five feet of it and would never realize it was there.

He then turned and gestured that the group should continue walking. Silently, they turned back to face the woods and disappeared into the foliage.

Tom fell in step with Leaf as he passed out of what was the clearing and into the woods. Tom glanced over at him as they walked and got his first good view of the tall, solemn man. He was close to seven feet tall, had brown hair, rough bark-like skin, and deep, emerald green eyes. All of his movements were deliberate, and he emanated a deep sense of peace.

In spite of the methodical feel to Leaf's pace, they made excellent time on the path they were following. They walked through more trees and dense shrubs to emerge in a clearing. Leaf and the others continued to press on. After going through the clearing, they pushed past a row of tree branches that briefly gave Tom an oddly nauseating lurching feeling, before suddenly falling away to reveal that they were all standing on a mountain path at the northern tip of a beautiful valley. It was gorgeous and seemed to be completely untouched by man. Tom would have stayed longer just to take in the sight but noticed he was already falling behind and hurried to catch up. After several minutes, they were down in the valley, and the dense underbrush gave way to old-growth trees that look like they were easily over a hundred feet tall. The area around the bottom of the trees was thick with tents and small buildings as well as people that were going about their business. Above, the canopy high overhead obscured the sky, yet still managed to allowed a soft green-gold light to filter down to shine on those below. To Tom, it was a scene that had an almost fairy-tale quality.

Leaf chuckled as he watched Tom's look of amazement. "Welcome to the Valley of the Cursed." He began a little ominously. "Well… Most people that live here call it the Settlement, but I can see you have many questions, my blue friend. Come, and we will exchange stories."

Tom was only able to nod his head in mute appreciation as he struggled to take in all of what he was seeing.

"Well then, we can start with mine, and maybe it will clear up most of your questions…" He began. "As you can see many of us would not pass for being *just* human. Like you, they have abilities that make it very obvious that they are different." At this, Tom glanced down at the glowing blue colors shifting in his hands. He had allowed his ability to remain visible, thereby protecting his identity from the group. He didn't know them yet and needed to assess if he could trust them or not.

"There have always been people like us" Leaf continued on as they walked through the small town. "and over the years, our numbers have grown. Some people would be born with an ability or would have something happen to them to trigger one. Whatever the cause, society would see them as different and would either shut them out or hunt them down. Whatever the case, many would take to the woods to either hide or to try to start their life over. Over time, people with abilities would run into one another and form little groups for safety and companionship, and that is how our little society came to be. For many years, we wandered without a home. Eventually, we reached a point that the group was so large that we needed a permanent place to call our own. It was getting too risky to move a group that large. That's when we thought up this place.

"You see, back then, we knew a mystic named Webster that said he knew a way that he could hide the Settlement for all time. His gift was that he could create gateways to pocket dimensions."

"Pocket dimensions?"

"Yes." Leaf explained. "He found this beautiful fertile valley, and he knew that it would fit our needs for a place to live. Webster was very old by then and knew that if the community he loved so much was going to survive, they needed a place that would be hidden from the world indefinitely, so he used all of his power to make the gateway to this place." Leaf saw that he needed to explain further. "Imagine a cabin floating in space. It has a kitchen, bedrooms, and a bathroom – all the things a cabin should have, but there is no way to get to it as it floats in space. Now imagine someone has built a brick wall. You walk around the wall and see that there is nothing on either side of it. It is just a normal wall. Then you notice that someone has built a door into the wall. Amazingly, you open the door, and you find yourself in the cabin. That is what a pocket dimension is like. It is a space that exists independently of the rest of the known universe and is somehow tethered to our physical world by some sort of a gate. Though the power required to do this for such a large space cost him his life, this is what Webster did to this valley. He permanently anchored the northern tip of the valley to the woods in southern Massachusetts. We unimaginatively call that opening the 'Gate,' and it is what caused you to feel nauseated a little bit ago when you stepped through it.

"Now, when people want to come here, they have to find the opening to the valley located in the woods. The challenge for us became how do we hide the opening from the "Normals?" During those early years the risk was pretty small, but as the decades passed, we had to actively take steps to make sure no one would stumble upon us. At first, we played pranks on the Normals and circulated stories that this wood is haunted. Our abilities and appearance made that part fairly easy, and they even started referring to the area around the opening as the Cursed Forrest.

Because of this, many of our early encounters with Normals became urban legends over the years, but we knew that a little fear alone would not provide us with lasting security from being discovered, so we sent our Will Breakers out into their towns. The Will Breakers "encouraged" the Normals to make our land, 5,441 acres right here in Southern Massachusetts, a protected park called Freetown-Fall River State Forest. That way we could prevent development and discovery from taking our home."

Tom had stopped walking and was just staring at Leaf's face as he talked. If it had not been for his open, honest face, Tom would never have believed a word of it. "But you talk about that story as if you were there for it."

"Yes."

"But that's impossible. You would have to be over a hundred years old." Tom objected.

"Actually, I am several thousand years old. The oldest by far of any of this company." Leaf admitted.

"Are you all… immortal?"

Leaf laughed a deep, rich laugh. "No, my friend. It is just me. My story is unique." He continued as they resumed walking. "I don't remember ever being human, and though I have had many names over the centuries – Igasho, Man of the Wood, Caminante Verde... I do not recall one that is my 'original' name. My earliest memory is simply waking up in the woods with my feet buried up to my ankles in dirt." They came to a stop outside a large tent. "This is our Council of Elders tent." He said with a gesture toward the tent. "I would like to invite you to come in for the meeting."

He didn't wait for a reply as he swept open the flap and entered the tent. Tom followed and froze. In a day full of unexpected surprises, this had to rank up in the top two. It was not a tent on the inside. Inside the tent was a great hall with chandeliers and oak-beamed walls. An enormous table that seemed to have grown right out of the floor was the centerpiece of the room. The ornate chairs that ringed the table were similar in design to the massive structure. Along one wall was a side table with coffee and all manner of pastries, vegetables, and cheeses, and was surrounded by people of all descriptions talking soberly as they snacked.

Leaf's low rumble of a laugh snapped Tom back to the moment. "Our illusionists decided long ago, that we should not lack for the finer things simply due to our isolation from the Normals."

"So, what is the illusion?" Tom asked. "The outside or the inside?"

Leaf raised an eyebrow. "Astute question my friend. In truth, sometimes it is a little of both." Then he turned to face the group within the tent. "Time for the council to commence. Please take your seats." He did not yell, but his baritone voice easily carried to all in the chamber. Glancing back at Tom "Please stay. Take a seat here." He gestured to the row of chairs toward the back of the hall.

Conversation died out, and people quickly moved to their seats. Leaf walked toward the head of the table where nine seats with different designs carved into them were lined up and took his place in the seat to the right of the middle chair.

Tom quickly found a seat and had just sat down when someone unceremoniously dropped into the chair next to him. It was the woman in white. She leaned in toward Tom, and he could see she was smiling through her mask. "What?" She asked him in a playful voice. "You helped save me from going too far with those agents, the least I can do is save you from being bored to death with our meetings…" She didn't wait for an answer as she turned back to face the group assembling at the head of the table.

An old man that looked like a caricature of every wizard Tom had ever seen drawn in a comic book came to stand in front of the middle chair. He picked up a gavel and wrapped the anvil sitting on the table just hard enough to be heard. "The Council of the Cursed will now come to order. Let all voices be heard, let the truth be known and let the future be decided."

Silence descended on the hall before the old man continued. "Today we have extended our hand in peace and understanding to the Normals and had that hand rejected with violence. The Council needs to know the details and desires of our people. Who would stand forth and tell of the day?"

"I would, Ward Nims." A woman with large grey eyes and sparkling blood-red hair addressed the old man. She turned and faced the hall and repeated the traditional words. "I am Scarlet Hawk, and I would speak for the people. I was at the rally at the Commons."

"Proceed."

"We did as we had planned – as the council had agreed." She began. "We set up a peaceful and informative rally to introduce ourselves to the Normals, and it was going quite well. I spoke to several that just wanted to meet one of us and seemed to bear us no anger. They were just curious." She paused. "Then the vans arrived, and men dressed in military gear came out. They had tranquilizer dart-guns, tasers and stun batons. They were obviously intent on taking us alive. I submit that they are likely the same group that has been doing the abductions throughout the country and that their organization is far larger and has more financial and political resources than we thought they did."

Several in the group nodded their heads and murmured their agreement.

"Leaf attempted to talk to them. He asked to see badges and to have them declare their intent, but the men in tactical suits simply opened fire with their dart guns. We defended ourselves. Then, the man in blue appeared, flying above the Commons." She gestured to Tom. "He joined our fight just as the other side sent in the one known as Stonehenge." Murmurs of disgust and anger filled the hall and the word "traitor" could be heard repeated from all quarters. "Stonehenge formed a wall to contain us, but the blue one knocked him back, knocked a hole in the wall and helped us escape. In the end, only three of our number were taken. It could have been far worse."

"Well spoken, Scarlet Hawk. Do any dispute this accounting of the day?" Ward Nims asked as she concluded her account. None responded. "So, where then do we stand?"

The woman in white jumped to her feet. "Our people have been taken! We need to find them and attack!" She yelled.

"Ghost Touch!" Nims admonished. "I know you are new to our society, but you know the rules of this council! You will show some self-restraint."

"I apologize, Ward Nims." She returned bowing her head. "I am Ghost Touch, and I would speak for the people. I have seen what this group does. They are kidnappers and killers. There is no telling what will happen to those that were taken. There is no reasoning with the ones that took them. They are evil and need to be removed as a threat to our people." There were several in the hall that called out "Here! Here!" in agreement.

"We all know of your point of view, my dear," Nims said with a voice full of sorrow. "And we all acknowledge that we need to do something to save those that were taken, but we are in the dark on this. Who are these men? Where is their headquarters? Are they a part of our government? Are they the same group that was in Vermont?"

"Stonehenge was with them!" Ghost Touch pointed out in exasperation.

"That doesn't mean it is the same group." Ward Nims countered. "And even if it is, we still don't know what we would be getting into. Blindly lashing out without knowing more could place even more of us in harm's way. If this group that is after us is part of the government, we could be starting a war that we can't win."

"Excuse me, Ward Nims." Tom interrupted. "I am… Storm and I can tell you, they are not part of the government."

To this, several people were on their feet shouting "Outsider!"

Ward Nims brought down the gavel again, and the room shook with the sound. "Silence." He commanded. He glanced to either side of his seat and saw them nod. "I know that outsiders do not normally address the council, but we would have the one that defended our people speak."

"I have been captured by these men before, and I think I have put together their game plan." With that, Tom recounted how he had been abducted and drugged. He spoke of how they had tried to use his brother as leverage and how they had wiped the minds of those that would have missed him. He told them about the TV interview with Greg Buckner and how he was fairly sure that The Wall was not part of the government, but could be a subcontractor of it. The only thing that he skipped was anything that would have tied him to his real identity. He never mentioned the fight in the streets of his home town.

When he finished, the room was silent for a moment. Then, Leaf stood up "You have provided us with a great service this day. First, you saved a great number of our people, and then you provided us with this valuable information on those that would harm us. Go now and let us ponder what this means."

Tom realized that he had been dismissed, so he nodded and turned to leave the council chamber. It was then that he realized that Ghost Touch was at his side. "Come on!" She smiled and lead him outside. "I'll show you where you can go wait for their decision."

It was evening by now, and the sun was starting to set in the valley as they began a slow-paced hike uphill into the woods. They walked for several minutes taking small footpaths that jack-knifed further up the hillside and deeper into the woods until they finally stepped out onto a large ledge that had a commanding view of the valley. Ghost Touch walked out to the very edge and with her back to Tom, reached up and removed her mask. Long dark curly hair spilled in waves down her back. "So, where are you from?" She asked as she turned back to face him.

But Tom was unable to answer, as he stared in utter disbelief into the bright green eyes of Reagan Hill.

"Oh, you can't tell me where you are from?" Reagan asked as she mistook his stunned silence for not wanting to give away his identity.

"Huh? Uh no…" Tom recovered. "I just can't believe it's you."

She looked puzzled. "What do you mean?"

"I mean, how did you come to have powers?" He changed topics to allow himself time to decide how much he wanted her to know.

"Oh, that." She smiled. "Well, I grew up in a small town in northern Vermont. I was sick – like horribly sick for most of my life. Half my class thought I had cancer and the other half just didn't like me. The doctors were convinced it was some sort of autoimmune disease – mostly because they had tested me for everything under the sun and couldn't figure out what was wrong." She walked over and sat down on the boulder, so she could dangle her feet over the edge. Tom came over and sat next to her so he could continue to hear her story.

"So, I ended up with lots of prescriptions that treated the symptoms but nothing that would treat the cause." She reminisced looking out over the valley. "Of course, it's hard to make friends when everyone is scared of getting puke on them. Very few people ever treated me like I was a real person with feelings. Well… except for one guy." She paused before continuing her story. "Anyway, one night in the summer between my freshman and sophomore years of high school, things got really bad. I was feeling like crap, like always, and had decided to go to my room after dinner to go to bed early. After a full day of puking, you'd be amazed at how tired you can get, but that night wasn't like all the others. Not long after laying down, I started to lose feeling in my legs and fingers. It was freaky, and I tried to get up to go for help. When that didn't work, I tried to holler for mom and dad to come and get me, but it was too late. I realized I couldn't move enough air to make more than a whisper. That was probably the most frightening moment of my life. I remember looking at my digital clock and seeing the time was 9:21 pm and wondering, how long can I go on like this. As it turns out, not long. I died at 10:47 pm."

Tom stared at her in open disbelief. "What…?"

"I remember floating up out of my body and traveling down a long tunnel with a light at the end. I remember touching that light and feeling bathed in warmth and peace. And like all wonderful dreams, this one ended when I wasn't able to pass into that light like the other beings around me were doing. I was forced to go back.

"My next memory was waking up at 5:20 am the following day. I was completely healed, and I don't just mean from the paralysis. I mean from everything. I have never had so much as a sniffle since that night. Even weirder, I wasn't just healthy. I was also strong. My body had been transformed. I could run like an Olympic athlete and punch harder than a pro boxer.

"In fact, I was at the local gym after having signed up for a self-defense class when I found out one of the other 'gifts' I had been given. I was sparring with my instructor's star pupil and – I have to say – he was kicking my butt pretty badly when I got angry, and it felt like my skin was vibrating. I was just getting up from a right hook he had thrown when he tried to knock me back down with an uppercut to the stomach. When he connected, I felt a wave of something leave me, and he flew backward. He was out cold.

"Later, I would call it the 'Ghost Touch.' I know this is going to sound corny, but I think every person has an energy that makes up their soul. Call it the 'breath of life' if you are religious, but most cultures and religions believe that there is more to being alive than the physical body. I believe my power disrupts the flow of that energy temporarily and knocks people out. I have since learned to wrap myself in a ball of it or shoot it out from me like a living stun gun."

"That's amazing!"

"Yeah, but it gets a little weirder. I was at a restaurant months ago, and this guy had a heart attack. They tried to do CPR on the guy, but it just wasn't his day. He died with me watching from two tables away. The weird thing is, when he died, my ability instantly felt like it was supercharged. I could barely contain power from knocking out every-one within a 10-foot radius! That's another reason for the name 'Ghost Touch.'"

"That is strange, but it isn't like you killed the guy," Tom said, not wanting her to feel guilt from something that didn't look like it was her fault.

"Yeah, I know. It's just odd – like me." She said and smiled at him. Tom was glad that his power obscured his features because he couldn't help but stare. Sitting on the boulder with the setting sun's light on her face, she was beautiful.

"If that was all in Vermont, how did you come to be here?" He asked trying to cover the awkward silence.

"Oh, that? I had a bad experience." She began. "Ever since I got my powers, I had been on the lookout for anyone that might have some of their own. What I found, surprised me." She got up and started to pace. "I found two others in town. At first, we just got together and talked about our experiences, but it didn't take long before we had located a place to go and practice using them. We really got into it and started to think of ourselves as superheroes. That's when we got the wakeup call.

"Right at the beginning of my senior year of high school, some stuff went seriously south. It was the second day of school, and I was in class. It was around 8:30 when the building shook from the first explosion. No one was sure what it was at first, but the administrators weren't taking any chances. They pushed the panic button and evacuated the school like they are supposed to if there is a bomb threat. Only I didn't go with the crowd. I snuck off and met up with my 'special' friends. We threw on ski masks to hide our identities and ran toward the explosions.

"That's the first time that I ran into the agents – except these weren't normal agents. These guys were all like that one we saw today that could move rocks with his mind, and they were all attacking this guy that I knew from school. I had no idea he had abilities too, but boy did he ever! He could fly and pick up cars with his mind. He was bulletproof and could form a shield around himself.

"Uh… wow!" Tom said feeling even more uncomfortable.

"Yeah. My team and I did everything we could, but it didn't matter. He died, and I was the only one from my team to walk away. Rhino was captured, and Blades was stabbed to death. I actually barely had enough power to stun the strongest of their group for a few seconds so that I could escape." As she talked, tears made their way down her cheeks. Tom couldn't tell if the tears were for him or for her fallen friends, but regardless, his guilt ratcheted up another couple of notches.

"So, I went back to school the next day, but I couldn't stand it. I couldn't get the fight out of my head. I wanted to go after those that hurt my friends, so I talked to my cousin in Florida, and she agreed to help provide me with a cover story. I told my mom I wanted to do the rest of my senior year in Florida so that I could help my aunt who is really sick. She agreed to let me, so I took a flight down, and when I got there, I went to the local school and took the GED exam so I could skip the rest of high school. Then, my cousin agreed to take care of our Aunt while I 'work through some personal stuff,' and here I am.

"It took me a while to get a lead on the agents, but then I read an article about this legend of a monster that lived around here, so I flew to Boston and started asking around. I thought it was the superpowered bad guys, but it turned out to be the Cursed Ones. It took me a month of looking through the woods to locate them. Well, it was more them finding me, starving and dehydrated, but you get the idea. I had found people that could help me in my search for those jerks that took out my friends.

"That is just incredible." Tom shook his head. He couldn't believe how strong she must be to have accomplished all that.

"So how about you, shy guy? Who were you before you went all blue?" Tom had known that she was going to ask who he really was. It was inevitable, and he knew that if he were going to work with the Cursed Ones for long, he would need to tell them his real identity.

"I'm sorry." He began.

"What? So, you aren't going to tell me after I just spilled my life story to you?" She was hurt, and Tom could see it in her eyes. "My intuition on men is total crap! I thought I felt a connection to you and I don't get that from hardly anyone!"

"Wait! Hold on!" Tom grabbed her shoulders just before she spun away from him and looked her in the eyes. His breath suddenly caught in his throat. Her eyes sparkled and danced in the fading light of the day. She was beautiful, caring and smart. He knew he could search a lifetime and not find another woman like her. She had trusted him with a very personal story, and now, she expected him to lower his guard too or possibly lose his chance with her. He could not bear that thought.

"I have learned the hard way that protecting my family and those that I love, means protecting my identity, so I don't know about telling everyone here in the valley, but you, I trust." With that, he pulled back his powers, and the blue light flickered and went out, leaving Tom standing on the boulder looking straight into Reagan's eyes.

At first, her face registered her shock. "Tom…?!?" Then, she started to smile, but before the smile was fully upon her face, she yanked her arms back out of Tom's reach. "You let me think you were dead!!" She yelled in anger, and the last thing Tom would remember that evening was Reagan raising her hand, and a bright flash of white light hitting him in the chest.

CHAPTER 18

James Gives His Report

i

James walked through the third set of scanners on his way into the Headquarters for GWI passing the double row of guards lining the walls with little more than a nod. The men knew him. James had trained half of them himself. In his wake, Trevor Merrola hurried to keep up with James and in the process, almost ran into the two Resource Agents that flanked the doors to the elevators.

No one looking at them would be able to tell that they had any abilities. They appeared normal. Other people, however, didn't always appear normal to them. They both were very powerful Changed. One could tell if a person had a talent and how strong it was. During his time as part of the Headquarters Guard, he had caught several Changed trying to get in to either learn what The Wall did or to attempt to destroy them. The second Resource Agent had a powerful, uncanny ability to sense trouble. The talent's accuracy was so fine-tuned that it verged on precognition.

His value showed itself when it was a normal person trying to do harm to The Wall. He had helped catch everyone from reporters to agents from the CIA and FBI, to parents of Changed that had disappeared. All had come with the intent to do harm in their mind, and all had been caught before they ever got past the reception area.

James checked his watch and tapped his foot as the elevator sailed up to the top floor where Greg Buckner held all the executive level meetings. They were getting close to being late, and James knew that would not go over well with Greg. "I wish this thing could move a little faster," James grumbled in anger. Again, Trevor marveled at how James was, at worst, irritated with the delay where others would have been at a near panic at possibly upsetting the CEO of the Wall.

"No worries, Sir." Trevor tried to reassure himself. "They need our report on the Boston Commons event. It's not like they are going to start without us."

James gave Trevor a scathing look. "You obviously have never seen someone thrown off the top floor for keeping the board waiting before."

Trevor went pale. "They've done that?"

"How do you think I became 'Lead Agent?'" He didn't wait for a reply. As the doors opened, James strode from the elevator and down the narrow hall. To an architect, the floor plan of the top floor would have made no sense, but to a student of warfare, it was a work of art. The elevator opened into what a strategist would call a "kill box." The hallway was all reinforced cement and rebar with a layer of graphite over that. It was nearly indestructible. The vents could release poisonous gas at the push of a button. In addition, the floor could release 100,000 volts of electricity after the sprinkler system had doused the intruder with water; if all else failed, the entire floor tilted, and the wall would open, dropping the intruder to their death, ten stories below.

As Trevor gingerly walked over the floor to the door at the end of the hall, he recalled what he had read about the headquarters building when he had become one of the top agents under James. He knew that the building had three top-level security areas. One was the basement where indoctrination and training were done. Another was the server room which was one floor down from where he currently stood. It held information on every one of the Changed they had ever encountered, every scrap of intelligence they had acquired through their network of spies and all the history of every project in which they had ever been involved. And the final area, of course, was the top floor with the executive offices and board room. In all three of these areas, it was easier to be killed than it was to stay alive, and as he crossed the floor, Trevor found himself seriously questioning his career choices.

After entering a code, a handprint, and an eye scan at the far end of the hall, the door opened into a modestly sized waiting room with chairs and a small table of magazines in it. There were no windows or doors other than the one they had just entered. It was obviously designed to disorient an intruder as to where to go next.

As soon as the door locked behind them, a section of the wall lit up and an image of a woman in a black, form-fitting, suit appeared. "Welcome back James. I see you are pushing the clock for the board meeting. I would have thought that the last time you were here, you would have seen how important being on time was…" Then turning to Trevor, she smiled. "Mr. Merrola. It's a pleasure to meet you. I am Lindsay McKay, the executive security officer. I will buzz you both through now."

With that, there was a light clicking noise, and part of the wall swung open to reveal a short hall with another door. Neither rushing nor wasting time, James cleared the hall and opened the door. The sight that met them was like nothing Trevor had ever seen.

The board room was a large room with a large oak table at its center. There were seven chairs evenly spaced around the table. Five of the chairs had video cameras and monitors in them. Four of those devices were on and showed the face of someone in a remote location. Greg Buckner stood at the head of the table with a large screen monitor taking up most of the wall behind him. Ensconced lights, tapestries, and paintings covered the walls. There were no doors or windows, but after seeing the security on the way in, Trevor knew that there must be an escape route somewhere.

"Ah." Sighed Greg as they entered the room. "There you are." He glanced at this watch. "Exactly on time." He chuckled. "Still living dangerously, huh James?"

"Always, Sir," James replied as he took up a position at the foot of the table.

"Well, that is the last of the group," Greg announced. "Mr. Eckwood is busy with the assignment we gave him during last week's meeting." He looked to the foot of the table and gestured toward James. "Without any further ado... Let's hear your report, James."

The devices on the seats quietly pivoted the cameras and screens to face James. Once all eyes were upon him, James began "As you all know, we recently had a rare opportunity. As we have long known, there is a group of the Changed living within a few hours' drive of Boston. They have always been quiet and kept to themselves, but after the Vermont incident when abilities became public knowledge, and our leadership started to openly talk about how dangerous they were, this cell became active and started to print propaganda pamphlets telling how they are 'just like you' and how 'we are your children, your friends, and your spouses.'"

At this point, Greg interrupted. "As you all recall, during the executive meeting in October, we decided to get ahead of the press on this. We wanted to make ourselves an authority on the Changed. We would then be able to get the public up to speed about the danger they posed to our nation and start controlling public opinion going forward. At the same time, we decided to separate our past business model from our future model by opening a new business front end: Max Protection."

"This strategic move was done so that if anyone had heard rumors of how we had recruited and operated in the past, it would not scare them off from contacting the new organization, and I have to say – it has worked flawlessly. Nearly two dozen Changed have applied to work for or received information from Max Protection in the past four months. Granted, that is not what one would consider a 'flood' of people, but it does beat our standard form of recruiting by about four times over. More importantly, assets found by this method are recruited willingly and with no force needing to be applied, no bloodshed and no need to do cleanup by our resources."

As Greg stopped, James resumed his report. "The pamphlets had no contact information and not nearly the audience that we had with our television ads, so we didn't worry about them growing their group. Well, that was until recently, when they decided to take a huge leap forward and hold a rally. They claimed that the rally was to 'raise public awareness that we are no more harmful than any other person you know,' but we highly suspected that by coming out in the open, undiscovered Changed would flock to others of their own kind."

"The decision was made in the emergency council meeting last week to send agents in and detain the rally members. Our mission objectives were two-fold. One, we were supposed to capture as many rally members as possible, and two, we were not to use lethal force doing it – no matter what the outcome."

"The morning of the rally we had plain clothes people plant video cameras throughout the Commons. Then, once the rally was in full swing, we sent a strike team in with tranquilizer guns, tasers, and stun nets to get the job done. On backup, if things went south was our Resource Agent, Stonehenge. His instructions were to prevent rally members from fleeing the scene."

"As you have all heard by now, things did go south. The rally members were not new to their abilities, and their reaction to being attacked was not what we have been accustomed to encountering. When we first started darting them, they were taken by surprise, and several of them fell, but then they quickly organized and began to fight back. We out-numbered them eight to one, but their abilities off-set that advantage – even though they were holding back.

"Holding back?" One of the remote board members asked. "In what way Agent James?"

"They weren't using lethal force, Sir," James replied. "The field officer, Agent Merrola will fill you in on the rest."

With that, James motioned for Trevor to take his spot in front of the board and continue the story.

"So, Agents started to notice the rally members fleeing the Commons as the heavy hitters for the group came out of hiding." He stepped up to the table and attached a portable drive into the USB slot. In less than a minute he had video from the Commons playing on the large screen behind Greg. He allowed the scene to play out until Tom's blazing blue form flew into the air. "Here you can see a newly Changed. We are calling him Blue. As soon as he comes on the scene, our men open fire, but he swats it away like nothing. Darts don't even get close to him. The other rally goers let him draw our fire and start running for the woods. We noticed this and had Stonehenge erect a wall to prevent any more escapes." The footage clearly shows the stone wall erupting from the ground around the group.

"As you can see there is a clearly defined leadership here." He uses a tool to circle the group around Leaf and Ghost Touch. "The tall plant lover is called 'Leaf' according to agents on the scene. The woman in white is 'Ghost Touch.' The mechanism of her ability is yet undefined, but essentially, she can stun someone for up to two days. Less if you don't come into physical contact." He clicked a button and pictures of Leaf's and Ghost Touch's face were posted on the screen.

"You said the biggest threat was the blue one? But he is not part of your leadership group?" Asked another board member.

"Yes, sir. Our analysts say that due to body language and such, the other two were not expecting him to show up." He rewound the camera footage to show Tom's blue form busting out of the hedges. "We first see him coming from here, but the cameras that might have caught his face going into that hedge were destroyed by the electricity coming from one of the other rally members."

Rolling the film quickly forward he froze it again as Tom blasted Stonehenge. "As you can see, Blue is the clear threat here." He skipped ahead to Tom knocking a hole in the stone wall and leading the escape.

"That section of wall he reduced to pebbles weighed about 6 tons…" His footage stopped with the rally members escaping through the hole. "At this point, I ordered our men to stand down and head back to base."

"And why did you make that call?" Greg asked, clearly not happy with the decision.

"I made that call because my orders were to capture what I could and not to kill anyone." He held his ground. "Continuing orders were for us not to be detained by police, and the state police were only 3 minutes from arriving on the scene. In my estimation, pressing our attack would mean continuing to risk lives, and while they didn't kill anyone on the field, we had several agents that needed immediate medical attention. Also, if we had stayed, we would have probably had agents arrested, and we definitely would not have been able to keep our haul of the Changed."

James smiled as he watched Greg nod in acceptance. "I see," Greg commented. "You were wise to do so."

"Thank you, Sir."

"And while I am not happy with the low number of subjects taken as a result of our mission, I am satisfied that we made the right choices along the way. At the very least, their message was stifled. Are we in agreement?" He asked the board members. Green lights lit up in front of each member's seat. "Good. Glad to see it." He commented as the last light came on.

Turning back to Trevor Merrola, "Here is what I want you to do. Pick two agents that were seen clearly on that video and have them killed. What powers did the rally members have? Shooting electricity? Throwing fire?" Trevor nodded quietly. "Good. Electrocute one agent and burn the other. Then release to the news that the Changed killed them. We need the public supporting us." He looked to James. "Make sure we triple the amount of money we normally compensate their families and maybe pay for their kid's college education. Then leak how well we took care of the fallen men's family. We will need the public's approval on how we are handling this."

Trevor was stunned as he watched James tell Greg how brilliant a move that was.

"Now on to what are we going to do next." He started to pace in front of the screen. "I will not allow these creatures to continue to undermine what we have built here with their 'meet a freak' days."

Trevor had heard the rumors that using Changed as if they were weapons and not people, wasn't just a business decision for Greg. It was personal. If the stories were true, back when they collected their first handful of Changed, Greg and his wife had been showing a group of potential investors in their Los Angeles facility what the subjects could do when one of them broke free and tried to escape. The subject had been listed as having a minor ability over electricity. As it turned out, that was nowhere near the full extent of the subject's ability. The spark the agents had seen was the flashpoint. When angered, the subject had the ability to set the very air on fire. None of the investors had survived that day. Most of the agents in the office were killed, and unfortunately, Buckner's wife had died three days later from third-degree burns to most of her body. That was the event that had crystalized Buckner's resolve to have control over the Changed, and if it were true, Trevor knew it was what was guiding Buckner's decisions going forward.

"We have come to a turning point in our company model, my friends." Greg began and pulled up some new slides on the screen behind him. "The Changed are public knowledge now, and we must work to contain their threat both privately and publicly. We cannot afford to have these creatures gain public support and become a legally protected group. I have seen many good men and women die at their hands. I know – they can talk as if they are one of us, but that is part of what makes them so dangerous. When we get upset, we don't level a city block or turn people into ice statues. The general public doesn't realize that many of these things are the equivalent of explosives in the hands of emotional children. Some of them need strong supervision and discipline, and some of them just need to be destroyed. It is too much power in random, undisciplined hands. Ultimately, they are a threat to national security, and I will see them all dead before I will allow them to trick our country into thinking that they are lambs, instead of wolves.

"So here is my proposed game plan for dealing with our current situation… First, I have heard that Senator Lucy Edwards has drafted a bill called the People with Abilities Act that will start to give protections to the Changed. This must be stopped before it ever sees the inside of a committee. Given that her cousin and best friend growing up have both come out as Changed, I don't see us talking her out of it as a possible way of changing her mind.

"My fallback plan is to let public opinion change her mind. We will have some of our resource agents carry out a couple of atrocities and see if that changes her mind. If not, we will have one of them remove her from office, permanently. One of the Changed killing a congressman should definitely get rid of that bill."

Trevor's mouth was open wide as he stared at Greg. He could not believe he had just heard him propose the murder a sitting senator. He had been a soldier most of his adult life and knew that the penalty for doing that was death – possibly by firing squad.

"Do you have a problem with that, Mr. Merrola?" Buckner asked him in no uncertain tone.

Trevor realized he was drawing attention and immediately set his face back to neutral. "Absolutely not Sir. I live to serve."

"That's right, Merrola. You live because I allow it." Buckner glared at the now blank look on Merrola's face. "I am not suggesting we start with removing the Senator, but I am saying that if this Senator is the key to keeping America safe from a domestic threat, then so be it.

"Furthermore, if we find that there are a large number of Senators that are of the same opinion, we should have one of our Resource Agents check to make sure that no one is using mind control on them. If there is, we may have to take more drastic steps so that the military takes over control of the government. If they have to take over because of people with abilities, I know that they will contact our organization to help them."

He paused for a moment to collect his thoughts and the silence in the room was palpable. Buckner had just floated an idea that would possibly result in his group essentially running the country. Trevor glanced at Neuwin and saw a slight curl of a smile at the corner of his mouth. Yes. This group had higher ambitions than Trevor had ever thought possible.

"Moving along… The second part of my plan involves the do-gooders from the Commons. We can't afford to have that group of poster children with abilities team up with anyone else – especially Senator Edwards. We will need to lure them back out into the open. Once that is done, we tag them and follow them back to wherever it is they live. Then, we can strike when they are not ready. I understand that these things have been living in the wild for a long time now and will not come peacefully, so I propose we take all of the agents and resources agents that we have on the East Coast and wipe this little community of abominations off the face of the planet."

"Whoa! Sir!" Interjected James immediately. "We have no idea who they have in their group, how many there are, what they are capable of or what they have for defenses! An assault on a group like that has worse odds than flipping a coin, even if we think we have them severely outnumbered – and we don't even know if that's the case!"

Greg glared at James, but he didn't flinch. "Agent Neuwin. We haven't been gathering the Changed for the past decade to have them retire on a company pension!" He snapped. "Find their hole and use our resources to rip them out of it. There is no way they are living around a populated place, or they would have been discovered by now, so you don't even have to worry about a lot of people seeing it happen. You can be as noisy as you want."

James shook his head. "I just want to go on record as saying this has the potential to blow up in our faces. From a military standpoint, it is rash and not well planned."

"In that case, Agent Neuwin, I would even authorize you to throw everything we have in the Lower Reaches of this facility at them. I think we both know what the outcome would be then." Greg finished smugly. "Now, how about a board vote on this course of action?"

"Wait, there really is a Lower Reaches?" Trevor asked innocently.

James just shook his head and looked at the floor while no one bothered to answer him.

"He is not thinking!" James fumed in the elevator on the way down to the fifth floor where his office was. "The Lower Reaches could be just as big a problem for us to control as they are for them in a battle!"

"What is down there?" Trevor asked curiously.

James stopped his fuming and hit the stop button on the elevator. "First off, the knowledge that the Lower Reaches even exists is so highly classified that if you had stumbled upon proof of its existence on your own, I would be sending a cleanup crew after you myself, so let me be clear: this is for your ears only. Anyone you tell is dead. Understood?"

Trevor nodded.

"You know the Strength Level Score that KIA gives to Changed?"

Another nod.

"You know that on paper we have only had a couple of dozen subjects that were over a 5 in the entire time we have been collecting them, and none of those were a 10?"

"Yes."

"That is a lie. The Lower Reaches are like the Radio City Music Hall of freaks. They are all chart toppers. We have 18 others that are eights and nines and one that is a ten locked up down there. The missions to capture or kill high-level subjects were always kept secret. We would send out two dozen of our resource agents and if we could subdue them, we would. If we couldn't… Well, digging the grave was easier than bringing them back here awake. These missions were real nail-biters. The entire trip back we would be worrying that they would wake up from their sedation. Then, we had to use a special tunnel to get them into the Lower Reaches without being seen. Of course, if all that worked out, we still had to figure out what to do with them once we got them back here.

How do you cage someone that can walk through walls? How do you keep them contained but also allow them to be studied by our scientists?"

"Studied?" Trevor asked. "Why do you want to study them?"

"Haven't you figured it out yet?" James snapped. "We are going to figure out what changed them and then we are going to apply the strongest of their powers to our most loyal soldiers. Our men will be unstoppable, and we will be able to charge whatever we want for our services."

"Who would you trust to give that kind of power?"

"To be honest, there aren't many people I would be willing to make indestructible. Maybe just a handful in the whole company – and nobody, that wasn't already loyal and vested in what we are doing here." James answered.

"Greg seems to really hate the Changed. Does he know about this plan?"

"Of course. It was his plan." James replied. "He knows that the Changed are not going away. He knows that a smart man gets ahead of the curve and if at the end of the day the only Changed left alive are ones that would take a bullet for him, I think he would be okay with that. Not to mention that getting rich out of the deal is a sweet bonus as well." He chuckled. "All we need to do is be able to harness the power of those already in the basement."

Trevor whistled. "I still can't believe you guys caught a ten." He shook his head. "I have to know – How? How can you contain something that powerful?" Trevor asked still trying to wrap his head around all that he had just learned.

"He is drugged. Heavily. And even with that, it is touch and go sometimes."

"Why take the risk of him getting loose here? Why not just kill him?"

"We tried. We gave him enough paralytics and sedation drugs to kill everyone within ten New York City blocks. He stopped breathing for three days. We were just about to bury him when he started to wake up. We barely got the IV back in him in time." James said shaking his head.

"My God…" Trevor breathed.

"No, Trevor. Even God doesn't go down there." With that announcement, James hit the button for the elevator to resume its trip.

CHAPTER 19

Time to Head Home

i

Tom had woken up stiff and aching the following day in a cot in an abandoned tent at the far end of the cluster of tents that belonged to the self-proclaimed "Cursed Ones." On the only other piece of furniture in the tent, there was a note with a white ribbon around it. Tom got up and walked to the small end table and picked up the note. He sat back down on the cot, slipped the ribbon off the letter and began to read it.

Dear Tom,

I am sorry that I hit you with my stun blast, but sometimes when I am very angry, these abilities have a mind of their own. I have been a wreck about not being able to save you for months now, then I pour out my heart to a guy that seems to want to listen, and I find out it's you! I felt betrayed and happy and pissed all at the same time. I thought you liked me in school, but how can I trust you or think that I mattered to you if you didn't even tell me you survived all this time. I obviously didn't matter enough for that basic courtesy. Okay, enough of this emotional crap. I have other news for you...

While you were "sleeping" the council finished up last night. They appreciate what you did and would like you to feel welcome to come and go as you please. However, they are not looking to have the public's first impression of them be pitched battles in their public parks, so they are not going to pursue The Wall at this time. They are going to keep their heads down and hope that no one will find them for a while. When things calm down, they will give making friends with the Normals another try. They have used this strategy several times over the last 100 years, and so far, so good.

Be well,
Reagan

PS. Please do not try to talk to me again. I need space.

Tom slid the letter into his pants pocket and stood up. *Yup. I really do suck with women. I have to be the only guy on the planet that could lose a woman he never had.* Feeling utterly defeated, he looked at his watch and found midmorning was closing in fast. He quickly released his restraints on his ability to conceal his identity again and left the tent in search of Leaf. After ten minutes of asking around for him, Tom found him in a field of flowers at the northernmost end of the valley.

He was standing on a knoll that gave him a good view of the field. Tom flew closer and noticed Leaf was actually standing and swaying with his eyes closed and his hands held up and out. Tom dropped to the ground and slowly approached his new friend as he tried to figure out what was happening.

It took a few seconds before he noticed it. Six feet in front of Leaf was a small sapling that seemed to be swaying in the same rhythm as Leaf. Even more interestingly, the sapling could be seen growing by the minute. Tom had seen this talent by Leaf before but had never seen him apply it so slowly and deliberately.

"Did you need me, Storm?" Leaf asked in his low rumbling voice as he continued to sway with his eyes closed.

"I just wanted to thank you and the Cursed Ones for your hospitality," Tom replied.

At this, Leaf chuckled. "Ghost Touch told us that you had retired for the evening… I stopped by the guest quarters and found you asleep. I am not sure what transpired between you two, but I am not so clueless that I couldn't sense the aftereffects of her talent. I will not embarrass either of us by asking what happened, but I hope it will not be a problem in the future?"

Tom was immediately uncomfortable. "No. It will not be an issue."

Leaf sighed. "That's good. She is what you might call an 'apprentice' here. She is learning our ways and has expressed a desire to swear the oath and become one of our people. It is a process that can take a few months to a couple of years…"

"I see. I would not interfere."

"That is good, Storm." Leaf breathed as the rhythm of his swaying changed slightly.

Tom watched with interest as the plant mimicked the change. "May I ask what it is you are doing with this plant? I have never seen one dance like that."

"Of course." Leaf smiled. "My talent isn't just making things grow fast. My ability is a profound connection to the planet and the ability to 'encourage' plant and animals to take on new attributes. This little beauty is my most amazing creation yet."

"Really? How so?"

Leaf stopped swaying and looked at Tom. "This little plant can grab carbon dioxide from the atmosphere with its leaves. It then transfers the gas to its deep, deep roots where it creates a carbon dioxide rich paste and excretes it."

Tom's eyes widened as he realized the real-world application of such a plant. "You mean this plant has the ability to…"

"Reverse global warming?" Leaf finished. "Yes. If I can get this plant to be seed bearing, it could completely fix what humans have done to this planet with regards to releasing greenhouse gasses into the atmosphere."

"That's amazing!" Tom marveled.

"Yes. This field is my lab. Here I design the nature-friendly solutions to the issues facing the planet. I even designed a fungus that eats radiation. Imagine what a few handfuls of those spores could do if you sprinkled them on spent reactor fuel!"

Tom looked around at the various plants growing with new found respect.

"It seems I have two things I am working toward in this life. Without a doubt I want people with abilities to be accepted and not to have to live in hiding. However, even more than that, my core motivation is to protect the planet from the horrible things that humans are doing to it, for I can feel every death of every plant and animal. Some days, it is almost too much to bear."

As Tom watched him work with the plant, he finally was able to feel how truly ancient and powerful the quiet man was. "I'm sorry," was all he could think to say.

Leaf looked over and chuckled again. "I believe you are my friend, and I appreciate that."

"You know that right now, I am working on the threat that The Wall poses, but you have my word that I will work to help you as best I can, and once I have resolved my issues with them, I hope you will let me help you with your quest to fix the damage we have done."

Leaf stopped and looked at Tom. "That would be most agreeable my friend." He smiled.

"I wish I could stay and talk more about this, but I need to get back home and make contact with my brother again." His face became somber. "I was forced to leave him, and I have been worried for him every day since. This meeting with Ghost Touch has just confirmed that I can't just assume that things went well when I left."

"Worried?" Leaf asked. "Why is that? Is he in danger?"

"Yes and no," Tom replied. "He has a really bad case of epilepsy, and I worry that he may be having seizures with no one around to help him."

"You are a good man, Storm. I can tell." He clapped Tom on the back. "I will share your worry as friends do." He offered, again slipping into his older way of talking.

Tom smiled back. "I appreciate that." Then looking around at the flowers a little more, "I still can't believe the things you can do! Would It be okay if I brought my brother here if I can get him to visit me? He would love it." He asked as he leaned over to smell one of the fluorescent yellow flowers.

"STOP!" Leaf yelled just before Tom sniffed the flower. Tom froze, not daring to move, before slowly standing back up with his hands up in the air in the universal "don't hurt me" sign.

"Sorry for raising my voice, but that is a flower that I made for our medics. It replaces the medicines of the Normals. It is a sedative and paralytic. One breath of that, and you will not be getting up for another day - unless you are exposed to the purple flowers with the red centers on the other side of the field. That flower would counter the 'yellow sleepers'"

Tom smiled. "Thank you, my friend." He chuckled. "No offense taken. I think I will head out now before I end up a lawn ornament."

Leaf joined in the laugh and then shook Tom's hand. "Be well my friend."

"Will do. See you soon." Tom confirmed as he gently floated up into the air above the field, before turning north and vanishing in a blur of blue light.

ii

It took only a week for Tom to set up the Craigslist advertisement and to get an email response from Levi. Tom replied right away with a response that included a phone number to the disposable "burner" phone that he had purchased from a kiosk in the local mall.

Within a week, they had everything set up. Levi had suddenly developed a love for money and had applied to a summer internship at a financial consulting firm called *Limitless Returns* in Boston. *Limitless Returns* just happened to be owned by one Thomas Ripley.

It didn't take Levi too many hours of pleading to get his mother's approval once she saw the elaborate web site for the company that clearly defined the entire paid internship as well as the testimonials of all the previous internship winners.

In truth, the site and site history had all been set up overnight by Tom and Iyr, and although it had cost Tom a princely fortune in bitcoin to get it done on short notice, the prospect of finally seeing his brother again made it completely worth it.

CHAPTER 20

Levi's Internship

i

A week later, found Tom waiting at the bus station for his brother to step off the mega bus from Burlington.

"Tom!!" He thought he could barely hear his brother calling out over the constant roar of people yelling and the rumble of the bus engines.

TOM!! Levi's voice screamed in Tom's head.

"Jesus! Levi! Tom shouted back. *Stop screaming. I hear you.*

Oh cool! Tom could hear the relief in Levi's thoughts. *Meet me at the coffee shop on the corner.*

Got it Tom affirmed and walked away from all the milling people to wait by the less crowded coffee shop.

When he finally saw Levi's beaming face appear through the crowd, he ran over and hugged him. "Good to see you, bro!"

"You too." Tom agreed. "I have so much to tell you."

"I can't wait." Levi started chuckling. "I wish I could say the same, but you know how things go back home. Nothing changes and even that happens slowly."

Tom smiled. "Okay, I have a taxi waiting for us around the corner. You aren't going to believe where I am staying…"

ii

Five minutes later, Tom was opening the front door to his apartment and motioning for Levi to go in ahead of him. Levi looked around in wonder. "Are you kidding me? This place is bigger than our whole house!"

Tom looked at the floor. "I wanted a nice place for us to stay."

"Oh, hell yeah!" Levi agreed. "Tell me it at least has two bedrooms."

"Actually, it has three and a loft where I have my home gym." Tom smiled again at his brother.

"Sweet!" He called over his shoulder as he headed down the hallway. "Which bedroom is mine?"

"Second door on the left." Tom hollered back.

A minute later Levi was back in the living room "No way!" He was shaking his head. "How Tom? How did you pay for all this? My bedroom has a view of Boston Harbor! Please tell me you aren't a supervillain that robbed a bank or something!"

Tom started to laugh. "Why don't you have a seat, I'll grab us some sodas, and I can get you all caught up."

"Sounds like a plan," Levi said as he landed heavily on the couch.

Tom flopped beside him and spent the next hour explaining everything. He spoke of the trip to Boston, his time in the homeless shelter, learning to turn coal into diamonds and even his recent encounters with the Cursed Ones and Reagan in the Settlement.

"I knew it!" Levi had burst out when Tom told him that Reagan was Ghost Touch. "I knew she was hiding something when she was talking to us. I just figured it was some mushy crap about you that I would never be able to un-hear, so I blocked it out."

Tom laughed, then frowned. "Well, you won't have to worry about that anymore. She is so angry at me for not telling her I was alive that I doubt she will ever speak to me again."

Levi sighed. "Don't sweat it, Romeo. I'm sure she can't be that mad."

"She knocked me out for almost twelve hours."

"Oh. Yeah. In that case, you may want to avoid her when we go to the forest tomorrow." Levi suggested.

"Huh?" Tom stopped. "I didn't say we were going to go see them tomorrow."

"Dude! Are you kidding me?!?" Levi protested. "You just told me that there is a secret society of superpowered heroes living in a magical woodland hideout. Do you think that there is anything in the entire world that I would like to see more?"

"Oh." Tom frowned. "Yeah, I guess not."

"Okay," Levi confirmed excitedly as he got up off the couch and headed toward the bathroom. "We should get ready for bed. I want to head out tomorrow morning, after breakfast." He paused before disappearing down the hall. "I still can't believe this place. It's so nice… Oh! I almost forgot to tell you, mom was playing the lottery three months ago and won a little over a hundred thousand dollars! She did some needed repairs on the house and car, but most of it just allowed her not to have to do overtime." Tom smiled, and Levi immediately looked stunned. "You aren't surprised!" He exclaimed. "Oh my God, Tom! That was you! You gave her the money."

"Stop reading my mind, Levi." Tom snapped.

His brother ran up and hugged him. "I thought that was too good to be true. We have never won anything before. Thank you, bro! That helped mom so much!"

Tom blushed. "Yeah. Don't mention it."

Levi was still smiling.

"No, really. Don't ever mention it to anyone." Tom clarified.

"Duh! Who am I gonna tell that my dead brother used his magical abilities to squeeze coal into diamonds, pawn them and hacked together a fake online lottery in order to anonymously give money to his mother who has had her memories of him erased…?"

Tom started to laugh. "I guess when you put it that way, my secret is pretty safe. Now, go get ready for bed. If we are going to the forest, we are both going to need a good night's sleep."

Tom smiled as he watched him go. Levi certainly hadn't changed much.

iii

"Oh my God, dude!" Levi exclaimed looking up from his breakfast to see his brother return from a five-mile run. "You are ripped!!" Tom looked down and noticed that the sweat was causing his running shirt to cling to him and that all of the workouts and martial arts training over the past five months had transformed his average build into that of an athlete. "You said you've been working out, but man!"

"Oh, shut up," Tom muttered. "You said back in Vermont we needed to up our game. We are up against soldiers and superhumans. We need every advantage we can get."

"Hey!" Levi jumped up from the table and blocked Tom from heading down the hall to the bathroom to shower. "I wasn't mocking you. I was just surprised. I don't think you know how much you have changed in such a short time."

"I'm the same person that you knew, Levi." Tom disagreed.

"No, you aren't." He persisted. "You are more confident. You have resources, and you have learned a ton of stuff."

"Maybe." Tom reluctantly agreed. "But we are still good, right?"

Levi smiled. "Of course."

"Cool. Then get dressed because the cab will be here to bring us to Boston Public Gardens in forty-five minutes." Tom playfully pushed past him.

"Why there? I thought we were going to the Cursed Forest?"

"We are, but I can't fly out of the same place every time," Tom explained as he paused outside the bathroom door. "If I develop a pattern of where I leave, or worse, I get sloppy and leave from here; someone will eventually catch on and figure out that I am Storm."

"Dude! Genius." Levi beamed.

Tom blushed. "Thanks bro, but speaking of protecting identities… You will find a large handkerchief, a pair of sunglasses and a hat in the top part of the closet in a box. You will need to put them on when we get to the Gardens so that no one can recognize you. Also, when we get there, you will need to call me Storm. What would you like to be called?"

"Oh man! You pop this on me now?!" Levi complained instantly assuming a perplexed expression. "Choosing a superhero name is a big step for me!"

Tom laughed. "Sorry, man. I never thought of how much work you put into mine. I'll help you."

Levi winced. "That's okay. I will work on it. I remember your attempts at names, and I would prefer a cool one."

Tom groaned. "Har. Har. Okay. Whatever. Just be ready for the cab" and disappeared into the bathroom.

iv

Tom and Levi walked into Boston Public Gardens and immediately headed toward the area with the most shrubs and trees.

"So how do we do this?" Levi asked looking around.

"Well, from what I have seen, the trick is to avoid cameras, not look conspicuous and to make the change quickly." Tom began. "I scouted this place days ago. The far corner has the perfect spot: no cameras and minimal foot traffic. If I am so unnoteworthy that people don't notice me, no one will be able to describe me after I change and fly out of here, so when I say 'go' throw on the glasses and hat. The handkerchief goes over your nose and mouth as quickly as possible. Then, I will go blue, and we are out of here. Cool?"

"Got it." Levi agreed and continued his casual stroll without looking at Tom.

A couple of minutes later, a man that seemed to be made of a shifting blue light could be seen rising above the treetops holding the hand of another man that seemed to float along beside him surrounded by a cloud of the same blue light. They hovered briefly as if gathering their bearings before turning into a blue blur that streaked West out of the city. Several miles out in the countryside, the blur arced south then seemed to split and head off in several different directions before they all seemed to disappear.

"That was so COOL!" was the first thing out of Levi's mouth as he and Tom gently landed in the middle of a large clearing in the woods.

"Thanks."

"I have to ask: why did we take that big arc to get down here? I mean, the sun was behind us for almost twenty minutes before it came back to be on our left… Did we take the scenic route? And what was with the fireworks display?"

"I'm surprised you didn't just pick the thought out of my head," Tom said teasingly to Levi and punched him in the arm.

"You said you hated that, or I would have."

"And you listened? Huh." Tom joked. Then, more seriously "I did that because if I head south every time I come here, people will start wondering what is south of Boston that is so interesting."

"Ooohhh."

"That's also kinda the reason that I shot balls of blue energy in multiple directions before we landed. If someone were tracking me from a satellite, they would have a tough time figuring out which of those landings was me." Tom explained. "Even with these precautions, I am not going to be able to fly here all the time. Eventually, someone will track me and get close enough that they will find the Cursed Ones." He sighed. "I really need to set up an alternate way of getting around."

"How about buying a car, genius?" Levi asked dripping sarcasm.

"Thomas Ripley doesn't have a license." Tom countered.

"Have Iyr make you one," Levi suggested. "Hell, have him make you fake insurance and registration too." He chuckled.

"No…" Tom countered. "The more things you fake, the easier it is to get caught. That is one of the first rules of hacking. A small footprint is better, but we could limit his assistance to just getting me the license."

"So, do that then."

"Yeah. Not a bad idea." Tom agreed and started walking toward the tree line. They hadn't entered the woods yet when they felt a slightly nauseating feeling and then realized they were walking back out into the clearing.

"Woah!" Exclaimed Levi. "Did you feel that?"

"Yes, I felt it, but did you notice what happened?" Tom asked.

Levi just stared at him.

"We are pointed the wrong way. We were walking that way." Tom stressed pointing to the trees that were now behind them.

"What the heck…" Levi asked.

"Either someone is playing tricks, or we have hit one of the Cursed Ones' defenses," Tom replied. "Well… let's see them redirect this." In a blink, he jumped into the air and shot back toward the tree line. Levi watched as Tom's blue form seemed to disappear into an invisible wall. There was a split second where he was simply gone. Then, a hundred yards to the right of where he disappeared, Tom came flying back out again and crashed into a stand of small birch trees, smashing them to pieces.

The blue streak of glowing plasma slowed, turned around and came back to land next to Levi. "Well, that didn't go as planned." Muttered Tom as he brushed himself off. "What did you see from here?"

"Dude, you just disappeared when you hit that barrier. It was like, bam! Gone! Then, poof! You popped out way over there!" Levi explained pointing.

"Well, this sucks," Tom muttered. "I know that the Settlement is a little over a mile that way." He pointed past the invisible wall.

"Why did we land so far away, anyway?" Levi asked. "Why not land in it?"

"I set down here because I couldn't remember exactly where it was when we were flying. It's weird though because as soon as I landed, I could remember."

"More shenanigans," Levi grumbled. "Somebody - or more likely somebodies are - playing with… Whoa!!" Levi exclaimed in midsentence. Then pointing, he asked, "What is that?!"

At first, Tom didn't see anything, but as he continued to look, something moved in the woods. It had a slow lumbering gait, and after a few seconds, Tom realized he was watching Leaf walking toward them. "Oh man! You had me nervous for a second." Tom told Levi. "That's just Leaf."

"Just Leaf…" Levi repeated staring at the large man as he made his way toward the brothers. "I wish you could see him the way I do, bro. The mental energy around him is intense! I could see the cloud around him way before I could see him. I've never seen anything like it. He must be incredibly powerful."

"Really?" Tom asked, but before Levi could answer.

"Hail, Storm," Leaf called from several yards off, waving his hand.

"Hi, Leaf!" Tom replied waving back.

Once Leaf was in the clearing and not stepping around plants, his long strides carried him to Tom and Levi quicker than either of them thought possible.

"Sorry about the confusion." Leaf apologized looking slightly embarrassed. "Normally, our telepaths warn us when one of our own are attempting to reach us so that we lower our defenses. However, all the stuff that is in the news this morning is stirring up so much emotion that floating around that they can hardly see out of the village - much less all the way to the far side of the valley!"

"News?" Tom asked. "We didn't catch the news this morning. What's going on?"

Leaf made a face. "It's Buckner again, but before we get into all of that, let's get you boys past the barriers and start our walk back to the Settlement." He gestured for the brothers to start walking back toward the invisible barrier. "Don't worry. This time, you will not be turned about. Once you started testing Floyd's displacement bubble defense, he became aware of you and notified me. I told him and the disorienters to stand down and hurried out here."

"We appreciate that you did." Tom smiled as he and Levi started walking in the direction that Leaf had come out of the woods. They were relieved to find that they didn't get spun around while Leaf was walking with them.

As they passed into the woods, Leaf looked over his shoulder and got a good look at Levi. "You must be Storm's brother. It is a pleasure to meet you...?"

"You can call me Wave."

Tom raised an eyebrow at Levi who immediately gave him the "shut up - we can talk about it later" look.

"Nice to meet you, Wave." Leaf finished his thought.

"Same here," Levi replied.

Then, Leaf made eye contact with Tom before resuming his story. "As for the news, all the major news stations were given footage of us defending ourselves against the agents in the Commons last week. Then, they interviewed Buckner, and he said that his men were there to provide security for us when we attacked his team. He even claims that we killed two of his men. Of course, the video is masterfully edited to cast our people and you in the worst possible light."

Tom seethed at hearing how the Cursed and he had been played by The Wall. "So, what are we going to do about it?"

Leaf glanced back at Tom and Levi again and smiled. "The council is in session right now trying to decide that. My suggestion was to allow me to do a television interview alone. That way, I am the only one at risk, and we can talk to a much larger number of people all at once."

"You *have* to know this propaganda by Buckner is a trap. He is baiting you into…" Levi started out and then trailed off as the small group stepped out of the thick undergrowth in the woods and into the golden light of the Settlement. "Hoooly sh…"

"Wave!" Tom interrupted. "I take it you approve?"

"Approve?!" Levi replied barely able to contain his excitement. "This place! It's…" He couldn't get any more out before he stumbled and fell forward, hitting the ground as his body was wracked with spasms.

It had been too much: the flight, meeting Leaf and now this. Levi's excitement was triggering his epilepsy, and a seizure had become inevitable. Levi's body quickly twitched faster and faster until he became as ridged as cement.

Tom dropped to Levi's side to briefly check him out before turning back to Leaf. "I need to put him somewhere he can be safe with anti-seizure medications, this is going to be a big one."

Leaf looked concerned. "Our medics have a tent."

"Perfect," Tom replied and touched Levi's shoulder causing him to float into the air on a pillow of blue light. "Please take us there."

CHAPTER 21

The Council Makes a Decision

i

It didn't take long before Levi was safely delivered to the medical tent. "I should stay here in case he is confused when he wakes up." Tom was telling Leaf as the larger man tried to convince him to give the medics some space to work.

"I am not saying that isn't a nice idea normally, but our medics have stuff available to them that, at the very least, will keep your brother relaxed as he comes out of his seizure." Tom looked unconvinced. "Storm, we also could use your voice at the council hall. I will have someone come get us as soon as he stirs."

"Okay, but as soon as he begins to wake, I will need to come back. No matter what goes on with the council."

"Agreed." Leaf then ducked his head into the medical tent and left very clear instructions with the medics before returning to Tom and beginning the walk toward the council tent.

"It is the decision of the council that we shall not risk more lives at this time on correcting how the Normals view us." Announced Ward Nims and the gavel fell with a loud boom signaling the end of the open discussion.

Tom and Leaf had arrived an hour ago, and both had argued that allowing Buckner's voice to be the only one that gets heard would surely lead to public opinion eventually being swayed in favor of treating the Changed as less than human. The opposition to that position was a group that believed that coming out of hiding would inevitably lead to more of their members being captured if not worse. It was an unacceptable risk, according to them, and in the end, there was no changing their minds. The council ruled four to three that none of the Cursed Ones would be allowed to speak publicly. The group would hide and wait for all the negative press to die down. Then, in a few years, they would try again.

"I will not let this stand." Leaf fumed as he and Tom passed out of the council tent. "The elders want to stick their heads in the sand and pray that these men will forget about people with abilities over time, but I have lived longer than all of them put together, and that is not what will happen."

"I have to say; I share your opinion. Buckner is not the type to let this all go with a shrug. His second in command, James, has hunted and killed our kind to make us do what he wants for years now. No, to people like Greg, our abilities mean power and money, and he will never give up either."

"True. No laws are governing how we are treated right now but given time and no opposition, that will change. You watch - if we run from our duty to be ambassadors of our people, they will come up with laws where we are less than human and need to be registered, like weapons or worse - locked up or exterminated! They will organize searches for us and devise ways to test for us - all in the name of protecting "the public." They will do their best to find every last one of us. As for the ones they don't find, someday they will come forth from their hiding places and find that the world has already made up its mind on them. That group will be easy prey. The Normals will do to us like the US did to Japanese-Americans during World War Two or like the Germans did to the Jews. They will do it out of fear or out of a false sense of duty if Buckner takes that approach next…"

"So, what can we do to prevent it?" Tom asked.

"I hate to say this, but I am willing to risk my place here in this community by violating the council's decision, in order to speak out against these false protectors of humanity. I will not stand by and be one of those that allowed the Germans to sell the Mein Kampf in my neighborhood without a fight. As long as I draw breath, I will not let them gain that kind of foothold unopposed. I will –"

But before he could say what he was going to do Levi, Reagan and another man came into view on the main path through the Settlement.

"Hey!" Tom shouted in amazement. He ran ahead and hugged his brother.

Levi hugged him back briefly before pushing him back slightly. "Sheez, man. You're acting as if you've never seen me have a seizure before!"

"But that was a Grand Mal seizure, and it was a bad one! You are normally down for days, not hours when that happens." Tom explained his concern.

"Yeah, but I have never had Doc, here, working on me," Levi said gesturing to the short, older man that was with him.

"Doc?" Tom asked.

"Hi." The man said as he shook hands with Tom. "Doc is what the younger ones call me. I suspect I remind them of the dwarf in that Disney story." He said with a chuckle.

"Oh." Tom smiled. "Well, it's a pleasure to meet you."

"He's a lot more than a fairytale character knockoff." Reagan asserted for her humble friend. "He is a board-certified intensivist that happens to be additionally gifted with the ability to heal most injuries or ailments with a touch of his hand."

"You are too kind, Ghost." Doc thanked her. "But I do have limits. I can only heal non-mortal injuries, and even that takes time."

"Limits or not, what you did was amazing!" Levi objected. "T – er… Storm…" He caught himself before he leaked his brother's identity. "Storm, you wouldn't believe what he can do! My seizure only lasted an hour, and when it ended, the headache was gone within minutes instead of days! He is a miracle worker."

"Levi! I hardly can perform miracles! If I could, you wouldn't have epilepsy at all anymore, but I can't cure that condition. It's just another ability like you reading thoughts or Storm being able to move things. It has its limits." Doc objected.

"Levi?" Tom asked, looking hard at his brother. "So, you decided to share your identity?" He couldn't believe how reckless his brother was being.

"I didn't have much choice! There are so many telepaths in this place that as soon as I was unconscious, and my defenses dropped, they couldn't help but hear my thoughts. Honestly, I was broadcasting them so loud; I'm surprised you couldn't hear them."

"So, does that mean that they know who I am also?" Tom asked, nervous for those around him.

"Actually, Tom, I watch the news, and as soon as I saw you with Levi, I figured out who you are." Doc interrupted.

Tom was stunned, but Levi immediately turned and faced Doc. "No. You *don't* know his real identity." Levi said forcefully as soon as he had eye contact.

Doc's face took on a daydreaming quality. "No. I don't know his real identity." He repeated.

"Woah!" Tom grabbed Levi by the shoulder and spun him around to face him. "What are you doing?" Leaf and Reagan both took a step back.

Levi relaxed. "I'm fixing the problem. You said you don't want people to know your identity and he found out… I made him forget."

"You can't do that!" Reagan objected.

"It is forbidden here." Leaf agreed. "Will Breakers need council permission to use their skill on others in our community."

Tom held up a hand silencing his friends. "Have you been using that ability since the incident with the Agent tracking you to the bridge?"

"I have only used it a couple of times, and that was to help mom. She kept finding small things that implied she had another child and it was causing her stress." Levi explained. "I couldn't give her back her memories, but I could give her a little nudge to not worry about it. At least she would have peace of mind and not be driving herself nuts wondering about it."

"You made her forget more stuff about me?" Tom was incredulous.

"I couldn't make her remember you, and the twins were sloppy when they erased you. They didn't clean up things. Like, remember your eighth-grade band trip to Maine? She remembered going. She didn't remember why she would go to Maine and listen to a grade school concert. It doesn't make sense without you being in the picture."

"I understand. That must have been hard to do." Tom sighed heavily. "Anything else?"

"Well… people recognized you from the news video and wanted to talk to mom about it, so they needed to be made to not recognize the person in the video as you."

"How many people, Levi?" Tom pressed.

Levi cringed as he replied "Maybe thirty or so…"

Tom sighed heavily. Then, looking at Doc's still dazed face. "Well… wake him up, and Levi…?"

"Yes?" Levi replied looking back over his shoulder at Tom.

"Give the man back his memories."

Levi sighed and shrugged. "Okay. It's your identity…" With that, Levi restored Doc's knowledge of Tom's identity and woke him up from the trance-like state.

Doc blinked and looked around at everyone staring at him. "Was I saying something?" He asked.

"You said you knew who almost everyone here is anyway." Leaf offered.

Doc looked slightly confused. "Yeah, well, there is no reason to worry about me telling anyone. I put identities in the same secret category as doctor-patient privilege. No one will hear it from me." He smiled at Tom and Levi.

"We appreciate that, Doc," Tom commented.

"Not a problem." Then, he looked at his watch. "I do have some other things that need attending to in the medical tent though." And a few minutes later, he was quickly walking back toward the medical tent while occasionally shaking his head as if to clear it.

iii

The group walked back to the guest tent at the far end of the Settlement. Once inside, Leaf rummaged through one of his bags and pulled out four painted rocks. He placed each one in a corner of the tent.

"There. Now we can talk without being overheard." He rumbled.

"What do you mean? We may be on the outskirts, but this is only a tent. People can still hear us from the outside." Levi questioned.

"No. Those stones have been spelled by our wizard. A very talented man named Bendati. He is an Ashtaari mystic, and I can assure you – as long as you stay within the square made by the rocks, no one will hear you." Leaf explained.

"That is soooo cool!" Levi marveled. "No one will hear us outside the tent? Even if I screamed?"

"What is all the secrecy about anyway?" Reagan asked brushing off Levi's question.

"I aim to violate the council's decision and do a television interview to get our side of the story heard by a larger number of Normals." Leaf stated in a calm voice.

Reagan was stunned. "But you'll be exiled!" She protested.

"I realize that my child, but as I was saying to Storm, some things that are worth the price."

"Damn it, old man, it's more than that!" She snapped. "This is exactly what The Wall is hoping will happen. They want us to come out in the open. They want us to fight amongst ourselves. The last encounter in the Commons was a setup to get damning footage of us and capture some of us. Who is to say that this wouldn't be the same, or worse?" Tom could see the anguish in her face and her voice.

"I'm sorry, but you will not change my mind on this matter." And in his words, all could hear the finality of his conviction. Silence followed as everyone absorbed the implications of defying the council.

"I'll go with you." Tom broke the silence.

"What?" Reagan was immediately furious.

"I know I can't change your mind, and I think this is a trap," Tom explained. "But I understand your reasoning. And if you are willing to put your life on the line to speak out in favor of people like us, then the least I can do is help protect you."

Levi immediately chimed in, "I'm in too."

Reagan glared at the three men. After a few seconds, she shook her head and smiled. "Well, if there is going to be a fight against those jerks, I'd hate to miss it."

CHAPTER **22**

Trouble at the TV Station

i

The group knew that stealth was going to be the key to getting through the interview in one piece. The following afternoon, Leaf lead the small group north through the valley and out of the protected area. The path was long and winding and abruptly ended in what appeared to be a wall of impassable vegetation. Leaf raised his hands and moved them to the sides as if parting curtains. Tom, Levi, and Reagan watched in amazement as the bushes and trees parted and moved aside.

"That's incredible!" Levi breathed. "Look! The roots are literally sliding through the dirt so that the tree can move out of his way!"

"Yeah." Reagan agreed. "No matter how many times he does that, I still get chills."

The process only took a minute or two, but by the time he was done, the bus was revealed with a clear path to the dirt road out of the Valley of the Cursed. They all piled on, and Reagan jumped in the driver's seat. "Now, let's just all pray that old faithful here will start." She said turning the key. The old bus protested loudly twice before the diesel engine revved into life.

Leaf smiled.

"And we are off to make history." Reagan crowed as the bus started down the dirt road.

ii

A little over an hour later, the bus could be found parked outside a television station in Needham Heights, just outside of Boston. In the seats of the bus there were three people sitting motionless, as if asleep.

"How can we help you?" The receptionist at the front desk asked of the large man standing in the lobby.

"Hi. Yes. I would like to do an interview." Leaf replied in his rumbling base voice.

"Okay. Do you have an appointment with someone?" She asked bringing up the schedules page on her computer.

"No." Leaf replied. "But I think that one of your reporters would like to talk to me."

The receptionist looked up from her computer and smirked at him. "And why would they want to talk to you, sir?"

"Because I can do this." Leaf replied and gestured to the small jade plant on her desk. The little plant shuddered slightly before growing two inches as the receptionist looked on wide-eyed.

"Uh. Um. Yeah." She stammered. "I. Uh. Hmm." Then, she regained her professional baring and dialed a number. "Hi. Tammy, this is Abigail in reception. I have someone here you need to meet." She paused listening to her headset. "No. You really need to come see this to believe it." She clicked a button ending the call. "She will be right down."

"Thank you," He replied. *That's it.* Leaf sent out the thought. *Now we wait.*

Okay. Came Levi's voice in his head.

I still don't like the fact that you are having us stay in the bus! Tom's voice was clear in all their minds. *If you need us quickly, it will take time to get to you.*

I understand that. Leaf replied to the group. *But like I said on the ride here, it looks a lot less threatening when there is only one of us going in for the interview and that person isn't wearing a mask.*

We still don't have to like it, Leaf. Reagan admonished him.

Objection noted.

Just then a tall blond woman dressed in a grey business suit came down the staircase behind the reception desk and out into the lobby. She walked up to Abigail, and they conferred briefly before she walked over to Leaf and held out her hand. "Tammy Orton, glad to meet you."

"People call me Leaf." He shook her hand. "It's a pleasure to meet you as well."

Tammy looked down at his hand and noticed the rough, bark-like skin. She smiled, knowing that this was going to be a great interview. "Would you care to come upstairs? We can discuss that interview you would like."

"Of course." Leaf replied and followed her up the stairs and back through a series of halls to one of the studio rooms with a large news desk in it. "Could you wait here a moment while I get someone to run the cameras?" She asked politely gesturing to one of the chairs next to the news desk.

"Certainly." Leaf replied. The woman smiled and quickly walked back out in the hall.

Okay. We are on the second floor in the far-right corner of the building from your position. There are no windows. He looked around the room. *This is obviously one of the rooms in which they film the news.*

Thanks, came Reagan's reply. *I am moving the bus to the rear parking lot now so that we are closer.*

Hey, just so that you know, I sense something. Levi's voice was loud in all their minds. *There are too many people thinking to narrow it down at this distance, but something is off. People are edgy, but I can't say they are up to anything in particular. Stay alert.*

Leaf didn't have time to reply as the door to the hall opened, and Tammy and a male coworker came into the room. He went straight for the lighting and cameras area, and she walked back over the news desk.

"While he works on getting the lighting and sound checks done, why don't you tell me why you would like an interview?" She asked.

"I represent a large number of people that have abilities, and I think that we are not being accurately represented in the news media." Leaf replied.

"How so?"

"Well, we have been watching the news, and all we see is Greg Buckner telling people that we are dangerous and that simply isn't true."

"Interesting." She mused. "I think that you were right to come here. Your side would make a great story." She turned to the cameraman and got his attention. "Frank are you ready?"

"One minute." He hollered back.

"Give me a three count when we are good."

"Okay." He held up three fingers. "Cameras are rolling in three, two…" As his last finger came down, he pointed at Tammy.

"This is ABC news with Tammy Orton, and with me tonight is a man with abilities. His friends call him Leaf, and he has told me that he and others like him are not a threat to anyone." She announced, setting the scene for the audience before turning to face Leaf. "It's a pleasure to meet you Leaf."

"Likewise." Leaf rumbled as he looked back and forth from the camera to Tammy.

"So, you say that you are not a threat like people in the media are painting you. You say that one of the top government consultants on the matter, CEO of Max Protection, Greg Buckner, is wrong in his assessment. How do you view yourself?"

Leaf looked at the camera when he answered. "I view us as a peaceful group of people that have traits that are not common. Just having that trait does not mean that you are any more dangerous than anyone else. Mr. Buckner wants people to believe that just because we have someone that can shoot lightning from his hands that this individual is going to go on a killing spree, and that is just not true. It is as absurd as saying that just because you own a gun that you are going to go shoot up a school! The lack of reasoning is laughable."

"Okay. But one of the things that Greg is suggesting is that each of the Changed is registered with the government so that we know what the extent of their powers are and where that person is. I mean – we register guns because they can hurt us, so doesn't it make sense that we register the Changed?"

WARNING! Levi screamed in Leaf's head. *She knows Buckner and is friends with him! She is using his term for people with abilities!*

Leaf shrugged off Levi's warning. "But Tammy, we are not faceless, lifeless guns, we are human beings with rights. If you believe that the ability to do harm should result in being on some registry list somewhere, then everyone in the world would need to be on it. People can look up how to make powerful explosives on the internet with supplies you could purchase from your local hardware stores! It is not the gun or the ability that makes a person dangerous. It is their intent."

Get out of there! Tom's voice yelled in Leaf's head. *There are SUVs coming up the –*

That was as far as the warning got before Tom's voice went silent in Leaf's head. He knew that he should get up and leave, but he also knew that this was the one chance he had to get their side heard, and he wasn't willing to let that go easily.

"I hear what you are saying Leaf, but we have footage of the Changed, including you, attacking police in the Boston Commons. It looked like your intent was to harm the police." Tammy was saying.

"The footage you were shown was very carefully edited." Leaf countered remaining calm. "Mr. Buckner wanted it to look like we attacked them, but it was his agents and not the police that were wearing those uniforms, and they attacked us first. We told them we had a permit for a peaceful rally and they opened fire. Did we fight back? Yes. We defended ourselves, and I am sure that looked frightening to someone who has never seen someone with abilities use them but let me assure you, we did not do anything more than stall their attack long enough for most of our people to escape."

"So, the reports of the deaths of two of those police officers?"

"I can promise you; they did not die at our hands." Leaf vowed. Just then the back door of the studio opened, and men in black suits started rushing into the room.

"Here he is," Tammy announced jumping to her feet and pointing at Leaf. "It took you long enough to get here."

Leaf stood up as the room filled with agents. He looked around. There were no plants or animals on which he could use his ability. He sighed and put his hands up in the air as every gun was pointed at him. "I am not armed. No need to get excited." He cautioned them.

Just then, there was an enormous crash, and part of the ceiling in the newsroom came crashing down. For a moment, there was chaos as dust and debris rained down on the room, and the agents struggled to understand what was happening. Then, blue and white lights started flashing, and the agents started dropping.

"Storm! Ghost Touch!" Shouted Leaf. "I'm here." He dropped to the ground behind the news desk as a volley of bullets ripped past him and into the wall. "Careful! Those are real bullets."

Reagan ran straight for Leaf's voice hitting agents with full strength blasts as she went. It didn't take her long to get to him with Tom only a second behind her, deflecting bullets as he went.

Once they were close to the table, Leaf stood up and waved them over. Reagan saw him first and ran toward him. Tom was trying to be everywhere at once as he blocked hundreds of rounds that were flying at them.

It was at that moment that Reagan saw it. There was a dark figure cloaked in black standing near Leaf. The roof had been blown open, and sunlight poured in, but around the dark figure, shadows seemed to gather making it hard to distinguish his features. The figure looked right at Reagan and began to move toward her. She froze as if ice-cold water had been thrown in her face. The figure leaned on its staff and reached a bone-like hand toward her. She spun around knowing what was coming next and saw the agent with his rifle aimed right at her head. He was less than thirty feet away. There was no way he would miss. He squeezed the trigger, and the rifle bucked as the bullet left the barrel. Then, a bright blue streak struck her knocking her to the floor. The figure in black was so close that the hem of his cloak brushed her leg as he stood over her. The sensation of his touch was like icy hooks digging into her. She sucked in a breath and passed out.

Pain exploded in Tom's chest as the bullet took him just below the collar bone and came out his back. He had seen the agent aiming at Reagan and had poured all his power into getting to her fast enough to push her out of the way. He had succeeded but at a cost. She hit the floor, the bullet hit him, and his momentum threw him clean into the far wall. There he struggled to rise to his feet when he heard the screaming start.

"Agents of evil! I am Hellbound, and I am here to deliver you to judgment." Her voice was filled with rage, and Tom watched as a woman in a black cloak and red suit with the symbol of a pitchfork on the chest came walking into the room. If the fact that she was walking straight into the agent's bullets weren't unnerving enough, the fact that her eyes were on fire as she threw flaming bolts from her hands definitely would have shaken Tom. Each agent that was hit by the flames screamed as he seemed to sink through the floor.

Tom rose to his feet and staggered over to Leaf and Reagan. "Come on!" He shouted over the screams. "You're going to have to carry her. We have to get out of here." Leaf reached down to pick her up, when a bullet hit him high in the stomach, sending him falling back into the chairs behind the desk.

Hellbound made it to where Tom and the others were standing and looked at them. Tom quickly raised a protective barrier between them as the woman raised one flaming hand. Then, she paused. "You are not a part of their evil." She lowered her hand.

Tom looked back to where Leaf had one hand pressed to his stomach as he struggled to get back to his feet.

Then, the building shook, and Tom heard a voice he had not heard since his battle in Vermont coming from the front portion of the building. "All right ya lil punks. Where are ya?"

Tom's blood went cold. "That's Maul!" He yelled to the others. "This guy is virtually unstoppable."

Leaf raised an eyebrow. "Unstoppable?"

"When I fought him in Vermont, I certainly couldn't get him to stop." Tom clarified with a thin attempt at humor. "And I asked him really nicely."

"Okay." Leaf said lifting Reagan as if she were a doll and heading for the door.

Tom made eye contact with Hellbound. "You are welcome to come with us." He offered. "You do not want to fight what's coming."

"Oh, but that is where you are wrong, my good-hearted friend." She almost cooed. "That creature is what drew me to this place. The greater the evil, the stronger the need is for me."

Tom stopped and shot a flaming ball of blue plasma at an agent that was aiming at Hellbound knocking him into the cameras. "It's your call, but we would welcome you."

Her eyes widened in surprise. "You have my interest, mortal. For now." She blasted another agent. "I will follow."

Tom! It was Levi's voice in Tom's head again.

Jesus Levi. It was one guy blocking your ability. Did it really take you this long to knock him out? Tom snapped as he held pressure on his shoulder. *We've been flying blind here with no communications.*

Sorry, bro! Levi called back. *It wasn't the one guy that was tough. It was the six agents guarding him that made it take so long. Let's not forget that I can't crack someone on the head with my abilities, okay?*

Okay. Where are you now? Tom sent out the question.

I just made it back to the bus. We are still parked in the rear corner. Why?

Maul is here, Tom explained. *We need to leave here now!* He turned to face the wall in the hallway. If he gauged it correctly, the bus should be through this wall and one floor down. *Tell me where to punch the whole.* Tom sent the thought to his brother.

Three more feet to your left or you will hit the bus, was Levi's assessment.

Tom was getting dizzy from blood loss but gathered his will and pushed hard against the wall. Bricks and mortar blew outward leaving a gaping hole in the wall just ahead of where the bus was parked. Tom staggered and leaned heavily against one of the walls.

"I will hold them back," Hellbound called back over her shoulder as she released blast after blast of fire.

"Put me down!" Reagan had come to and was struggling to get down from Leaf's shoulder. Once he had set her down in the hallway, he turned and raised his hands out the window. In seconds, a small spindly maple had grown thirty feet right up past the hole in the second floor. The tree notably had no branches aside from those at the top.

Leaf looked back and called to the group "Follow me." He quickly wrapped his arms around the tree and slid down like it was a fireman's pole.

As he stepped away from the pole and waved for them to follow him, Reagan got her first look at the blood soaking Leaf's shirt. "Both of you?" She demanded of Tom pointing to Leaf's wound.

Tom gave a weak smile, but Reagan was already moving. She was hurt, and now she was furious. Her power was rooted in her emotions, and now she felt that power building as she channeled all the anger, pain and fear she felt into that power. As she walked toward the doorway, she no longer thought like Reagan. She was Ghost Touch, and her touch was almost lethal.

Hellbound took one look at Reagan and backed out of her way as she stood in the doorway to the newsroom. All the agents were firing at her and Maul had just made it to the back of the room. She should have been cut down countless times, but the bullets seemed to bend in their flight to just miss her. Drawing on her power, she glowed a dazzling white as she held her ground and continued to build up her energy. As the glow became too bright to look at, she raised her hands before her and finally, released it. The blast blew the cameras, furniture, and agents into the far wall, smashing lights and cracking the walls. All of the agents in front of the blast on the second floor were knocked unconscious for days, and even Maul staggered backward and was driven to one knee.

When it was over, Reagan sagged slightly from the effort. She turned back to see Tom finally lose consciousness and fall out of the hole in the wall. Her heart went up in her throat, and she bolted toward the opening just in time to see a gust of wind catch Tom's falling form and gently lower him to the ground.

Looking around she saw the woman with fire in her eyes making a gesture with her hands as Tom's limp form changed direction on its bed of air to float toward the bus.

Reagan breathed a sigh of relief. She knew that her blast had bought them a few seconds. Only the agents upstairs were unconscious. All the ones downstairs and the ones that were still arriving would be in pursuit in no time. She quickly dove out the opening and slid down the tree. Knowing that seconds counted, she hit the ground running and made for the bus. She was barely inside when the first bullets hit the side of the bus.

"Come on boys! We need to get out of here now!" She urged as she looked up and saw Levi trying to get the bus started.

"I'm trying, but this piece of crap won't start." He gave up trying to turn the key. "It's possible I may have flooded it." He confessed. "Sorry. I've just never driven a diesel before." Then, much quieter. "Or… anything else for that matter."

"Then why did you try to drive the bus?" Reagan yelled at him.

"Because you guys kept saying hurry and everyone was hurt or late getting here!"

"Is this really how you people got here?" Hellbound asked in disbelief as she surveyed the ancient bus.

"And who the hell are you?" Reagan snapped.

"Hellbound is how I am known on this plane." She replied coolly.

Reagan hadn't waited for the answer. She made her way to the driver's seat after Levi had got up and was now trying to start the bus as the sound of bullets hitting the bus wall became a steady rapping.

Levi had come back to the seat his brother was in and was looking critically at him. "I think he just passed out."

"That's good." Reagan acknowledged. "Any idea how we are going to get this thing moving?"

Levi sighed. Then he deliberately reached over and pressed on the bullet wound in Tom's shoulder. Tom screamed and sat up in the seat. "Don't do that!" He yelled punching his brother in the arm.

Levi fell off his seat and into the aisle. "Deal, but first could you make the bus go now before we all get killed?"

Tom glanced around and then, wincing in pain made his way up to stand next to Reagan at the front of the bus. "Get ready. You are going to steer and use the breaks. I'll make us go." With that, he placed his hand on the dashboard of the bus, and the cloud of bright blue plasma around his body seemed to expand to surround the bus.

As soon as the bus was completely encased, it began to move forward through the parking lot. Reagan looked around in amazement. The engine still wasn't on, but here was the bus moving faster than it had ever done as Tom poured his energy into it.

Behind them, the agents jumped into their SUVs and attempted to keep up, but in minutes the bus was going faster than any other vehicle was capable of matching. Reagan and Tom weaved the bus in and out of traffic, first heading east toward downtown Boston before taking Route 3 and hugging the shoreline south all the way to Ellisville. It was there, just as they were about to hook back west toward the Cursed Forest that Tom's strength finally gave out. The blue cloud that was encompassing the bus flickered and went out as Tom sagged to the floor.

"Tom!" Reagan shouted in alarm as she struggled to pull the coasting bus to the side of the road.

"I'm o-o-okay." He stuttered as he sank from his hands and knees to a laying position on the floor. Levi was already beside him.

"Oh damn." Was all Levi could say as he looked at the amount of blood Tom had lost.

After getting the bus to a stop, Reagan asked, "What can I do?"

"Drive the bus," Levi replied absently.

"We can't keep going." Reagan snapped looking from where Leaf lay unconscious to Levi. "They are both going to die if we keep going." Then, she leaned in closer to Tom and put her hands around his neck, pressing her head to his chest. "Why did you do that anyway?" She scolded Tom.

"He would have killed you, Reagan." He answered quietly. "I didn't think you'd mind that much." He smiled dryly.

She pulled back and looked at his face earnestly. "Tom, I was only mad that you didn't tell me because I thought we had the beginning of a connection and I really liked that feeling. You were the first person that has ever made me feel like they liked me for me."

"I did, and still do."

"You two are a friggin mess." Levi cut in abruptly. "I would love for you two to have a meaningful talk about your feelings, so that I could finally puke up my breakfast which has been dying to come out since I first saw all this blood, but first, I gotta ask, can we get this piece of crap moving again before Tom or Leaf dies?"

"I agree with the sarcastic one." Hellbound chimed in, "Death will come for them if we linger."

"Fine." Reagan turned beat red and jumped back into the driver's seat. She turned the key a couple of times, and the engine reluctantly came to life. "What hospital is closest?"

"No." Leaf objected as his head bobbed with his ragged breathing.

"Wow. I thought you were out cold." Levi said, surprised.

"No hospitals." Leaf repeated. "We must make haste to the valley. Doc and his team can help us."

"Leaf, I don't think you can make it that far," Levi said as he got a better look at the man and instinctively knew that the older man was in far more immediate danger than his brother was.

"I would rather die myself than go to a hospital and have all of us caught or killed. Our group is in no condition for a rematch." He explained. Then, he reached down and slid his finger into the hole made by the bullet.

"What are you doing?!" Levi yelled in disgust.

Leaf's face registered no pain as he dug around. Then removed his finger with the small metal projectile attached to it. "I knew it." Leaf commented holding the bullet up for all to see. "Look." The bullet he held up was slowly blinking.

"What is that?" Reagan asked.

"A tracking bullet," Hellbound commented. "They aim to find your home and kill you all." She said casually. "It's what I would do."

"You are one scary b…" Levi began.

"Reagan." Tom interrupted. "We need to hurry."

She nodded as she quickly pulled the bus back on the road and made for the valley at the bus's best possible speed.

Hellbound casually walked over and plucked the bullet from Leaf's hand. She stared at it until it burst into flame and melted into a lump on the bus floor.

The bus shuddered as the engine came to a stop in the field at the far north end of the valley. It was as close as anyone could park to the Settlement.

The bus doors were thrown open, and the group came out as quickly as they could. Reagan had her arm around Tom to help support him, and Levi and Hellbound both supported Leaf as he half staggered across the uneven ground in the woods.

"Anything yet?" Reagan called back to Levi.

"No. We must still be too far away for me to reach any of the telepaths at the Settlement." He replied as he slid closer to Leaf to take on more of his weight.

"Okay. Crap. Everybody keep moving." She encouraged, not knowing how much further Tom and her mentor would last.

It was Leaf that gave out first. They had passed the clearing that marked the opening to the valley only a few minutes before when he stumbled, and his legs finally gave out. Even with two people to support him, his weight dragged both Levi and Hellbound to the ground.

"Ghost Touch!" Levi shouted to her and Tom who were already a dozen yards ahead. She looked back and nodded her head before turning Tom around to walk back to where Leaf lay.

I think I can hear others now! Levi announced to everyone in the party.

"Then tell them to haul it here!" Reagan urged sinking to the ground with Tom.

Levi stood and turned facing south. *We need help here! We have injured people that are dying!* His mental voice was a roar through the woods that sent all the animals running and flying away from the small group on the ground.

Tom crawled over to Leaf and got a good look at his appearance. The shallow breathing and pale skin spoke volumes. "Stay with us Leaf!" He encouraged the ancient man.

"I don't think that is possible, Tom." Leaf weakly huffed out between gasps. "I didn't make it home, but it looks like we made it to my lab."

Tom glanced around the clearing and realized it was the same field that marked the northern tip of the Valley of the Cursed. It was the same place where Tom had talked to Leaf a little over a week ago. Twenty feet away was the carbon burying plant with which Leaf had been dancing. Tom smiled at his friend. "Help should be here any second."

"It will not be soon enough my friend, but before I go, I would like to give you a gift."

"You don't need to do that." Tom deferred. "Save your strength."

"It is a gift I made last week and I have just been waiting for it to bear fruit." He whispered. "In the southeastern corner of this field, is a plant that has a fruit growing on it that is yellow and orange and about the size of a lemon. It will cure your brother of his affliction." As he talked, he pulled himself up to a kneeling position.

"His epilepsy?" Tom asked unable to believe what he was hearing. "It will cure his epilepsy?"

"Yes." Leaf confirmed. "You, he and Reagan are some of the best of what humanity has to offer. I want you to find good people like you and bring them to the Green Mountain National Forrest in Vermont. They will be safe there." As the others watched, Leaf's skin darkened and seemed to become even more like tree bark.

"What do you mean safe there?" Reagan asked, not understanding.

"I have known for a long time that a change has been waiting to happen inside of me. I was scared of what that change would do to me.

Now, it seems that I will need to hibernate to heal from this wound. When I come out of that hibernation, I will be different, and far, far more powerful than I have ever been." Small tendrils slid out of Leaf's legs and into the ground.

"That's a good thing though, right?" Levi asked trying to understand why Leaf seemed so worried about healing.

"Transformations like this alter personalities too. I may not remember you. I may only have my convictions, and lately, those convictions have been a wave of growing anger over how humans are destroying the planet. My worry is that when I wake, I will no longer be a friend of humanity." More and more of his body took on the aspect of a tree as he quietly explained his situation to his friends.

"What are you saying? That the only people you won't attack will be those in the forest in Vermont?" Levi asked, incredulous.

A second bullet emerged from the hole in Leaf's abdomen and the bleeding finally stopped. "I am saying: beware humanity. They have abused this planet for too long. They have taken the Earth's lack of response for a free pass to continue their abusive behavior. When I awaken, I suspect there will be no more free passes. Even now, I can feel the certainty of this outcome solidifying."

He paused and looked at the worry and sorrow on the faces of his friends. "I am sorry, my friends. I don't want this, but it is what is happening to me. One cannot fight the pure will and force of nature itself." And with that, the change that had been creeping up his abdomen to his chest, finally overtook his face ending any further conversation.

"Holy crap!" Levi breathed. "That doesn't sound good."

"No. It doesn't." Hellbound agreed, reaching over and picking up the second bullet. She looked at it briefly before melting it.

Reagan was wiping tears from her eyes. "It is a worry for another time. We need to get Tom to the medic tent." She immediately tried pulling Tom up to his feet, just to find that he no longer had the strength to rise.

Just then, the air next to them shimmered, and a group of four men stepped out of that space and into the clearing.

"Doc!" Levi yelled, recognizing the short man in the front of the group. "Here! We need you here." He indicated to where his brother lay.

The small group ran forward, and Doc placed his hand on his brother's shoulder. "I sense nothing major has been hit. This will take time, but you will be fine." Then, he looked around. "Where is Leaf? I figured he would be with you."

Tom, Reagan, and Levi all looked down still trying to cope with the pain of losing their friend.

"He got shot and turned into that tree," Hellbound announced bluntly pointing at the tree. Reagan glared at her. "What?" She snapped at the younger girl as her eyes flared with fire.

Reagan huffed at her and turned her back as she refocused on Tom. It was less than a handful of minutes before the group had Tom laying on a green wool blanket. Doc touched one of the symbols written in marker on the blanket, and it gently rose to hip level, neatly lifting Tom in a magical litter.

"Woah!" Levi breathed in amazement. "How did you do that?"

"I didn't do anything." Doc corrected. "This is a gift from the sorcerer, Bendati."

"I gotta meet this guy," Levi muttered under his breath as they all started walking toward the disturbance in the air. "Oh! Hold up a sec." He exclaimed, snapping his fingers as he ran off to the edge of the clearing. There he looked around and found the tree he was looking for – the one with the orange and yellow fruit. Reverently, he plucked a fruit from the tree and clasped it to his chest as he ran back to rejoin the group. "This little baby is mine."

CHAPTER 23

The Council Convenes Again

i

It was a full two days later before the council convened again, and Tom had spent most of the time in the medic tent being healed by Doc and his team. The first night was a haze of pain and people checking in on him. Levi, oddly, was not among them. Although, the following morning, Levi was sitting on his cot when Tom woke up.

"How are you doing?" He asked immediately.

"I'm sore, but I think I'll live," Tom answered as he took stock of how severe his pain was.

"That's good." Levi looked relieved. "Sorry I didn't come sooner, but I got hungry on the walk back here and had a couple of bites of Leaf's fruit he made for me."

Tom was all ears, but they both just looked at each other.

"Well come on little brother!" Tom finally caved in first. "Don't make me beat it out of ya."

Levi laughed. "Well… Let's just say no one is going to go after one of those for the taste." He shuddered. "It's like a mixture of raw fish and peanut butter." He made a retching motion. "I almost puked it up twice."

Tom smiled. "And…?"

Levi shrugged. "And I stopped taking my meds, so we will see in a day or so." Then he looked closer at Tom. "You are looking pretty pale bro. I think I'm gonna get Doc back…"

But Tom didn't hear the rest. He had already passed out.

Over the next two days, Tom improved, and during that time, Levi was his eyes and ears in the Settlement. From what he learned, the entire group was in disarray once word of Leaf's fate had reached the close-knit group. The reactions ranged from shock and disbelief to profound sadness and rage.

In the morning, on the day of the meeting, Reagan walked into the medic tent and found Tom resting in the cot that had become his bed for the past three days.

"So how is your patient doing, Doc?" She asked.

"He is doing quite well. He heals remarkably fast." He commented as he took stock of the cupboards in the tent. "If he would stop bursting into blue flames every time I inspected his wound though, it would help." He commented absently.

Reagan chuckled and walked over to Tom's cot. She sat down on the edge of it and looked down at his sleeping form. "What am I going to do with you?" She murmured under her breath.

"Go out on a date with me." He whispered back as he cracked one eye open.

"You're awake?" She playfully shoved him.

"Ow!" He winced immediately guarding his shoulder.

"Oh man!" She pulled back as her hands went to cover her mouth. "I am so sorry."

Tom groaned and sat up in his cot. "It's okay." He shook his head a bit to clear the last cobwebs of sleep. "I am almost all healed now. Just achy."

She smiled at him as she absently brushed some of his hair from his face.

"So…?" He asked.

"So, what?"

"So, would you like to go out on a date?" Tom asked, exasperated.

"Well, look at you." She smiled at him. "One bullet in the chest and all of a sudden he finds the nerve to ask me out!" She shook her head. "If I had known that was all it took, I would have shot you in our sophomore year."

Tom groaned. "You aren't making this any easier."

"Easy and me are two words that should never be used together." She chided him. "But to answer your question, yes. I would love to go on a date with you." She stood up and tossed his shirt at him. "Now, get dressed. Ward Nims wanted me to make sure that you attended the council meeting, and it starts in five minutes."

Tom sighed, pulled on the shirt and got up to go. "I guess I can't spend the whole week in bed."

"Aren't you forgetting something?" Reagan asked as he walked toward the opening of the tent.

Tom looked back at her quizzically.

"Your identity, genius." She reminded him. "Aren't you going to go all blue flames?"

Tom frowned. "No. I don't think so. If what Levi says is true about these folks, most of them already either know or suspect who I am. No sense in being insulting by trying to hide it."

"Speaking of your brother, where has he been the past couple of days anyway?"

"He has been waiting to see if he has a seizure now that he has taken Leaf's cure and is off his meds." He smiled at her. "So far, so good." He stopped and faced her. "Of course, you know Levi, he has been checking out the Settlement a bit, but most of his time he has spent in the caves where the telepaths and Will Breakers live," Tom explained.

"They live in caves?" Reagan was taken aback. "I've lived here for almost half a year, and I had no idea."

"From what Levi says, some of them are so powerful that they can't shut out other people's thoughts. The caves act as a natural insulator for them so that they can shut out the voices." Tom explained.

"Huh. You've been stuck in one tent for two days, and you seem to know more than I do." She looked down at the floor.

Tom caught the look. "What's going on? You keep making small talk, but you only come in and check on me for a handful of minutes once a day. Even during that short an amount of time, I can tell there is something wrong. Care to talk about it?"

"I wouldn't even know where to start." She admitted.

"Try starting with our latest adventure. I can tell something happened at the television station that is eating at you."

She smiled at him. "I can't seem to get much by you."

Tom just smiled back and waited.

"So, during the fight, you saw me run toward Leaf and then freeze, right?"

"Yes."

"I froze because there was someone else in the room."

"There were a lot of 'someone elses' in the room." Tom grinned.

"Tom now is not the time to stop listening. You were about to make some serious points for paying attention."

"Sorry."

"Anyway, I was looking at Leaf when I saw this guy wearing a black cloak walking straight toward me. I could sort of see through him. Like he was a shadow or something."

She now had all of Tom's attention.

"As he got closer, I realized that I knew him. I knew he was the Angel of Death and that he was there to collect me." Tom looked stunned as she pressed on. "I knew that he would not be the one to kill me, but something was going to do it. That's why I spun around and looked right at that agent."

"I remember that part." Tom agreed. "I remember thinking it odd that you spun around before he shot you. Like you knew what he was about to do."

"That's because I did know something was going to happen, and I would have died, right there, but you intervened."

She was pacing now. "I was thrown to the floor right next to the figure in black. I was so close, in fact, that the hem of his cloak touched me, and that's what brought it all back."

"Brought what back?"

"My memories the night I died in high school," Reagan answered.

"Like 'post-traumatic stress reliving it' sort of thing?" Tom asked.

"No." She disagreed. "Like I had memories that someone suppressed for me that happened while I was dead that night."

Tom kept quiet and let her get out what she needed to say. "I told you back when we talked on the ledge about that night. I died and couldn't go into the light. Something pulled me back, and then I woke up." Tom nodded. "Well, what I didn't remember is that the Angel of Death was the one that pulled me away from the light!"

"Oh man!"

"Yeah. I was in spirit form with him, and we sat on my bed as he told me about an offer he had for me. He said that his time as the Angel of Death would someday end, and he would need a replacement. He said his replacement would come from one of his apprentices. His apprentices were chosen because they are good people with a strong sense of duty. These people had been spared an untimely death and been granted special powers. If they used those powers wisely, they would be a candidate for his position once it came open. If they were not chosen at that time, they would go back to being normal human beings and live out the rest of their lives as usual. But if they were chosen, they would become the next Angel of Death."

Tom's eyes were almost coming out of his head. "And you elected to possibly become the next Angel of Death?"

"Tom, you forget – I was dying. If I said no, he would have released me, and I would have died right then." She looked in his eyes for understanding. "It wasn't my dream job, but I was fifteen and didn't want to die that night. It seemed like a good way to live a little longer."

He looked into her eyes and saw how much this new information was upsetting her. He pulled her to him and held her. "No. You made the right decision. Just being an apprentice doesn't mean you will become the next Angel." He squeezed her tighter. "And for totally selfish reasons, I am very glad you are alive."

Reagan melted into his arms and squeezed him back. Then, she remembered the time. "Oh! We are going to be late." She said turning away from Tom, so he couldn't see her dabbing the corner of her eye with the back of her hand. "Come on Blue Boy, let's get moving!"

She didn't wait any longer for him and stepped out of the tent.

Tom glanced briefly at Doc who still stood in the far corner of the medic tent busily cleaning a large table they used for procedures before following Reagan outside.

"Good luck with that." Doc chuckled under his breath as they left.

ii

As Tom and Reagan entered the council chambers, people were just settling into their seats. Tom was surprised to see Hellbound sitting in one of the chairs closest to the door. Levi was on the opposite side of the room motioning for them to sit next to him. Tom could see that Hellbound was not the type to get up and move and no one was sitting near her. He gestured for Reagan to sit down next to her, then turned and waved at Levi to get him to come over too. Reluctantly, he did.

Once in his seat next to Tom, Levi caught his brother's eye. *I don't see why you want to sit next to that thing.* He glanced at Hellbound.

Hey! That's not cool. She saved our lives back at the TV station. Tom admonished his brother.

I don't care if she floated down from the sky and solved every problem we will ever have — she is not cool. Levi protested strenuously. *You don't see her the way I do, Tom. Her power is incredible but dark, and it acts like it would lash out on its own if something weren't reigning it in, and as for her mind… Even beginning to touch on her mind is like walking through a blast furnace naked. She is not to be trusted! She is evil.*

She doesn't act it. Tom defended her.

Doesn't act it? Levi was incredulous. *Do you think she sent those agents on vacation in the Bahamas when she hit them with her fire? No. They went somewhere much worse.*

Before the boys could debate any further, Ward Nims struck the gavel and intoned the words that called the council to order. "The Council of the Cursed will now come to order. Let all voices be heard, let the truth be known and let the future be decided." He looked grimly down at Tom and his small group. "It is my understanding that a group from this Settlement violated the will of the council and attempted to be interviewed by the Normals."

There were grunts of ascent from several places throughout the chamber. Reagan stood. "That is true, Sir."

"And you did so knowing that it would mean your exile?" Nims asked.

"We did so because Leaf said he was going to do it even if he had to do it alone. He knew he faced the possibility of exile if he had succeeded, but he said that the council was incorrect in its decision to withdraw from the world of the Normals. He felt that due to his extremely long lifespan he knew such a move would ultimately cost the Cursed Ones their freedom or even their lives, so he was willing to risk it." Reagan turned and made eye contact with those around the room. "He was willing to risk his life to protect yours, and we were willing to risk ours to protect him."

"And in doing so, you will share what would have been his punishment," Nims concluded.

"No!" Several people stood up and started shouting. "Let them speak!" and "What happened out there? Why is Leaf dead?"

Nims pursed his lips in frustration. "So be it. Who wants them to speak?"

A full three-quarters of the room stood and said "Aye."

"Then speak and tell the council what happened," Nims commanded.

Reagan began with how Leaf had experienced propaganda warfare before, how it is possible for a small group of determined people to change the minds of a population against a minority, and how that never ended up well for that minority. She explained how they had planned to do an interview with a television reporter to get their side of the story heard by a more substantial part of the population.

Tom joined her explanation and told about how they had gone to the television studio and how Leaf had gone in alone so that the others would be able to maintain their identity and keep watch for him. When he told how the television reporter had called The Wall, the angry murmuring began in the hall again. But when the story of how many agents there were and how they were shooting real bullets came out, several in the crowd started yelling their opinion. "This is an act of war!" "This cannot go unanswered!"

Tom held up his hand, and the crowd quieted as he resumed his story. He told them of the flight from the television station and the ominous warning in the clearing. At the end of the story, everyone started talking at once. Most of the voices continued to call for revenge on The Wall.

"Order!" Ward Nims yelled, banging his gavel until there was silence in the hall. "In spite of this unfortunate incident, nothing has changed. We knew that bad things would happen if we went head to head with The Wall. That is why we agreed to go to ground not two weeks ago in this very room! Don't you all remember that?"

"But Leaf died!" An older woman in the front row protested.

"After we told him to stay put!" Nims countered. There was a large amount of grumbling, and people shifted in their seats at this. Nims looked around the room and realized that it was a topic that needed to be discussed again. "Fine. If you all want to open this discussion for a second round of debates, I just need someone to make a motion."

"This is pointless," Hellbound announced in a voice that carried throughout the council hall as she stood up.

Nims looked at her as if noticing her for the first time and started to tremble. "Wh-who allowed this abomination into the hall?"

"I do not need your permission to determine where I go, old man. That is my choice alone." Then she turned and looked directly at Tom. "And I am no abomination. No more than any other child born of violence is."

"We know exactly what you are." Came Nims voice from across the chamber. He now stood with his staff in hand and the light on the end of it glowing orange. "You are the product of a demon and a witch. You are a child of two worlds and are accepted by neither. Tell us this, monster: why are you here?"

Hellbound's expression turned sad for a split second before going back to her expressionless norm as she turned back to face Nims. "I am here to help save you all."

Nims laughed out loud. "One of hell's bounty hunters is here to help us? And why should we be willing to ally ourselves with the likes of you?"

"Because Leaf was shot with two tracker bullets. The second one was active all the way to the edge of the clearing at the northern tip of this valley. If The Wall was following it – and you know they were – then they have spent the last two days gathering reconnaissance and satellite photos of this area. I estimate in two more days they will attack this place in force."

At this announcement, there was silence in the chamber. Then Nims spoke. "Why have you waited to tell us this?"

"Because The Wall has some of the most evil men on the planet working for them as well as several low-level demons. Having them attack you is the easiest way to bring them to me so that I can send them back where they belong."

Tom was stunned. She was willing to risk all their lives so she could pursue her prey. He had thought that she wasn't all bad. During their conversations over the last two days, she had told him how the majority of the beings she relocated were demons or creatures too powerful to be held in human jails. Tom had told himself that she was performing a service to the world, but more than that, he had felt like they were starting to establish a friendship… How could she be his friend, but be willing to risk all their lives to get to The Wall?

"Our apologies if we don't allow you to use us as bait." Came a voice from the back of the hall. All eyes turned to see a small man in a black cloak stand up from his seat. The people on either side of him sucked in their breath as if just realizing with whom they had chosen to sit.

"Ashtaari." Hellbound spat the word out and backed away from her friends.

"Hellbound." The man in black greeted her. "You may call me Bendati."

"I will call you several things, but Bendati is not one of them." She quipped.

"I have been watching you for several years now." He told her.

"Years are just the blink of an eye for me."

"Oh, I know. The older your kind gets, the more powerful they become, and you are quite powerful." He smiled.

"Good. Then you know I am powerful enough to know that you are merely a novice in the Arts of the Ashtaari. I can feel your magic. It is strong but untrained. I have ward spells that are capable of blocking anything you might try to throw at me." She smiled. "You won't be able just to wiggle your fingers and make me disappear."

"Oh, I figured you would have wards against my magic. That's why I have Floyd." He smiled back.

"What's a 'Floyd'?" Hellbound looked confused.

An overweight man in a plaid flannel shirt stood up sporting a beard and a baseball cap that read "Normal ain't no fun".

"Meet Floyd." Bendati gestured to the man.

"Bye," Floyd said, and with a gesture and slight popping noise, Hellbound was gone. Everyone in the hall continued to stare at Floyd. "Aw. Don't worry y'all. She's not dead. She's sitting in a field just south of Paris, France. 'Sides, now that I know she ain't welcome, she won't get past my displacement bubble agin."

The room immediately burst into conversations and hollering until Nims was able to get everyone's attention again. "Okay. This makes our discussion about whether Leaf and his team were right or wrong something of a moot point. We can discuss that later – if we survive. At this point, we will have to assume that the hunter was right about the tracker bullet and that we are looking at maybe two days before The Wall can assemble a group to attack us. To assume otherwise, we risk our lives. If it turns out we are wrong, we can always stand down later."

The mood in the room immediately shifted from division to one of unity. "The way I see it, we need to defend this place to the last. We cannot rely on the displacement bubble to keep us safe. Storm and Ghost Touch, you have both been in two encounters with the enemy and so have the greatest breadth of knowledge about them. I want to make you two responsible for the defense of the Settlement. I expect you will need the ability to make decisions quickly over the next few days and you will not be able to come back and check with the council every time you make one. Consider yourself generals with our blessing to make all decisions necessary to defend our people from this threat."

Tom and Reagan looked stunned.

"Do you have any directions for us now?" Nims asked, knowing that he had put them on the spot.

"Um. I guess we will need to talk to everyone to get an inventory on what powers everyone has since those will be our primary weapons." Tom began uncertainly.

Reagan chimed in, "And we will need to talk to members of the Settlements' security team to get a rundown on what our current defenses are."

"I think that we should erect a tent in the green in the middle of the Settlement to act as our command tent." Tom finished.

Nims pointed to a couple of the men in the hall. "Make it happen gentlemen." Then, turning to the rest of the group. "Everyone else: I would like you to call in everyone you know – regardless of if they have abilities – that would be willing to stand with us. It is the only way we stand a chance against them."

CHAPTER 24

Preparations Begin

i

As soon as the council was finished, Tom and Reagan had Levi contact the council's telepaths so that they could announce to all the Cursed Ones that they would be opening a temporary tent in the middle of the Settlement as the command tent. Each member would be expected to drop by the table in front of the tent as soon as possible so that a list could be made of who was capable of what. It was the first step in creating a defensive plan.

Tom and Reagan had been working the table for two hours when there was a loud pop, and fifty yards away from the table a sharply dressed young man with dark greased back hair and a neatly trimmed goatee appeared out of nowhere. He looked slightly startled at first. Then he looked around and saw the table and walked over to Tom. "Hi. I am John Muertos. Bendati told me to register here." He explained.

"It's a pleasure to meet you." Tom greeted him shaking his hand. "I'm Tom."

"Hey. I understand the first step is we are letting you know what we can do?" He asked.

"Yes. Please."

"Okay. I can take emotional energy and turn it into electrical energy." He explained.

Tom looked at him blankly.

"So, if you get pissed at me, I can shoot lightning from my hands." He clarified. "I imagine that will come in useful since everyone here is angry already about Leaf and they are getting anxious about the upcoming fight. I can already feel the power starting to build." He held up his hands, and sparks shot out connecting his fingertips.

"Do you have any weaknesses or important points we should know about?" Tom asked as he quickly wrote down John's power.

"Yeah. If I build up too much and don't release it, I might explode."

Tom jumped. "Explode? How do you know that? I mean… It seems like something you could only learn once."

John frowned at him then shrugged. "Yeah. My twin brother had the same power, and now he is a pile of ash I buried in my back yard."

"Oh. I'm sorry." Tom apologized.

"No worries. You are just doing your job."

"I appreciate your understanding. I believe the others have opened a sleeping structure for the new people coming into town. It's down by the council tent."

"No need, my friend. I used to live here. I still have a place a little further back in the woods." John flashed a quick grin and walked off toward the trees as the next person in line stepped up.

"Hi. My name is Trebuchet, or you can just call me Trey." He said extending his hand.

"Like the catapult?" Tom asked shaking his hand.

The stranger with blonde curly hair and a quick smile grinned at Tom. "Exactly."

"And what is your talent?" Tom asked after writing down his name.

"The faster I go, the more indestructible I become." He declared.

Tom looked at him and waited.

"If I run as fast as I can, a bullet will not puncture my skin, but if I am going sixty-five miles an hour in a car, I become so molecularly dense that I could drive into a brick wall and I would be fine." He explained.

"Okay. Do you have any weaknesses or important points for us to know?" Tom asked.

"Yeah. When I am standing still, I might as well have no powers at all."

"That's okay, Trey. Several people have already registered that don't have any abilities at all. They are just going to help us any way they can." Tom explained.

"Cool." He smiled. "Glad I can help." He said as he moved off toward the sleeping structure.

The next man in line stepped up and very meekly mumbled something from under his hoodie.

"I'm sorry." Tom stopped him and leaned in closer to the small, thin man. "What did you say?"

He worked his hood down to reveal a pale face with mousy brown hair. "Hi. They call me Captain Livid" he squeaked with an asthmatic wheeze.

"You're kidding…"

And so, the morning went, with person after person lining up to tell about their powers. Some of the registrants walked up to the table and some popped into existence a few feet from the tent. All of them were willing to defend the community, most in tears after finding out about the loss of Leaf. By noon, Tom and Reagan had collected dozens of names and had even recruited a couple of volunteers to take their place so that they could go back into the command tent and work on strategy.

ii

"This is crazy, Tom!" Reagan was complaining. "If Hellbound is right, there is no way we are going to be ready to defend this place in time!"

"I was thinking about that as we were taking notes this morning and I have a few thoughts." He replied scribbling in a notebook.

"And?"

"And, the way I see it is this… First, we have no real confirmation when or if The Wall will be attacking us. We need that confirmation. Second, we need to prepare our defenses. Third, we need to make sure that this doesn't come back to bite us with more bad publicity, and finally, we need to make sure that this doesn't happen again by doing something about The Wall."

"Jesus, Tom!" Levi scoffed from his chair in the corner of the tent. "You were supposed to simplify things, not add to the to-do list."

"The 'lil feller is right." A heavy-set man agreed. "We barely have enough folks to defend ourselves, and you're tellin' us to send some of 'em off to run errands?"

Tom turned to face the bearded man. "Who are you again?"

"I'm Floyd. The security feller you wanted to talk to." He replied dryly.

"Oh," Tom remembered him from the council hall that morning. "Sorry, Floyd. There has been a lot on my plate, lately."

"Don't sweat it, son. My feelin's are perty hard to break." He said patting Tom on the shoulder. "Now, let's have that plan."

"Okay. Here are my thoughts. I am going to reach out to a resource of mine and see if he can't comb the dark web to see if and when The Wall is gathering its forces to attack us. That should give us the answer we need without committing additional resources from here.

"We also need to get the name of every member that can scramble electronic devices. We do not want anyone able to videotape this fight and play it for the news to make us look bad. They have done that to us twice already. We do not need a third time. Since this scrambling will take out all our cell phones and other communication devices, we will need to employ the telepaths to keep us all in contact with each other. We need to send someone to their caves and get them up here."

"I just called them." Levi interrupted and then paused looking at the ceiling. "They are on their way."

"Good." Tom smiled. "We will also need to get in touch with the government and see if they will do anything about Buckner's private militia."

Everyone started talking at once.

"We don't have time to start making phone calls to the FBI to see who in that organization we can trust." Reagan's voice pointed out as she shouted above the rest.

"I don't propose doing that," Tom explained. "When I was searching around the dark web, I found a bunch of old contracts between The Wall and the FBI. They are years old, but there used to be a connection there. I don't know how close they still are, so I propose we go higher than that. I want like to make contact with the director of homeland security, Lance Thornton."

Floyd let out a low whistle. "You don't go small do ya, boy?"

"We aren't going to survive if we don't go for the throat. We need a high-ranking person on our side." He paced the room. "We need to show the world what The Wall has been doing, and we need to wipe out their organization."

"Woah!" Levi protested. "Wipe out?"

"In the end, we need the law on our side," Tom explained. "If we can collect proof of what they have done to us, we will surely have that support. Then we can think of it like a game of capture the flag. We capture as many as we can of their top people, we destroy any data stores of information on what we can do, and we cripple their fighting ability. That should show the rest of their satellite offices that we are not to be messed with and their organization should collapse."

"That's a little on the wishful thinking side," Floyd said dubiously.

"Maybe." Tom agreed. "But it's a start."

"It's a start if we survive their attack here." Reagan countered.

Tom sighed. "That will be the most difficult part of all. We need to take this list of powers and analyze them to see how we can make the best use of each one of them." He turned to Reagan. "Leaf told me on my first walk through this place that one of the tents belonged to a group of Gypsies that could occasionally get strong feelings about what was going to happen in the future. What do you think about asking them to come here and help us work on a battle strategy? If they get any hints, we can use them to our advantage."

"Sounds like a good idea to me." Reagan agreed watching Tom pick up his backpack and sling it over his shoulder. "Where are you off to?" She asked.

"I need to contact my internet resource, and I need to touch base with Lance Thornton. I will be back by nightfall or not at all." Tom explained as he released the restraints on his power and burst into blue light. Turning to Levi "Keep listening for my return. I want you to be able to tell Floyd to lower the bubble, so I don't get stuck outside our defenses."

Reagan was stunned. "You are leaving the defensive strategy to me?"

"I can't think of anyone better." Tom smiled at her, slipped from the tent and shot into the air.

"He, he, he…" She sputtered.

"Hasn't learned anything about women." Levi finished.

iii

Tom's first stop was at his house. As soon as he connected to the web and pulled up the chat program, Iyr immediately popped online.

▶ Where have you been!?

◊ I was busy.

▶ Hanging with your new friends at the Settlement?

◊ How do you know about them?

▶ Tsk. Tsk. Tsk. Someday you will figure out that there are no secrets from me.

◊ Then, why ask where I have been?

▶ Because I couldn't track you guys after your bus disappeared in the woods and I was concerned that you might be dead.

◊ You care about me?

Tom was surprised at the uncharacteristic show of compassion.

► As long as you pay me to care. Computers aren't cheap you know.

Ahhh. That made more sense.

◊ Nice.

► So, what was the goal at the television station anyway?

◊ We tried to get an interview on TV about people with abilities not being monsters. You know – counterpropaganda stuff. Why do you ask?

► Let's just say that whatever you did has made them frantic enough to be sloppy online.

◊ I guess that's a good thing. Were you able to learn anything?

► Well, thanks to Greg Buckner going on TV and telling us that he is the new owner of *Max Protection*, I started monitoring them for network traffic too, and their security isn't anywhere near as strict as The Wall. What I found is that they have been transferring massive amounts of people and weapons to Moon Island.

◊ Where is this Moon Island?

► It's a small island at the end of a causeway. Hmm. Maybe that makes it a peninsula and not an island anymore. Oh well. Anyway, it's located on the northwest tip of Quincy Bay, on the Southern end of Boston Harbor. Of interest to us – there are three things on that island. One is an outdoor shooting range for the local police departments. Another is a firefighter training facility, and the third thing is a wastewater treatment plant that hasn't been used in 50 years.

◊ How are any of those interesting?

► The treatment plant has been closed for 50 years, but fifteen years ago it got a facelift. The original two-story cement structure was replaced with a ten-story-tall glass building. On the building permit, they had the nerve to say that the extra space was for 'historical records'! That's a LOT of records about poop! Even more fun is the fact that this 'abandoned building' uses more power than an equivalent sized shopping mall.

◊   So, put it all together, and we have a black site for The Wall?

►   No, we have *the* black site. I think it's their headquarters.

◊   Then, that is where we need to focus our efforts. We will need to get some eyes on this facility so that they can tell us when the agents all head out. That will give us a little over an hour before they arrive at the Cursed Forest and start their attack.

►   Look, if you are thinking of putting boots on or around that island – even if it's just to observe, there are things that you should know. First, Moon Island only has one way on or off from it unless you are going there by boat or flying. That land bridge is *heavily* guarded – and that's just the stuff I can make out with cameras and satellite images. For you, that may not be an issue, but it would be difficult to get a group of any size in there.

►   Second, is the fact that this is the headquarters of a company that gets contracted out by other governments as hired muscle. Their defenses will have defenses, and I can promise you, they will have dozens of people with abilities fighting on their side.

◊   Are you saying it will be impossible to monitor this place or are you just warning us not to attack it?

►   I am saying that this isn't some empty building where you can hide in the neighbor's bushes. They will be on high alert, armed to the teeth and looking for trouble. If you feel the need to spy on them, do it with extreme caution. If you are considering a preemptive strike to cripple their ability to get their troops to you, I would seriously reconsider that. From what data I have been able to gather, they could take out any assault team you could muster without breaking a sweat.

◊   Noted. So, do you have an idea on if they are going to attack, or better yet – when?

►   They are definitely going to attack, and according to internal communications within the sister company, Max Protection, they will have everything they need at Moon Island by the day after tomorrow.

◊   What will they do then?

►   What does any army do after they gather their troops and munitions? They march.

iv

Lance Thornton was running late. In spite of telling his staff that he was not to be bothered unless it was a national emergency, it had still taken him much longer than he had anticipated to get through all the information the FBI had given him. In fact, he had already pushed his two o'clock meeting with them back to a three o'clock and now he was considering canceling it all together and rescheduling for another day. He shook his head thinking about it as he stuffed the security brief in its folder and jammed that in his briefcase. No, now that he was up to date on the information the FBI had obtained from Greg Buckner about the threat posed by the Changed, he knew that some interim decisions must be made about how the government would respond if there were an event. These would have to be in place at least until the matter was discussed and decided upon by Congress.

Lance had risen quickly through the ranks in his career. He had started as valedictorian of Paul Robeson High School on Chicago's south side before becoming one of only three African American's to be named

293

a Rhodes Scholar two years later. Ultimately it was his experiences in the poorest, most violent parts of Chicago that shaped his choice to get into law enforcement. He spent years in the FBI before joining Homeland Security. Now, as the director, he found himself smack in the middle of one of the most significant decisions of his career. What to do about people with abilities?

There was a lot of pressure from some very influential people on both sides of the fence encouraging him to either lock up or protect the group. Lance had always been a fair man that weighed all the evidence impartially before making a decision, but after reading the brief that had been provided by Buckner and his associates, he could not imagine anything that would make him think that it was a good thing to allow such dangerous individuals to run around loose.

Three minutes later he was just clearing the back door of the building when he noticed a bright blue light across the parking lot. At first, he thought it was a light from a police car, but then, no, it wasn't flashing. In fact, it seemed like it was growing. Fast!

"Ooof!" The wind left Lance's lungs as he was grabbed around the waist and pulled up into the air at high speed soaring out over the Potomac River. He instantly went for his gun that was strapped to his under-arm holster.

Tom felt the shift in the director's weight and knew what he was doing. He immediately let go of him. The lack of contact stopped Lance from drawing the weapon and caused him to instinctively reach toward Tom who he thought was the only thing holding him up.

"Whoa!" Lance hollered as he hovered in a blue haze of energy next to Tom above the river.

"My sentiment exactly, Mr. Director." Tom agreed. "Let's not jump to conclusions here and pull that sidearm."

"Or what? You are going to drop me to my death?" Lance asked as he continued to stare, wide-eyed, at the empty space between himself and the river.

"Don't be ridiculous, you're over water, and more importantly, I have no intention of dropping you." Tom corrected him. "I just need a few moments of your time. I tried going through the front door and waiting to see you the conventional way, but your secretary told me that you would not be available for days. My people and I do not have days to wait."

"Your people?"

"People with abilities," Tom explained. "Let's go somewhere that you will feel more relaxed and we can speak." Without waiting for a response, Tom and the director started to float toward the roof of the Office of Homeland Security. Once they were on the roof, Tom made a gesture and a dome of blue light that was too dense to see through formed around them.

"What's that?" Lance asked pointing to the dome.

"Just protection in case your coworkers see us and decide you need rescuing." Tom picked up a rock off the roof and tossed it at the barrier. The rock bounced back and landed at their feet. "I don't like being shot at, and as long as we are not moving beyond the range of this barrier, I can keep us safe."

"That's wonderful. Now, why are you kidnapping the Director of Homeland Security? You have to know that this is going to make you and 'your people' look like terrorists?"

"I am very sorry about that, Sir, but we are running out of time, and we don't know who we can trust." Tom began. "Every time we reach out to someone, The Wall has anticipated the move and is waiting to attack us."

"The Wall? I have heard of them. They used to do wet work for the FBI until about ten years ago when they dropped off the radar."

"That is the group, but they didn't disband. Instead, they started taking Americans with abilities hostage and forcing them to work for The Wall by threatening to harm them or their families."

"And you're saying that they have been kidnapping U.S. citizens and developing their own enhanced military force for a decade and no one has ever heard of it?" Lance was skeptical.

"That is exactly what I am saying. Are you saying that Homeland Security has nothing to do with them? They don't work for the government in any way?"

"No," Lance confirmed. "As far as I am aware, they haven't done any contract work for the U.S. since they disappeared." He started to pace.

Lance couldn't help but think that something stunk here. The thing that he hadn't been able to put his finger on in the briefing material was now taking shape in his mind. Why had Buckner – a man that had run Great Wall Incorporated, a known assassin-for-hire group – gone all soft-touch and opened a bodyguard boutique? How had he gathered so much information about people with abilities when no one else had even known they existed? He knew he needed more hard facts and not just stories. He paused and chose his next words carefully. "Now, if I were them, and I was a self-proclaimed authority on people with abilities, I would be using that status to try to maneuver into a place of trust within the government."

"That is our worry, Sir." Tom agreed. "It's the first step in his plan. He gathers a bunch of superpowered people under his command. It gives him the appearance of being an authority on something no one knows about yet, and it gives him a tactical advantage that the regular government doesn't have. Next, he manufactures a common enemy – us – so that the government will want to hire his group to protect normal citizens. When that happens, he will offer his company's resources to hunt us down. He stands to gain a ton of money and power from this move. Because of this threat, we need to have our side of the story heard before we are declared an enemy of the state."

"I have seen the TV footage of the fighting and the dead bodies. It looks pretty damning." Lance said doubtfully. "If you are going to go up against someone like Buckner, you are going to need a lot more than accusations and suspicions. You are going to need some bulletproof evidence."

Tom considered his next move carefully. Then, he reached out and restrained his powers. Lance blinked as he suddenly found himself standing on the roof talking to an ordinary eighteen-year-old boy. "I know that by showing you my face, I am risking everything – for myself and my family, but I need you to believe what I am saying."

Lance realized what a huge risk Tom was taking. "You have my attention. Why don't you tell me your story?"

Over the next two hours, Tom told Lance about who he was and where he had been. He talked about how he got his powers and how The Wall had found him and tortured him in their field office. He talked about what really happened at the battle in the Commons and the fight at the television station. Lance listened and occasionally asked for clarification of some of the details.

"So, you are saying that there is a large group of people in a place called 'the Settlement' that is currently preparing to be attacked by an army of mercenaries and Changed – oops – people with abilities right here on the East Coast of the United States?" Lance summed up the last few minutes of Tom's story. "And these people are not a threat to US security?"

"Yes," Tom replied. "To both questions."

Lance let out a low whistle. "That is a tall order to believe. How can I believe he has an army when no one has reported any large troop moments? If large numbers of soldiers were gathering around Boston, someone would notice. And how can I believe you are the victims when no one has any evidence of the dozens of people being tortured and brainwashed?"

Tom looked slightly exasperated.

"Don't get me wrong, I want to believe you, but all you have is your word, and I'm sorry to say, that isn't going to cut it when Buckner is feeding people video images of people with abilities that *look like* they are attacking and killing the police."

Tom hung his head. "Yeah. I know."

Changing the subject, Lance asked, "How long do you think you have before they attack?"

"Our best intelligence says tomorrow or maybe the day after."

Lance winced. "At this point, I have to remain impartial, but it is only fair to tell you, that doesn't give us much time to get some evidence showing that Buckner has done any of the things you claim. Without evidence he is torturing citizens or gathering military forces on US soil, the government can't step in to protect you and your group." Lance warned. "And if I get that evidence, I would need to mobilize a group large enough to stand a chance against the group you just described that he has gathered. That's no small number of federal agents."

"I know."

"So, let's pretend that I believe you for a second. The only thing I can tell you is that you should evacuate the Settlement." Lance offered as he walked in a circle around the inside of the dome. "Live to fight another day. Get me what I need for evidence and the government will be on your side when you confront him."

"We have already considered leaving the Settlement, and it is not a great idea," Tom explained. "If they have someone watching the valley, they could always follow us and attack us wherever we go. They have overwhelming numbers so that we wouldn't stand a chance. At least in the Settlement, we have defenses put up. We may not win, but at least it wouldn't be the complete spanking we would get if we tried to run for it."

Lance looked at Tom with a reappraising eye. "That is a very astute assessment. You and your group are a lot more than I expected."

Tom shrugged.

"If you aren't going to run, how do you expect to win?"

"That was part of what I have spent today researching," Tom explained. "I was trying to get your help, but it seems you can't do anything without evidence. I understand and respect that, but I can't get that evidence because it is currently locked up in their headquarters and guarded by hundreds of trained killers."

"Yes. Without evidence, I really can't do anything for you." Lance apologized.

Tom released his power and Lance stepped back as Tom seemed to catch fire. "Then that is what I will bring you." He waved his hand, and the dome dropped revealing three men in tactical gear with weapons leveled at Tom and Lance. "Somehow…"

"Wait!!" Lance yelled to the men while holding his hands above his head.

"Mr. Director get down!" The closest would-be rescuer yelled as he aimed at Tom.

"No! He's with me" was the last thing Tom heard Lance say as he suddenly launched into the air at a speed that would have caused a normal man to black out.

Once safely out of range, Tom turned north and poured on the speed as he raced back toward the Settlement.

CHAPTER 25

Tom Returns

i

Levi! Tom mentally yelled out into the woods. *I'm here. Flying above. I can feel someone disorienting me. Tell them to stop and lower the protections so I can fly to you.*

He had attempted to fly south over where he knew the gate to be, but every time he got close, he would get nauseous and confused about what direction he needed to go. *Levi!*

Yes. Yes. I hear you! Came Levi's voice in his head. *I am working on it. These are really old wards you are having us drop for you. If we weren't in such a time crunch, we would make you walk.*

Oh. Sorry. Tom apologized. He slowly made his way south until he felt the ward drop and the nausea left him. Then, he picked up speed, flew through the gate and continued on just above treetop level until he came to land at the northern tip of the Settlement.

"Nice of you to come back and join us." Reagan snapped as she walked out of the woods to Tom's left.

"Jesus!" Tom jumped. "How do you do that?"

"Do what?" She asked.

"Appear out of nowhere. You don't even make any noise when you walk. It's unnerving." Tom complained.

"At least I am not the one that disappeared this morning…" She countered as she fell in step on the walk toward the command tent.

"I am sorry, Reagan." He apologized as he got eye contact with her. "I truly am. I just realized that we lacked certain critical pieces of information, and I knew that you are just as capable of setting up the Settlement's defenses as I am, so I felt like I should bust butt and get the info we were missing."

They arrived at the command tent and walked inside. "Where is everyone?" Tom asked as he walked over to the sat down next to the large table that dominated the center of the room.

"They are at dinner, then they will be coming back here," Reagan answered absently. "So, I get it. You were showing that you trusted that I am a capable leader by leaving so that you could do some important reconnaissance mission." She sat down next to him at the table. "What I want you to get is that I don't work that way. I consider it disrespectful for you to leave me stuck doing all the work while you fly out to do God-knows-what."

"If it helps, it wasn't a joy ride." Tom offered. "I found out a lot of useful intel."

"Okay. Let's hear it." Reagan clearly was not impressed.

"First, I spoke to an associate of mine that is good on the internet. He was able to give us an estimate of one more day before The Wall will be in a position to attack us. He also was able to determine that their Headquarters is on Moon Island in Boston Harbor."

"Not bad." She conceded. "How did you meet this guy? Why is he trying to help us?"

"Because I pay him to," Tom replied. "That's part of the reason I trust him."

"You have someone working for you?" She was stunned. "For money?"

"Yes."

She shook her head. "Did you win a lottery or knock over a bank or something? You couldn't afford hot lunch in school back in Vermont."

"Nothing like that." Tom chuckled. "I will explain it later after all this is done, but for now I also need you to know that he informed me that agents have been arriving at their HQ for days. He doesn't even advise trying to monitor the island because of how much firepower they have there. It's about an hour and fifteen minute drive from here. That means that even if we were watching them, we wouldn't have much time to react once they started transporting people."

"True." She agreed. "But we could use all the warning we can get."

"He says they are dug in like a tick on that island. His concern was that they would notice if anyone tried to watch the island." Tom cautioned. "However, I thought that we could station normal scouts along Marina Bay and North Quincy. These people should not have abilities so that the Wall's agents that look for enhanced people won't even see them. They will have to rely on catching people showing an interest, and in heavily populated areas they won't be able to scan every person's thoughts in the crowd. It's too much. We will just have the scouts look for a large number of troop vehicles heading south. That's how we will get our one-hour warning."

"Not bad, Blue Boy." Reagan agreed. "What else ya got?"

"I met with Lance Thornton." Tom began.

"The director of Homeland Security? *That* Lance Thornton?" She was incredulous. "You actually got in to see him?"

"Yeah."

"And he just happened to have time to meet with you? With no appointment?"

"Umm… No." Tom admitted. "I kinda grabbed him and took him up to the roof." Reagan rolled her eyes, groaned and held her head in her hands. "We *needed* someone, Ree! We can't pull this off on our own. We are outnumbered over twenty to one and obscenely outgunned. They have battle strategists that have seen actual combat that have been planning this raid for days now. I needed to see if the government would get involved and defend us."

"Okay. You kidnapped someone. Yeah. Sure. What could go wrong?" She looked up, almost talking to herself. "Did he at least say he would help in the end?"

"Well… no." Tom admitted as Reagan's head sank back into her hands even deeper. "He isn't able to offer us help because right now it is just my word against Buckner's video evidence that we are trouble. Also, there is the fact that no one has seen Buckner's private militia gearing up to do anything. It seems too far-fetched. However, he did tell me that if we could get some hard proof that what I told him about The Wall and Buckner was the truth, he would take that to Congress and go after Buckner himself."

"So, he needs proof." She looked back up at Tom. "What proof? Where would we find it?"

"I imagine there is all the proof we need in the Wall's HQ."

"The place your friend said was too dangerous to even put under surveillance?" She asked.

"Yeah."

"So what you are saying is that you pissed away half a day finding out that we are on our own with this massive attack and that if we survive – which there is no way we should – we would still have to attack an impenetrable fortress to get the evidence we need to clear our name and get these jerks off our butts in the future?"

Tom looked at the ground. She was obviously still not impressed. "Yes."

Reagan patted his right leg hard enough to make it sting. "Nice job, hero. You left me here without talking about what you were going to do. You did not treat me like an equal. Then you were gone for most of the day while I worked my butt off and all you did was confirm what we already knew. They are coming in a couple of days." She shook her head at him again. "If we are done, I am going to go see where the commanders I appointed are hiding." She got up and started walking toward the opening of the tent. Tom got up to follow, but as soon as he put weight on his right leg, he discovered the reason it had stung when Reagan had slapped it. She had subtly discharged some of her power and put his leg to sleep. His hands flew up as he pitched forward, and he landed with a crash on the floor. By the time he made it to his hands and knees, all he could hear was her chuckling from the other side of the tent flap.

ii

The evening meeting started as soon as the last of the seven commanders arrived back at the command tent and was seated around the table. Tom looked around the table noting the people he recognized – Levi, Reagan, Floyd, and Bendati. The remaining three were new to him.

"Let's get started guys," Reagan called the meeting to order. "First, some introductions. You all know me. I am Reagan, also called Ghost Touch. This man" she gestured to Tom "is known as Storm. He turns into blue plasma and can move non-living things with his thoughts. He is also one of the co-leaders of this group." Touching Levi's shoulder as she walked behind him "This is Levi, also known as Wave. He is a telepath that can also do mental domination." Moving to Floyd "You all know Floyd. He can displace matter and is one of the primary security defenses for the Settlement." Then she motioned to Bendati. "This Bendati. He is an Ashtaari mystic. Some people would call him a sorcerer. At his current level of training, he has the ability to place spells on objects." He nodded at her brief description.

"Next is Rowan." She indicated the green-tinged, waif of a woman that stood dressed in what looked like a suit made of leaves growing around her body. "Now that Leaf is gone, she is the leader of the Green Folk. They can communicate with nature." Finishing her loop around the table, she stopped behind the last stranger. "Finally, there is Simon Reynolds also called Psyman, the leader of the telepaths. He is the strongest of their group."

Reagan walked back to her seat and held the back of her chair. "Tonight, we are going to hammer out the details of our defense plan. By the end of tonight, we need to know every step of how we intend on saving this place. How are we going to repel a group that outnumbers us twenty to one? How far are we willing to go? Equally important, if we can't hold them off, and we are losing, what are we going to do?"

"How far are we willing to go?" Tom asked. "What do you mean?"

"I mean just what I said. These people are coming after us in our home. They are going to be shooting real bullets, and they mean to kill every last one of us." She was clearly angry. "Are we going to be willing to kill back?"

"No." Tom stood up. "Look, I understand that these guys are not going to hold back. I understand that it would be easier for us not to hold back either and just to kill every one of them that we can, but that isn't what we should do."

"Really Tom?" Reagan asked. "Why not? I didn't see them holding back when they wounded you and pretty much killed Leaf." There were grunts of agreement from around the table.

"That is true. They didn't hesitate, but I will say this, if we kill them, we make their accusations about us true. That makes us murderers."

"People die during a war, Tom." She corrected him. "It's not called murder when you kill in self-defense."

"You may be right about that, and we can argue the morals of taking a life by slapping the get-out-of-jail-free card label of 'war' on a situation, but there is another even more important reason not to kill them. It would undermine our efforts to win over the government." He looked pleadingly from person to person. "Think about it. If we can do this without killing anyone, we will be able to testify that we are not dangerous and should be protected and not hunted. If we kill, they will not line up to protect us."

"You make a valid point." Reagan conceded. "What do the rest of you think?"

"I don't want to kill anything," Rowan spoke up. "The loss of life is abhorrent to our kind."

"Same here." Chimed in Psyman. "I have been in another person's head right up to the last moment. Death is horrible and there is no undoing it."

"Are we all in agreement then?" She asked. Each face nodded in turn as she looked around the table.

"Okay, then on to the next order of business. How do we defend ourselves from a bunch of killers?"

"I know!" Rowan piped up smiling and raising her hand like she was in grade school.

Reagan laughed. "Just say it, Rowan. No need to hold back here."

"We – the Green Folk – have a stockpile of what we call gugerda root. When boiled, it releases a toxin that will effectively immobilize anyone that gets it under their skin within seconds, but it doesn't impair their breathing. We could dip arrows and darts in that, and they would make formidable non-lethal weapons."

"Good." Tom agreed. We will need a lot of that stuff and a lot of darts and arrows. We should also place that stuff on every twig and sharp stick in the forest between the Gate into the valley and the tip of Leaf's clearing."

"We can do that." Rowan agreed.

"Cool." Tom pressed on. "Now, what was this about what to do if we are losing? I thought that once The Wall controls the Gate, there will be no way out of this little pocket dimension. We will have to fight to the end, right? There is no way to escape if they hold the gate."

"Not by conventional means," Bendati spoke. "I have found a way to spell stones so that they can transport you to another stone."

Tom blinked. "I don't understand." He admitted.

"Imagine that I make a destination stone and place it in the Green Mountain National Forrest in Vermont. Now imagine that I spell another rock. We can call it a 'go-stone,' and I hand it to you. When you think we are about to be overrun by the Wall's agents, you touch the go stone, and you disappear only to reappear at the destination stone in Vermont an instant later."

Tom smiled. "That would be awesome! I didn't think we could do that."

"We couldn't." He agreed. "Floyd here can only control where people end up if they are being ejected from the bubble he creates. When he tries to move them any farther than that, he loses accuracy."

"So, Hellbound going to France?" Tom asked.

"Pure chance," Floyd confirmed. "She coulda ended up in the ocean, but from what I understand, that wouldn't have been a bad thing either."

Tom shook his head. "I still don't think that she is evil. She had plenty of chances to do harm here, and she didn't."

"Son, we are jus' gonna have ta disagree on that one." Floyd stopped him.

"In any event, we didn't have the ability to move people to a specific place until about a week ago," Bendati interjected. "Now, we can accurately move people to any place that has a destination stone as long as we have a go-stone matched up to it."

"Perfect." Levi chimed in, "but how many people can one go-stone move?"

Bendati smiled at him. "Insightful boy, you are." He placed a stone with a strange marking on it on the table. "I don't know yet. I know that it will take one person and whatever they are holding, but I am not sure if it will take another person if that person were holding on to you, and to be honest, I haven't been around anyone I don't like enough to test it."

"What do you mean by that?" Tom asked.

"Well, the other person might go with you, or maybe his hand will go with you, or maybe none of him will go at all… He might all disappear and not reappear on the other side. I just don't know."

"So, one rock per person," Reagan noted.

"Yes." Bendati agreed. "And just so you know, they disappear after they are used, so don't expect to show up with the rock still in your hand."

"Where do they go?" Levi asked.

Bendati shrugged. "Rock heaven?"

"Jesus. I'm working with children." Reagan muttered under her breath.

"Okay guys!" Tom spoke up trying to get everyone on track again. "We have been running on the assumption that we would get caught if we try to run, but now that we can flee without being seen, should we?"

"No." Psyman offered. "I don't think we should. I think that if they show up here and we are gone, they will immediately start looking for us again. Our next home would take years to hide as well as this one – if ever. God knows we don't have anyone with the same kind of power that Webster had back in the 1850s to provide us with another pocket dimension solution…" He stood up at his spot at the table and made eye contact with each member of the group. "They would start looking for us, and they wouldn't stop. No, we need to at least bloody their noses bad enough that they wouldn't ever pick another fight…"

"That is going to be messy," Reagan advised. "There is no way we will make it through without losing members of our little cursed family."

"You can call it a 'family' if ya want, but it's purty dysfunctional, and really pissed off 'bout losing our brother Leaf," Floyd warned her. "An' I gotta say, this is *not* the family I would want to be pissed at me."

"I agree," Tom added. "I think that this is the kind of a decision that needs to be voted on. All those in favor of staying and fighting, raise a hand."

Psyman, Reagan and Floyd immediately raised their hands. Slowly, Tom, Bendati, and Levi raised their hands as well.

"I do not agree with fighting if we could flee." Rowan disagreed. "But I will not abandon my brothers and sisters." Then, she too raised her hand.

"There you have it," Reagan announced. "Now let's work out how we are going to stop but not kill, a large number of heavily armed, experienced soldiers."

iii

The morning came far too soon to suit Tom. He and Levi quietly walked out of the guest tent at the far south end of the Settlement and arrived at the small tent that on the outside looked like it would not fit more than three people standing up. He pushed back the opening as they stepped inside to find the vast banquet hall with tables of food and drinks. People milled about grabbing food and sitting down to enjoy it while the quiet of the early morning softened people's voices to a whisper.

Even the coffee tasted bitter as he looked around knowing that this was possibly the last morning he would ever see this valley with all its wonders again.

"Good morning boys." It was Reagan. She was dressed in her white spandex suit with the red sash. Her skull-like mask was tucked into the sash as she sat down at Tom's table to eat with him and Levi. Tom was again struck by how beautiful she looked. Her dark curly hair framed her pale face, and her green eyes seemed to glow in the muted light of the tent.

Levi kicked Tom under the table. *Say something, moron!* Levi snapped in his mind, breaking him out of his reverie.

"G-good morning Reagan." Tom stammered. Then to Levi, *I need a couple of minutes with her.*

Got ya. This wingman is taking off. Levi grabbed his plate of fruits and roasted vegetables and stood up to leave. "I gotta see a guy about a thing. Later."

Jesus! You suck at subtle." Tom shot out at his brother as he walked away from the table.

Bite me, bro. Now say the right things to this woman so you can make up. If one of you doesn't survive today, you do not want to part on a sour note, came Levi's reply.

He hadn't really considered one of them not surviving the coming invasion, but thinking about it now, he knew that was naïve.

Reagan looked at Levi's departure with mild interest and then looked at Tom. "You must have something you want to say to me in private?"

"I do. Was it that obvious?"

"Well, the last time I saw Levi leave anywhere near that fast is when he pulled the fire alarm at school, so he didn't have to take a quiz in Spanish class." She chuckled.

"You knew about that?" Tom chuckled. "He hates those."

She smiled back encouragingly.

"I just wanted to apologize for my behavior. In my push to get the information I knew we needed, I didn't take the time to communicate with you the way you deserve." Tom caught and held her eyes. "I would never intentionally hurt you, Reagan. You mean too much to me to risk losing you – again." The last was added with a smile.

Reagan smiled back. "Apology accepted." She said softly. "And when this is over, I have some ideas about this date…" Tom blushed to the roots of his hair.

iv

It wasn't even seven when everyone assembled outside the command tent to wait for orders. Bendati walked up to Tom and handed him a stick with carved markings on it. "Take this and hold it in your hand. Touch the ruin that looks like a square with a dot in the middle and your voice will be heard by everyone here without shouting."

"Thank you." Tom was relieved that there was a way around not having a microphone and amplifier in their technology-challenged little group.

Reagan nudged him forward to begin talking. He placed his thumb on the correct rune and started talking. "Good morning. As you know, the six other commanders and I have been working around the clock since we found out about this attack to get us ready to defend ourselves. We know that the temptation when being shot at will be to retaliate with lethal force. We need you to fight that urge with everything you have. If we do that, we may win the battle, but we will lose the war. None of the Normals will stand with us against evil men like Buckner in the future if we act like we deserve to be treated like criminals now."

"Leaf would not have wanted us to become like them. He wanted us to be better than that. He knew we have abilities, so we are different. We stand out. Like any that stand out, we have a choice. Do we become a scary thing to a child? Or do we become a role model that they wish they could meet? Making sure that they know we are the good guys here, will ultimately save our lives, so don't go too far in a moment of anger."

"Now, on to the business of preparing for today's battle. We have a lot of work to do and very little time in which to do it. Last evening, you each got a number from one to seven assigned to you. That number represents the commander with which you are assigned to work. We are each going to hold up a flag with a number on it. Please come stand with the commander that has your number, and you will receive specific instructions for what your group needs to do to prepare." Tom placed the stick in his back pocket and held up his flag with a number two on it and walked off to one side of the town square area. Ten people quietly made their way up to him.

"Okay, this is about right. Each commander should have about ten people." Tom nodded.

"You mean that our entire fighting force is only seventy people?" A young lady wearing brown and green cloths and sporting a bird feather in her hair asked.

"Actually, it will be more like only fifty of us fighting." Tom corrected her. "There are some people here that have refused to take part in the actual fighting but have agreed to help us prepare the valley for the attack."

"And The Wall, I heard has over five hundred men coming." Tom could hear the nervous tremor in her voice.

"Actually, they have close to double that, but we are not sure how many people they are bringing here." Tom corrected. "Yes. The numbers that we will be facing are the scary part, but you also need to consider that we have the home court advantage, we know the land, we have had time to prepare for them, and we have a far better reason to fight then they do. We are fighting for our homes and our right to survive." He looked around the group and watched as looks of determination replaced their looks of fear.

"Now let's start checking things off our part of the preparation list." Tom grabbed a note pad with his list on it. "I need Sparrow to step forward." To his surprise, the girl with the feather in her hair stepped forward. "I hear you have the ability to turn into a bird and get other birds to do your bidding." She nodded. "Good. I need you to run a couple of errands for me. The first one is to drop this rock in the Green Mountain National Forrest in Vermont." He held a small black rock with a carved design in it out to her. She shimmered, and in her place stood a powerfully build falcon.

"Huh. I thought she would have been a sparrow." Tom muttered.

"Sparrow is her name. She can turn into any bird." One of the others in the group corrected him. The falcon squawked its agreement as it grabbed the rock in its talons.

"Okay. Once you are done that errand, please see me for the next, more difficult one." The falcon squawked a second time and launched into the air.

Tom sighed. Today was going to be a very long day.

CHAPTER **26**

The Wall Makes Their Move

i

Two hours before dusk, James stepped out onto the balcony over-looking all the Agents that had assembled at the headquarters location. There were almost seven hundred men and over a hundred resource agents assembled on the grounds below. All waited silently in ordered rows for their field commander to speak.

James grabbed the microphone to address the crowd below him as the amplifier squawked to life. "Good afternoon agents." He began. "It is good to see so many of you turn out for this raid. As you know, the Changed that have been running the Boston terrorist cell have been slowly gathering in a secret location. Until recently, we had no idea where, but thanks to the ingenuity of some of our team, we have discovered their location, and now we have the opportunity to wipe this threat from the face of the planet. We are not taking captives. We are not leaving witnesses. Some of these terrorists have the ability to change how they look. They could make themselves look like children or even a plant for all we know. Because of this, we will be bringing a large number of explosives with us. When we leave their lair, there will be nothing but dust left for a mile in any direction."

"As for intel on that location, Agent Sanchez has been using his ability to go undetected to monitor it for the past week. The area in question is located in the middle of a national park. Specifically, there is what appears to be an invisible doorway or gate located there. We are not sure where it goes. It could be connected to any location on earth. For that matter, it could go to another time or even planet. There is no way to tell until we step through. What we do know is that there are a large number of these terrorists using that gate and we need to put an end to it."

"Our mission will begin with a standard vehicle deployment at a mile out from the gate. We will proceed with caution heading in from there. Keep in mind that these are the Changed! It is highly unlikely that they will use standard battle tactics or weapons! We will be using some of our resource agents that can sense the Changed and eliminate any ambushes before they are triggered. If any agent runs into something that you can't get past, please communicate that to the resource agent assigned to your squad."

"We are expecting them to attempt to block our communications. Our new coms use a special type of ultra-low band wavelength to communicate. They will be impervious to standard jamming. However, if they are somehow able to knock out our communications, we will revert to hand signals as we did in Nicaragua when we took out the magnetic threat there last year."

He paused to try to read the mood of his men, but he may as well have been trying to read the emotions of the cement on which they stood. "I cannot stress enough the importance of this mission. We have fought this group twice already, and they are dangerous. I have heard some of the talk about being uncomfortable doing an assault on American soil, but each one of you has been in the military and taken the oath to defend against all enemies foreign *and domestic.* This group is a domestic threat that we can't allow to escape just because Congress is still getting briefed on the threat. Once they see what you have been up against, you will be honored as heroes and patriots! Keep that in mind when you encounter these terrorists, and make no mistake, if you hesitate, they will kill you." He could tell they were ready. "Okay! Now get on the transport pad! We have a country to protect!"

A loud "Hurrah!" went up from the assembled agents. Then they all quickly crossed the yard and climbed into what looked like a hastily erected three-story structure. Each floor was simply row after row of chairs bolted to the floor with seatbelts attached. A ladder was mounted to each side of the structure so that the agents could climb up to each floor and get in the seats. Once all the seats were filled and the munitions stowed on the lower level, James spoke into the mic one more time. "Microman, could you do the honors?"

With that, a man in a green and blue suit walked up to the front of the transport pad. He took a deep breath, closed his eyes and raised his hands. At first, nothing seemed to happen, but after a couple of seconds, the entire transport pad seemed to shudder. The agents looked at one another in alarm for a second before they all seemed to disappear – along with the transport pad.

By then, James was walking past the other man. He casually strolled into the middle of the field where the pad had been located and bent over. He walked back to where Microman stood and carefully lowered the miniaturized transport pad full of agents into a wooden box and closed the lid over it. "Perfect. Now you are sure you will be able to return them to the normal size?" He asked Microman.

"Relatively. I told you, I've never done anything this large and complex before." The man in blue and green said as he panted from the effort he had just exerted.

Well, let's hope – for your sake." James warned him. "Now get in the truck with the others." He instructed him. "And bring this." He ungraciously handed him the box.

ii

In the wake of the amazing ending to James' speech, no one noticed the seagull taking off from the edge of the island where the dirt from the shoreline, gave way to the manicured green grass of the lawn in front of the Wall's headquarters. It had landed there earlier when the assembly had begun to form up into rows and had stayed throughout the entire speech. Now, it spun out over the ocean, flying low and seeming to look for fish before slowly turning southwest and increasing in speed.

iii

James rode in the front of the transport truck. The decision to move the troops and equipment by shrinking them had been borne out of necessity. There was no other way to move that many troops and all that equipment without attracting attention. Now the mission was to get the troops safely to Sanchez and get them back to normal size without tripping over any defenses the Changed may have devised. In truth, he was a bit nervous about what awaited him at Sanchez's location. He had lost contact with the agent hours ago, and he had been in enough conflicts to know that silence could mean anything from broken communication equipment to Sanchez having been discovered. However, James had known him a long time now, and if he had to place bets, he would bet that it was a communications issue.

As the van made the left turn from South Main Street in Freetown onto Copicut Road, James started to feel that familiar pre-battle tightness settle in his stomach. Five minutes to go. He turned around and faced the others in the van. "Okay, Stonehenge, Maul, Trevor, Microman, be on alert. We will be there in less than…" He didn't get the rest of the sentence out at the van came to sudden stop.

"Why are you stopping?" James began as he spun his seat around and looked out the front window. What he saw cut off any further questioning. A hundred and fifty meters in front of the van was a huge gaping chasm. It looked like a sinkhole 30 feet across had opened up stretching 50 meters into the woods. James smiled. "I knew they would do something." He muttered as he stepped out of the van to get a better look.

He walked to the side of the road and picked up a rock as the others got out of the van to look at the road. "Looks like they know we are coming. This might get interesting." James chucked the rock at the sinkhole and watched as it sailed out into the air and landed with a "thunk" a few seconds later in the bottom. "Huh," James commented. "Not an illusion." Then he turned to face the others. "Stonehenge, make us a bridge." He barked out his order while jerking a thumb over his shoulder before climbing back into the passenger seat of the van.

Stonehenge slowly walked up to the edge of the sinkhole before planting his feet, closing his eyes and raising his arms. Almost immediately, a low rumble started to build from beneath their feet. In a matter of seconds, a foot-thick ribbon of rock the width of the road burst forth from the near side of the sinkhole. The ribbon shot across the expanse and slammed into the ground on the far side.

The van pulled up next to Stonehenge, he got in, and they continued straight forward over the newly created bridge. Another mile and a half down the road and the van came to a stop again as the GPS built into the dash indicated that they were less than a mile from the area that Sanchez had reported noting the gate.

"The report states that there is supposed to be a road off to our right that ends in a clearing." The driver informed James as he looked at the dense forest next to the road. The shrubs and trees grew in so close that it was impossible to see more than a handful of feet into the woods.

James chuckled. "Pathetic attempt to block us." He reached over and grabbed the handset to the speaker system attached to the outside of the van. "Sanchez! If you are out there - get down!" Not waiting for a reply, he looked back over his shoulder into the van. "Chaos Song. You're up."

The van door slid open, and a short, lean Asian woman stepped out. She walked up to the side of the road and eyed the forest. After planting her feet and checking that everyone was behind her, she took a deep breath and opened her mouth. What came out was not a song or a sound. It was as if a bomb had been detonated, but the blast seemed to come from her mouth. The trees and shrubs closest to the road were ripped out by the roots and sent flying. Trees as far as a hundred feet away were flattened. As soon as the roar of Chaos Song's power died down, she turned around and smiled back at the group. "I found that clearing you were looking for Mr. Neuwin."

"Strong work." He congratulated her as they all piled out of the van. "Now that everyone in a fifty-mile radius knows we are here, we should hurry the hell up and get started." He walked over to Microman, who was still holding the box containing almost eight hundred agents and grabbed the box from him. He strode out to the middle of the clearing, removed the platform from the box and placed it on the ground.

"Micro…?" He indicated to the box as he quickly walked away from the area.

Microman walked up to the edge of the clearing and stared hard at the platform. At first, it jumped, and then the wooden sides holding the three-story transport pad burst outward revealing the rapidly growing transport pad, troops, and equipment. The growth back to the correct size was much slower than the shrinking had been. At about the half-way point, Microman paused and took a deep breath before finishing the process. Once done, he shook slightly and then passed out. Two of the agents were violently ill over the side of the platform, and one just screamed for a few seconds before going still. A quick inspection by one of the medics in the group confirmed that the man had not survived the re-enlargement process.

"Only one death…" James muttered under his breath. "Not bad." He reached back into the van and grabbed the handset for the speakers as all the agents collected their gear and formed up into their pre-assigned groups. "Okay people. Follow your section commander's leads. We have already established that the enemy knows we are coming so they could hit us at any time. Be ready." He dropped the mic and opened his handheld GPS to reaffirm the coordinates of the gate. As soon as he flipped open the GPS lid, a deep, loud tone resonated from deep in the forest pushing a slight breeze in front of it.

James instinctively crouched expecting an attack to follow. When nothing happened, he stood back up and looked at the GPS. It was completely fried. James attempted the power button twice more and then checked his cell phone. It was dead also.

"Sir." Trevor began. "It looks like they hit us with an electromagnetic pulse weapon. Everything electronic is dead."

James smiled savagely. "It's a good thing that bullets aren't electronic then, isn't it?"

"Hoo-rah!" Merrola replied back as he chambered a round in his HK416 assault rifle. "You have to admit though…" Trevor looked at the woodline at the edge of the clearing that Chaos Song had made. "They are a plucky little group." He looked over at James as they started their walk toward the gate and noticed James giving him a questioning look. "If they know we are coming, they have to have some idea of what kind of trouble we are bringing with us. If I were part of their group, I would have encouraged them to start running and don't ever stop, and yet, here they are - doing their best to make it so that we can't reach them."

"And you think that makes them brave?" James scoffed. "I think that collection of freaks knows damn well that if this hideout is discovered, there is no place on Earth they will be able to hide from us. No, they have no choice but to stay and fight…" James and Trevor both felt it at the same time. It was an overwhelming sense of disorientation and nausea. Both men froze in their tracks. Trevor heard the squads of men that were closest behind him groan, and some of them threw up. Trevor tried to turn around to see what was happening but only succeeded in making himself fall to the ground as he lost his ability to tell up from down.

James took two more steps toward the woods, but the sense of vertigo and nausea was so overwhelming that he had to stop.

"Hey guys," Sanchez said walking casually from the woodline in front of the agents.

"Jesus." James remarked from between clenched teeth. "What the hell, Sanchez?"

"I don't know." He replied. "It looks like they have someone that can make you feel disoriented and nauseous. The men that I brought with me were sick too at first. Then I did this" he touched James' arm, "and they were fine."

As soon as Sanchez's hand made contact with James, all the vertigo and nausea stopped. James stood up and composed himself. "Right then." He brushed off and straightened his bulletproof shirt before looking back at Sanchez. "So how many people can you shield and for how long?"

"I have no idea," Sanchez admitted. "I didn't even know this was part of my abilities this morning. I thought all I could do was be invisible to telepaths and other forms of detection."

"Okay. It looks like we are going to find out. Why don't you go high five the men?" He gestured to the growing group of men that could barely stand behind him.

"Looks like finding the person that can do this is going to be a priority then," Trevor stated after Sanchez clapped him on the back. "We would be crippled if Sanchez's ability gives out at the wrong moment."

"True." James agreed already walking forward. "I think that…" And then he disappeared only to reappear a second later twenty feet to the left of where he had been and headed in the opposite direction.

"…we should - Holy crap! What was that?!" James exclaimed realizing that he had been completely spun around.

Trevor had immediately frozen when James had disappeared and was now staring at the place where it had happened with a critical eye.

"Looks like you found their barrier." Sanchez was sweating from the effort of protecting so many people as he came running up to James.

"This is the thing you warned me about?"

"Yeah," Sanchez confirmed. "It's a sphere that completely surrounds the gate in the middle. If something passes into that space, it spits it back out somewhere else along the perimeter. We even tried tossing rocks on top of it, but they just shot out over there." He gestured to the right of their location.

"Can it be overwhelmed?" James asked.

"I didn't have the manpower to attempt it."

"Well, you do now," James informed him.

"Sweet." Sanchez smiled. "You men!" He hollered, getting the attention of a large group of agents that was closest to their location. "Form up beside me. I want you to line up twenty men wide, five rows deep."

The men lined up as instructed with weapons at the ready.

"We are going to try to break through this wall by all of us charging it. Most Changed have a limit on what they can do. Our goal is to overwhelm this one so that the barrier drops. Got it?" The group grunted their agreement. "Good. On the count of three. One. Two. Three!" Sanchez dropped his arm like a man waving a green flag at a race and ran flat out at the wall with one hundred agents right behind him.

As the agents hit the barrier, they all disappeared, leaving James and the rest of the group to look about for the place where the men were going to rematerialize. A second later it was raining agents as they started to reappear from the top of the displacement bubble some twenty-five feet in the air.

Men landed on top of one another, breaking bones and occasionally firing off weapons that had been ready to shoot if the barrier had fallen. Screams of the falling and groans from the wounded filled the air.

James smacked his forehead with the palm of his hand. "You've gotta be kidding me." He muttered. Then to he turned to Trevor "We didn't know that they could rematerialize up in the air I take it?"

"No Sir," he confirmed. "It was always at ground level before."

"Okay. That is enough of that." James motioned to one of the other commanders. "Go through the group and see how many of them are not injured and can continue with the mission. The ones that can't should be sent to the hospital if you can get the vehicles running after that EMP." He then turned to and walked back into the milling agents and came back with two of them.

"Mindicator." He addressed the woman dressed in black tactical gear. "Can you sense the man projecting this barrier?"

She paused, looking thoughtful for a moment. "No. Not from here. If this gate leads to another place, I may need to go there to bring him down."

"Crap!" James fumed and paced back as he thought. "Okay. I think we can get you in there if we have Jumpfoot use his teleporting ability to get you past this barrier."

James grabbed the short man by the ammunition strap on his back and shoved him slightly closer to the invisible barrier. "You know the drill. Jump to the other side of the barrier, get through the gate and then protect Mindicator at all costs. Her job will be to mentally locate the person generating this barrier and destroy his mind. If she can't do that, you two will be on your own."

Jumpfoot sighed heavily. "For the record, I really don't like this plan."

"Noted." James acknowledged chambering a round in his SCAR assault rifle. He noticed as Jumpfoot looked back at him nervously and smiled. "Don't worry. This is for the terrorists, not you."

Jumpfoot visibly relaxed. Then he grabbed Mindicator's hand and asked: "So, are you ready?"

She didn't have time to answer. One second, she was standing a foot away from James and Trevor and the next she was twenty feet ahead of them still holding Jumpfoot's hand. As James watched, he saw her let go of Jumpfoot, look around to get her bearings and immediately drop into a crouch. Jumpfoot took one last glance back at all the agents amassed on the other side of the barrier and then motioned for Mindicator to follow him as he got up and ran forward. They had only taken three strides when the air around them rippled like they had just dove into an upright pool of water and simply disappeared.

Trevor looked on with interest. "Now what?"

"Now we wait and throw rocks."

"Throw rocks?" Trevor asked.

James picked up a small rock and gently tossed it at waist height at the barrier. It blinked out of existence only to reappear as it fell from twenty feet up. "Yeah. When they stop doing that, we rush the gate."

CHAPTER 27

The Attack Begins

Sparrow had met up with the seagull she had sent to Moon Island and returned to the Settlement half an hour ago with news that The Wall had started to move troops. They had immediately dispatched most of the commanders to tell everyone to be ready. Only Reagan and Tom remained in the command tent to coordinate the defense.

"Are you okay?" Tom asked after watching Reagan pace rapidly in the confined space of the tent.

"Yes." She quickly answered. "No. I don't think so." She muttered wringing her hands as she continued her pacing.

"Okay. As long as we have that clear." Tom chuckled.

Reagan made a rueful face at him. "How can you be so calm?"

Tom shrugged. "We have made all the preparations that we can. Our plan is a sound one. If we fail… At least I will fail standing against those that would harm those I care about." He looked at her as closely as a thought occurred to him. "Hold on. You *love* to fight. Normally, you would be dancing around this tent, and we would have to assign someone to hold you back. Why are you really nervous?"

She exhaled sharply and smiled at him as she realized that he knew she was holding back. "You sure do pick weird times to gain insight into women Thomas Woods." She walked back to the table and sat in the seat next to him. "Do you remember the talk we had about seeing the Angel of Death?"

Tom's eyes grew wide. "Do you see him? Is he here now?"

She laughed a warm, throaty laugh and looked at him with her heart in her eyes. "No silly. But thank you for that. I really needed something to break me out of my funk, and a good laugh was perfect." She leaned forward and squeezed his hand. "I have been thinking about the things he told me that night when he granted me my powers."

"Oh." Tom knew that she had been busy the past couple of days as they crammed to prepare the Settlement. Her energy had seemed limitless, but now he suspected the reason she was doing so much was to keep herself from thinking about the revelation she had about where her powers originated. "Care to talk about it?"

She made a face. "I guess I should. Internalizing it is just making me sick." She pulled her seat in closer to his not wanting anyone to overhear her worries. "I just can't help but think about what he said. He told me that the other apprentices and I would prove ourselves through how we use the gifts he gave us. I think that means that the more I use my powers, the closer I will get to being the one chosen as the next Angel of Death!"

Understanding hit Tom like a bucket of ice water. "So if you kick butt in this battle, you think you are going to dramatically increase your odds of becoming the next Angel?"

Tears started to come unbidden from her eyes. "Yes, Tom, and I don't want to do that! I *can't* do that!" She was shaking. "I can't even look at it when a raccoon gets hit on the road! How am I supposed to…?" She couldn't finish as she started quietly sobbing as she covered her face with her hands.

Tom stood and pulled her close holding her shaking form in his arms as all her fear passed out of her through her tears.

After the worst of it had passed, Tom pulled back and looked in her eyes. "I hear you, and I get it. I would be nervous too."

"What am I going to do though?" She asked, almost pleading. "I can't sit this out. All my friends, my new home and… you. I won't lose you again. I have to fight."

Tom shook his head. "But if you fight, you will still lose us." He said realizing what an impossible situation it was. "People don't just get to hang out with Angels."

"Then what do I do Tom?"

"I don't know. I don't want to lose you either." He held her close again as he thought it over and this time, she slipped her arms around him and held him back. "I may not know how to deal with the Angel issue, but I do know this: you need to do what is right – no matter what you fear might be lost. If something bad is going to happen either way, then you should choose the thing that you will be able to live with later."

She looked at him curiously.

"What I mean to say is, would you be okay with not fighting if it meant that you would not be selected as the Angel of Death? Would you be able to live with letting your friends fight and possibly die?"

"Obviously not." She scoffed.

"Then there is no decision to make," Tom concluded. "You should stand with your friends, and we will deal with the problem of the Angel on another day."

Reagan looked up at him and smiled. "Leave it to you to make a choice so full of greys, a black and white decision." She stood up and kissed his cheek.

Just then the tent flap whipped open, and Levi, Floyd, and Psyman burst into the tent. "Tom! They are at the edge of the displacement bubble!"

"Are you sure?" Reagan asked.

"Yes," Floyd replied. "Diz almost passed out a couple of minutes ago."

Reagan immediately was concerned. "Why? What happened to Karina?" She asked using her friend's birth name instead of her public one.

"She was projecting her vertigo ability out past the displacement bubble when she felt a massive number of people walk into her field. The drain on her from affecting that many people almost knocked her out." Psyman explained. "She could only hold it for a few minutes then she had to stop projecting her vertigo power. She is in the medic tent recovering now."

"That means that they should hit the displacement bubble next, right?" Tom asked Floyd.

"Oh, they already have. I bounced one guy at street level. Then, I moved the exit into the air a bit." He chuckled. "They tried to overwhelm me too by charging the bubble, but my power doesn't work like Diz's does. I'm fine with moving large numbers of people."

Reagan smiled. "They rushed the bubble at ground level and came out in the air?"

Floyd's smile was smug. "Yup. Not sure how many attempted it exactly, but it was a lot, and they all came out on the second floor of nothing."

Floyd was still chuckling when he suddenly grabbed his head and cried out.

"No!" Yelled Psyman reaching for Floyd as he pitched forward, unconscious.

"What just happened?" Tom demanded.

"Psychic attack!" Psyman answered. "I shielded him after it first hit, but I am not sure how much damage she did." He quickly grabbed one of Bendati's go-stones for the medical tent and placed it on Floyd's chest. Then he picked up Floyd's limp hand and dropped it on the stone. As soon as it made contact, the large man disappeared. "I hope Doc is ready because I think he is going to have a full tent before tonight is over."

"That's it!" Reagan exclaimed. "Psyman – tell those close to the gate to brace themselves. The attack is starting now!"

"On it." He replied as he took on a distant look again.

Reagan looked back at the large map on the table, taking in for the thousandth time the layout of the valley. "The gate makes a natural bottleneck. All of their agents have to pass through it. If we can hold them there or even just hurt them bad enough, we might stand a chance of saving this valley."

"Levi – have Rowan pass word to the plants," Tom instructed. "If anything gets past the people we have stationed at the gate. The plants are the next line of defense."

Before Tom had time to say anything else Reagan grabbed him and kissed him soundly on the lips. Everyone froze as half smiles crept across their faces.

"What was that for?" Tom asked as Reagan broke the kiss.

"In case I don't get a chance to do it later." She smiled at him as she pulled her mask down to cover her face. "Now that I know what I need to do, and those monsters are at the gate, I have to go!"

"Wait!" Tom called to her as she moved quickly toward the tent flap. "You can't just leave."

"I don't need to stay. Everyone knows the plan. There is nothing left to do but do it." She explained. "Levi, Psyman." She called over her shoulder. "Listen for me. I know your abilities don't work on electropaths like Muertos, so I am going over to his place to make sure he is ready. God knows – if he fails, we are all in trouble."

The two telepaths didn't even have time to reply to her, and she was gone.

Levi whistled. "She's completely insane." He turned to face his brother with a huge grin on his face. "She's perfect for you. You should start naming your kids now…"

"Levi –shut up." Tom snapped as Psyman tried to cover his smile with his hand. "She is right though." Everyone in the room shielded their eyes as Tom released his ability and burst into blue light. "The planning phase is pretty much done. The defenses at the north end of the valley are as good as they are going to get, but if they make it this far, they are going to make short work of the wall we attempted to erect. I know there is a group that is working on reinforcing it. I am going to help them. Levi – remember, I am assigned to the defenses at Yoman's Creek. Let me know when they hit John's house, and I will fly to that position." He walked to the tent flap. "Don't forget – as soon as the agents pass through the north, we will need the telepaths to come out of those tunnels they are hiding in and evacuate any of the survivors that couldn't escape to

Doc's tent." Without waiting for a reply, he shot through the door of the tent and out into the dusky light of the evening sky.

Levi shrugged. "Sheez! You'd think, I have no idea what I am supposed to do here."

Psyman chuckled. "So, this isn't your first invasion?"

Levi smiled at him ruefully. "That's not what I meant. I meant that I can read everyone's thoughts within two hundred yards - further if I concentrate. I can't forget because I can hear everyone reminding me all the time!"

Psyman looked at Levi very critically. "Please tell me you are not leaving your mind that open." He walked over and got eye contact with Levi. "Don't think for a second that we are the only telepaths in this valley anymore! If you don't be careful, Floyd won't be the only one in Doc's tent with a mind that is turned to mush."

Levi blushed to the roots of his hair. "I'm sorry... Master."

"Don't be sorry." Psyman admonished him. "You are a good apprentice, and you are one of the most powerful telepaths and Will Breakers that I have seen in a generation. The fact that you have only had these abilities for such a short period of time and you already have this level of mastery is nothing short of a miracle. However, that doesn't absolve you from needing to learn control. Quite the opposite in fact. Without control, it is just a matter of time before you harm someone." He sighed as he sat back down at the table. "It's just a shame that you didn't have more time to study with me before this attack. The things I could have shown you!"

Levi smiled. "We will have to make time after. I really do want to learn."

"I know." The older man smiled. "One thing at a time, though. Let's make sure that none of the bad guys are able to sneak up behind our friends."

CHAPTER 28

James Goes West

i

Jumpfoot and Mindicator had lasted less than a minute after stepping through the gate. A barrage of darts filled with gugerda root had them unconscious before the first agent stepped through the gate to help them. Unfortunately, they had managed to do their job before they fell. With Floyd down, agents poured through the gate. At first, they barely had time to notice that they were through the gate before they fell with darts in their necks or legs, but subsequent lines of agents came through the gate with riot shields raised. The darts made the sound of heavy rain on a tin roof as they bounced harmlessly off the plastic shields.

Within a matter of minutes, the agents had set up a foothold at the mouth of the gate. James and Trevor came through and stood to survey the layout of the valley from behind the riot shields. It didn't take long for them to establish a plan of attack. James got the attention of his sub-commanders and signaled for them to follow him as he moved them along the edge of the hills that formed the western border of the valley. Trevor did the same taking his half of the troops to the steep ledges on the eastern edge of the valley. The plan was simple. Stay to the high ground and encircle the valley. If they could flush all the Cursed Ones into the middle, they would be surrounded, and the agents could rain death down on them from the higher vantage point.

James paused long enough for Sanchez to catch up with him. "I have had enough of this crap! Get the resource agents up front. I am not going to be ducking blow guns for the rest of this invasion!"

After a couple of quick hand gestures were relayed through the group three agents made their way up to James while using the shields as cover.

"Chaos Song and Maul – clear our path," James instructed.

Chaos Song took a deep breath and stood up. The blast that came from her shattered darts in midair and knocked over trees. The defenders of the Settlement that were closest to her position fell to the ground with blood pouring from their ears and noses as her song of destruction ended. A split second later, the skies seemed to part as lightning struck the upstretched hand of one of the Cursed Ones only to fly out of her other hand and strike Chaos Song in her chest, hurling her backward through the air and into the bushes behind the group.

"Oooh!" marveled James. "It looks like some of these tree-huggers have teeth. Maul…?" He asked turning to the large man.

All that Maul had needed was a direction. With his eyes fixed on the lightning wielding defender, he ran straight at her. She looked up to the heavens as a second bolt hit her, charging her body with power. Just as she looked for Maul so she could release her bolt, he grabbed her. With no place to aim her energy, electricity flew off from her in all directions lighting up the evening sky for miles.

Even with the electricity flooding through his body, Maul picked the small living lightning rod off her feet and threw her hard into a tree. On contact, the tree burst into pieces as the remaining power of the lightning was discharged. The defender never moved again.

ii

"What the hell do you mean, they split up?" Levi was so stunned that he spoke the words out loud.

I mean — they have so many people that they split their forces at the gate. Now, instead of coming straight at us, they are surrounding us! Came Rowan's thought as Levi and Psyman attempted to coordinate the battle from the command tent. *They poured through the gate like bugs. There was no stopping them. We probably knocked close to two hundred of them out between using darts and our abilities.*

Listen, we need to drive them back toward the middle. I don't care what you have to do, but we can't let them take the high ground and surround us!

Okay, came her reply and then she was gone.

Levi looked over at Psyman. "They are…"

"I know." He replied cutting off the other man. "I sense them pushing southeast toward the cliffs. That natural barrier will force them to come back toward the middle of the valley. They should be pushed right into Leaf's lab."

Levi's eyes grew wide with alarm. "They might hurt him if they notice he isn't a normal tree!"

Psyman smiled. "I wouldn't worry about that. I had Rowan look into moving him yesterday. When she showed up, he was gone."

"Gone?" Levi looked at the older man in disbelief.

"Yes. Completely gone. Only some odd markings in the ground where his roots used to be. Before you ask, I have no idea what happened, and we just don't have time to look."

Levi still looked concerned.

"So, Rowan is going to try to turn James and his crew back toward the middle?" Psyman asked trying to get Levi to focus again.

"Yes. She sounded determined, but I have no idea what she is going to do."

iii

Rowan followed the progression of James' group as they blasted their way uphill toward the ridge on the west side of the valley. Levi was right. With so few people to defend their home, they had to make use of the area's natural defenses that lay in the middle of the valley. Not only would the ridgeline be the least defended, but it is the tactically a superior position to be in when it comes to fighting.

No one knew the wood like Rowan. Her connection to the power of the earth was second only to Leaf, himself. Branches moved out of her way as she bolted through the trees on an intercept course with James and his agents.

When she was still several hundred meters in front of them, she came to a stop. She could not see them yet, but the earth beneath her bare feet screamed to her about the outsiders that broke of branches as they marched, crushing plant and weed alike as they scrambled blindly through her forest at night.

Rowan quietly took a deep breath, pulling in the energy from the wood. She exhaled and felt her life energy mix with all the forest around her. Every plant, animal and insect were connected. *Listen to me, my friends! You have allowed the other Cursed Ones and I to live in peace with you, but now something evil comes. They have no respect for this place, and I fear for you!* She felt the energy of the wood turn as a cold ripple passed through the air. *None of us is safe this night! So, wake up! Wake up and stand with us!*

iv

James looked up at the night sky as the wind shifted and foul stench filled the night air. They had been walking for twenty minutes through the trees as they fought constant running skirmishes with assailants both seen and unseen in the woods. But now, something had changed. James looked nervously around at the trees as his fine-tuned battle-sense warned him that something fundamental had shifted. Both James and Sanchez had taken a knee and were surveying the area.

"Do you see anything?" James whispered.

"No. But you *feel* that, right?" Sanchez asked.

"Yup." James agreed. "Something just happened, but that only means that we need to move faster. I don't want to give whatever that is time to develop a game plan." He stood and motioned for the agents to start pressing south again along the western ridge.

That was when the screaming started. One of the men on the left-hand side of the column, dropped his assault rifle as he held up his right hand in his left and screamed until he threw up.

"Jesus!" James exhaled. "What's wrong with him?" He had barely got the words out when another man, this time in the rear of the column on the right fell over clutching his leg and screaming. James spun around to see what was going on, but two more men dropped.

As one of the screaming men was lifted to a standing position again, the agent that had helped get him back upright cried out and snatched his hand back from the man. A large leaf drifted to the ground between the two men.

James ran over and shined a flashlight on the leaf. It was large and almond shaped with sharp needle-like spikes all over it. He recognized the leaf immediately as a dendrocnide moroides, also known as a suicide plant. They usually lived in Australia, and the needles secrete a potent neurotoxin that causes excruciating pain that can last for years. Normally, the plant only grew to a maximum height of about six feet. Slowly James looked up and shuddered as he realized that every tree in that entire area of the forest were hybrid suicide plants. He and his men were standing underneath thousands of leaves.

James stood. "On me!!" He yelled as another man dropped screaming. The next several minutes were total chaos. All of the remaining men ran toward James position.

"Shields above your heads, men!" James instructed just as the trees seemed to shudder and the leaves rained down on them in sheets. The smell of death and rotten meat intensified and that was when the first wolf showed up. Typically, they were fairly common in the northeastern portion of the country but didn't tend to attack humans. The second wolf was much larger and seemed to possess an almost human look of intelligence in the eyes. Then, the bats and insects started flying in and out among the agents. These too seemed to be deliberately trying to fly up their noses and into their ears and eyes causing them to miss what would have otherwise been easy target practice on the wolves.

"Enough!!" Screamed one of the agents suddenly breaking free from the rest of the group. "I am Agent Wither, and I will not be brought down by a bunch of bugs!" He screamed and raised his hands. A black pitch seemed to flow out of his fingertips and everything that came in contact with it instantly decayed and turned to ash. Trees, insects, and animals all changed to powder as the other agents looked on in awe. "Die!" He snarled as he continued to project black smoke all about him laying waste to the piles of crippling leaves.

Two other agents with hand-held flamethrowers joined him and aimed at the trees, setting fire to everything in sight.

As another row of trees fell, a small female figure clad in a living suit of leaves walked forward out of the wood. Agent Wither paused his attack as she stepped forward to face the group. "I am Rowan of the Green Folk. Lady of this wood. Stop this and go back. We will give you safe passage back to the gate, but the destruction of this wood will not be allowed."

"Not allowed, little girl?" James sneered. "I don't take orders from your kind." He informed her as he quickly raised his weapon and fired.

Quicker than humanly possible Rowan moved to one side, but she was not quite fast enough. The bullet took her high in the shoulder spinning her around and pushing her back.

A small cheer went up from the remaining agents until she slowly righted herself. *Levi! Tell Storm I am sorry.* With green blood dripping from her shoulder, she stood and raiser her hands. A green light seemed to emanate from her eyes as the wind in the woods rose to a howl. All the remaining agents took aim but were too late to fire as a row of bamboo, too dense to shoot through, shot up from the ground creating a layer of protection for her. Immediately following that, more razor-sharp foot-long bamboo erupted from the ground underneath the agents, skewering feet and legs. Men fell screaming in pain all around James.

Agent Wither refocused and was about to release his jet of black decay when a bat carrying a leaf from the suicide plant flew directly into his face. His screams joined the other men as he fell to the ground clawing at the leaf that was stuck fast to his face.

"Maul! Do something!" James screamed as he watched his men dropping at an alarming rate.

Maul had been trying to find his target. Bamboo spikes shot out of the ground only to break off as they hit the solid mass of his feet and legs. Leaves clung to his hair and shirt just to be brushed off when the poisonous needles failed to puncture his thick skin.

"She's through there!" James yelled pointing at the row of bamboo.

Maul didn't need to be told twice. He put his head down and ran like a bull straight at the bamboo. It shattered as he pushed forward. As he came through the other side, four enormous wolves ran at him and attempted to sink their teeth into his hamstring, but they too could not puncture his skin. Not breaking his stride, Maul grabbed the wolf that had tried to bite his neck and slammed it into the wolf biting his legs with enough force to break bones. Then, he was on Rowan. He snatched the tiny girl up with one hand around her slender neck as her legs kicked in the air.

"You cannot kill… me… brute." She managed to choke out as he slowly squeezed his hand until he felt the bones in her neck snap beneath his fingers.

"Looks like I can, witch." He mused as her body went limp in his grasp. Just as her struggling stopped, he heard a thump and looked down. She had dropped something. He tossed her body to one side and looked down. There on the ground was a black rock with a strange mark carved on it.

"Maul! Get back here!" hollered James from the other side of the broken bamboo. Maul quickly pocketed the black stone and ran back to help the remaining agents.

Trevor's March East

i

Trevor's group had hiked through the woods almost unimpeded as it hugged the eastern side of the valley. It didn't take him long to see why. Directly ahead of them was a sheer cliff over two hundred feet high. If he were going to continue to hug the eastern edge of the ridge as he made his way south, he would need to have almost three hundred men climb that cliff.

Of course, there was one other way… "Get Stonehenge up here," Trevor commanded. A couple of minutes later the two men were looking at the cliff silhouetted in the moonlight. "Well?" Trevor asked without preamble. "Can you get us up that cliff without us having to scale it?"

Stonehenge grunted. "Yeah. But it would leave us exposed and vulnerable to attack. A schoolgirl with a slingshot could defend that summit for a year."

Trevor shook his head. "Yeah. I was afraid of that. It's too big a risk. We will have to go around, slip up behind it and regain the high ground."

The group of almost three hundred made their way through the trees and had nearly made it around the westernmost tip of the cliff when one of the agents yelled out a warning and pointed to the cliff. A large bucket of sedative tipped darts had been launched by catapult off the clifftop. It would have been catastrophic if one of the resource agents hadn't intervened. Metanite stepped forward and projected a barrier around the group. The darts bounced off and landed harmlessly in the woods. Trever knew that if they could launch that, they could just as easily launch something harder to deflect, so he had the group move further out toward the center of the valley.

All at once, they stepped out of the dense tree cover and into a large clearing. Trevor called a halt and used night vision goggles to get a better look at the clearing in the dark. "Something is off with this clearing. Some of the plants are putting off weird lights."

"If you think that is odd, you should see this place in infrared." An agent named Pitfall commented. "Some of the plants light up like microwave ovens."

"Well, there is no help for it. Avoid the ones that look suspicious and let's get out of here as soon as possible."

The group pressed forward and made it three-quarters of the way through the clearing when Stonehenge thought he saw something move. He quickly reached over and grabbed for it only to come up with a handful of fluorescent yellow flowers. "Crap!" He exclaimed. "I swear I saw something move." As he turned the flower over in his hand a large puff of yellow powder erupted from the bloom into his face. The large man sneezed once and then fell over with a crash as the medicinal flower sedated and paralyzed him in an instant.

"Holy crap! Did you see that?" An agent that Trevor couldn't make out in the dark asked. "We gotta get out of here!"

"Calm down, people," Trevor warned them. "We need to keep our heads."

That was the moment the screams of James' men could start to be heard in the distance.

"What's that?" The agent asked again. "It sounds like they are being tortured!" He edged forward preparing to make a run for the woodline.

"Stop! Do not run!" Trevor warned, but it was too late. The row of agents closest to the woods rushed forward. In his haste, the leading agent stepped on a glowing plant. There was a bright flash of orange light, and everyone within thirty feet of them froze like they were caught in a picture. Some of the frozen agents were in mid-stride – not even touching the ground.

More men turned to run off toward the trees to their left but stopped when Trevor quickly turned and shot one of them in the back of the head. "I said 'Stop!'" Trevor clarified. "I will not have you men losing your nerve and getting us all killed or frozen. Now, carefully, get back in formation and let's get through this – alive and together."

The men that had been fleeing reluctantly turned and joined the others. Pitfall fell in step next to Trevor. "What do you think that orange thing was?"

"My best guess is something that creates a localized time trap, but I would need a lot more research to be sure."

Pitfall considered it for a moment. "After we clean up here, I want to see if there are more of those things. They would make a sweet weapon."

Trevor shook his head. "You're an idiot. You don't know anything about them. If you want one, you should capture the person that grew them, but that isn't going to happen."

"Why is that?" Pitfall asked.

"Because Microman back there is carrying enough miniaturized explosives on him to blow an aircraft carrier into space, and I aim to back all these Changed into a corner somewhere and pull the pin."

Pitfall let out a low whistle. "Brutal."

"Effective." Trevor corrected him as they passed back into the woods.

Pitfall listened as the screams in the distance intensified. "I hope so because from the sounds of things, we may be the only ones left to fight."

He had barely got out the word when shouts went up from the rear of the column, and the sounds of fighting could be heard.

Trevor dropped to one knee just as something flew overhead and shattered as it bounced off a nearby tree. Explosions rocked the clearing. The first one hit the rear guard of the column, and they simply floated up into the night sky. When the second one detonated, the men standing closest to it looked at each other in confusion for a second, then dropped their guns and started hitting, scratching and biting each other like they were children fighting on a playground. Some of the agents close to them had to tie them to a tree and leave them there.

By the time the third explosion hit, the group had learned it meant something awful was happening. They looked around in fear but still couldn't locate the person setting off the detonations.

Trevor grabbed one of the resource agents. "Ethereal Jackal – this attack is coordinated from somewhere. Find it and take out the person in charge." The man in black nodded once and then ran off into the night. "Let's pick up the pace." He called.

It was when everyone started to march again that they discovered what the third explosion was. Four of the men no longer had feet. Their feet had been transformed into roots. The rest of the group were visibly shaken. No one wanted to imagine life as a tree.

"I said MOVE!" Trevor yelled. They didn't need to be told twice. Before they got very far the fourth explosion rocked the group and five of the men found themselves stuck in an invisible sphere. They pounded on the wall and even fired bullets at it, but it didn't break. They too were left behind.

When the fifth explosion detonated the entire group launched into a full run, there was no stopping it. There was no thought. They simply ran for their lives.

ii

The Cursed Ones setting off the explosions behind them were from a group of wraiths. They had the ability to step into their own shadow. They made no sound as they moved and at night, they were almost impossible to see. The only time they could be hurt is when they became solid. To interact with the physical world, they had to take physical form. They would step out of their shadow, hurl an explosive and dive back into wraith form. All in all, they were having a fantastic time until they heard a sharp command in their heads. *Stop! Do not pursue them! They are close to the home of Muertos.* The wraiths silently broke off their attack and sullenly started their walk back to the command tent.

iii

As Trevor and the others ran through the woods, they saw a small light and ran toward it. It was the window of a small log cabin set back against the hillside. Trevor got within a hundred feet before he came to a stop to assess if it was safe to get closer. As his men caught up, they took their shields off their backs and formed a wall in front of the group. The men in the back did the same, praying that the chaos that had followed them from the clearing would come no closer.

Just then, the door to the cabin swung wide open spilling light from a fireplace into the surrounding woods. "Gentlemen. I am John Muertos, and I have felt you coming for some time now." An immaculately dressed middle-aged man with a goatee announced as he stepped out into the night. "Your fear… Your anger…" He continued as he walked closer to the line of shields. "I am afraid it has been quite exhilarating for me." As he continued to approach, small streaks of electricity curled off his body in all directions. A few more steps and they flew off his hands to hit the ground next to him.

One of the closest agents fired a shot at him, only to have the electricity vaporize the bullet in the air before it struck him. "Gentlemen. I will not kill you, but this is not going to feel pleasant. My apologies."

With that, he let loose the enormous charge that had been building as the emotions of those in front of him fueled his ability. The blast shattered the shields in the front row of men knocking them over and quickly dancing into the following rows. Pitfall, who had been standing next to Trevor, bent over and touched the ground. It immediately fell away into a six-foot-deep trench swallowing both Pitfall and Trevor just as the electricity sizzled through the air where they had been crouching.

Trevor turned to face Pitfall in the trench. "Can you extend this thing? Get us a way out of here, before he fries us all."

Pitfall turned to the southern wall and placed his hand on it. Immediately, the ground fell away, and the trench extended hundreds of yards into the woods.

Trevor yelled to the men above. "Metanite, cover us and get as many to follow this path as you can." As the agents dropped down into the safety of the trench, Trevor grabbed a grenade off one of the men's bandoliers. He pulled the pin, counted to five and flung it as hard as he could in the direction of the electricity.

The explosion from the grenade was nothing compared the blast of heat and electricity that blew past the trench. Trevor did not wait to see if the man in the suit was dead or not. He yelled for his men to follow him and ran to the end of the trench.

iv

Reagan had checked on John to let him know the attack had begun and to be ready. Then she had circled back to the southern side of Yoman's Creek to wait with the other defenders. At a few minutes past midnight, there was an amazingly bright flash of light from the direction of John's cabin.

Levi — tell your brother to bring his blue butt down here, or he is going to miss all the fun! She sent the thought out into the night.

On it, she heard Levi's reply just before the ground on the north end of the creek sank exposing the opening of Pitfall's trench. A moment later agents covered in dirt started pouring from the mouth of the opening.

Reagan didn't wait. "Light 'em up, boys!" She yelled as she stood up and white bolts of stunning energy flew from her hands as she laughed at their surprise.

351

The effect was amazing. The agents emerging from the trench had just survived a terrifying run through a haunted forest filled with invisible attackers who lobbed horrific weapons at them. After escaping that, they had run into what appeared to be a beatnik college professor that could throw electricity with his hands. Now they stood at the mouth of a trench, and some of them were too terrified to raise their weapons at what appeared in the cold moonlight to be the walking incarnation of death. Her pale white clothing and grinning skull mask laughed at them as she advanced toward them firing bolts from her hands.

The effect didn't last long though as agents were forced out of the trench before it emptied out near the creek. The agents in the woods ran to the edge of the trees and used them for cover. Bullets were just starting to fly when a loud female voice rose above the rest. "STOP! She is mine."

The agents at the opening of the trench moved out of the way as a woman dressed all in black stepped out of the opening and strode confidently into the clearing.

"I am Lady Death, and I have felt your approach. Who are you?" She demanded.

"I am Ghost Touch," Reagan replied holding her ground. She hated to admit it, but she too had sensed the other woman approaching, and now that she was in front of her, the sensation was intense. "I don't suppose you would care to surrender?" She asked dryly.

The other woman scowled at her. "You are a child."

Ghost Touch stuck out her tongue and fired a white bolt straight at her.

She barely had time to raise her arm when it struck her. Reagan looked on, stunned as she realized her power had no effect on the other woman.

The Lady Death didn't hesitate and raised her hand. Black bolts flew from them and struck Reagan square in the chest but had no effect. She sucked in a breath. "How?" The dark lady demanded, but Ghost Touch already had an idea.

"Oh… I think I know." She smiled under her mask. "You didn't happen to die and come back to life anytime recently, did ya?"

Lady Death looked stunned.

"I thought so. I am willing to bet you and I are apprentices to the same creature." Reagan started.

"I am an apprentice to NO ONE!" The woman in black shrieked.

"Easy sister. It was a hard pill for me to swallow when I first found out too."

Lady Death had heard enough. She ran forward and swung her fist at Reagan's face. Reagan ducked under it and shoved the other woman sending her pinwheeling to get her balance.

"Oh, you want to do this old school?!" Reagan asked bringing her hands up in self-defense.

Lady Death was beyond reason, she screamed again and rushed at Reagan with her arms up reaching for her neck. Having been in dozens of fights when she was younger, Ghost Touch knew this move well. As soon as the other woman's hands got close enough, she grabbed her by her forearms and held on as she bent and allowed the other woman's momentum to send her into a backward roll. With one quick shift of her feet, Ghost Touch had them in Lady Death's abdomen and kicked upward sending the woman in black sailing past her to land in the creek.

Sputtering, she stood up and turned to face the other defenders on the far side of the creek. Seeing the smiles on their faces, she raised her arms and fired her black bolts at them. This was the queue to open fire that the agents in the woods had been waiting to see. Bullets flew, and Ghost Touch would have fallen if a bright blue wall of shimmering air had not spread out to protect her.

Lady Death's aim was horrifically accurate. As her bolt struck its first victim, he staggered backward. With his hands in front of himself, he watched as his hand and then his entire body turned black. He was dead before he hit the ground. She, on the other hand, relished in his death as the dark force around her seemed to grow more intense and expand.

Just then, one of the agents got off a lucky shot and killed one of the Cursed Ones. As the defender breathed his last, Ghost Touch could feel the energy being released. It flooded into her, and she knew that her abilities were now stronger. She turned to face the agents in the woods. She took a deep breath and shoved forward with her ability. The men attempting to take cover behind the trees were blown backward, unconscious before they hit the ground, as leaves rained down on them.

Looking for a new target, Lady Death looked up and saw Storm firing balls of glowing blue plasma down at the agents in the woods. Without a second thought, she aimed and fired a stream of black energy at him. Due to her position below him, the shot hit his leg. The bright blue power he emanated immediately started to dim as he dropped toward the ground, unable to continue to fly.

Storm could feel his leg go numb and shifted his balance to his other leg while attempting to project a barrier of air molecules between himself and the constant stream of dark energy coming off Lady Death, but nothing worked. The stream passed through his barrier as if it wasn't even there. Within seconds, he could feel himself losing strength and was no longer able to even attempt to erect another shield.

"No!" Screamed Ghost Touch. As she watched, the blue glow in Storms arms and legs flickered and went out, revealing a t-shirt and jeans. She turned and ran at her.

The effect of Lady Death's dark power hitting Storm was terrifying. The dark force swirled and crackled growing stronger by the second as the life was being drained from him. "Yes!" She cried out in triumph.

Just then, the shadow of a wraith moved on the edge of the creek bed heading in a straight line to Storm. Bullets slammed ineffectively through it and into the dirt as the agents tried to stop it. Just as it was about to pass Storm, there was a flicker of movement, and the physical person flew out of their shadow to tackle Tom, sending them both sprawling into the trees.

"Aarrgh!" Screamed Lady Death as her feeding was interrupted.

"Hey, bitch."

Lady Death turned around just in time to see the tree limb as Reagan swung it for all she was worth into her head. She landed unconscious in the sand by the edge of the water.

"Not good enough," Reagan muttered in a fury and ran over and started kicking her.

The rest of Trevor's group was now surging out of the mouth of the trench, and bullets whizzed past Reagan as she continued to kick Lady Death's limp form. "You… could… have… *killed…* him… witch!" She screamed ignoring the bullets, but then, a huge hairy form appeared next to her.

"Commander." It growled in a voice that was barely human. "We go, now!"

"Hold on Wolfblood…" She continued kicking.

Without any further warning, the creature picked her up, still kicking, and bolted off to the southern side of the creek and the safety of the trees. The remaining defenders fired darts and used their abilities to slow the advance of the agents, but there was no holding the creek.

Wolfblood let out a single chilling howl, signaling the retreat, and the defenders started moving back toward the Settlement in pairs.

"Put me down, puppy or I will drop you where you stand!" Reagan squeaked as the massive creature loped back a few yards before picking up a rock and hitting one of the agents in the head with it from a distance no human could have matched.

Looking down at her, and seeing that she was serious, he unceremoniously dumped her on a bed of moss.

Reagan landed in a pile. "Where is Storm? Did one of the others grab him too?" She demanded.

"Back there." He gestured back at the creek. "With wraiths," Wolfblood growled.

"You *left* him!?" She was furious.

"You not die." He shrugged.

She grumbled under her breath and turned around to go back, but before she could start working her way to where Tom had fallen, a barrage of bullets hit the trees and ground all around her sending up a shower of bark and dirt. She immediately dropped to the ground next to Wolfblood for cover. "You had better hope he is not dead, or I will never forgive you."

He looked at her with understanding in his canine eyes. "No time" he growled. "Home or die."

Reagan froze for a minute. Her heart screamed for her to run to Tom just as her mind screamed for her to lead her group back to the relative safety of the settlement. "I'm sorry Tom" she whispered under her breath. *Levi, tell the others in my group to retreat to the Settlement.*

CHAPTER **30**

The Siege

i

There were only five of the original ten defenders that made it back to the Settlement.

"Holy crap! I guess they did reinforce the wall!" Reagan marveled after she finally caught her breath from the run. Normally, she would still be walking through trees, but they had all been cut down for one hundred yards in every direction surrounding the settlement. Reagan had known that this was the plan and had seen a lot of the work done before she ran off into the woods, but seeing the project completed was both impressive and upsetting. She knew that the archers and catapults needed open space to fire at the attackers and she knew that all the wood had gone to good use building the twenty-foot wall that surrounded the settlement. It didn't matter. She still acutely felt the loss of the trees, many of which she had sat under as she received training from Leaf about what it meant to be a member of the Cursed Ones. Now, instead of the cozy feeling of being hidden under the protective golden canopy of the ancient trees, she felt exposed and vulnerable walking up to the three-story walls of the fortress.

The gate swung open at their approach and Levi came jogging out to meet them. "You made it!" He exclaimed as he ran up and hugged her. Then, looking at the small group with her. "Where's my brother?"

"What do you mean?" Reagan asked as fear gripped her. "You can't contact him?"

"No. Not since he was knocked out in the battle at the Creek." Levi explained.

Reagan grabbed her skull mask that had been hanging from her sash and pulled it back down over her face. "That's it! I should never have left that place without him!" She spun on her heal and marched straight into Wolfblood's lower chest.

"No." He growled. "You lead."

"I *am* leading fur-ball!" she snapped, looking up at him as tears of anger and frustration welled in her eyes, "but I am doing a crappy job! I never should have left him behind!"

Wolfblood reached down to grab her shoulders. "Don't!" She snapped. "Don't touch me! I am so pissed right now, you wouldn't wake up for days."

Wolfblood snatched his paws back and took a step backward.

"Reagan, listen – I know you are upset, but Tom knew the risks going out there," Levi interjected as he cautiously approached her. "We have thought he was down before." He reminded her. "The guy is fairly hard to kill."

Reagan chuckled through the tears. "Oh! This sucks!" she snapped, wringing her hands. Levi walked toward her like he was going to attempt to hug her. "Do you not like being conscious?" She asked him critically. He instantly backed up. "I don't know why it is that every time a woman has tears in her eyes, some man wants to hug her and 'make it better!'"

"Sorry." Levi apologized.

"No need to be. You just need to be enough of a telepath to know that sometimes these are tears of anger or frustration," she explained, "those kinds of tears will get your ass kicked if you try to 'hug them away.'"

"Noted." Levi agreed. Then, in a more business-like tone, "Okay. Let's get inside and button this place up. You were the last group we were waiting to have come back from your mission." He started walking back toward the gates, and they fell in step beside him. "In addition to the group you have been fighting, we have a group that has managed to hug the northwestern ridgeline. We believe that group is led by James Neuwin. He took out Rowan just south of the gate and a fairly large group of defenders that we had waiting to ambush him. He currently has only 84 of his original three hundred with him, and he is setting fire to everything on his way here."

"Why is he doing that?" Reagan asked.

"I am not entirely sure. All I get from his men is that they are terrified of the trees." Levi smirked.

"Pity," Reagan commented. "How about the group that hit us?"

"From what the shapeshifters can gather, that group is led by someone named Agent Merrola. This little aspiring sociopath is a subordinate to Neuwin, but just as ruthless. I heard he actually shot one of his men when they tried to bolt on him."

"Ouch." Reagan murmured. "Tough love." Then looking around "Hey. Where's Psyman? The last telepathic update I got was that he was going to work the eastern group while you worked the western one."

Just then, they passed into the lighted area inside the walls of the Settlement and Reagan got a good look at Levi. He looked sad and fatigued, and there was blood on his shirt.

"He was, but they got an assassin past our defenses and into the command tent." He explained as tears rolled down his cheeks. "Some guy dressed in black. He just materialized out of nowhere and cut Psyman's throat while he was talking to me! That's what all this is." He gestured to the blood on his shirt. "The guy in black shoved Psyman aside and came at me!"

"Oh my God..." Reagan looked at him, horrified. "What did you do?"

"Froze." Levi's chuckle was cold and filled with self-loathing. "I guess Bendati had sensed a presence in the camp and was trying to get the guys location, but it wasn't until he became solid in the tent that Bendati could pinpoint him. It was spooky. He just appeared and whispered something in the guy's ear." Levi shuddered. "I will take getting shot or stabbed any day over what happened to that man."

Reagan stopped in her tracks. "You mean Bendati killed him?"

"No." Levi shivered again. "But I am sure, that would have been far better for the attacker."

Reagan looked at him quizzically.

"Don't ask. Just know that justice was served." Levi resumed walking toward the tent. "Where were we? Oh yeah, Merrola has been trying to hug the eastern ridgeline but with much less success than Neuwin had. He went through Leaf's lab, John's house, and he ran into you folks at the Creek. Of his original two hundred and ninety, he is down to 61 men with him."

Reagan sighed heavily. "So, we have just under a hundred and fifty converging on this place?"

"That's what it looks like," Levi confirmed.

"And how many people do we have left?"

"About thirty-three," Levi said quietly. "Some of those are wounded, and all of them are fatigued."

"Jesus. How long before they show up here?"

"They should start showing up in about ten minutes." He confirmed.

Shaking her head, she asked, "Do you have any good news?"

Levi smiled. "There's fresh coffee in the command tent."

ii

"Attention! You in the Settlement!" The man's voice rang out in the still air of the night carrying to all those behind the wall.

Reagan, Bendati and Levi climbed the ladder to the walkway erected around the inside of the wall. Poking her head over the top of the fortification Reagan looked at the ring of torches and bonfires that the invaders had placed around the far edge of the clearing and yelled back at the man. "What?"

"I am Senior Agent James Neuwin. My agents and I have you surrounded. You and your group have been determined to pose an immediate threat to the safety of the United States. If you surrender now, we can guarantee your safety and a fair trial. If not, we are prepared to level this place." Trevor looked over at James with a question in his eyes.

Turning back to the others on the wall "You two are the last of the seven commanders other than me." Reagan stated looking back at the Bendati and Levi. "What do you think?"

Bendati chuckled. "You would not be in charge if you were so gullible that you would believe that monster."

Levi nodded. "He is completely lying. He intends to butcher us."

Reagan smiled and nodded back. She turned back to face the men in the field. "Umm… Let me think about it." She yelled back and disappeared behind the wall.

"You have five…" James began to yell back when two of the men standing next to him fell. One with an arrow in his leg and the other with a dart in his neck.

James didn't wait for another volley. "Attack!!" He screamed, and the sounds of the night were replaced with the sound of automatic weapons fire.

A group of fifteen agents immediately started working their way across the one-hundred-yard clearing under cover of their shields. They were halfway across when a catapult launched two baskets of darts at them. Five of the men dropped, but the rest kept pushing on.

Bendati then stood at the top of the wall directly in front of the group. Several of the agents targeted him with sniper rifles only to find that they were unable to see clearly to fire at him. As he lifted his staff, he looked at the sky and clouds gathered overhead. The wind picked up, but it only seemed to blow on the group approaching the wall. The shields of the men acted like sails and one by one they were lifted and tossed back into the trees. When the last one was gone, the only thing they left behind was a box they had obviously been concealing.

Levi spoke in Reagan's and Bendati's minds. *That box is full of explosives. I could feel their fear of it blowing up if they held on to it in the wind. They were supposed to blow the gate open with it.*

We will have to keep his men away from it. Bendati's voice replied.

Okay. We have a brief pause here so let's make the most of it. Levi called out.

I'll help with reloading the catapult. Reagan called.

I have some special arrows for the archers. Bendati offered.

They scrambled to help the other defenders, but it was less than five minutes later when shouts went up from the back wall as the second wave of men rushed the wall. At the same time, a lookout in the front noticed two shadows flying across the clearing.

We have incoming on north and south sides! Levi announced to everyone in the settlement.

A loud sound rang out from the back side of the Settlement. *Ignore it!* Levi's informed all the defenders in the front. *That is Infinity doing her thing in the back. As long as she can hold that, the attackers can run forward forever and will never reach the wall.*

In the meantime, darts and arrows peppered the shadows as they crossed the clearing to the north of the Settlement. Nothing had any effect on them.

Those shadow things are not stopping, and they will hit the wall in less than a minute! Levi shouted to Reagan.

She had been helping to reload the catapult and had to hand off to another defender. Running back to the top of the wall she saw the first of the shadows flit up the side of the wall and land next to her on the walkway at the top. She dropped into a crouch, and her hands started to glow when suddenly, the shadow seemed to split and change, becoming a solid person – a person with his hands raised in front of him.

"Don't shoot!" He begged.

"Jesus, Mason!" Reagan snapped at the man. "You should have told someone the wraiths were going to join us!"

"We're not," Mason explained. "I'm just returning something you lost in the woods." He looked over at the second shadow that was stretching and morphing. A moment later, Tom stepped out onto the walkway.

"Tom!" Reagan exclaimed as she ran and hugged him.

Yes! Levi's excitement could be heard and felt everywhere.

Tom hugged her back and whispered in her ear. "Sorry for worrying you. I will make it up to you later." She hugged him fiercely one more time before letting go.

"I will hold you to that." She smiled.

A small explosion rocked the wall bringing the fight back into focus. "I checked out their positions before I came in," Tom told Reagan. "I have an idea." Then he spoke to Levi. *Hey bro. Sorry, you couldn't reach me when I was in wraith form. I would have changed so I could let you know I was okay, but the woods close to the Settlement was crawling with these guys, and it took me a while to get my ability back after Lady Death did her thing.*

No worries. Levi replied, just happy to hear his brother. *Are you back to normal yet? I mean — you're normal?*

Tom laughed. *Yes, brat. Now get to the front wall and bring Bendati.*

In no time at all, Levi, Bendati, Reagan, and Tom were all standing on the wall, just out of sight of the agents on the other side. "Here is what I am thinking. We have been at this less than an hour. Neuwin is a lot of things but stupid isn't one of them. He tried for the quick fix of blowing the doors open. That didn't work, so he has spent the last half hour testing our defenses and counting our people. It won't be long before he attempts a full-blown, well-planned assault. I would rather not give him that chance. If we can attack him hard and fast, there is a chance that we can win this thing."

"Win?" Reagan asked. "They outnumber us by over four to one!"

"True." Tom conceded, but from my calculations, he has lost about 80% of his fighting force, and we have only lost 40% of ours."

"Dude." Levi cringed. "You know I hate math."

Tom rolled his eyes. "You know what I am saying though. If we can keep this up, they will lose!"

"That cannot be deduced from the available information." Bendati objected. "A lot of our wins were traps and guerilla tactics. This is a straight up fight."

"Humor me," Tom begged. "Let's hit them hard and see if we can get them to see that it will not be worth it. I think it may be time for Captain Livid." Then he looked around. "Wait. Where is Reagan?"

"Heeeyyyyy bad guys!" Came a yell from the front of the wall.

"Oh crap," Tom muttered as he looked up to see Ghost Touch flipping her middle finger in the direction Neuwin was last seen.

Bullets flew, and the wall splintered next to where Ghost Touch had been sitting a moment before.

Tom burst into blue light and shot up into the sky above the walls. *Levi – tell him to get ready.* Tom threw the thought at his brother as he found the pale, wheezing boy dumping a basket of darts into the eastern catapult. As Tom watched, the boy dropped his basket, looked up at Storm and gave him the "thumbs up" sign.

Close enough. Tom thought as he wrapped the young man in a protective shield and used it to lower him over the wall.

As soon as his feet touched the ground, he started to run toward the closest agents. It was obvious that running was difficult for him. His breathing was labored, even at his slow pace and he had a hitch to his gait. As the agents targeted him, Tom dropped the protective shield and prayed that Captain Livid's abilities didn't suffer from any sort of performance anxiety. As the first bullet flew at him, his ability engaged. The small, pale boy suddenly filled his baggy clothing. Muscles bulged as the adrenaline that triggered his talent coursed through him.

It didn't stop there. At ten feet tall, bullets bounced off his hardened skin. Seconds later, at twenty feet tall, he plowed into the line of agents picking them up and throwing them into the woods. One of the resource agents ran at him and punched him. It was apparent he had enhanced strength as Captain Livid staggered back a couple of paces. This just fueled his rage even more.

Now at his maximum size of twenty-five feet, Captain Livid's hands were almost as large as his opponent. Looking down at the other man, he growled in rage as he brought both hands together in a clapping motion with the resource agent in between them. The blow ruptured both of the man's eardrums and threw off his inner ear. He staggered and fell as dizziness and vertigo made it impossible to stand anymore.

Infuriated at the interruption, Captain Livid stepped over him and continued to open hand slap agents into unconsciousness. He had almost made it to Neuwin's command area when Maul ran out of the woodline to his left using Captain Livid's own shadow from the fires to hide his approach. In the dark, Captain Livid barely caught a glimpse of Maul before his fist made contact with the side of his knee.

With a sickening crunch, Maul crushed the cartilage and toppled the larger man. Captain Livid, dropped to one knee, holding the injured leg out to the side. Seeing Maul running in closer for another blow, the huge man grabbed Maul in one hand, lifted him above his head and slammed him as hard as he could into the ground shaking the walls of the Settlement. Not stopping there, Captain Livid leaned all of his weight onto his tiny adversary and ground him into the earth.

He was still leaning in when he noticed his hand was no longer touching the ground. Maul was now standing, unharmed, holding Captain Livid and all of his weight over his head. Grabbing the edge of the giant hand, Maul quickly bent it under, flipping the giant onto his back. He then ran up onto his chest and swung a fist with all his strength at Captain Livid's face. The fight abruptly ended as the unconscious giant, began to resume the form of a small teenage boy.

During the fight with Maul, Storm had continued throwing balls of energy that detonated like bombs just feet in front of the attackers, knocking them back and destroying their weapons.

Bendati took his staff and made a chopping motion, and the first row of trees that the agents were hiding behind were all cut clean through. Agents looked up in time to see the trees falling. Leaving everything, they bolted further back into the woods to avoid being crushed.

Ghost Touch hit several of the agents closest to the wall with bolts of her stunning energy, dropping them where they stood.

Levi encouraged all the defenders on the wall to open fire.

After several minutes of the intense exchange, Storm circled the Settlement to get everyone's attention.

"I am Storm, and I want to talk to Agent Neuwin." Storm yelled from his vantage point back on the wall.

A moment later, a figure walked out of the barricade the attackers had erected at the edge of the woods. "You have my attention. What do you want?"

"Look around you. You have a fraction of those you came with and even that number is dwindling fast. Surrender now, and we will not harm your men. We will grant them safe passage out of our valley."

"Oh, you think that you are winning?!" James replied laughing. "You may want to count again."

As Tom and the other defenders looked on, the air between the Settlement wall and James shimmered, and a sea of agents materialized in the dim light of the scattered torches.

"We have been holding an additional five hundred men in reserve." James jeered. "They are fresh and ready to fight."

"Levi?" Tom asked questioningly.

"No, they are real. It's no illusion. I can feel them, and bro… almost half of them have abilities."

Tom's head bowed at the news. "That's it then." He murmured under his breath. "We cannot win this."

James had been waiting for the additional troops to be in position and to finish collecting information on the strength of those in the Settlement. Content that he now had the information and numbers he needed, he turned to Maul. "It's time to crack open that can of worms. Go open the door."

"You got it, boss." Maul grinned wickedly as he started his slow jog across the clearing.

Reagan saw him first. "Crap! They aren't waiting, and they are sending the big one."

Darts, rocks, and arrows hailed down on Maul as he closed the distance to the front gates. Storm flew off in a streak out into the woods, reached down and ripped an enormous oak tree from the ground. Pouring his energy into the tree, he aimed and launched it into the air.

Maul heard a whistling noise that grew louder and louder. At the last minute, he looked over his shoulder just in time to see the ancient tree hurtling toward him. In a crash like thunder, the tree came to rest on top of him.

A cheer went up from the walls of the Settlement as silence replaced the thudding sound of Mauls heavy footsteps.

The cheers died on their lips as the fallen tree suddenly shook and snapped in half as the huge man resumed his approach to the gate.

Maul struck the gate once with his shoulder and leaned in as he continued his forward run. Timbers cracked, and chains snapped as the human battering ram tore the gates from their hinges.

"My God! He's through!" Storm breathed as he watched the gates fall.

A cheer went up from the hundreds of new agents assembled in front of the gates. Then, like water gushing through a crack in a dam, they all started running for the doors.

"No, no, no!" Tom was frantic as he crossed the distance between the woods and the Settlement. On the way, he happened to glance down and saw the crates filled with explosives that The Wall was going to use to blow up the settlement. It immediately gave Tom an idea. He reached out with his power and grabbed the crates, floating them into the Settlement.

Tom! What the hell are you doing! Came Levi's voice. We risked our butts keeping that particular form of death out of here!

I hear you Levi, but I think it is time to activate our fall back plan. Tom sent out the thought.

No! We can salvage this! We don't have to switch to plan B yet! Levi insisted.

Tom landed next to the explosives on the walkway on top of the wall just in time to see Ghost Touch shrug and jump off it to land on Maul's back. The excruciating pain of physical contact with her would have been enough to knock any other person into unconsciousness. Maul staggered and hit one of the support beams for the wall with enough force to snap it into splinters. "Get... off... me!" He managed to grind out between clenched teeth.

"I don't think so, big guy." She cooed into his ear as she wrapped her legs around his waist and put him in a chokehold. "I am feeling very snuggly!"

Maul screamed as the pain tore through him. "I... I..." He began.

"I'm listening. Spit it out big guy." She taunted as she pulled back on her choke hold in what seemed to be an honest attempt to pull his head off.

"I..." But that was all he had. The energy from Ghost Touch crackled as sparks between her and Maul. Finally, he dropped to one knee and then fell to the floor. Ghost Touch nimbly rolled to her feet as he went down to avoid being pinned under him.

"We should continue that talk when you aren't so sleepy." She offered as she walked away from him.

"Are you done playing yet?" Tom called down to Reagan.

"Why? Do you have something more fun?" She called back up to him.

He looked down at the crates. "Umm. Yeah. These should be fun." Then, calling out to his brother. *Levi. It's time. Get Phoenix up here and spread the word. It's time for plan B.*

Crap! Levi mentally fumed. *Your call bro. Doing it now.*

From his vantage point at the woodline, James could see the gate hanging in tatters, and his agents all prepared to rush the gate. The thing that had caused him to issue the order to hold the advance was when Storm had snatched up the crates of explosives that he had initially planned on using to blow the gates.

Even in James' modest opinion, the amount of explosive power in the crates was a bit much. Not knowing how big the Settlement was, he had opted to err on the side of being overly prepared. The bomb they had been sliding up to the gate probably had enough power to not only open the gate but to obliterate over half of the Settlement in one enormous ball of flames.

With that much explosives inside the walls of the fortification, it may be worth holding back a number of the men in case they decided to suicide bomb the place.

James shook his head as he thought the entire situation over for the hundredth time. He was still amazed. This small handful of Changed had inflicted heavy casualties on his experienced mercenary group. Even more impressive, was that they had not killed any of his agents. Part of him almost wanted to thank them since this kind of training for his men was invaluable. It was almost a shame the people of this valley all had to die.

He looked back at the walls around the settlement. It was all green wood. Untreated. That meant the walls had all gone up recently. The amount of labor involved would have taken a typical group of people months to do. Yet here it was – complete and strong enough to handle all but his most powerful resource agents. Speaking of which, where was Maul?

James didn't have any time for further musings, as he watched Storm appear at the top of the wall.

"Neuwin! I know you can hear me. Call your men back. You have come here looking to kill us, but we will not allow you the honor of ending our lives. We choose when and how we die. And we chose to do so as free men and women here in our valley home."

"Oh shi…" James muttered running forward. "Get back! Get back!" He screamed to his men. As he watched in horror, the man in blue made a motion, and the gates to the Settlement opened, revealing a red-haired man standing on top of the crates of explosives. James snatched up a pair of binoculars to get a closer look and noticed Maul in the far corner of the opening shaking his head as he started to get back up.

What in God's name could knock him out? James marveled, just before turning his gaze back to the red-haired man. The man held out his arms as if he were praying. Off to his right, he heard one of the sniper rifles fire, only to see the bullet disappear in a puff of smoke three feet from the red-haired man.

It happened swiftly from there. Flames burst from the man's eyes and ears just before the entire area burst into flames. A large image of a red dragon made of fire reared up over the Settlement. Its hungry eyes glanced at the agents that were now dropping their weapons and running as fast as they could. One fiery blast hit the field right behind the slowest of the agents sending him hurling through the air.

The second blast was directed at the crate of explosives. As soon as James saw the creature draw in a breath and take aim, he screamed out to this troops "Get down!!" and dropped to the floor.

The explosion that followed was, to put it mildly, excessive. The entire front wall of the Settlement was blown free as a massive ball of flame soared over a thousand feet into the air. All of the tents and buildings inside the wall that made up the Settlement were incinerated. The only things left other than the back wall were made of rock. Even the sand was melted into glass.

The dragon that had started it all roared once and then seemed to curl up in the flames and disappear.

iv

As soon as the flames died down, James stepped out from behind the forcefield projected by Metanite. At the midway point between James' position and the Settlement, Maul was slowly climbing to his feet and patting out his burning clothing. Shaking his head, he fell in step with James as they approached the location of where the Settlement had been just minutes before. Now that space was just ash and ambers swirling in the superheated air.

Then, they heard movement. A scrambling noise could be heard somewhere ahead. James nodded in the direction of the sound as he and Maul pressed forward. Then, they saw him. In the light of the full moon, a red-haired man with smoldering cloths was frantically pawing at the ground looking for something. "Come on! Come on!" He was whispering impatiently as James and Maul approached.

"Hold on there, lil fella," Maul said.

The man looked up, and his eyes were glowing the same color red as the dragon. "No. I need to find it." He patted around some more.

"You need to stop moving," James told him raising his weapon and pointing it at the man covered in soot.

Just then, the red-haired man snatched something up from a pile of ash. "I found it!" He exclaimed. "I left it in the tent, but everything burned. I should have known that would happen." He admonished himself as he held up an object in the air above his head.

"Woah there," James instructed him. "Slowly, now. Put whatever that is down. Nice and slow."

The man slowly brought his hands down to chest level. James could just make out the carvings in the small black rock by the light of the fires at the edge of the clearing.

The red-haired man smiled at James, and in that instant, he knew that the man was not going to comply with his request. Acting on instinct, he shouldered his rifle and grabbed the man to wrestle the object away from the man.

Maul was only a step behind, yet before he could close the distance, both men disappeared with a faint popping noise. "What the…?"

Spinning in a circle, Maul realized what must have happened. "Crap." He muttered and sat on a large rock to wait for the rest of the agents to catch up. He was barely sitting when he had to shift his weight in discomfort. Then, he stood and reached into his back pocket to see what was so uncomfortable and pulled out the small black rock with the carving on it that he had picked up when Rowan fell. "Hmmm…"

CHAPTER 31

Breaking In

i

The first thing Tom felt after the nausea passed was the cool, salty ocean breeze. He looked down at his hand where the go-stone had been to find nothing left of the magical device.

"You made it!" Levi announced in an excited whisper clapping him on the back. "Welcome to Moon Island bro!"

Tom smiled back in the dim pre-morning light, as he looked around and got his bearings. He was on the northeastern side of the island, a short distance from the northern tip and a few feet into the woods. Around him was a small group of volunteers from the Settlement.

"Thanks!" Tom smiled. "Did everyone make it?"

"Everyone but Phoenix. He may just be finishing up though."

"Good." Tom was relieved. "You know, when you came up with this idea, I thought you were nuts, but it might actually work."

"I told you – this may be the only time all the muscle is out of this building, so we will have a chance to get the evidence we need." Levi was obviously proud of himself.

"So, how do their defenses look?" Tom asked as made his way to the edge of the trees to take a look at the Wall's headquarters building.

Levi's smile dropped. "Well… A little less than perfect." He explained. "As soon as the first person showed up on the island, a two-foot-thick cement door was lowered, closing off all access to the ground floor, and it's anyone's guess what is in there once you get past the doors. On the up side, they didn't have enough people left to mount an attack when we triggered the alarms, and that tells me, they only have a skeleton crew left running the place."

"Well, it's a good thing that we brought our industrial strength lock pick." Tom laughed. Then, he walked out beyond the trees, in plain view of the headquarters building to get a better look.

"Storm!" Reagan whispered loudly from the trees. "They can see you!"

"Ghost Touch – we tripped the alarm when the cement door dropped." He explained, no longer whispering. "Even if they called for help and the agents in the Cursed Forest repaired their communications devices from the EMP, their reinforcements are still over an hour away." He smiled and rubbed his hands together. "We have an hour to crack this egg and get the hell out of here."

The rest of the crew came out of the woods. Reagan, Levi, Bendati, Trebuchet, Breacher, Wolfblood, Siesta and Alchemy gathered around Tom. "Okay guys. Here it is – our one shot. Trey and Bendati will get us in. Levi, Bendati, and Breacher – your job is to find their servers and grab all the evidence you can find about their illegal activities. Reagan, Wolfblood and I are going after Buckner. Trey, Alchemy, and Siesta

– Anything short of bringing the building down would be great for a distraction. The heavier the damage to property the better. But we will all still abide by the one rule: no killing. I think we have done well so far with this, but if we are going to prove our innocence to the authorities, we cannot be murderers." He looked around the small group, and they each nodded their agreement.

"Okay." Tom looked at the huge cement door. "Trey, ready to open the door for us?"

"If you can get me going fast enough." He agreed.

Tom's grin was fierce. "Not a problem. Do you have the payload?"

"Yup."

"Then, let's do this." The blue plasma flared as Tom rose into the air above the others. "Hold on to your fillings," Tom advised Trey as he grabbed the air around the young man and lifted him up. Once up above the heads of the others, Tom began to spin, whipping Trey around like he was attached to the end of a rope. Faster and faster he spun.

I don't know Tom. Levi cautioned. *How hard do you have to throw him to get him through that door?*

Iyr and I calculated that last night. If it really is two feet of just cement, he needs to hit it with about 11,000 pounds of force. I am going to throw him at least 500 mph just to be sure.

I know he becomes more indestructible the faster he goes, but dang – I hope his ability doesn't have an upper limit or he is going to be a pancake! Levi marveled.

Too…late… now… Tom squeezed out the thought as he and Trey blurred into what looked like a giant sparkling blue roulette wheel in the air. The wind he generated pushed the small group back toward the trees as it climbed to a screaming pitch.

Holding her hands over her ears, Reagan watched in amazement as the blue light grew brighter and brighter as Tom fueled the inhuman speed with his power. Just as she was needing to look away, Tom took aim at the door and released Trey like a rocket-powered slingshot.

Flying through the air like a streak of blue lightning, Trey struck the door with earth-shattering force. The doors blew inwards pulling the hydraulic lifts that supported them and a portion of the walls with them.

Not stopping there, Trey continued through the reception desk, past the armed guards in the lobby and through several interior walls before coming to a stop next to the back wall. Once there, he dropped the destination stone in one of the plant holders and ran back toward the front of the building.

An instant later, the other seven members of the group appeared standing next to the plant holder in the back of the building, their hands still tingling from activating the go-stones.

"That worked surprisingly well," Levi commented. "We are inside and not a shot fired." He no sooner spoke the words when he heard gunfire from the front of the building. "Crap. What do you suppose that is?"

"Maybe the distraction we told Trey to make?" Bendati offered.

"On it," Siesta commented and ran toward the sound of the gunfire.

He had barely left the room when four agents with automatic weapons burst into the back room. Tom threw up a barrier, and Wolfblood lunged under it, grabbing the legs of two of the men and hurling them across the room. Reagan hit the third with a white bolt. Bendati was about to take care of the last assailant when Levi yelled. "Wait! We need him."

Alchemy held up a hand, and a silver ball materialized in it. She flung it at the remaining agent. It shattered on contact with his clothes and transformed them into a gummy substance that stuck to the floor and table on which he had been leaning. In seconds, the goo had crystallized into a hardened plastic.

"Ooohhh." Reagan approved as she walked closer. "Creative. I like it." She complimented the other woman as she got closer to inspect the frozen agent. "It doesn't explode or anything, does it?" She asked from behind the man as she winked at Alchemy.

"Not for another three minutes." Alchemy replied with a complete poker-face.

"Still haven't worked that out yet, huh?" Reagan asked, smiling.

"It's on my to-do list." She replied dryly.

"That gives you about two minutes left to tell us the things we want to know," Reagan informed the agent. "We need two things. One — where are the servers located in this dump? And two, where is Buckner?"

The agent continued to struggle against the crystalized goo that use to be his clothes.

"No use in struggling," Levi advised. "The last agent broke his arm and still couldn't get out of that stuff. Just tell us what we need to know, and we will let you out."

"You're bluffing!" The agent spat. "I read the briefing on you freaks. You don't kill people."

"Really?" Bendati asked. "Have you heard back from a single person you sent against us last night?"

The agent grew frantic. "Okay! Not that it will help you, but Buckner is on the top floor, protected by dozens of guards, and the server room is right below him on the ninth floor — in the second most heavily guarded room."

"See?" Reagan asked tapping his shoulder. "That wasn't so rough." On her last tap of his shoulder, sparks flew, and the agent slumped, unconscious.

"That's it then," Tom announced. "You all know your missions." Alchemy nodded and ran down the hall toward the front of the building where Siesta had gone moments before.

Breacher smiled after her. "Those are three highly volatile people to let loose with instructions to do damage. I hope we get out of this building before they fully embrace their mission."

"Good point. We should probably hurry." Levi commented. "I saw the sign for the stairs down there." He pointed down the hallway on their left.

Reagan, Tom, Wolfblood, Breacher, and Bendati all followed Levi toward the stairs. The stairwell required a handprint to get in, but Tom with an extra push from his ability knocked in the door.

"Ugh," Levi muttered, as he took the first flight two at a time. "I hate stairs."

As they rounded the fourth floor, Levi suddenly came to a stop. The door to the fifth floor flew open, and a man dressed all in grey stepped out from the opening. "Good to see you again, Reagan." He greeted Ghost Touch.

"Who?" She asked, but the man had already lowered his head and was charging the group. "No..."

Storm grabbed a piece of cement from the wall and yanked it in front of the group. The man smashed clear through it and slammed into Storm hard enough to send him flying backward into Wolfblood. If not for the huge man's reflexes and larger mass, they all would have been knocked back down the stairs.

"Rhino?" Reagan asked. "Is that you Jimmy?"

"That's not my name anymore." The man in grey replied. "Now I am Cyclone."

"You were captured!" Reagan ran toward him. "We thought you were dead."

"You mean you treated me like I was dead." He turned to face the others and lowered his head again.

"Don't do it young man," Bendati warned. "I am not some piece of furniture you can push across the floor."

Cyclone didn't seem to hear him. Instead, he started to run right at him.

"Don't hurt him!" Screamed Reagan.

Bendati watched as Cyclone started running and casually drew a line in front of himself with his staff. He whispered something under his breath, and as Cyclone tried to cross the line to slam into Bendati, he seemed not to be able to pass it. It was as if he had dived into a piece of glass or a mirror. He had height and width, just no depth, and he was stuck.

Reagan rushed to her former friends' side but didn't dare to touch him. "What did you do to him?"

"I trapped him in two-dimensional space," Bendati explained.

"You can you do that?" Levi asked trying to see Cyclone from the side.

ii

Back on the ground floor next to the potted plant, there is a small popping sound and a rush of air as Phoenix and James suddenly appeared in a cloud of smoke. James rolled immediately to one side and fired his assault rifle. The bullet hit Phoenix in the head throwing him back into the plant holder.

"What the…?" James looked around trying to get his bearings. "I'm back at headquarters!" Then, he heard the shouts and gunfire, and he knew what had happened. "Those sneaky little… They used our invasion of their home to plan an assault on our headquarters!"

Keeping low, he crept into the closest office and logged into the computer. He quickly pulled up the security video of Trebuchet's spectacular entrance through the front door and the ensuing firefight through the first floor. Changing from security videos to the alarm system, he noted that alarms had also been tripped on the ninth and tenth floors.

"Oh no!" James breathed. "This has to stop. They can't leave here alive with whatever they came for!" But he knew that reinforcements were all hours away in the valley and they couldn't even radio them for help. The agents that had been left behind were not going to be strong enough to stand up against whoever the Changed had sent here. There was only one possible solution. He immediately ran for the stairs leading to the basement.

As he descended the stairs, he passed the door leading to the training center where new Changed were indoctrinated into The Wall's fighting force. Further down, he passed the door that lead to the experimental weapons department. Finally, several stories down from that he reached a locked door with a hand and retinal scanner. He quickly entered his passcode and scanned his eye and hand. The light outside the door turned green, and the door popped open.

He knew this was the only way he could win against this level of infiltration. He needed the strongest of the Changed, and he needed to be strong enough to control them without any assistance. The level nine and ten Changed in the Lower Reaches could change the tide of this fight, and in his desperation, he was willing to risk letting them loose.

First, though, he needed to be strong enough to control them, and that meant becoming one of them. The scientists in this section had been working on creating a way to transfer abilities to ordinary people. The Wall's current model of finding people with abilities and forcing them to work for them was an obviously flawed model. They hoped that they would be able to take the strongest of the abilities and give them to soldiers that were already loyal to The Wall.

James knew that they had a prototype that had been successful in transferring abilities in a lab setting and that they had petitioned the board to begin trialing the drug on volunteers. Well, now they had their first volunteer.

"Hurato! Where are you?" James called out as he ran past cell after cell of sedated prisoners with abilities. Glancing at a clock, he realized that his chief scientist would not arrive to work for hours yet. "Fine. I'll do it myself." He had read the reports. He knew what the names were of the chemicals that had the five strongest abilities. Running to the secure chemical locker, James entered his security passcode into the pad. A red light blinked indicating he did not have access.

Grumbling, James unshouldered his rifle and aimed at the locking device. Two shots rang out, and the door opened, and a cold, frosty vapor spilled onto the table. James watched as a security monitor lit up indicating that an intruder was making their way through the training center, just two floors above him. Wasting no time, he grabbed all five chemicals and laid them out on the table in the lab. Grabbing a syringe, he quickly loaded it with the experimental power of one of the Changed. Then, looking at the other four vials, he shrugged and loaded them into the syringe as well. "Gotta be strong enough to control them *all* once I release them." He muttered and plunged the needle into his arm.

iii

Back at the plant holder, Maul suddenly appeared in a puff of smoke. Looking around the room he shook his head. "Gotta say I wasn't expectin to show up here." He rumbled. Then, hearing an explosion down the hall, he realized what was happening.

"Aw man. Headquarters is under attack." He knew he had very specific orders on what to do if that ever happened, and he immediately ran for the secret elevator located behind a false panel in the janitor's closet. After scanning his palm, he stepped into the small device that would bring him to the executive offices.

CHAPTER 32

The Tables Turn

i

Wolfblood tapped Levi on the shoulder. "Go now." He urged looking up the stairs.

"Aren't you the least…?" He began to say as he looked at the two-dimensional Cyclone. "Ah. Skip it."

The group ran up the remaining stairs to the ninth floor where they paused to catch their breath.

"This is where it gets fun." Reagan giggled, barely able to control herself.

"Dear God," Bendati muttered. "Go turn her loose upstairs. She is unbearable to be around when she is like this." With his index finger, he drew a symbol on the palm pad scanner that unlocked the door.

"Levi." Tom called to get his brothers attention. "Be careful."

"I'm always careful, bro." He smirked.

Tom rolled his eyes and waved for his group to continue following him up the last flight of stairs. When they arrived, Wolfblood walked up to the palm scanner. "Got this." He growled and ripped the device off the wall.

Reagan sighed and tried to open the door leading onto the floor. It remained locked fast. "I was afraid of that. Breaking the keyhole didn't break the lock."

"No worries," Tom said as he slid up next to her. "Buckner is on this floor, and there is no way I am letting him escape." The bright blue surrounding him seemed to brighten as he held his hand up toward the door. With the sharp squealing protest of metal being ripped apart, the door came loose and fell into the hallway.

As they stepped into the hall next to the elevator doors, they all cautiously looked around at the long empty room. The hall had a wall of windows on the right and a door at the far end. Other than that, it was completely devoid of decoration or apparent purpose.

"Don't move!" Reagan warned as they all stepped into the hallway.

Tom and Wolfblood froze.

"What?" Asked Tom, barely moving his lips.

"Haven't you ever seen an Indiana Jones movie?" She asked amazed. "Look at this place! Everything about it feels weird. There's gotta be traps!"

"Go." Wolfblood indicated the door at the far side of the room.

"I think we need to think this through…" She began, but Wolfblood was already walking across the hall. He hadn't proceeded more than fifteen feet when the row of vents along the bottom of the wall opened with a noticeable click. The group all looked down at the vents in time to hear the telltale 'hiss' of the poisonous gas being released.

"Not this stuff again," Tom muttered as he reached out and crushed the pipes that were feeding the gas into the room, sealing off any contamination before it started.

"Huh." Reagan looked at the vents. "You would have thought they would have tried something a little tougher."

As if on cue, the sprinkler system activated and soaked all of them before shutting off.

"That makes even less sense than the vents." She commented. "It's not like we are going to melt."

"Unless…" Tom began looking at the standing water on the floor. "Move!" He yelled suddenly as he grabbed Reagan around the waist and flew into the air.

Wolfblood didn't need to be told twice. With supernatural speed, he jumped into the air and sank his claws into the wall, holding himself off the floor as the first crackle of electricity shot through the layer of water on the floor.

Tom created a ball of swirling plasma in his free hand and threw it at the door on the far side of the hall blowing it off its hinges. As the floor dropped open in a move that would have killed anyone not flying or clinging to the walls, he glided over and landed in what looked like a mid-sized waiting room. As he set Reagan down, Wolfblood landed lightly on the floor next to them, his tongue lolling out to one side in a lupine grin. "Fun."

Seeing the claw marks all across the wall, Reagan chuckled and made the "tsk, tsk, tsk" noise. "Barely house-broken, I see."

Wolfblood's look was withering.

She blew him a kiss, bounced into the waiting area and glanced at the four identical walls. "Well, this makes no sense. There are no doors to this room."

"Not for your kind." Came a crisp, feminine voice as the wall to the left of the door suddenly lit up, and a middle-aged woman in a grey form-fitting suit appeared.

"My *kind?*" Came Reagan's reply an octave higher. She got up in the projection's face. "And just what *kind* is that, ya racist old…"

"Ladies!" Tom intervened. "How great to see we have some communication going on here." He smiled at them both. "Can I get your name, ma'am?" He asked looking at the projection.

"My name is Lindsay McKay." The projection replied with open disdain. "I am here to tell you to go back. Mr. Buckner is not here, and even if he were, you would not be able to get past this room. The walls are all layered with graphite and four inches of steel. You are effectively cut off."

Wolfblood pounced at the image projected on the wall. With his enhanced strength and claws, he shredded and bent the metal like taffy. "Open door, lady!" He roared as he peeled the metal wall to find more cement behind it.

Storm walked up to the next section of wall, held out his hands, palms down, and lowered them toward the floor. Blue energy glowed around the top of the wall and slowly started to crumple the metal wall toward the floor. Halfway down, he stopped realizing that there was a second wall behind the one he was opening.

Ghost Touch walked up to the section of wall in front of her, placed her hands on the wall and closed her eyes. Then, as Wolfblood and Tom watched, she slowly sank through the wall like a shadow passing into a dark room.

A moment later, a section of the wall made a clicking noise, swung open, and Reagan stepped out. "Found it."

"You never told us you could walk through walls." Tom admonished her.

"I didn't know that I could. I knew I couldn't use my stun bolts on them, but I figured that the Angel of Death would need to have a way to get past something as simple as a wall." She smiled thoughtfully. "I just needed to be quiet, listen and I somehow knew how to do what needed to be done."

"Nice work!" Tom complimented her as he and Wolfblood followed her through the door.

The hallway they entered was short and barren of any decoration. At the end of it, they pushed the door open and stepped into a large room with an enormous oak table in the middle. Sitting at the far side of the table were two men. One was Greg Buckner. The other was Maul.

"How the…" Storm started to ask as he saw Maul sitting there with smoke stains all over his shirt.

"You really need to work on puttin locks on your fancy rocks, boy," Maul advised him as he stood up from his chair.

"Now, children. Let's not have this turn ugly." Buckner advised as he stood and backed up toward the wall.

"Shut up old man!" Reagan snapped. "You already made this ugly when you had our friend Leaf shot." White energy crackled around her as her emotions ignited her powers. "You have been a pain in the ass for too long. Inciting the public to think we are the dangerous, crazy aggressors while you torture and kill our kind for profit!"

Several agents slipped into the room through doors located behind the curtains on the walls carrying strange looking rifles. "As you can see, you are outnumbered and outgunned." Buckner gloated as he gestured to the agents.

"Outnumbered, yes." Storm agreed. "The rest we will have to see about." The next few seconds were a blur as Tom raised a shield around his companions and himself just as the weapons fired.

Wolfblood dove over the barrier picked up one of the agents and threw him into a second agent, knocking them both into the wall hard enough to leave an imprint of their bodies in the cracked plaster.

Ghost Touch opened fire sending white bolts of energy into the agent closest to her. She turned to the next man just in time to see him firing at Wolfblood's unprotected back. He howled and went down. She ran at the man, grabbing him by the front of his shirt, his body stiffening as she made contact. "You should not have done that!" She hissed between clenched teeth and threw the man into another agent that was trying to get in closer to get a shot off without hitting the fellow agent.

Tom sent balls of charged plasma into the three agents in front of him, leaving them twitching from the electrical blast. Knowing that there was still one more agent, Tom dropped and rolled into a crouch. A gust of hot ozone sailed past him as she heard the electrical weapon scream out it's shot. Tom threw a hand behind himself without looking and sent a plasma blast out, dropping the remaining agent where he stood.

Standing, Tom looked around and found Wolfblood on the ground, stunned. Then, Tom saw Reagan holding her stomach and realized that the blast he had just dodged had hit her. Her eyes wide and looking at Tom, she staggered and dropped to the ground.

"Okay, lil man. You're next." Maul warned as he grabbed the massive oak table separating him from Tom with one hand and shoved it against the wall.

The blue energy swirling around Tom, flared a bright shade as his fear for Reagan and anger that someone had hurt her charged his energy. Waves of power radiated off him, and a powerful wind sprang up with Tom at the source. The granite tiled floor cracked, and the walls seemed to bend away from him. The room seemed suddenly too small to contain his power. As bolts of electricity arced off him blowing out the fluorescent lights in the room, all thoughts of being the boy from Vermont washed away. He now fully embraced his power as Storm.

"Pretty lights and some wind ain't gonna save ya." Maul rumbled as he marched toward Storm.

Storm turned and threw a blast of energy at Maul. Maul never even tried to duck. The bolt slammed into his chest, but he just kept walking. Storm reached out with his mind, grabbed a section of the cement walls from either side of Maul and brought them together with a thunderous noise that shook the building. The pile of rubble only stayed still for a heartbeat. Then, with a loud cracking sound the rubble split, and Maul continued his advance toward Storm.

Tom held out a hand, and a bubble of blue energy appeared around Maul's head. The air molecules being manipulated by Tom were so tightly packed that no air could pass in or out. Maul's hands immediately came up and grabbed onto the dome of air. Digging his fingers in, Maul pulled hard. Tom staggered backward as the pain of Maul ripping the bubble of energy open tore through his mind.

Smiling at him Maul rumbled. "Nice try, kid, but I don't need to breathe, eat or sleep so I would never pass out from lack of oxygen."

Now, only an arm's length from Storm, he reached out and grabbed Tom by the throat, easily lifting him off the ground. "Now, you are going to learn why I am called Maul." He pulled back one huge fist and punched Storm in the face.

Had Storm not projected a barrier that absorbed most of the force, the one punch would have taken his head off. His vision blurred, and thoughts scattered as the pain coursed through his body. He knew he had seconds before he was knocked out by another punch or he passed out from lack of oxygen due to Maul's stranglehold around his neck.

Storm looked around frantically as Maul started to bring his hand back for another blow. As he raised his fist, Storms mind seemed to settle as he accepted the possibility that he would die. In that moment of clarity, the answer came to him. Calling on his remaining power, he flew upward bringing Maul up with him. At close to the height of the elevated ceiling, he forced a blast of energy out in front of him blowing a hole through the roof.

Accelerating as fast as he could, Storm and Maul blasted through the hole like a cannon fired at the sky. Before, Maul had time to react he was hundreds of feet in the air and climbing. Tom knew that no matter what happened, Maul would survive. If he fell to earth, from any height, he would just get up and come at Tom and his friends again and again. Nothing could hold him. No cell would be strong enough. No needle hard enough to puncture his skin to drug him, and with him not needing to breathe, no gas could sedate him.

Tom was rapidly approaching a blackout. In a moment of inspiration, he faked passing out and allowed himself and Maul to begin to fall. It worked perfectly as Maul's grip instinctively loosened as he began to fall. Tom seized the opportunity and threw a powerful blast into Maul's midsection sending him flying as air flooded Storm's burning lungs.

Knowing what his next move had to be, Storm quickly grabbed the air around Maul and began whirling the large man around in a circle as he had Trebuchet just a few minutes earlier. At seven thousand feet and climbing, the blue power flying off Storm lit up the morning sky as he whipped Maul at an ever-increasing speed. At just under eight thousand feet, Storm released Maul straight up into the only prison that could hold him – a low orbit around the planet.

ii

Levi, Bendati and Breacher ran down the hallway on the ninth floor. Levi was in the lead holding an unlit lightbulb in one hand.

For the second time, Levi paused and asked Bendati "Are you sure this is really necessary? It isn't even attached to a power source."

Bendati frowned. "Yes. I am telling you, that bulb will light up if we are about to spring a trap, and I certainly don't need a battery to make it light up. Now move."

Relying more on speed than stealth the small group continued down the labyrinth of halls. "This way." Breacher directed as they were about to pass by a reinforced door.

"Did you have to pick the thickest door?" Levi asked as they slowed and looked at the huge metal structure that attached to the wall so tightly, not even a piece of paper could slide past it.

"They are in here," Breacher confirmed rubbing his hands together. "I can feel them."

"You're sure?" Bendati asked.

"Absolutely." He confirmed.

"Good. I had Alchemy whip us up a little something before we left. She said it would make it easy to get through something solid." He reached down into his robes and pulled out a small silver orb. The colors on the surface danced under the fluorescent lights. "Step back."

"Wait," Breacher cautioned. "We don't want the wall to turn into crystal. We'll never get through."

"That's not her only gift," Bendati explained. "She can turn any material into any other material with one of these little guys." Without any further explanation, he threw the ball at the door. The silver coated the door and seemed to pull and stretch. In a matter of seconds, the heavy reinforced metal door had been transformed into a door made of spider webs.

"Oh, come on!!" Levi objected. "That's disgusting."

Breacher was already pulling the webs apart with his hands and stepping through into a room that was floor to ceiling server racks, power supplies and fire suppression systems. "Damn! This is my kind of candy store!" Breacher cooed as he looked around.

Bendati looked back down the hall. "How long do you need?"

"At least twenty minutes," Breacher answered as he pulled two high-density solid-state drives from his backpack and plugged them into the main console. "I will need at least that long to crack their security and copy the data." Levi expected him to sit down at the keyboard, but instead, he reached out and laid his hand on the monitor and closed his eyes. Images, letters, numbers, and symbols all shot across the screen faster than any normal human could follow.

"Cool. We will…" Levi began.

"Step back." Bendati urged pushing Levi back behind him with a protective arm. Before Levi could ask him why, Bendati reached down with a marker and made two small symbols on either side of the torn spiderweb door. A second later, the huge metal door was back in place.

"No way!" Levi exclaimed. "You fixed it?"

"No," Bendati confessed. "I don't have that ability – yet. However, I did make an illusion that it is fixed so that when the guards walk by on their patrols, they most likely will not investigate further."

"Dude! That's genius." Levi complimented him. "Just one thing – what are they going to say when they see us?"

"We will need to hide," Bendati told him.

"Too late." Levi pointed down the hallway behind them. "I can feel them. They know someone set off the stairway door alarm." He frowned at the other man. "Sloppy."

"We can talk about it later," Bendati told him hurriedly. "We need to move."

"We'll never get past them," Levi held up his hand. "I got this."

The three men rounded the corner and saw Bendati and Levi. "Hi… John." Levi greeted the first man. "We are just a couple of guards you know."

The man in the lead faltered slightly then smiled. "Hi. It looks like our watch commander got us mixed up again. Both squads are watching the same place."

"Yeah." Levi chuckled. "I think having most of the heavy hitters gone today on that mission has all of us a little spooked."

"No kidding." The guard on John's right agreed. "With what we have in the basement, we don't really need much more to make us nervous, right?"

Levi's eyes went wide. "No! I guess you are right about that." Then, looking back at Bendati. "Come on Frank. Let's go ask watch command why they doubled the rotation. If this is a screw-up, I'm going home and back to bed!"

Bendati nodded and followed behind Levi.

"Later, guys," Levi called as he waved his hand over his shoulder.

"Take it easy," John called after him.

Levi kept up the act until he rounded the corner. Then he staggered and leaned against the wall. Bendati rushed to his side. It was only then that he noticed that Levi was awash with sweat. "Controlling what someone sees and thinks is harder than it looks." Levi breathed shakily.

"You did well." Bendati commended. "Come on. Keep walking."

iii

The twenty minutes Breacher needed to copy the data had dragged by, but Bendati and Levi had managed to stick it out without being seen again. Even so, several times they had to turn around when the enchanted light bulb lit up and find another route. However, when the alarm started going off indicating that the executive suite on level ten had been compromised, all that changed. Agents poured out into the halls with weapons drawn. Levi could sense them but only when they were almost on top of them.

"You are sure this is the way back to that server room?" Levi asked running down one of the hallways.

"Yes." Bendati panted. "I'm positive."

They were just coming to a fork in the hallway. "Left, or right?"

"Right."

"Okay." He turned and faced Bendati. "The most important part of our mission is to get those files out of this building. Eight agents are coming down the hall to our left. There is no way we can avoid them.

I will cause a distraction, you keep going and pick up Breacher and the prize. Do *not* come back for me!"

"This is not a good plan," Bendati told Levi.

"It may not be a good one, but it is the only one we have right now." He agreed. "On three."

"May the Mystics watch over you." Bendati patted his shoulder.

Levi didn't wait any longer. "Three!" He stepped out around the corner where all the agents could see him. He swallowed hard. He knew there was no way he could pull off another detailed mental domination as he had done to the three men earlier in the evening. He also knew that simpler stories were easier to push on someone, and fears were the easiest. As the guards raised their weapons, he held up his hands in surrender. Walking forward to get as close to them as possible, he planned out his next move.

When he was within six feet of the closest guard, "You have bugs crawling all over you." The man dropped his rifle and started clawing frantically at himself. "You are being tickled." The second guard dropped his weapon and started laughing. Then as quickly as he could... "You are blind. You are paralyzed. You have diarrhea. You're falling. You're naked."

Amazingly, he was past them. They all were incapacitated by the beliefs Levi had pushed on them. Just as Levi passed the last man, he sensed something. "Wait. That was seven. Where's the last guy?" Without warning, the final agent jumped out from around the corner and lunged at Levi with a large combat knife.

Levi's eyes grew huge as he felt the blade bite deep into his stomach. Blood poured down his shirt as he grabbed his assailant for support to stand. Levi pulled the man in close and whispered in his ear. "You're on fire." The man flinched as if a fly had landed on his nose. Then, he held his hands up in front of his face and started screaming. Frantic to escape the pain, the agent bolted back down the hall, not even stopping when he ran through the large picture window at the end.

"Oh crap," Levi muttered as he sank to the floor. "He wasn't supposed to do that. Tom's gonna be pissed."

The Lower Reaches

i

Wolfblood bent a metal piece of rebar from the caved-in section of the ceiling around Greg Buckner's wrists, just as Storm was floating back down into the room.

The energy weapon had not been able to subdue the superpowered man for long. He had woken to find Buckner desperately scanning security cameras as he tried to find a way out of the building that wouldn't involve the possibility of a firefight.

"Ghost Touch?" He asked not wasting words.

Wolfblood motioned to the corner of the room where he had laid her out with a rolled-up curtain under her head. Tom ran over to her and dropped to his knees to get a closer look. "Hey. Wake up, beautiful. We aren't done yet." He whispered holding her close.

She moaned and wrapped her arm around him. "I promise I will never drink again, mom." She moaned, half awake.

"What?" Tom asked. Then shook his head in disbelief. "You scared the crap out of me." He scolded her.

"Sorry. This pillow is just so comfy." She purred.

"But we need to get up and go beat up bad guys." Tom teased her.

"You say the sweetest things…" She mumbled and started to get up.

She got to her feet and looked around the room. Seeing Buckner in Wolfblood's custody, she beamed. "Looks like you caught a *big* one."

His answering smile was contagious.

Tom was about to suggest they start back down the stairs when Levi's voice rang out in his head. *Tom! Something is happening far below us. Three basements deep I sense mortal fear and an insane amount of power waking up.* His mental voice sounded funny in Tom's mind. Brittle.

Are you okay? Tom's mind questioned.

You need to stop asking questions and get down there. The others are on their way too.

Okay. Tom replied. *We are on our way.*

Hurry Tom!

"Are you ready for battle?" Tom asked Reagan.

She smiled. "Always."

"Good. Levi just contacted me. We are needed now in the third sub-basement." He announced loud enough for both her and Wolfblood to hear.

"Did you say the third subbasement?" Buckner asked looking very nervous.

"Yes," Tom answered. "Why?"

"Nothing." He answered testing the bar that held his hands with increasing anxiety. Then looking at Wolfblood "So, you caught me. Let's go. I don't care where, but can we go *right now?*"

"It doesn't take a genius to see that whatever is in the basement isn't good," Reagan commented blandly. "Wolfblood - If you have him, Tom and I should probably go now."

Wolfblood nodded, and they headed for the door.

ii

Tom and Reagan could hear the sounds of battle growing louder as they approached the doorway to the basement. The door itself hung in tatters from one hinge looking as if it had been made of cardboard and not reinforced titanium. They ran into the lab and froze trying to make sense of what they were seeing.

The lab was a large open area with a row of cells along the left-hand wall. The cells were made of what appeared to be a crystalline glass substance that was several inches thick. There was a bed, sink, and toilet in each cell. All the cell doors were open and less than half of them were occupied.

The rest of the large room was in disarray. Computers, centrifuges, microscopes, tables, and chairs were all tipped over or thrown against the wall. One section of the wall had a huge scorch mark on it. Below the scorch mark was the burned body of Trebuchet.

Standing protectively next to his friend's smoldering body, Siesta was firing blasts of his stunning power at a large man that looked only vaguely familiar. He had the remnants of tactical pants on, but it looked like his upper body had ripped through his shirt. Flames danced down his forearms toward his hands as he advanced on the large wooden table that Siesta was hiding behind.

Movement further in the room caught Tom's eye as Alchemy squared off with two figures he couldn't recognize. One was half encased in what looked like diamonds, which slowed her down. The other was bleeding from cuts to the forehead and his right arm. Alchemy herself was limping on what looked like either a badly turned ankle or a broken leg while whirling three silver balls in one hand and short sword in the other.

"I've got Alchemy," Reagan told Tom as they both started running.

The large man in tactical pants was almost at the overturned desk by now. Tom grabbed one of the lab's centrifuges with his mind and hurled it at the flaming man. A normal man would have been thrown across the room, but when the device hit him, it bounced off like it was made of styrofoam. The giant turned and faced Tom. That was when Tom finally recognized him. "Neuwin?"

James chuckled. "Well, well, well. It finally comes down to this." His words were difficult to understand as they rumbled past his fang-like canine teeth.

"What happened?" Tom asked staring at him.

"I knew that normal people stood little chance of ever beating you animals in a fair fight. That was made painfully clear last night." James explained. "But now, I am the most powerful Changed ever, and this war will die with you – right here and right now." Flexing his enhanced muscles, James started to advance on Tom.

Tom threw a blast of swirling plasma at James only to have him swat it away like it was nothing more than a bug. James raised his hands, and a searing hot blast of fire flew out, smashing through a hastily erected barrier Tom had put up and slamming into Tom's chest, throwing him back into a rack of servers. The computers melted as James kept advancing.

Seeing Tom was in trouble, Siesta ran up to James and fired his stun blast at him with all of his strength. James staggered slightly at the unexpected force, then, quicker than is humanly possible spun around and backhanded Siesta. The blow from James massive hand connected with Siesta's right arm and chest, breaking bones and throwing him into the cement wall like a bug hitting the windshield.

The distraction was all that Storm needed. This was the man that had ordered his abduction. The man that had overseen his torture, ordered his brother's capture and his mother's memory erased. Tom had always used restraint when using his powers. He knew he had to so that he didn't kill someone. But at this moment all thoughts of that were gone. Tom seemed to brighten until his eyes were like beams from a laser. Intense winds blew in all directions from Storm. The fury inside him built until it felt too large to be contained in his body. At the height of his building rage, two beams that were so bright they were almost white shot from his eyes and slammed into James. The huge man flew through the air and crashed into the cement wall as the force of Storm's eye beams continued to push him into the cement.

iii

Reagan had continued to run as Tom engaged the man advancing on Siesta. She had almost made it to her friend's side when Alchemy slipped in some liquid spilled on the floor. Unable to use her injured right foot to catch herself, she landed on her back with her short sword poised in front of her as the bleeding man reached for her.

"Move!" Reagan bellowed. Alchemy heard her and rolled to her right to give Ghost Touch a clean shot. The bleeding man looked up just in time to see the bolts of white light erupt from her hands. In an instant, he was gone, and Reagan's blasts harmlessly hit the back wall. In that same moment, Alchemy quickly lifted her sword as if using it to point at something on the wall. The bleeding man suddenly reappeared, right where Alchemy was pointing her sword – materializing with the blade now protruding from his thigh. The man screamed and dropped to the ground with the sword firmly stuck in his leg.

The woman covered in diamonds saw her opportunity and pointed her hands at Alchemy. Small glands in her palms opened and a green liquid shot outward. Alchemy threw one of her silver spheres at the liquid and instead of acid hitting her, water splashed harmlessly off her shirt.

Reagan didn't hesitate. She ran at the diamond covered attacker. As she ran, she called on her power, infusing her body with crackling white energy. At less than ten feet she dove and connected with the other woman's midsection. Sparks flew, and the woman screamed as the power of Ghost Touch ripped through her body causing every nerve cell to shriek in pain. Reagan spun away from the woman and rolled to her feet, noting that the other woman was unconscious.

"Thank you, Ghost Touch." Alchemy was trying to get up. "Now to help Storm."

Blue light flooded the room making both women shade their eyes.

"Looks like Storm is *pissed!*" Reagan noted. "We may need to help the other guy, so he doesn't end up dead." Then, she frowned as Alchemy hopped on one foot. "I don't think you should be trying to help anyone."

"I'm still good," Alchemy argued.

"You can't even stand."

"I can more than stand. I can fight." The young woman was determined.

Reagan had been looking through the small bag that hung from her waist. Gingerly she removed an object. "I bet you can, but I don't want you dying because you couldn't get out of the way. This guy is too powerful to go after if you aren't 100% and you mean too much to me to risk it." Not waiting for a reply, she tossed the small black rock at Alchemy who caught it in midair and suddenly disappeared. Like the aftereffects of a camera flash, Reagan could still see the anger in Alchemy's eyes as she realized she had just inadvertently activated the go-stone that Reagan had tossed her.

"Yeah… I'm gonna have to really suck up to her to make up for that." Reagan muttered under her breath as she started to go back to help Tom. She turned just in time to see blue-white beams from Tom's eyes shoving an enormous man into a wall. The man couldn't pull himself away as the cement cracked from the continued force of the impact.

Just as Reagan was about to fire a volley of her power at the man Storm had pinned, the man used his talon-like hands to tear out a fist-sized piece of cement and throw it at Storm. Had Tom not been using his power to protect himself, the impact would have been fatal. His eye beams winked out as he flew backward smashing into a large filing cabinet.

Reagan slid to a stop and fired at the man clawing his way out of the rubble of the wall. He rolled to one side and came up on his feet.

Facing the man, Reagan smiled. The effect while wearing her mask with the skull painted on it was chilling. "Fee, Fie, Fo, Fum." She mocked him. "Just who the hell are you?"

"I am the end of your kind." He rumbled.

Ghost Touch looked puzzled. "My kind? Why do people keep saying that? It's offensive" she taunted. "Besides, don't they allow mirrors down here in the basement? I hate to break it to you, sunshine, but you are one of us."

"No. I am not. I am Agent James Neuwin, and I hunt your kind." He roared throwing a ball of fire at her head.

"Jesus." Reagan ducked and muttered. "That's all I need. A super-powered bad guy having an identity crisis." She cautiously maneuvered over toward one of the open vacant cells. "How about you have a seat on this nice bed in here, and you can do some soul searching?" She gestured toward the cell.

James raised his hands and spikes shot from his palms. Reagan dove to her left and rolled back to her feet narrowly avoiding being impaled on the spikes as she continued to maneuver James closer to one of the open cells. "James Neuwin… I thought that was the name of the Lead Agent that attacked the Settlement." She mused trying to draw him into a conversation.

"It was." He agreed. "I mean, it is." He walked a few steps closer, and his arms ignited as he prepared for his next attack.

"You sure did get here in a hurry. How did you swing that? And what's with the 'roid-rage?" She looked past him and saw Tom had dug himself out of the smashed filing cabinets and lined up behind Neuwin.

"Now!" Tom yelled and flew full speed into James' back. Reagan dropped to the floor as James sailed over her head and into the crystalline jail cell. Ghost Touch quickly jumped to her feet and slapped the button on the wall causing the cell door to slide shut.

"Wooohooo!" Tom crowed as James got to his feet and punched the cell door.

"Yes!" Reagan ran up to Tom and hugged him. "We got him!"

James' second punch was much harder, and the entire cell shook. "You think this thing can hold me?" He bellowed. "I have all the powers of the five most powerful Changed on record. This cell won't hold me!"

Just then, a light flared at the far end of the room. Flames danced across the water that was on the floor.

"Whoa," Tom cautioned. "Is that a gas fire?"

Before Reagan had time to answer, colors started to shift in the reflection on the surface of the water. Tom looked down and the shifting pattern resolved into a nightmare landscape. Lifeless dirt for miles with barren mountains in the background. Fires raged without pattern or cause. Then, he saw movement. A figure dressed in a red suit with a black cloak came striding toward them. When the figure got to the edge of the image in the pool, she kept walking and stepped out of the reflection in the water, up into the basement.

"Greetings, mortals." Hellbound greeted Tom and Reagan as she pulled the cowl of the cloak back so her fine features could be seen. "I am here to collect the evil ones." She announced.

"Evil ones?" Reagan asked. "Could you be more specific? There is an awful lot of evil in this place."

She sneered at Reagan. "I have come for that one." She announced pointing at James. "Even from Hell, I can sense him. His deeds demand my attention."

James looked on and smiled. "I'm not scared of you, lady." He yelled. "Just wait until I get out of here." He looked down at his hand, and it changed suddenly becoming metallic looking. Then, he smashed his fist into the crystal walls of the cell.

Reagan watched as James' blows began to crack the walls around the cell. "She may have a point, Storm." She looked back at Hellbound. "If this cell can't hold him, I don't know of one that could. Sending him to Hell might be the only way to confine him."

"I don't like it." He disagreed. "This isn't just a jail sentence." He turned to face Hellbound. "Do you torture people in Hell?"

"The human myth of Hell is not the reality. Hell is another dimension. If there is torture, it is only from being separated from those you care about in this dimension." She explained.

"Then why do you bring bad people there?" He pressed.

"Where else can you have an eternity of solitude to figure yourself out? Where else are the creatures that live there better able to defend themselves against evil? No. All the creatures of that realm would be considered apex predators in any other place." James' last blow caused the cell to shudder, and a hairline crack appeared in the crystal. "Now, stand aside, I come for my prize."

Reagan and Tom backed away as the crack deepened with each successive blow. Finally, tired of waiting Hellbound raised her hands and uttered a phrase in a language neither of them could recognize. Glowing spirals and patterns appeared in the air. They glowed once and faded to nothingness taking the door to the cell with them.

"It's about time," James growled as he stepped out of the cell and back into the lab.

"Indeed, monster," Hellbound greeted him. "Now, it's time to send you to Hell." With no further prelude, she raised her hand and engulfed him in flames.

As Tom and Reagan watched in amazement, James started to laugh from inside the flames. "You are going to have to do better than that, witch!" He yelled and leaped at her.

He was inhumanly fast, but Hellbound was faster. She sidestepped, narrowly avoiding his clawed hand that was reaching for her face and drove her knee up into his abdomen. The blow knocked the wind out of him, but he was already on the attack again before she could get in another shot. He reached out for her neck but missed as she danced back. Unfortunately, her cloak didn't have time to get clear. With one huge arm, he yanked her off her feet by her cloak and flung her into the cement wall.

Reagan looked over at Tom. "So, what do you think? Do we help her out?"

"Absolutely." Tom agreed. "But how? I hit him with everything I had and he chucked a brick at my face!"

"At least he didn't hurt anything important." She patted him on the back. "Look – I'm not saying we can stop him, but maybe we can distract him enough that she can do what she has to do."

"Agreed."

James was moving over to where Hellbound was clawing her way out of the rubble when both Reagan and Tom hit him in his side, throwing him toward the back of the room. As they walked past Hellbound, they saw her finally stand up. She ripped the cloak from her shoulders, eyes blazing with fire. Her skin now closely resembled the red of her suit. She was furious. Small glowing runes appeared on her skin, and a small set of horns could now be seen atop her head.

"I will destroy you for that, beast." James was just regaining his footing when Hellbound leaped at him. She was smaller than him, but her demon powered rage was limitless. She pounced on his back, wrapped her legs around his waist and started savagely punching his ears and neck. The huge man staggered back across the water-soaked floor before crashing into the row of freezers on the back wall as Hellbound rolled free.

James rose, dripping with water as Hellbound, Ghost Touch and Storm positioned themselves between him and the door.

"I think it may be time for me to go out and see the world," James said as he sized them up and glanced at the door.

"Not gonna happen, Neuwin," Tom said firmly.

James ripped the remains of his shirt free and roared in anger. As he started to run at them, all three focused all their power on him. Reagan's white blast mixed with Tom's blue and the yellow flames from Hellbound slammed into James' chest and pushed him back as his claw-like toes scraped the tiled floor for purchase.

The three poured on the energy, and as James' foot touched the water on the floor for the second time, flames erupted, and colors swirled. "You may be able to stop me from teleporting you there, beast, but you can't stop me from opening a gate between realms and pushing you through."

James looked back over his shoulder as he continued to lose ground and saw the nightmare landscape coming into focus. "No!!" He screamed. "You can't bring me there!"

"It's no worse than you deserve monster," Hellbound told him. "You have taken innocent lives – including those of children. When you weren't killing people, you were brainwashing them or ruining their lives. You have made this life a hell on Earth for many people, and now is the time for your atonement."

With that announcement, the images in the water solidified, and James sank to his waist in the inch-deep water.

"Hey James!" Tom called as he stopped firing his blue blasts of energy at him and watched him struggle in an attempt to stop sinking into the image. "When you see the devil, don't forget to tell him who sent you." With that, Tom ripped up a huge section of the cement floor and threw it with all his strength at James. The cement block caught him in the face and threw him back through the gate. "There. Let's see how you like getting hit in the face."

Hellbound and Reagan both stopped firing, and as Hellbound closed her fist, the gate between realms slammed shut.

"Holy crap!" Reagan looked around at Tom and Hellbound in amazement. "We got him!" She started to dance in place. "For a minute, I thought we would still be fighting his ass tomorrow!"

Hellbound didn't answer but started walking toward the door to the lab.

"Hey," Tom called to her. "What's the rush? We did it."

"Not quite, Storm." She countered. "I still need to collect Buckner, for it was he pulling Neuwin's strings."

"Whoa, whoa whoa!" Reagan interjected. "We can't let you do that."

Hellbound stopped walking toward the door and slowly turned to face Reagan. Her eyes still burned with fire and the runes on her red skin glowed an unholy yellow. "You can't *let me*...?"

"She's right, Hellbound." Tom cut in. "We appreciate you taking James, but Buckner is a human and needs to be held accountable for his actions here in this realm."

"I do not need your permission to collect those that perform evil on this scale. He is damned, and so he is mine."

"No. I won't allow that." Reagan said calmly.

Hellbound looked at her like she would look at a cat hissing before she kicked it out of the way. "And are you saying that you have the power to stop me?" She turned to face Reagan, and her entire body seemed to catch fire. "For I am not in the mood to play around further."

Reagan closed her eyes and pulled her hands together as if she were in prayer. "No. We both know I don't have that kind of juice." A cold wind suddenly blew through the lab that chilled to the soul. It put out fires and froze the layer of water on the ground. "But He does." She finished.

Hellbound's eyes grew wide as she watched one of the shadows in the room coalesce into a figure draped in a cloak so black that it seemed to have a life of its own. Beautiful, full black wings protruded from the back of the cloak, and he held a staff with a pulsating black gem at its top. The face was hidden in the cowl of the cloak, but no one needed to see more to feel the immense sense of power radiating off the creature. Hellbound froze in place for a moment before dropping to her knees.

"I see you have some sense of what I could do to you?" The dark figure's voice seemed to come from a long distance away.

"Yes." She answered quickly. "I meant no disrespect. I am just doing what the codex said I must if I am to survive. The hunters must collect all those that violate the Agreement."

"And you have done well, but you must not collect the one called Buckner yet. I have been told he still has more that he must do before he becomes yours to play with." The cold, dead voice rasped out.

"Understood." She agreed.

"Good. Now, go." As he spoke the last word, he brought the butt of the staff down on the tile. Reagan and Tom bowed their heads as it struck. The sound echoed loudly throughout the chamber. When they looked up again, Hellbound was gone.

The dark figure walked over to Reagan and looked at her. "You have done well this day, apprentice." He commented. Before she could say anything, he was already beginning to dissolve. "I will see you again, soon."

"Soon?" She asked nervously, but he was already sinking into the shadows that played across the floor. Reagan looked at Tom with tears in her eyes. "Does that mean, I'm going to die soon?"

"I don't know what it means," Tom admitted. "But there is something that you should know."

She looked at him quizzically, and he pointed down at her suit. What had been white spandex with a red sash was now a light grey with a slightly auburn sash. "What the?" She looked at her suit. "What does this mean?"

"I could hazard a guess, but you may not like it."

"Spit it out." She urged.

"His uniform is black, and yours was white. After him telling you that you did well, your uniform is now darker. Maybe you got promoted?" He offered.

She groaned and leaned on Tom.

"If everyone is done killing people," came a faint voice from a far corner of the room "could someone help me out of this cell…"

iv

Walking out of the headquarters building for The Wall, Reagan, Tom and a gentleman in his late thirties ran into Greg Buckner being escorted out by a young Native American man just as police cars started to arrive.

"Who are you?" Tom asked immediately. "I told Wolfblood to stay with Buckner."

"I did." The young man answered smiling.

"You're Wolfblood?" Tom asked incredulously. "You talk differently."

"You should try talking with a mouth full of wolf-sized teeth!" He countered. "You didn't think I looked like that all the time, did you?"

414

Tom blushed. "Well, yeah. How was I supposed to know?"

"Another racist against werewolves." Wolfblood sighed theatrically with a slight smile on his lips. Then, looking at Reagan, he asked. "So, who is your guest?"

"This is Boost." Reagan introduced the other man. "He was one of the level nines that was locked up in the basement."

"Really?" Wolfblood asked. He turned and offered his hand to Boost. "Nice to meet you. What is your gift?"

"If I want to, I can increase someone's power for a short period of time."

"Sweet, but please don't make me more of a wolf. I enjoy being able to run upright." Wolfblood joked.

"Storm!" Bendati came running up to the group. "We have a problem!"

Tom looked at the usually reserved man and could see his concern. "What is it?"

"Your brother." He started. "He is with the medics. It isn't good." He held out his hand for Storm to take it.

Tom gestured for him to wait. "Can you carry two of us?" He asked.

"Yes."

"Good." He grabbed the Boost by the arm. "Let's go."

"Where are we going?" Boost asked, but Bendati had already grabbed Tom and activated the stone. The world blurred and Tom, Boost and Bendati were standing in the middle of the medic tent in Green Mountain National Forest in Vermont. Boost took one sharp breath in and dropped to one knee puking.

Tom looked around and got his bearings in what looked like a trauma center. There were white tiled floors and fluorescent lighting. Signs on the walls listed which hallway went where. Orderlies were pushing patients to different areas as the injured continued pouring in from the Valley of the Cursed. Bendati already was walking quickly down the hall. "He's in here." He motioned for Tom and Boost to enter the room.

Inside, Tom found Doc leaning over his brother. Levi had been laid out on a cot after his shirt was cut away. His breathing was shallow and rapid, and his skin was pale. Doc was holding both of his hands over Levi's abdomen, and they were glowing a cool light as he attempted to heal him. "How's it going?" Tom asked quietly.

"Not good," Doc said through clenched teeth. "He was brought in a while ago. We sewed up what we could, but he has lost a ton of blood and continues to lose more. If we don't stop the bleeding soon, your brother won't make it."

Tom stood looking at his younger brother as tears streamed down his cheeks. "No…" He turned and looked at Boost. "Could you help?"

Boost looked over at Doc and understood. "For the man that got me out of that hellhole? Absolutely." He walked over and put his hands on Doc's shoulders. "Now, whatever happens, don't stop focusing on healing."

At first, nothing seemed to happen. Then, Doc seemed to stiffen, and the light from his hands increased from a dull glow to a light that hurt the eyes. Healing power exploded out of him. No longer able to confine it to just the patient in front of him, Doc's ability had an effect on everyone in the medical tent. Levi, of course, was the one most affected. As they watched, his wound stopped oozing blood, the skin mended, a scar formed and then healed, his breathing slowed and deepened as his color improved.

Boost let go of Doc's shoulders, and the light from Doc's hands flickered and went out.

"My God! That was incredible!" Doc breathed.

Tom was still looking at Levi. "So, he is going to be okay?"

"Okay?" Doc laughed. "He isn't even going to have a scar. I think he is completely healed and just sleeping now."

Tom's body sagged in relief, and the rest of the group cheered quietly so as not to disturb Levi's rest. It was then that they started to hear all of the voices from other rooms in the enchanted trauma center. Tom walked out into the hallway and saw Captain Livid walking down the hall with a smile on his face. "What happened?" Tom asked.

"I was in my room, and then my knee, eye, and wrist healed when no one was even there!" He was almost jittery. "I think my asthma may even be cured."

Tom smiled as he realized how much Doc's healing power had been amplified. "A level nine..."

ʊ

Feeling recharged from Doc's overpowered healing, Tom walked out of his brother's room and down the hall. There he saw an opening partially covered with a canvas tarp with an exit sign over the top of it. He pushed past the canvas to find himself standing outside a tiny one-person tent in the middle of the woods. There under one of the trees was the sorcerer Bendati and with him, the technopath, Breacher.

Tom walked over to them. "You guys still awake?" He asked. "I would have thought you would have gone for some shut-eye by now."

"We would have, but we have something that we need to pass on," Breacher answered, reaching into his backpack. From there, he pulled out two hard drives and showed them to Tom. "They are full – almost five terabytes of data. It includes videos of tortures, methods of brainwashing, and experiments performed on captives going back years. It also had detailed records of every place they had their money, and man, did they have a lot of money!"

"Past tense?" Bendati asked.

"Well, I did transfer a substantial amount into one of our accounts so that we could make reparations for some of the lives they ruined. Then, I introduced a virus into their system. It not only deletes their hard drives, but it writes over them and deletes that too." They both gave him blank looks. "It's almost impossible to recover that way."

"Oh," Bendati said understanding. "Good job then."

"Yeah. Strong work." Tom complimented him as he took the two hard drives.

Breacher just shook his head knowing they still didn't understand.

"Okay. I guess that means there are just two more things to do before we drop this off with Thornton, then." Tom commented.

"What's that?" Bendati asked.

"First, I will need a destination stone made for Thornton so that we can get to him quickly. Second, we need to make a video, pleading our case to Congress." Tom explained.

"Let's do it." Breacher smiled.

CHAPTER **34**

A New World

i

Days had passed since the attack on the Settlement and the subsequent battle on Moon Island. Levi's knife wound appeared to be healed but had left him physically exhausted and too weak to stand. Doc had explained that healing still requires a lot of energy from the body, and now Levi's body was paying that price. Tom and Levi thanked him profusely for his work, and the following day Tom took Levi back to his apartment to finish recovering. Not surprisingly, Reagan had accompanied them as well. She ended up adopting the third bedroom at Tom's condo. When asked, she insisted that she was sticking around to help care for Levi "just until he is better." She claimed it was so that Tom could do things like run errands and not have to worry about leaving Levi alone.

"She does realize that I can simply call out to you telepathically if anything were to happen, right?" Levi asked Tom one evening when Tom was helping him get back to his bedroom. Tom just smiled.

ii

Roughly a week later, Tom got a text from Lance Thornton.

> My rooftop. 14:00 today.

Tom's stomach flipped. This meant that Congress had made a decision on how they would proceed with protecting people with abilities. "Oh man…"

"What's up?" Reagan asked as she sipped on her coffee across from Tom on the balcony table overlooking the harbor. The table had become her favorite space in the condo. It had a beautiful view of the ocean, and in the late summer, the cool wind coming off the water was very welcome. She would frequently have breakfast there with Tom as Levi slept in late.

"I just got a text from Lance. He wants to meet this afternoon to talk about the decisions that Congress has made."

"Ouch." She winced. "That already, huh?"

"Yeah." Tom agreed. "I feel like I am the attorney for an entire race of people and if they get locked up, it will be my fault."

"Don't forget to add in the fact that you would end up going to jail with them." She chimed in cheerfully.

"You are not helpful." Tom's look was sour.

"Well… Nothing we can do about it now, so why waste the energy being scared?" She reasoned as she sipped her coffee.

Tom continued to replay the video he had sent to Congress in his mind. He had talked about his experiences with The Wall and James Neuwin in particular. He had told them about Leaf getting shot and how The Wall had attempted to exterminate them entirely. He mentioned how Buckner had used his position with The Wall to try to convince people that those with abilities were evil and needed to be arrested or killed. In an act of stochastic terrorism, he had striven to make the people he called the Changed into "enemies of the people."

Tom shuddered. He hated the term "Changed." That was the language of their oppressors, and it made his anger rise to hear it. He had been very clear that from now on the acceptable terms were "people with abilities" or "enhanced Americans."

He had finished the video by challenging them to change their position and motivate them to take action.

"Evil was allowed to flourish because good people sat back and did nothing. My friends and I paid the price in blood for your lack of resolve! Going forward we need strong leaders who will no longer be satisfied living on the sidelines. We are a good, loyal group of your citizens and we deserve leaders that will defend our rights to life, liberty and the pursuit of happiness again."

"Part of that defense will have to include protecting us from people that would incite violence against us through their words or actions. In world history class, we learned that a charismatic man in the late 1930s influenced a large group of people to commit horrible crimes by playing on people's fears and loyalties. He got them to fear each other, and he subverted their patriotic side into something ugly that made them willing to do the unthinkable. This incident with Buckner is no different. I spoke to the men that worked for him, and they all thought that they were protecting this country from an imminent threat. This misconception was allowed to fester unmatched because there was no opposing view to be heard, and you are all partially guilty in your silence."

"My friends and I do not harbor any ill will to the country, but we do humbly beg you not to be silent any longer. We know that you could not have foreseen the evil in Buckner's heart, nor could you have anticipated him trying to control us for his own financial benefit. But now that you do know that this sort of manipulation is possible, we are asking you as our representatives to please protect us."

iii

When Tom instantly appeared next to the destination stone he had placed on Thornton's roof; the director was so startled that his sidearm was in his hand before Tom even had time to see him.

"Whoa!" Tom threw both hands in the air in the universal sign of surrender even as he raised a shield to protect himself from the bullet. "Easy Sir." Tom cautioned.

"Why didn't you tell me that you could do that?" Lance demanded stuffing his firearm back in the holster.

"Sorry. No one else around me seems to mind much when people come and go that way." He explained.

"Their reflexes must be fried," Lance muttered.

Tom laughed as he created the solid blue barrier around both of them, dropped his personal shield and restricted his powers so that he and Lance could talk face to face. "I guess so. I never thought of it that way." Turning around to inspect the dome he had created on top of the building he noticed that there was a picnic table up there now. "That's new."

"Yeah. My men thought I had lost it when I told them that I wanted a picnic table on the roof." Lance chuckled. "I have been eating lunch up here just to justify them hauling it up here."

Tom sat down. "Well, I do appreciate having a place to sit."

Lance shrugged.

"So, what's the verdict?" Tom asked bluntly. "Should we all start running now?"

Lance laughed. "No, but I am glad that I went through your video before I showed it." He shook his head. "You really didn't pull any punches, did you?"

"How do you mean?"

"I mean you fell just short of calling some of the most powerful men in the country lazy and stupid."

"Oh. I guess I never thought they would take it that way." Tom admitted. "Sorry. I am not a diplomat."

"That is a point I stressed to them before pressing 'play' on the video." Lance smiled. "The final verdict on whether or not to list your group as a protected entity with the full rights of a citizen was 65% in favor and 35% against."

"Yes!" Tom jumped up from the table in his excitement.

"Hold on," Lance warned. "There were conditions."

"Conditions? What conditions?"

"Well, there was some fairly heavy opposition, and some quarters wanted to insist that people with abilities must work for the government and be registered like a weapon," Lance informed Tom.

"No way!!" Tom yelled cutting off Lance. "That is not acceptable!"

"I figured you would say that." Lance agreed. "And I hope you understand that this discussion lasted days and the entire time I was the one arguing loudest for you." Tom grew silent as Lance continued. "I recognized the fact that you and your group had already performed an enormous service for this country and that it is we, in fact, that are in debt to you at this moment. I then went on to search for some middle ground. Now before you open your mouth to protest me wanting to compromise, you need to understand this — there is no way in hell that group was going to allow a group of people with abilities to walk around and effectively make the government the *second* most powerful organization in this country."

Tom was silent for a moment as he considered it. "What was the compromise?" He asked, already dreading the answer.

"We had to agree that there would be a group of people with abilities that worked for the government. They would be charged with dealing with crimes and enforcing the law where enhanced Americans were concerned."

Tom was stunned. "That is the opposite of what I wanted! Another group of agents that are assigned to keep people with abilities in line?"

"I know. But try to understand things from their point of view. Some of these abilities are terrifying. No normal person stands a chance of arresting a person with abilities if they break the law, and God forbid they form a group! They would be all but unstoppable." Lance paused while Tom thought about it before plunging forward. "I told them you would never go for it… Unless you were the head of it." He finished as he watched Tom's face for his reaction.

"What?!? No way!!" Tom was stunned.

"It's the only way you will be able to make sure it doesn't get subverted again. This way you can make sure there are no more free-range government-supported groups like The Wall." Lance reasoned. "And you would answer directly to me."

"But I am not a police officer or anything like that." He objected. "I don't have any training in the field."

"Training you on the law and how to conduct yourself is easy. The self-defense and ability to subdue without killing, you have already proven you can handle."

"This is not what I envisioned doing with my life," Tom told him as he continued to try to think of a way out of it.

"It may not be the life you would have chosen, but it is the life that's chosen you."

Tom paced the roof in obvious frustration. "If that is the only way, then I agree."

"That is wonderful news! I will notify them of your decision."

"Uh huh," Tom mumbled still stewing.

"That just leaves one other small order of business." He dug through his briefcase and brought out a picture. "There is one person with abilities that has been hurting people and needs to be brought in for her crimes." Tom could already feel his heart sink as Lance slid the picture of Hellbound across the picnic table.

"Oh man…"

www.ingramcontent.com/pod-product-compliance
Lightning Source LLC
Chambersburg PA
CBHW071932130726
47908CB00015B/185